That fact registered immediately. None on the dry concrete surrounding the bodies and none on the one nude body he could see. Unusual.

The nude girl lay flat on her back, head tilted to one side, hands cupping her breasts as if testing for firmness and heft. Her legs were drawn upward, knees spread, held in position by a small round stick of firewood propped against the side of each kneecap. Auburn hair fanned out from the small round head, a precise pattern that could not have happened by accident. . . .

ONLY WHEN SHE CRIES

Praise for Edward Mathis:

''Mathis has a fine sense of plotting!''
—**Pittsburgh Press**

''Edward Mathis is one of the best stylists among a new crop of hard-boiled writers.''
—**Virginian-Pilot/Ledger-Star**

''Well worth your attention.''
—**San Diego Union**

''Mathis will undoubtedly gain more fans!''
—**Publishers Weekly**

ONLY WHEN SHE CRIES

EDWARD MATHIS

B

BERKLEY BOOKS, NEW YORK

To Randy, Janet, Brian
and Casey Davis

ONLY WHEN SHE CRIES

A Berkley Book/published by arrangement with
the author's estate

PRINTING HISTORY
Berkley edition/September 1989

ISBN: 0-425-11851-7

A BERKLEY BOOK ® TM 757,375
Berkley Books are published by The Berkley Publishing Group,
200 Madison Avenue, New York, N.Y. 10016.
The name ''BERKLEY'' and the ''B'' logo
are trademarks belonging to Berkley Publishing Corporation.

PRINTED IN THE UNITED STATES OF AMERICA

10 9 8 7 6 5 4 3 2 1

PROLOGUE

NEW YORK

Amanda Price turned away from the open kitchen doorway, the fragile, early morning sunlight imparting a golden blush to auburn hair the color of well-polished cherry wood. She was smiling, dark blue eyes alight with an inner warmth that mirrored the contentment of the moment, the promise of a beautiful new day and an overwhelming rush of love for the two wonderful males in her life.

"Esmerelda's brought her babies out into the sunlight," she said, crossing to the bubbling coffeepot on the counter. She poured a cup of coffee and gave her husband an amused glance. "He's sitting on the ground, and they're crawling all over him. He's entranced."

"Hmmm," Webster Price said, wetting a thumb, turning a page of the *Wall Street Journal* spread open on the table in front of him. "What did you say?"

Amanda set her coffee on the table across from him. "I said he's playing with Esmerelda's kittens. They fascinate him. This is the first time she's brought them out from under the house."

He looked up quickly, brows knitting, then relaxing, a series of deeply etched furrows fleeing across his narrow forehead like the fleeting shadows of worrisome thought. "Aren't you a little . . . I mean, are you sure it's safe?"

The amused smile came back, a flash of white, even teeth behind shapely lips. "Don't fret so much. Their claws are tiny. Don't worry. If one of them gets him, they'll hear him over in the next county."

He cleared his throat, long, slender fingers worrying one corner of the paper, the frown returning, dissolving, dark, expressive eyes seizing and holding hers. "I wasn't thinking about that. I was thinking about . . ." His voice hesitated, faded.

"Hoppy," she said, clucking, shaking her head in mock-exasperation. "Honestly, Web, you're a worrywart. Besides, Hoppy was the stupidest rabbit I've ever seen, and Spencer was only two and a half then."

"I know, but . . ." He broke off, his restless fingers smoothing the creases they had made in the paper. He looked up again and tried out a lopsided smile. "You're right, I'm a worrywart . . . but don't you think you'd better bring him in now? He's been out there quite awhile."

She laughed and stood up, dipping her head in defeat, the luxurious mass of hair spilling across copper-toned shoulders, luminous ends curling inward and upward as if striving to reach the lovely face. She came around the table and plopped in his lap.

"All right. But first, where are you going to take us today? You've been promising him the zoo for a long time now, and it's going to be such a beautiful day . . ." She trailed off suggestively, sliding her arms across his shoulders and nuzzling his neck, exhaling audibly into his ear.

"Oh, Christ, all that walking, the smell—"

"Come on now, you promised him. He never gets to see you during the week. He waits all week long for Sunday to be with his Daddy—"

"Okay, don't nag," he said, sighing, distracted by the smooth swell of flesh above the square yoke of the colorful sundress. Firm flesh, yet silky soft, a pleasing paradox he found immensely stimulating.

"Hmmm," he said again, transforming his critical survey into a salacious leer, "maybe we ought to leave the little guy out there for a while. Do him good probably, consorting with nature, gamboling with the wee critters—"

She nipped his ear, chortled, wriggled lithely, and broke out of his embrace. Rosy-cheeked, eyes darkly shining, she leaned forward and wagged a finger under his nose. "Don't start something we can't finish, buster," she said sternly. "I don't want to spend the rest of the day waiting for tonight."

He laughed. "Jezebel."

"Lecher." She ambled back around the table, hands on her hips, bottom half swaying. She picked up her cup and sipped, watching him, daintily dragging the tip of her tongue across the moisture of her lower lip. She stood hipshot, breasts outthrust, smiling.

"You better cut it out," he said softly. "I'll lock the little bugger out, and the only animal you'll see today will be me."

"Oh, wow," she said, shivering delicately, but heading, nevertheless, for the kitchen door, tossing her head, watching warily over her shoulder as if expecting pursuit.

Webster sighed resignedly, tasted the cold dregs of his coffee, and made a face. He was reaching across the table to steal her cup when he heard the scream.

A small scream—a harsh, sobbing sound quickly escalating into a shriek—cut off in mid-note as Amanda's hands flew to cover her mouth, bringing it down scale to a ululating moan, then rising again, piercing, shattering.

"Oh, my God! Webster! Oh, God! Oh my God!" The sheer horror in her voice broke the rigor holding Webster Price contorted across the table, brought him lumbering across the spotless linoleum to where she stood rooted, unable to move, her body numb, responding only to some incomprehensible compulsion that would not allow her to close her eyes or turn away.

She felt his warm hands on her ice cold arms and began shaking uncontrollably, heard the rasping hiss of his undrawn breath, a hoarse, guttural curse, and still could not look away from her son, the short, sturdy leg rising and falling relentlessly, doggedly, a flushed, intense look of utter fascination on the round, angelic face as the hard leather sole crushed a twitching ball of calico fur beneath his foot.

Webster pushed her aside, cursed again in futile anger as the storm door latch defied his fumbling fingers. Finally it yielded; he stormed through to the porch, bellowing:

"Spencer!"

The boy stopped, poised, his leg uplifted; his face raised, eyes bright and shining, but uncomprehending. A splash of blood across one cheek gave him a rakish appearance, a look of devilish glee as he grinned brightly and lifted his arms.

Each hand contained a dead kitten; blood dripped sluggishly through chubby, clenched fingers.

"See, Daddy," he cried happily, his voice high and shrill with excitement, "I squished them! They're all flat!"

LOS ANGELES, CALIFORNIA—FOURTEEN YEARS LATER

Dr. Millford Stromb swung open the door to his abbreviated waiting room and advanced one pace forward, smiling at the room's two occupants.

"Mr. and Mrs. Price. So good of you to come. I'm sorry I'm running a few minutes late—"

"That's quite all right, Doctor." Amanda Price lifted effortlessly to her feet and extended a slender hand to the portly doctor. "We want you to know how much we appreciate your call, and your concern." She gave him a fleeting smile, then turned to the lanky man beside her, flashed one quick look at his scowling, handsome face, and went on hurriedly, "I don't believe you've met my husband."

"A pleasure, Mr. Price," Stromb said heartily, stepping forward again, taking the limp, clammy hand in his and resisting an instantaneous impulse to drop it.

Webster Price dipped his head in a perfunctory nod. "Likewise," he said, managing, in two syllables, to convey irritation, arrogance, and impatience.

Not a mean feat, Stromb thought, moving to the side of the door, inclining his body in a movement that was almost a bow, symbolic inference that his visitors were persons of worth.

Webster Price passed in front of him with no perceptible change in his irascible expression, walking quickly, a light, bouncy gait often affected by small men overcompensating.

Amanda Price flicked Stromb a small smile, a soft grimace, before following her husband into the room.

Stromb waited until they found chairs before seating himself behind his free-form walnut desk. He wasted a few seconds fiddling with the items on his desk top, feeling a little disconcerted at Webster Price's obvious antagonism, something he had not anticipated since the couple had no certain knowledge of the reason for the meeting. Or had they guessed? Or, perhaps, Webster Price simply didn't like psychiatrists.

He folded his hands and cleared his throat. "As you are aware,

Spencer will be eighteen in two more weeks. Accordingly, his probation will end at that time. So will, of course, his mandatory treatment at this clinic.'' He stopped and briefly scanned the two silently watching faces. ''I asked you here to discuss the possibility—'' He broke off abruptly and waved a pudgy hand in a half-angry gesture of repudiation. ''No, I won't dissimulate. I asked you here to *urge* you to continue your son's treatment, either at this facility or some other. I would further urge that treatment be intensified, preferably on an in-patient basis—''

''In-patient?'' Price echoed incredulously. ''Are you suggesting we commit our son, Doctor?''

Stromb met the tall man's dark, burning gaze head on. ''Yes. That is my sincere recommendation. Spencer is a very disturbed young man, Mr. Price. Far more than anyone realizes, I think. Far more than I myself realized when I began seeing him sixteen months ago.''

Price made a hawking, disgusted sound. ''Nonsense! Spencer's a high-spirited boy, a little wild, maybe, a little too prone to self-indulgence, maybe even a little too conceited and overbearing when it comes to girls. But, hell, Spence's a big, good-looking kid. The girls chase after him. Show me a seventeen-year-old boy who wouldn't take advantage of that, and I'll show you a wimp—or a homo.''

''That isn't the point, Mr. Price,'' Stromb said quietly. ''And I think you know it. You know what happened to the Evans girl as well as I do. That cannot be dismissed as simple high-spirited behavior. Your son wasn't drinking; he wasn't on drugs. What he did he did deliberately and with full awareness of his actions. I'm very much afraid he would have done more if the girl's neighbors hadn't happened along.'' He paused, then went on doggedly. ''He told her in precise detail what he intended doing after he raped her. That is a part of the record.'' He paused again, his tone softening. ''He has since admitted as much to me.''

''I don't believe it,'' Price said bluntly. ''He told me what happened, how the girl led him on, teasing and enticing, then backing off when it was too late to stop, when he was so worked up he didn't know what he was doing. Hell, so he slapped her around a little. It happens all the time. If he hadn't been my son, if he'd been a poor kid, they'd have slapped his wrist and sent him to bed without his supper or something. Hell, he was all torn up about it. He couldn't talk about it without crying.''

He settled back into his seat, the lean, handsome face flushed with righteous anger. "There's nothing wrong with Spencer that a few groundings can't cure."

"Dr. Stromb," Amanda said, her voice hesitant, her lovely face pale and taut. "I don't understand. Your last report a few months ago said Spencer was making progress. You said he appeared to be facing up to the consequences of his actions, that he acknowledged culpability in the Evans case, and that he seemed genuinely contrite."

Stromb took a deep breath, expelled it, and nodded. "And so I believed. I must confess, Mrs. Price, that your son can be extremely convincing at times, when he cares to. I must confess also that for almost a year he manipulated me as adroitly as he seems to manipulate everyone around him. He is glib, witty, and persuasive. He can be very charming; he is extremely intelligent. He is, I'm afraid, fundamentally flawed."

"Flawed?" Price demanded. "What do you mean?"

Stromb sighed again. "It's not an easy thing to explain. It's even more difficult to admit that he fooled me for so long. The only excuse I can offer, if indeed there is one, is that the standard tests are woefully inadequate when we are dealing with an antisocial personality, particularly a personality as brilliant and cunning as Spencer. He has over the years observed and absorbed to an almost perfect degree the needs and demands of society and, while these requirements are as antithetical to him as a bubble bath is to a cat, he has programmed himself to reflect the responses necessary to maintain an appearance of normalcy."

"I don't know what the hell you're talking about," Price said angrily. "This is all a bunch of psychiatric bullshit!"

"I'll try to be more specific," Stromb said, keeping his voice carefully even, feeling a drumbeat of anger of his own. "Your son, Mr. Price, is emotionally crippled. He is not complete, not a whole man—or boy, if you wish, although he is as much of a man as he will ever be. He was, in all likelihood, born the way he is, and I suspect if you and your wife had been totally candid at the time you filled out my questionnaire, his background would be much more revealing. As I said before, he is an antisocial personality. The current label in favor is sociopath. There are many sociopaths around. To Spencer's affliction we must add yet another label: sexual psychopath. Combination of the two produces a terrifying reality. In Spencer's case, we find a man who has no conscience, no human compassion, a man who has found that he can achieve unbridled joy by inflicting trauma on other living creatures, a man who can experience intense sexual ecstasy only by ignoring the needs and rights of others, by imposing his own will, by degradation and humiliation, and finally, by committing the ultimate atrocity—inducing death.''

He stopped and looked at them through a silence so absolute he thought he could hear the splash of Amanda Price's tears. She stared straight ahead, glistening slicks beneath her eyes, shiny smears across her cheeks, hands coupled in her lap like two dead brown birds.

"You're crazy!'' Webster Price lurched forward in his chair, lean face alive with undifferentiated emotions, breath rasping like a faulty engine. "You've been around loonies too damn long, Doctor! Shit! You're crazy as hell if you think I'm going to put that boy in some damn institution with a bunch of nuts. He's as normal as I am.''

"That may well be,'' Stromb said, his pale eyes glinting, annoyance segueing into anger despite his usual iron control. "But if that is true, sir, then I'd suggest you seek help at once.''

Price lunged to his feet, his face choleric. "You can forget it, Doctor. Spencer has one more visit, I believe. I'll see that he comes. After that you're out of the picture.''

Stromb pushed to his feet. "Very well, Mr. Price. I can only advise. I will, of course, recommend that the court retain control of Spencer, that he be remanded—''

"You do that,'' Price said harshly, crossing to the door in long, springy strides. "I'll damn well guarantee you it won't do any good.'' He yanked open the door and went out. Seconds later, Stromb heard the outer door close with a crash. He looked at Amanda Price, then walked around his desk as she rose to her feet.

"I'm sorry,'' he said. "I'm afraid I handled that badly. I seem to rub your husband the wrong way. Perhaps I should not have been so blunt.''

She shook her head, her face distraught. "No. It isn't your fault. We hadn't discussed it at length, but I'm sure he suspected you would say something along the lines of what you did say. We've know for a long time there was something different about Spencer. But Webster refuses to discuss it. He attributes everything to youthful exuberance, sowing wild oats . . .'' She trailed off, giving him a small, weary smile. "Perhaps it will all work out for the best. Spencer is going into the army as soon as he's eighteen.'' She extended her hand. ''Thank you again for your kind efforts.''

''Not at all,'' he said, shaking the slender hand. ''I'm afraid I've accomplished very little.''

Not a damned thing, in fact, he thought morosely moments later, watching her lissome figure disappear through his outer office door. Sixteen months of fencing with a brilliant teenage psychopath who had manipulated him as easily as a doting mother for a good part of that time. Belatedly, almost reluctantly, he had come to the realization that Spencer Price was more and less than he pretended to be. Then one day, three months before, his sluggish metamorphosis had crystallized into a painful, blazing epiphany.

Spencer Price, apparently in the throes of some irrepressible inner compulsion, had seized the conversation and revealed with terrifying clarity the shadow world that had been a part of his existence since early childhood. Horror-filled tales of depredations against the animal world, the cold, matter-of-fact voice pointing out with quiet pride his cunning and resourcefulness in avoiding detection, in picking his victims with calm, logical precision.

And later, graduating to a higher level of accomplishment, forays against the female population. Generalities only, no specific detail of time or place. Shocked into hypnotic silence by the piercing eyes, Stromb had listened with a growing sense of dread, a coursing thrill of fear, a dry, empty feeling in his stomach.

At the end of the fifty minute hour, they had stared at each other; Stromb with difficulty, Spencer with a taunting, wolfish grin that eventually exploded into wild, braying laughter and a hilarious renunciation of all he had confessed. A put on, he had said, a way to spice up an otherwise boring appointment.

But Dr. Millford Stromb did not believe his recantation. He had sensed truth in the boy's didactic recital of atrocities, sensed an underlying excitement, passion, behind the toneless voice, the glittering eyes.

And now, closing the door behind the youth's handsome parents, he felt the return of creeping dread. He moved back to his desk and sat down. He took his pipe out of a drawer, packed it, and lit up.

He would fail; he was convinced of that. Webster Price was too powerful, too much money and too many good lawyers. So in a few more days, Spencer Townsend Price would be away free and clear. He puffed a ball of smoke toward the ceiling and sighed.

He would hear of Spencer Price again; he was certain of that . . .

1

PRESENT

Narcotics is a miserable damn business, Cloud thought, fishing the last cigarette from the pack on the car seat beside him. He cupped his palms and lit it from the dash lighter, then crushed the box and dropped it into the white paper bag with the half-eaten hamburger and soggy fries.

Inhaling deeply, he felt a dry, burning sensation in his throat and realized with a small pang of dismay that he had opened the pack at the beginning of the stakeout at nine o'clock. He glanced at the luminous face of his watch. Eleven forty-five. Jesus Christ. Twenty cigarettes in two hours and forty-five minutes. That was almost seven an hour, one every eight minutes or so. He scanned his section of the Seven-Eleven parking lot across the street and wondered glumly if he should quit—if he *could* quit. He stirred restlessly behind the wheel of the unmarked Chevy. Thirty-seven and he had been smoking since he was fifteen. Twenty-two years. Jesus Christ.

He stubbed out the cigarette and looked at his watch again. Ten more minutes. To hell with it. The buy had been set for ten-thirty, and such things usually went on time or not at all. Dealers were notoriously capricious people, had been known to abort over something as normal as a man walking a dog in the area of the buy. Or a wino staggering down the street.

And maybe that's what happened, he thought. Maybe they

picked up on one of us. Strobish was sprawled on a bench in the small park at the end of the street, dirty and ragged, a brown-bagged wine bottle conspicuously displayed, and Rafferty was somewhere in the parking lot of the apartment complex behind the small, self-service grocery story. He had seen neither of them since nine o'clock and had only the keyed signals at ten and eleven on the walkie-talkie for assurance that he wasn't maintaining a solitary vigil. Parked behind a yellow, front-end loader, sandwiched between a Dempster Dumpster and a flatbed trailer loaded with lumber, he felt reasonably secure in his own position.

He took out a fresh pack of cigarettes and ripped off the cellophane and the cardboard lid. He stared at it for a second, then slipped it into his shirt pocket without taking one. He picked up the walkie-talkie and stepped out of the car. He moved back into the shadow cast by the stacked lumber and relieved himself against one of the trailer's huge tires. He watched a brilliant display of ragged lightning in the west, counting the seconds before a roll of thunder and guessed the storm was entering the western edge of Fort Worth. The faint smell of ozone drifted past his nostrils; wind rattled a loose board on the stack of lumber.

He zipped up and keyed the walkie-talkie.

"Sucker one to sucker two and three. I've had about all the fun I can stand for one night. I reckon I'm gonna mosey on into the barn. Coming?"

Jake Rafferty's chuckle preceded his voice. "I guess. Sorry it was a bust. Wanted to give you a little excitement for a change."

"Next time I'll stay home and work a crossword puzzle. Strobish? You with us?"

Strobish's answer was a loud, liquid belch. "Oops . . . shorry fellers, I'se just finishing up the Ripple."

Rafferty's laughter crackled through the box. Strobish, his new partner, was black, and since Strobish seemed compelled to make a lot of racially oriented jokes that Rafferty didn't always understand, in the interest of harmony, he laughed a lot.

Cloud punched in. "I'm going on home. It's a lot closer than the shop. Tell Buckley I'll turn this bucket of bolts in tomorrow."

"I'll do it," Rafferty said. "Hey, man, thanks for the assist. I owe you one."

"Good. I'll remember that the next time I get a rash of killings."

Rafferty laughed again.

Strobish broke in. "Hey, don't I get any thanks for laying on this cold, hard bench all evening?"

"You get the wine, man," Rafferty said.

"See you guys later," Cloud put in quickly.

"Okay, Ben, thanks again."

"Take care, Lieutenant."

Cloud tossed the walkie-talkie inside the car and retrieved the paper bag. He crushed it into a ball and made a one-handed push shot into the Dumpster on the other side of the car. He took in a deep lungful of moisture-laden air, watching the expanding outline of the approaching thunderhead and feeling a sharp disappointment with the outcome of the evening.

He suddenly realized that he had been on a high without being aware of it; he could feel the curious mental and physical interaction that signaled winding down: a sense of outrage, deprivation, anger.

It had been a long time since he had worked narcotics with Jake Rafferty as his partner, longer still since he had participated in a bust yielding as much as a kilo of cocaine. A key of prime Colombian white, ninety-four percent pure. Sammy Keeler had whispered it into the ear of Jake Rafferty, and Sammy Keeler had been the first and best snitch Benjamin Cloud had ever recruited.

So what had happened? Cloud wondered. A dozen possibilities. Keeler had had an extraordinarily long run. Maybe he had been set up. Cloud hated to think about that, hated to think about little Sammy Keeler lying dead in a ditch.

He backed the Chevy out of the pocket and maneuvered across the littered lot and jumped the curb into the street. He turned east on Northcross Street.

Large, fat raindrops splattered on the windshield, and by the time he stopped at the Grapevine Highway intersection, the car had become an empty drum, an uneasy sanctuary in a sea of pounding rain. He switched on the windshield wipers, watched their lackadaisical sweep across the slippery surface, and snorted an oath.

Overhead, the hanging signal became a pale-green blur. He muttered another soft curse, counted to ten, held his breath, and eased out into the intersection. Driving by instinct and memory, he slowed to a crawl and angled toward the curb once the light was safely behind him. The car immediately to his rear flicked its lights then blared its indignation and swung out and around him, low-slung pipes blatting a song of pure power, wide tires sending a graceful arcing sheet of water to further overwhelm his wipers.

"Asshole," he said, gliding into the curb, straightening, and coming to a halt. "Stupid damyankee," he added, smiling a little, thinking it was more likely a Texan, one of that curious breed who believed their mastery over a driving machine was total and absolute, the state of the weather notwithstanding. As a patrolman he had picked up the pieces of more than a few whose bad judgment had been exceeded only by their stupidity.

He shut off the motor and glanced at his watch. Good. Thirty minutes since his last cigarette. Two an hour wasn't bad at all. He shook one free and lit it with his lighter. He sat smoking for a moment, staring at the opaque windshield, feeling isolated inside his small cocoon, a timorous thread of claustrophobia squirming around the edges of his consciousness. An almost imperceptible shiver rippled through him. He snorted softly, reached forward, and flipped on the radio.

Instant cacophony. Blaring static and a female voice with the clipped, staccato resonance of an M-16. He winced and turned down the volume.

". . . think I'm some kind of bloody clairvoyant? I've been trying to raise him. He's not at home, and he's got his flippin' radio turned off if he's in his car. You'll bloody well be the first to know when I . . . *if* I find him." Cricket Bloom's rapid-fire Bronx rhythm overlaid with British solecisms left over from an aborted, eight-year marriage to a former dockworker from Liverpool.

"Bloody crap," an indistinct voice muttered, and the radio hissed and crackled emptily.

Cloud stared thoughtfully at the water cascading down his windshield. The indistinct voice had sounded like Rosie Simple's rumbling bass, the third and latest addition to his small Homicide Division. A six-year veteran of the streets, Rosie Simple was still obviously uncomfortable with the nondescript uniform of a detective. He missed the psychological reassurance of the instant identification afforded by a highly visible gun and the jingling, weighty accoutrements of the street cop. Nevertheless, Cloud thought he had the makings of a good detective. Slow-moving, methodical, he had the twin advantages of intimidating size and a disarming countenance, a boyish grin that inspired confidence. And most of all, he enjoyed the sludge work of an investigation: knocking on doors and asking the endless questions.

Cloud frowned. If it had been Rosie on the line, then he was probably the one they were looking for, and Rosie wouldn't need him for something ordinary like a knifing down in Willowville.

He picked up the mike.

"Cricket, Ben Cloud. What's going on?"

A moment of earthy crackling silence. "Well, saints be praised if it ain't himself! And just where would your lordship be shacking up the whole blessed evening?"

"I'm off duty, Cricket," he said, a little amused, a trifle annoyed. "But I've been giving Jake Rafferty an assist on stakeout. It's on the board, if anyone had bothered to look."

"Yes, sir, I understand, sir. I'll look next time, sir," she said, her voice crisp and cool, an indication that someone higher than a lieutenant had entered the dispatch room. "It's Detective Simple, Lieutenant. He's been sitting on two db's for over an hour—"

"What?"

"Dead bodies, sir. A ten . . . ten . . . well, two dead bodies, sir. That address is two-nine-four Crescent Lane. Repeat, two-nine-four Crescent Lane."

"I've got it," Cloud said, glancing at the windshield. The rain had slowed. "I'm less than a mile away. Call Detective Simple and tell him I'm on my way." He started the car and rolled down his side window far enough to reach out and slap the revolving light on the roof. He felt the snap as the magnetized base took hold.

"Okay, Ben." Cricket's voice had softened, a sign that her visitor had departed. "Rosie's flipping out, Ben. It's a couple of young women. Out."

Cloud made a sliding U-turn on the wet street, slipped past two cars waiting at the signal, and cautiously ran the red light. He picked up the mike again.

"Cricket. You said Rosie's sitting on the bodies. What time did the call come in?"

"Ten-forty. A Mr. Harold, neighbor. Chasing his dog. He said they were still . . . warm."

"What's the current situation?"

"M.E.'s been there and gone. Rosie's holding the tech squad, Russell and Stovall, until you get there. And, of course, the bodies."

"Thanks." He dropped the mike and concentrated on his driving, feeling a tightening in his solar plexus, a gradual diffused warmth as his heartbeat slowly accelerated. He roared by the deserted Seven-Eleven store without a glance.

2

The driveway to 294 Crescent Lane was effectively blocked by two squad cars and an ambulance, all with lights flashing, revolving, a psychedelic intermingling of pulsing color against the backdrop of towering trees and thick shrubbery. Across the street a black-and-white television news van sucked the life out of its battery with blazing headlights. A small knot of people huddled near its gaping rear doors. A small cluster of press cars lined the street behind the van.

Cloud braked to a stop behind one of the squad cars. He lit a cigarette and climbed out, noting automatically that the small brick house's nearest neighbor was at least a hundred and fifty feet away, the large expanse between studded with trees and divided more or less equally by a thick, head-high row of ligustum hedge.

The rain had dwindled to a steady drizzle. He cupped the cigarette in his hand and turned up the collar of his dacron Windbreaker as he circled the car and walked toward the driveway. The door on the squad car opened, and a patrolman stepped out. He lifted a hand in a halfhearted salute. The revolving lights licked surrealistic patterns across his broad face, pinpricks of multicolored light pinwheeling on the convex surface of his left eye.

"They're around in the back, Lieutenant," he said. "That's where it happened, I guess, around back."

Cloud nodded. "Thanks, Charlie. Bitch of a night for it."

"Ain't no good night, Lieutenant," Officer Charlie Gosdin

said, then stalked past Cloud to intercept two raincoated figures who had broken away from the group near the van. He met them in the center of the street, arms widespread.

"Lieutenant! Lieutenant Cloud!" A feminine voice, vaguely familiar and plaintively supplicating.

Cloud stopped at the crime-scene tape stretched across the front yard between wooden stakes and looked back at a pale blur of a face beneath a floppy, plastic rain hat.

"Amy Reed! Remember me? I interviewed you once before on that—"

"I remember," Cloud said. "But I'm sorry. New policy. Captain Summers handles all press releases." He spread his hands and shrugged apologetically, then turned and ducked under the tape. He remembered right enough. His one and only shot at being a TV star. He shuddered. Caught between her lovely, disconcerting smile and the unblinking, round eye peering over her shoulder, he had been instantly traumatized, seized by gut-swooping fright, dry mouth, swollen tongue, a tingling numbness spreading slowly throughout his body. It had been a total disaster, but the heartless witch had run it anyhow, and had been mean enough to call and offer him a copy.

He glanced over his shoulder. She was trudging back toward the van. Charlie Gosdin stood in the center of the street watching her, hands on his hips, legs widespread.

He turned back, smiling, and saw Rosie Simple coming down the driveway to meet him.

Five inches taller than Cloud's six feet, he had shoulders that looked at least a yard wide inside the loose-fitting yellow slicker. He looked and walked a lot like John Wayne, Cloud thought, and wondered sometimes if he secretly practiced the stilted, almost mincing stalk that had been the dead actor's trademark. He carried a three-cell flashlight in one huge hand; the other held a clipboard and pen.

"Sorry about rousting you out, Ben, but I thought you'd want to see this the way we found it." He pocketed the flashlight and ran a hand across his wiry bush of dark hair, flipping away moisture.

"I wasn't asleep," Cloud said, sucking on the cigarette in his cupped hand and discovering it had drowned. He crushed it into a ball, started to flip it away, then stopped. "This area been swept?" It was a statement more than a question. Rosie was thorough.

Rosie nodded. "Everything inside the tape." He turned as

Cloud came abreast of him. "As good as we could before the rain hit."

The two men neared the corner of the house. "How's it look?" Cloud asked, not really expecting an answer. He could already see part of a sheet-covered lump on the wide expanse of concrete between the house and the garage, and one good look would be worth a thousand of Rosie's words.

"Weird," the big man said, slowing down as they reached the protection of an aluminum patio cover that extended across the rear of the house almost to the two-car garage a half-dozen yards away. A small red Ford, blistered with raindrops, sat with its nose a few inches away from one of the double doors.

Two men in street clothing sat side by side on the edge of a tiny concrete porch, looking tired and wet and glum, the paraphernalia of forensics scattered on the concrete around them. A uniformed policeman leaned against the brown-and-white brick of the rear wall. Cloud nodded at the men, then reluctantly turned to the bodies illuminated starkly by a high-wattage bulb hanging from the center of the patio cover.

3

There was no blood. That fact registered immediately. None on the dry concrete surrounding the bodies, and none on the one nude body he could see. Unusual.

The nude girl lay flat on her back, head tilted to one side, hands cupping her breasts as if testing for firmness and heft. Her legs were drawn upward, knees spread, held in position by a small, round stick of firewood propped against the side of each kneecap. Auburn hair fanned out from the small, round head, a precise pattern that could not have happened by accident. She was tanned all over. Except for barely discernible smudges on her neck, she appeared unmarked.

Cloud walked around the body, squatted at her head, and gently turned her face to the light. Her skin was blotched, darker in spots behind the tan, the small even features almost composed: eyes closed, lips parted slightly, the tip of her tongue pressing against a tiny crack between small white teeth. Cloud straightened and looked at Rosie.

"Strangled? She shouldn't look like that."

Rosie nodded. "Doc Milbourn said he musta worked on her, closed her mouth, shoved her tongue back in, smoothed her face, like that."

"Raped?"

"Yeah. Semen tracks there in the crease . . . yeah, she was raped." Scowling, he flipped a page on the clipboard. "Named Laura Sue Elliot. Eighteen. Not married, according to the neigh-

19

bor who found them. Worked for some outfit named Cinetex in
Dallas. Her and the other one rented this house together. The
other one wasn't raped. She was savaged, neck broken like a
dead stick, headlock and a snap, looks like. She's got some faint
burn marks on her cheek that could have been the fabric of the
guy's coat sleeve.''

"Was she covered like that?"

"Yeah. Can't figure that one. He had to go in the house to get
that sheet. Ripped it off one of the beds. Don't make any sense.
He leaves the Elliot girl spread out like a whore at a carnival,
and lays the other one out like Sleeping Beauty. She's still got
her robe on.''

Cloud walked reluctantly toward the other body. "No idea
which one went first?" He scanned the area around the body,
stalling, not wanting to look at another dead girl. Not just yet.
He took out a handkerchief and mopped at water trickling out
of his hair.

Rosie mopped his own brow. "I got a kind of theory," he
said diffidently. "Milbourn couldn't say. They died too close
together." He hesitated, then looked away, his broad face noncommittal. "I think he followed the Elliot girl home, maybe
parked out on the street or maybe drove right up behind her.
Anyhow, I think he caught her right here on the patio and made
her take off her clothes.''

"Why not take her inside? Be safer. Less chance of the neighbors hearing.''

"I don't know why. Maybe he knew she had a roommate.
Maybe he likes the open air. But, for whatever reason, he did it
right here. The light was probably off, it switches on inside the
house. Hell, maybe he did it with the light on. Anyhow, we're
pretty sure he did it right here, raped and killed her. Three of
her nails are chipped and broken, and Stovall found some loose
matter under them that looked like concrete dust. The nail chips
will probably show up in the vacuum." He paused and took a
deep breath. He looked down at the sheet-covered body. "I think
this one heard them—heard something—and came out to check.
He jumped her, broke her neck. There's no evidence that he did
anything else.''

"He did enough," Cloud said, bending down and lifting the
sheet. Blond hair in curlers caged in a brown fishnet, a cold,
pale, immobile face, a swollen neck. A familiar odor of voided

bowels spilled out from beneath the sheet and caught in his nostrils like a noxious mist.

He froze, awkwardly transfixed by thudding shock. "Jesus Christ," he breathed.

"What?" Rosie moved a step closer.

"I know her," Cloud said harshly. "Ramona . . . I don't remember her last name. I only met her once."

"That's right," Rosie said. "Ramona Butler, age twenty-six. Ticket agent at American Airlines." He gazed quizzically at the shorter man's tight-lipped handsome face as he slowly straightened. "I'm sorry, Ben. Was she a friend?"

Cloud shook his head. "Not a friend, no. Not yet. But she might well have been one soon. She was engaged to marry a friend." He took out a cigarette, lit it with unsteady hands.

"Who?"

"Jake Rafferty."

"Jake?" Rosie expelled his breath in a gusty rush of air. "Bloody hell!" Another time Cloud might have smiled at the big man's appropriation of Cricket Bloom's favorite expletive.

"Two months ago. I double-dated with them. It was an engagement party of sorts. He gave her a hell of a rock—" He broke off, glanced at Rosie, then bent and lifted the sheet.

"It's not there," Rosie said. "No jewelry at all. Son of a bitch must have taken it."

Cloud leaned closer and studied the long-fingered hands folded beneath her breasts. "Give me your flashlight." He switched on the light and lifted her left hand, bringing his eyes close to the pale, smooth skin.

"Marks," he said, after a moment. "Faint, but they're there. He ripped it off. It scraped her knuckle in two or three places. I remember it was a pretty tight fit." He replaced the hand and covered the body again. He gave the flashlight to Rosie.

"Were there any signs of robbery inside?"

"None at all. In fact, the Elliot girl's purse was in the pile with her clothing. Seventy-five dollars and some change."

"Who caught the squeal?"

Rosie's head swiveled toward the cop leaning against the house. "Mulligan over there and Peters got here about—" He broke off, his eyes coming back to Cloud's. He frowned. "Hey, man, you don't think one of them took it?"

"It wouldn't be the first time, Rosie. That diamond cost Rafferty almost two thousand."

"Shit, Ben, they're cops! If they can't be trusted—" He stopped, his square face clouded with belligerence. "Hell, I was here almost as soon as they were. You think I might've taken it? You wanta search me?"

"Not all by myself," Cloud said, smiling faintly.

"Well, dammit, Ben, you know the killer took it."

Cloud shrugged again. "No, I don't. Not for a fact. Neither do you, Rosie. But there's not a hell of a lot we can do to prove otherwise." He looked down at what was left of Ramona Butler and wondered if it would be left up to him to tell Jake. They were friends. Everyone knew that. And that's what friends were for. He knew that, believed in it, but he still didn't want to be the one to tell him.

"How about Jake?" Rosie was saying quietly.

Cloud nodded. "I'll tell him."

"No. I meant . . . well, you know eighty percent of all killings are committed by—"

Cloud's cold-eyed stare stopped him. "Forget it. I was with him and Strobish tonight from nine to twelve." A little ashamed of his brittle tone, he softened his features.

"Good," Rosie said happily. "I didn't really think . . . oh, I haven't told you. We know what time they were killed; close, at least." Watching Cloud light another cigarette, he shook his head in disapproval. "You're smoking way too much again."

"Are you through with us, Lieutenant?" David Russell rose from his seat on the porch and stood waiting, his lean pock-marked face impatient. "We finished a half-hour ago." He threw Rosie a truculent glance.

"How about inside?"

Red Stovall stepped forward. "We lifted a bunch of latents in there, Ben, but we'll have to wring them out, compare them with the dead women." He shrugged. "Maybe we'll get lucky."

"I wouldn't count on it," Rosie said. "This bastard is careful. Or maybe he wore gloves. The only article of clothing that would have handily taken prints was the Elliot girl's shoes. He obviously had them in his hands when he stacked them beside the girl's other things, but Red here went over them with a fine-tooth comb and didn't find a usable print."

Stovall nodded. "I'd say they were wiped down."

Cloud turned to Rosie. "Anything else turn up inside?"

The big man shook his head. "Nothing that jumped out at me. We turned the place upside down, bagged a lot of stuff like checkbooks, old check stubs, some letters and photographs, two personal phone books, and the Elliot girl's diary, but I couldn't see any real connection with the murders. At least the phone books will give us a quick starting place."

Cloud nodded. "Anything on parents, other relatives?"

"One of the letters was from the Elliot girl's mother. She lives in Dallas."

Cloud looked at Stovall. "Okay, you can take off. Tell them to come on in for the bodies." He watched the two men gather their equipment, walk hump-shouldered into the rain. He sucked on the cigarette, then whirled back to Rosie. "Well? What are you waiting for, a drum roll? How do you know the time?"

"What?" Rosie did a momentary double take. "Oh, yeah, the Elliot girl's watch. It was smashed—crushed I guess was more like it. The glass wedged the hands at 10:01."

"It was still on her wrist?"

"Yeah. It's a battery-powered type. I told Stovall to check the battery, make sure it hadn't stopped on its own."

Cloud's gaze drifted back to the girl. He whistled softly through his teeth, his dark brown eyes squinted. He took a last drag on the cigarette and flipped it out into the rain.

"You'd think he would've noticed," he said.

Rosie rolled massive shoulders in a shrug. "What difference would it make to him? She probably broke it flinging her arms when he was choking her. Or he coulda stepped on it. There's some dark smudges on her wrist, on the inside. Could be heel marks." He shifted his feet and cleared his throat. "You haven't said what you thought about my theory."

"It sounds all right, Rosie. For now, at least. Until we can find out where the Elliot girl was tonight, how the Butler woman spent her evening." He walked to the edge of the patio and stood looking into the dark, weeping night, thinking of all the things that had to be done. And as swiftly as possible. Time was an enemy, an implacable, relentless foe that could easily defeat them. The first few hours were the most important. Out there somewhere a man was waiting, bloodlust gone, his frenzy abated. He would be riddled with uncertainty, perhaps conscience-stricken, certainly filled with a steadily growing dread as he recounted his black deed, wondering frantically if he had made some mistake, many mistakes, left his signature at the scene in some unfathomable manner. Killing another human is an awesome and eternal thing, Cloud thought, a festering malignancy of the soul, and no one is totally immune to its effect.

Cloud moved restlessly, stirred by a sense of urgency. "What makes you think he followed her home?"

"No real reason. It just seems logical—"

"Maybe he was already here waiting for her. Maybe hiding there in the shrubbery, at the corner of the house . . . in the garage."

Rosie nodded somberly. "He could have, I guess. We checked the garage. The Butler woman's car is in there—the motor stone-cold dead, by the way. I'd say it hadn't been moved in at least six hours. The walk-in door was unlocked all right, and Stovall picked up a few prints, but my guess is they'll turn out to be the women's."

"Could be he killed Ramona Butler first. Maybe a robbery at that."

"Nothing disturbed in the house except the bedspread where he got the sheet. It's balled up on the floor."

Cloud shook his head. "There wouldn't be. He killed her quickly, savagely. No time for her to resist or try to get away."

"Then why would he bring her out here on the patio? Why not leave her where she fell if he killed her inside? It don't make sense, Ben."

"Maybe that's why he did it this way," Cloud said, a tingling wash of old familiar feelings creeping over him, a mixture of frustration, weariness, and anger. "Because it doesn't make any sense to us doesn't mean it didn't make sense to him. Maybe he's a nut."

Rosie nodded slowly, as if the thought had already occurred to him. "Let's hope not. Because if he is some kind of psycho, then he's liable to do it again."

They stared at each other through the heavy, almost liquid, air. After a moment, Rosie walked over and laid his clipboard on the concrete porch. He looked at Cloud and shrugged. "Historically speaking, nuts are repeaters. I don't have to tell you that."

"Then don't," Cloud said crisply, turning back to face the dripping night. "We've got all we can handle right here and now."

4

Car tires squealed out in the street. Cloud turned to look down the driveway as Rosie came up beside him. Two men in white uniforms protected by clear, plastic rain gear halted halfway up the drive as a tall figure in a flapping, tan raincoat rushed past them.

"Shit," Rosie said, "it's Rafferty."

"Yeah." Cloud reached automatically for a cigarette, relieved. He wouldn't have to tell him, after all.

Jake Rafferty pulled up a few feet away, his gaze sweeping over Rosie, finding Cloud's, locking. His square, open face was pale, dark patches under his eyes that Cloud had never noticed before. His mouth pursed in an involuntary movement, then pulled thin across strong, white teeth.

"It's not true, is it, Ben?" It was a hoarse, pleading whisper.

"I'm sorry, Jake."

Rafferty's square shoulders rounded, his hands going deep inside the raincoat's pockets. His springy salt-and-pepper thatch of hair was gradually succumbing to the weight of the rainwater, a wiry patch slowly uncoiling over his right eye. Water streaked his cheeks; he blinked his eyes twice, rapidly, then walked stiffly past the silent detectives.

He stopped a few feet away from the two bodies and stood, swaying. He moaned softly, then seemed to break at the waist, bending forward, dropping to his knees. He came to rest with his head touching the concrete, shoulders shaking, a small puddle of water beginning to form. He made raw, painful sounds, almost obscured by the soft, steady drumbeat of rain on the aluminum roof. The two men from the ambulance came onto the patio and stood quietly, watching.

Cloud lit the cigarette, avoiding Rosie's gaze, feeling a deep, genuine empathy for his friend and a tiny stir of uneasiness at seeing a strong man cry—whatever the reason.

They stood for minutes, not certain what to do, not sure how much grief was enough.

Cloud finished the cigarette; he looked finally at Rosie. The big man shrugged, his expression noncommittal. Cloud zipped up his Windbreaker and put his hands on Rafferty's shoulders.

"Come on, man. Come on, buddy, this is no good." Surprisingly, the grieving detective's shoulders moved easily under his hands. Cloud helped him to his feet. He stood, swaying. "I think . . . I think I ought to . . . see her," he said dully. "Is it . . . is she bad?"

"Not like you think," Cloud said. "She's dead, Jake, but he didn't''—he groped for a word—"mistreat her."

Rafferty's head shifted toward the naked girl. "Not like her?" he said, his voice almost childlike, plaintive, seeking something good out of the monumental bad. He took a hand out of the raincoat pocket and wiped his cheeks, squeezed the bridge of his nose.

"No, not like her," Cloud said reassuringly. "The girl was the one he was after. Ramona just happened to get in the way. He just killed her, Jake. Quickly, we think."

"Who, Ben?" His voice was back to normal, beginning to clot with anger. He turned to Cloud, face pulling taut, piercing blue eyes hot and bright with tiny, dancing flames.

"We don't know, Jake. Not yet. We'll find out."

Rafferty's gaze switched to Rosie. "Nothing? You don't have anything?" The anger in his voice was full-blown now. He could vent it on Rosie; Rosie wasn't his best friend. "Goddammit, Rosie, nothing?"

"We're investigating, Jake," Rosie said, his own face tightening, making allowances for pain, for friendship. "You're a cop. You know the drill—"

"Hell with the drill! I want this son of a bitch caught!" His hands came out of the raincoat pockets, clubbed fists swinging in a wide arc. "What about the neighbors? They must have seen

. . . heard something. Dammit—'' His voice chopped off, ended in a choking sob. He turned abruptly away.

"We've canvassed the neighborhood, Jake," Rosie said, his voice gentle. "We still got men out there working. Her next-door neighbor found her—them. He's the one called it in. Other than that, nobody saw or heard a thing. That's not surprising. There were no gunshots.''

"How about the neighbor," Jake Rafferty said. "Maybe—"

"He's seventy-four years old. Weighs about a hundred-ten. He couldn't have done this with a platoon of marines helping him.''

Rafferty's shoulders slumped; he turned his head and looked toward the bodies, his face set and hard; his lips twitched, crimped together, then went slack. He whirled and crossed to the driveway, walked back the way he had come, shoulders hunched, head drooping.

Rosie shook his shaggy head and looked at Cloud. "Bad. He took it bad.''

"What the hell did you expect?" Cloud said sharply. He motioned to the ambulance attendants still standing silently at the corner of the house. "Let's get it cleaned up.''

He walked over and sat down on the edge of the small porch, abruptly aware that he was exhausted. A long day, the three-hour stakeout, and now this. Too much. He wasn't a young man anymore. He glanced at his watch and tried to figure out how many cigarettes he had had since midnight. His mind wouldn't compute. He took out the pack and started to count, stopped, shook one free and lit it.

He stood up abruptly. "We need to look this over again in the daylight. It's too easy to miss something at night, too many shadows. Bring Stovall and Russell with you. I'll have Graves cover the autopsy.''

Rosie nodded. "I'll hang around for a while. We've still got some men working the neighborhood. I think I'll talk to old man Harold again. He's the guy who found them.''

They walked down the driveway together. Officer Gosdin was back in his prowl car. The Channel 5 news truck was still parked down the street. The press cars were gone. A familiar yellow-clad figure broke away and started toward them.

"Damn," muttered Cloud.

Rosie grinned. "Want me to handle her? I already dusted her off once tonight. I think I intimidate her.''

"Yeah. But be gentle, Rosie. Remember our new PR image, firm but courteous."

"Uh-huh. She gets feisty with me, I'll turn her over my knee and paddle her. Come to think about it, that might be fun." He stepped over the sagging crime-scene tape and angled across the grass with a long-legged, purposeful stride.

Cloud ducked his head and turned left at the street, feeling cowardly but righteous, a bit annoyed at her persistence, more than a little surprised at his own reaction to a dimpled smile and flashing green eyes. A pleasant encounter, he acknowledged ruefully, but once a night was enough.

5

Spencer Price paused at the rear entrance to the apartment. Key in hand, he turned to look back along the dark, narrow walkway he had just traversed, a five-foot wide passageway formed by two six-foot cedar fences. It was one of the main reasons—if not *the* main reason—why he had taken the shabby little one room efficiency apartment-with-bath, and he had come to regard it as part of his private preserve, the secret entrance to his little domain.

From his vantage point on the small, square, concrete stoop, he could see over the wooden gate at the far end, the jumble of cardboard boxes and general refuse behind Mack and Mabel's Sack and Save grocery store. He could see his battered car in the adjacent apartment parking lot, and a portion of the street beyond, deserted at this time of night. The grocery was closed, as were all the shabby businesses that comprised one of Trinity Square's oldest strip of shopping centers. Oldest and crappiest, he thought.

Satisfied that he had not been observed, he opened the door and went inside. Pausing only to relock the door and put on the chain, he made a beeline for the half-sized refrigerator built into a rickety square of cabinets in the section of the room purported to be a kitchenette. A three-legged hot plate graced one end of a short, chipped and torn Formica counter. A four-slice toaster sat nearby, its cord fuzzy and frayed, one prong of the electrical plug missing. Rusty water streamed from the single faucet into

the small sink, leaving a rat's tail of dirty gold across its yellowed enamel bowl.

But Spencer Price hardly noticed. He didn't live here. He
didn't eat here, and only occasionally fell asleep across the
lumpy, sagging bed or on the couch before the TV.

This was his retreat, as mean and uninspiring as it was, his
secret place to come to when life overwhelmed, when his mind
reeled with images of what once had been, stagnated with what
was *now*.

He took a bottle of beer out of the refrigerator, popped the
cap, and drank deeply. He crossed the room with loose, heavy
strides, threw himself into the overstuffed chair with the musical
springs and dirty, exposed stuffing.

He stared sightlessly at the blind eye of the cheap portable
TV, the events of the evening tumbling across his mind's eye in
a kaleidoscopic rush, bringing heat to his loins and a kind of
savage, soaring joy.

Once again he felt the bound-up hair against his chest; once
again he heard the sharp unbearably loud crack of vertebrae, the
soft, womanly feel of her rounded buttocks against his tumes-
cing loins.

He remembered holding her tightly long minutes after she was
dead, dark, wicked desires holding sway, teasing him with wild,
hypnotic impulses as his free hand explored her unresisting body.

But in the end, cool reason had prevailed. He had put her
away from him, covered temptation with a sheet.

The ritual is the thing, he had kept reminding himself, over
and over.

Now, slowly, deliberately, he forced the runaway projector
inside his head to slow, to stop, to proceed again in stop-and-go
motion, concentrating this time on the younger one, the one with
the heavy mass of auburn hair he had so meticulously arranged
around the sleeping face, the delicate pink tongue he had jammed
behind her teeth. He had carefully wiped away the tears and
worked her lids down to hide the once beautiful eyes, now
marred by tiny red ruptures that were the sad and inevitable
result of strangulation.

He had worked swiftly but well, humming under his breath,
stopping only once to indulge himself again on the still-warm
corpse, a rapid exchange that took only minutes, seconds really,
and left him panting and empty, shivering with a sudden surge
of self-disgust.

But then he had sat erect and breathed deeply, forcing the self-loathing to fade, go away. Such thoughts were self-destructive and illogical.

This was the body he had been born with. He could no more control his compulsions than he could control the urge to eat, and his mind and emotions had come along with the body. At last it was clear that he was destined to serve his own gods, as old and dangerous as they may be. He had dwelled among the living dead far too long. Now, once again, he was alive, living the way he had been meant to do from the beginning.

He was only a man, but he had been given the power of life or death, endowed with the remorseless instincts of a true predator.

It was his mandate, and he would use it wisely and well—and often.

Later, when his seething thoughts had slowed to a placid murmur, he got up and left the apartment, still exhausted but somehow refreshed, cleansed, chastened, the one sensation he felt above all others a sense of rejuvenation, a thrilling feeling of rebirth.

6

Watching the early-morning furor outside his office windows begin to dissipate as his detectives, singly and in pairs, vacated the large, airy squad room, Capt. Eli Summers yawned prodigiously and thought about the coming day with more than normal trepidation. Elbows propped on his desk, his first mug of coffee of the day trailing a nauseous vapor into his short pug nose, he sourly considered the ramifications of a double homicide on the equilibrium of Trinity Square, Texas.

And not just a double homicide, a good old-fashioned, drunken brawl that got out of hand, a couple of pimps gutting each other over a valuable pross, two winos clubbing each other to death with a bottle of muscatel. Hell no. Sex murders, for chrissakes. Ritual sex murders at that: One laid out like the Madonna, the other propped open like the town pump. How the hell did you work up a press release on that?

A shitstorm, he thought morosely. With one-fourth the population of Trinity Square female and under thirty, it was going to be a veritable shitstorm and, as usual, he would be the one without an umbrella. He allowed himself a long moment of discontent, screwing his round, freckled face into a doleful mask of self-pity.

He took a healthy slug of coffee, then lurched backward and sprayed the bitter brew into the wastebasket, exhaling gustily to cool seared membranes. He swore and yanked open the middle drawer on the right side of his desk. He tugged the cover off a small rectangular carton labeled "staples" and took out a bottle of Irish whiskey.

Imagine forgetting something like that, he thought ruefully, dumping a generous dollop of amber fluid into the coffee, swishing it carefully, sipping cautiously, adding a bit more, then looking up in annoyance as his office door burst open without the customary courtesy rap. Seeing Jake Rafferty's pale, stormy face, he suspected the shitstorm had begun.

"Hello, Sergeant," he said casually, capping the bottle and putting it away. "Have a seat," he added politely, covertly studying his subordinate's face, understanding his agitation, the obvious pain, noting the belligerence banked just below the surface, realizing the reason for that and dreading the coming confrontation. A gentle man himself, he had long ago come to terms with the volatile nature of most cops, had, in fact, used that predictable trait on occasion in his own somewhat meteoric rise in the department. Small in stature, wiry of frame, he had learned early on that big men were soft clay in the hands of a small man with brains.

He took a sip of coffee. "Sorry about your fiancée, Jake," he said quietly.

Rafferty nodded jerkily, caught in the peculiarly male dilemma of having to reluctantly acknowledge and accept pity and make an appropriate reply in return. He avoided it by charging head on.

"I want a transfer, Captain. Temporary. A temporary transfer to Homicide."

Summers sipped, stared thoughtfully at the plate-glass window behind Rafferty's back as if he were seriously considering what both men knew was a hopelessly absurd request. He squinted pale green eyes and made his face pucker gravely. Finally, he sighed and shook his head.

"I'm sorry, Jake, I can't do that. If you were working Homicide now I'd have to keep you away from the case. You know that. You're emotionally involved. Emotion crowds out logic, clouds the reasoning process." He shook his head sadly. "You know I can't do it."

"I want a leave of absence then."

Summers shook his head again. "It wouldn't matter, Jake. You still couldn't poke around in the case. We'd have to stop you."

"I can quit," Rafferty said tightly, his lips pulling thin in an involuntary rictus.

Summers leaned forward earnestly. "Don't do that, Jake. You've got six, seven years you'd be throwing away. Even if we took you back later on, you'd lose your time in grade, have to start all over. You're a good detective, a good cop. You've done a great job in Narcotics, maybe one of the best yet. Leave homicides to Cloud. Cloud and his group. Let them do their job. They'll get the bastard for us."

"I want him myself!" It was a hoarse, rasping growl wrested painfully from a tormented soul.

"See!" Summers was almost shouting. "See! Dammit! That's why I can't let you near the case. You blow that asshole away and we'd be standing lip deep in shit for a year! The goddamned bleeding hearts would come down on us like the plague. I don't care if he's a mother-mauling baby-stomper, we got idiots out there'd scream blue murder if we busted a pimple on his ass. You know damn well how the courts are today. One whiff of personal involvement with an investigator on the case and the bastard would walk. If we caught him limp and dripping over a dead girl, he'd walk." He stopped, breathing heavily. "And, dammit, you know it!"

"No, he wouldn't," Rafferty said sullenly, "not very far."

"And you'd spend the rest of your bloody life in a bloody jail." Bloody? Hell, Cricket Bloom was infecting the whole damn department.

Rafferty stood up and strode to the window, anger and frustration evident in the taut, strained face, the rigid lines of his slender, compact body. He stood stiffly erect, staring out across a sea of monotonous rooftops, the sterile, unimaginative apartment complexes that housed more than forty percent of Trinity Square's eighty thousand people.

"Will you give me access to the file?" He whirled before Summers could answer. "I have to know what's going on, Captain. I—I just have to know." Despite his obvious effort to keep it out, there was a note of agonized pleading in the husky voice.

Summers felt a rush of empathy. "I think that can be arranged—if Lieutenant Cloud agrees, of course. I think he will."

Rafferty nodded, his face revealing his relief. He turned away from the window and crossed to the door. "Thanks, Captain," he said, and went out quietly.

Summers stared at the door. He sipped at his cold coffee, suddenly realizing in the small blaze of a minor epiphany that the somber detective had achieved exactly what he had expected to achieve. All the rest had been window-dressing bullshit, throwaway points in a cleverly manipulated game.

He smiled wryly and lifted his mug in a salute to the departed detective, moved Jake Rafferty up a notch in his estimation.

7

Cloud called a halt at six o'clock. He glanced at the three weary faces around him and wondered if he looked that bedraggled. They had been going like racetrack greyhounds since nine that morning, compiling a list, two lists actually: relatives and friends of Laura Sue Elliot. Beginning with the murdered girl's parents, a web of names had been steadily growing, each person they managed to contact by phone supplying additional names until their list had grown to over fifty. The one name Cloud had been most interested in had been obtained from Laura's mother: the name of her current boyfriend.

Twenty minutes later, Cloud had scratched him from the list of possible suspects; a flight engineer with a major international airline, he had been somewhere over the Atlantic Ocean when Laura Sue was killed. Confirmed.

Ron Graves, the third man on Cloud's Homicide Squad, pushed back from his desk and stood up. He stretched and pumped at his left ear with the palm of his hand. He shook his head and grinned at Cloud. "Jesus, I don't feel right without that damn phone stuck in there."

He had flaming red hair and a dense camouflage of freckles. A weightlifter by avocation, he was partial to tight, faded jeans and tank tops. He had a magnificent body, a shy, crooked smile, and a bouncy, somewhat feminine walk that had led more than one misguided redneck to the unfortunate conclusion that he was gay.

Elsie Locklear, civilian, a tall, square-shouldered blond on loan from the computer terminal, lit her fortieth cigarette of the day and sagged into her chair in mock-exhaustion. "I haven't worked this hard since I left the streets." A trifle to the right of pretty, she had a well-formed face with a bit too much nose, and crooked teeth. But her wit was dry, her humor contagious, and she worked conscientiously and well, and that was what mattered to Cloud.

Rosie Simple insisted on making one more phone call, and Cloud left the small room alone, wondering how much of the long day's drudgery would prove fruitless. All of it, most likely, he thought, shrugging to throw off the pall of weariness that had clung like a wet shirt since he had forced himself out of bed after only four hours of sleep. And another day of the same tomorrow.

After that would come the interrogations, endless driving and endless questions, lies and evasions and half-truths arising from the very human need to put oneself as far away as possible from the creeping tentacles cast by the dark shadow of the dead girl's murder.

But that was the drill, and sometimes it worked. Not always, but sometimes. Often enough to make it worthwhile.

Once, during a routine neighborhood check after the murder of two elderly pensioners, Cloud had knocked on the door of a small frame house two blocks away from the murder scene. Hot and sweaty, he had reached for his handkerchief at the instant a tall, gangling youth opened the door and, seeing Cloud's hand back there near the gun, the boy had thrown up his hands and screamed, "Okay, you got me! I give up! Don't shoot!"

As easy as that. Not often, but what the hell else was there?

He drove west on Commodore Avenue past a bustling phalanx of fast-food restaurants. Near the extreme western edge of the city, he turned into the macadam parking lot of a sparkling white colonial mansion that had been recently renovated and converted into a cafeteria-style steak house. Good food in a homey atmosphere.

Completely disenchanted with the plastic, assembly-line foods of the more flamboyant chains, Cloud had been eating at The House, as it was called, on an average of three nights a week since it had opened. It was run by a husband and wife team who compensated for a bad location and lack of advertising with well-cooked food at reasonable prices. Cloud had noticed a steady increase in customers until it was now sometimes necessary to stand in line.

He ordered sirloin strip, medium rare, baked potato, and built his own salad at the well-stocked salad bar. Two pieces of Texas toast, a large glass of milk, and a slice of chocolate pie seemed about right to his hungry eye.

A simple meal for a simple man, he thought, selecting a two-person table tucked into a small natural alcove formed by a bank of live rhododendrons and an immense wooden pillar sporting a gleaming coat of beige paint that failed to conceal the checkered tracks of time. A huge, old-fashioned candle chandelier with subdued lighting dominated the main eating area, and muted murals depicting western ranch life in the 1800s covered the area above dark, waist-high wainscoting. A pleasant room, conducive to leisurely dining and good digestion.

Cloud buttered his toast and baked potato and was reaching for his steak knife when the brown, pleated skirt billowing smartly above knee-high brown boots came into his peripheral vision. He watched, head down, cutting into his steak, not at all surprised when the boots stopped in front of his table.

He had seen the black-and-white news van behind him all the way down Commodore Avenue, but had dismissed it as coincidence when the van had zipped busily past the restaurant parking lot. Now he knew, and he wondered how she would handle it.

"Well, hello!" Surprise, and just the right amount of cheerful delight: a trace of reticence and a dash of coquetry. "Imagine seeing you here?"

Cloud didn't look up. "Why? You didn't think cops ate?"

Amy Reed laughed gaily. "Not that. In the movies and books you cops are always grabbing hamburgers and hot dogs while you're waiting to pounce on the bad guys." Her bright chatter seemed a trifle strained, Cloud thought, the trailing laugh more for the benefit of possible onlookers than for him. He chewed steak methodically, took a bite of salad.

"Well," she went on, obviously undaunted, "we both seem to be alone. Shall I join you?"

Cloud looked pointedly at a nearby empty table, then, a little ashamed of himself, nodded and said, "Sure. Why not?" He moved his salad bowl a token half-inch closer in and finally, reluctantly, looked up.

"Don't get up," she said sweetly, and he found himself choking on a laugh. Green eyes sparkling, that incredible smile on full candlepower, she stacked her food on the table and deposited her tray on a nearby cart. She settled across from him and leaned forward to look at his plate, heart-shaped face alight with amusement.

"My, that looks good. I wish I could afford to eat like that." She surveyed her own meager meal, a large bowl of salad and crackers, a small cup of yogurt and iced tea, and made a pretty, dimpled face.

"It isn't expensive," Cloud said awkwardly, feeling a need to make up for his churlishness. "Could I get—"

She chuckled and shook her head. "It isn't that. I can't afford the calories. I'm forever dieting."

Cloud surreptitiously surveyed what he could see of the slender shoulders, modest breasts, and short, well-rounded arms and decided to leave well enough alone. Personally, he preferred women with a little more meat on their bones, but he had always suspected that was because the first burning passion of his life at the tender age of thirteen had been a ripe, buxom, unapproachable young lady of sixteen years.

"This is a nice place," Amy Reed said. "This is my first time. Do you eat here often?" Not beautiful in the classic sense—nose a bit too short and upturned, full-lipped mouth a smidgen too small for that—there was an arresting quality about her, a warm, eager vitality that suited the glowing, honey-tinted skin, complimented the smoldering intensity behind emerald eyes. Cloud found the combination devastating and, was discovering with a faint flush of resentment, that it had not been the naked eye of the camera alone that had proved his undoing at their first meeting.

"Sometimes," he said brusquely, suddenly aware that he was sitting straighter, had removed his elbows from the table, was chewing more slowly, methodically, wiping his mouth after each bite—shit! Woman power. It was pervasive, insidious.

She finished eating a bit of salad, took a sip of tea. "What I meant before, when I came in, is that it's hard for me to visualize you eating out alone. You look like the home-cooked meal type, pipe and slippers and the evening paper before the news comes on the tube. I can't imaging why, but you have a sort of . . . of married look."

"I can't imagine why, either," he replied dryly. "I'm not."

"Ever been?" She bounced the rim of the tea glass off the

plump fullness of her lower lip, her eyes bright with candid inquisitiveness.

"Only slightly, I think," he said, realizing with a tiny blip of surprise that that was exactly the way to describe his three years with Diana, a light and casual bonding, two human organisms coming together only for purposes of mating, drifting, going their separate ways until the atavistic urges brought them together again.

She laughed. "Me, too. It's only been three years, but it seems like a bad movie I didn't like at the time and can't understand why I even remember at all." She lifted the glass of tea. "Here's to the panacea of our generation—divorce."

He met the lustrous eyes squarely for the first time. "Our generation? You don't look thirty-seven to me."

"That's how old you are, huh?" she said, smiling, unabashedly pleased at his frankness. "Well, I'm twenty-eight. How much is a generation, anyway? It's certainly more than nine years."

He shrugged. "A generation is a state of mind. Goes right along with that other old cliche: 'You're only as old as you feel'." He pulled his gaze away from her, reluctantly shearing the flowing lines of magnetic flux. He attacked his steak again, feeling a foolish, adolescent thrill as her booted foot brushed his under the table.

"Hmmm," she said humorously, "a philosophical cop." She waited a moment and, when he didn't rise to the bait, she bent over her dinner.

8

The silence grew, built rapidly, became oppressive despite the muted undercurrent of noise from the other patrons. A bubble of silence Cloud soon found intolerable. He swallowed a half-chewed piece of steak. "Isn't it about time you began pumping me about the Elliot-Butler murders?" he said abruptly.

"Is that why you think I came over here?"

"In here," Cloud corrected. "You followed me from headquarters. Premeditated surveillance of a police officer. There's probably a statute against that somewhere."

"Why don't you arrest me?" A creeping flush had deposited a rosy spot high on each cheekbone. "Or have you made your quota for the day?" She flashed him a small slice of her smile, insolent and provocative.

"I always have time to handle one more good bust," he said, then grinned at the unintended double entendre.

Her flush deepened. "This is one bust you won't be handling, mister."

He looked directly at her chest and allowed his grin to grow. "That's a rotten shame. I missed my chance with Dolly Parton, too."

Her laugh burst spontaneously, throaty and full, raising startled heads all over the room. She covered her mouth with her hand, her eyes squinted merrily, tiny slits of emerald fire as she shook silently in an effort to confine her laughter.

He watched her and smiled, suddenly feeling very good, witty, in charge.

Tears welled, spilled over onto her cheeks; she waved away his proffered handkerchief and dug in her purse for a wad of Kleenex. After a while, she dabbed her eyes free of moisture and removed her hand. She shook her head, a thick swatch of hair spilling across a flushed cheek. She brushed it over her shoulder in a singularly feminine gesture.

"Jesus," she said. "That was funny. Nasty, but funny." She still refused to look at him.

"Me and Bob Hope," he said, wishing he could think of something else to say that would bring back that delightful sound, that enchanting, rosy look.

"All right," she said severely, "you can't put me off by making funny remarks. I want to—let's see, what were we arguing about?"

It was his turn to laugh. And she joined in, low and husky this time. Intimate. Even more enthralling, he thought.

"Well, I guess we're not going to fight," she said, taking a cigarette from her purse, holding it poised, looking at him expectantly, a tiny smile tilting the corners of the small mouth.

He took out his lighter. "Not liberated, I see," he said, holding the flame for her, lighting one of his own.

"Absolutely. But there's no conflict in wanting to be treated like a lady." She let smoke dribble from her nose. "Besides, I know a male chauvinist when I see one, and since we've decided we're not going to fight . . ." She let it drift away with the smoke.

"What are we going to do?"

She smiled without showing her marvelous teeth. "I don't know what you're going to do, but I'm going home, take a hot, hot bath, and settle in with whatever trashy movie's on cable."

He looked past her, out into the parking lot. "I don't see the van." He brought his gaze back to hers. "Did they drop you off?"

She made a face. "Damn detective. Yes, they dropped me off. I was planning on taking a cab if—" She broke off and shrugged, the crooked smile returning.

"If I didn't take you home, you mean?"

"Something like that," she said coolly.

"Just on the off chance you might learn something more about the murders?"

"You've got it. But, one thing, the ride would have ended at my door." She huffed a ball of smoke at him. "Anyway, it's right on your way."

"You know where I live?"

"Sure. Is it a secret?"

"No. But I—"

"Remember when we had that on-camera interview? I ran you through our files. It was there, address, rank, and serial number." She cocked her head and laughed at his disgruntled look. "You cops aren't the only ones who keep records, you know."

"Why did you bother? That interview was a disaster, and you know it. I looked and acted like a stagestruck ten-year-old."

Her eyes widened in indignation. "You did not! You did fine. I wouldn't have put you on otherwise. I'm not in the business of embarrassing people—even cops. You did great. You spoke slowly and seriously, the way a cop should. Anyway, it was a serious subject."

He shook his head ruefully. "I thought you were being sarcastic when you offered to run me a copy of the tape." He doused the cigarette in the remnants of his milk.

"Never happen," she said, a mocking edge to her voice. "I have nothing but the utmost respect for most cops—even the ones who preen and beat their chests. Male machismo and arrogance are the same, wherever they're found. It's the ones who think violence is the solution to every problem that make me want to upchuck."

"I can't argue with that," he said, standing, picking up both checks. He noted that she made no attempt to replace her lipstick at the table, simply used the wad of Kleenex to wipe her mouth clean. He liked that, and the comfortable silence that followed them to the car.

He shook two cigarettes loose from his pack and she lit them from the dash lighter. Smiling, she handed him one. "No herpes."

"I'm sorry," he said, feeling an absurd tingle as he slipped the cigarette into his mouth.

"What?" She gave him an incredulous smile, wide eyes and dimpled cheeks.

"I'm sorry I don't have anything to give you about the murders."

"No sweat," she said lightly. "It was a dumb idea, anyway.

I get them occasionally. I generally count to ten and they go away.'' She smiled, and they lapsed into silence again.

She lived four blocks from him, a small, three-bedroom brick house in a neat middle-class neighborhood that had weathered well thirty years of harsh Texas elements.

She told him she had been born there, had spent almost every night of her life under its roof, including her honeymoon. Her father had died when she was six, her mother when she was twenty and, except for three odd years of her marriage, she had lived there alone ever since.

She told him good night, patted the back of his hand on the wheel; he waited until she waved to him from inside the door.

He drove home to his empty condominium. Sadly. Alone. Sadly alone.

9

The forensics report revealed little that had not been obvious to the eye at the murder scene. A few shreds and chips of broken fingernails identified as belonging to the Elliot girl; the dry residue collected from behind the nails, as suspected, turned out to be cement. No fingerprints, no bloodstains.

A check of the dead girl's watch battery proved it to be in good working order, indicating the crushed lens had indeed stopped the hands at 10:01 P.M.

An expensive watch, according to Laura's mother, with nine small but excellent quality diamonds studded around the tiny face the size of an almond. A real glass crystal and a twenty-four-carat gold case. Since it was worth at least half as much as the Butler woman's diamond ring, Cloud wondered why the killer had left it behind. Maybe because it was broken; maybe in his frenzy he hadn't noticed it. Or maybe he had a thing for diamond rings, a girl friend to give it to. More likely the flashy sparkler had caught his eye, and it had been a momentary impulse. A souvenir. Cloud would have wagered a year's salary the crimes had not been motivated by robbery.

The Medical Examiner's report also contained few surprises. Cause of death: asphyxiation by strangulation. Surprisingly little damage to larynx and trachea, hyoid bone intact. Instrument: human hands, moderately sized, powerful. Semen present in vagina, throat, and stomach, indicating sexual activity at or about the time of death. Semen samples indicating blood type O.

45

One anomaly that brought a light, thudding shock to Cloud's solar plexus: five smooth stones extracted from the Elliot girl's vagina. Of various sizes ranging from three-quarters of an inch in diameter to the size of a pea. A notation in parentheses identified the small rocks as creek gravel, more commonly known as pea gravel.

Cloud rocked back in his chair, reaching for a cigarette. He was alone in the office. Elsie Locklear had begged off for a couple of hours to attend her computer terminal, and Rosie Simple and Ron Graves were working the seemingly endless list of potential suspects. Relatives and close friends first, radiating outward to encompass casual acquaintances, fellow employees, ex-suitors, and anyone else whose name cropped up during the interminable questioning.

Staring at the ceiling, smoke drifting past squinted eyes, he tried to remember if there had been gravel anywhere in the vicinity of the slayings. He closed his eyes completely, hoping to aid the recall process. Nothing came. He stirred restlessly.

Something about the five smooth stones bothered him. He could almost see it, sensed it teetering on the edge of his awareness, quivering there like the last leaf on a winter oak.

He sat without moving, trying not to think about it directly, seducing his recalcitrant subconscious with trivial nonsense and whimsical musings. It wouldn't come, hovered teasingly—like bright green eyes and a soft, pouting mouth, a slender, supple frame undulating in amorphous frailty—shit. His head began to ache. He heard footsteps approaching.

He relaxed and rocked forward in the chair. He opened his eyes and stared up into the sober face of Jake Rafferty, a quizzical twitch at the corner of his mouth, blue eyes darker than Cloud remembered, deep-sunken, rimmed with purple.

"Catching a few Z's?" Rafferty asked lightly, lowering his slender frame into Cloud's straight-backed visitor's chair. He wore chinos and a checkered sport shirt, scuffed brown loafers, and a yellow cloth baseball-type cap advertising Bell Helicopter.

"Sherlocking," Cloud replied, just as lightly. "Only it isn't working for me. Maybe I need a line of coke to sharpen up the old amino acids or whatever the hell—"

"That the lab and M.E. reports?" Rafferty interrupted quietly.

Cloud nodded reluctantly. "Only on . . . only on the Elliot

girl,'' he said. "We don't have the Butler woman's yet. Lab report's no help at all.''

"Could I see them?''

"Jake,'' Cloud said, then stopped and crushed out his cigarette, groping for the right words. "I know you have Eli's permission, but . . .'' Seeing the hard cast to the roughhewn, handsome face of his friend, he realized that words would be futile. He sighed inwardly, passed the papers over without another word.

He lit another cigarette and watched Rafferty skim through the forensic report, face expressionless, the twin lines beside his nose deep and shadowed as he tilted his face in intense concentration.

Cloud closed his eyes again and tried to bring back his mind's eye vision of Amy Reed. She was there, tauntingly elusive now that he was actively pursuing her; he could see her at the edge of his imaginary vision, but when he tried to look at her directly, she dissolved.

A sound brought his eyes open with a snap; Rafferty sat upright, staring at him fixedly, his mouth a saber slash across a suddenly ashen face, eyes wild. The M.E.'s report rattled in his hand.

"It's him,'' he said, his voice barely above a whisper. "The stones . . . his trademark . . . the way she was laid out. Goddamn! I should have remembered sooner . . . but I couldn't! I didn't know about the stones, Ben, not until just—Jesus, the dirty son—''

"Whoa! Jake. Slow down. Who? What are you talking about? What about the stones?''

Rafferty closed his eyes and breathed deeply, once, twice, three times. Then he opened them again, his face back in order except for rapidly blinking eyes.

"Quantico . . . the FBI school at Quantico, Virginia. Last year when I had that fractured arm, when I was on sick leave . . . you remember . . . I went to that psychological profiling class. Like the one you and Rosie went to before. Arrowstone . . . his name was Arrowstone . . . Julius, no, Julian Arrowstone. A goddamned psycho who'd killed maybe twenty-five, twenty-six girls. He was one of our class subjects.'' His voice had gained volume, laced with vitriolic acerbity. A convulsive shiver rippled through him. "He killed only . . . redheads, only auburn-haired . . .'' His voice dwindled again, his face contorting as if he might cry.

"What about him?" Cloud asked softly. "What makes you think—?"

"The stones," Rafferty said dully, "the stones and the way he left her. He always left them like that, propped open . . . like that. And the stones, always five smooth stones. Maybe I should have realized when I saw her, but I wasn't thinking. I—I was only feeling."

Cloud fished his keys out of his pocket and unlocked the center drawer of his desk. He took out a pint of Wild Turkey. From the large drawer he obtained two small paper cups. He poured the cups half-full and put the bottle away. He handed one of the cups to Rafferty.

"Drink," he said, showing by example what was required.

Rafferty gunned half of his. He thumbed the corners of his moustache, thick and dark against the sallowness of his skin. He nodded his thanks and tried out a fleeting, sickly grin that projected more pain then humor.

"Tell me," Cloud commanded.

10

Rafferty nodded perfunctorily, then drank the rest of his whiskey. He made a sound halfway between a sigh and a sob and dropped the cup into the wastebasket.

"Julian Arrowstone. Here. God help us. When I was at Quantico he was in the news. That's why they used him as a profiling subject. After fifteen years in a psycho ward, the son of a bitch ups and kills a doctor and walks out in the doctor's clothing. That was six months or so before I went to Quantico. They were looking for him in and around New York. And then young girls started dying in Chicago. Five or six, I can't remember. Exactly the same . . . the stones and the same position. Strangulation. Rape. Sometimes sodomy. They said he was killing his mother—his stepmother, to be exact. That's all they learned for sure about him in all those years. An incurable psychopath. He went in when he was nineteen or so, and the psychologists and psychiatrists had a field day. Very controversial. Some called it dissociative reaction." He paused and winced apologetically. "I remember the terms, I'm not sure I remember what all of them mean. I think dissociative reaction refers to a split personality."

Cloud nodded. "We can query New York. If it is him, I don't give a damn why he's doing it. What I need is a description, pictures, prints, background data . . . well, you know what we need as well as I do." He lit a cigarette and studied the other man for a moment. "Maybe it isn't this guy Arrowstone. Maybe it's a copycat."

49

Rafferty looked back at him somberly. "It's possible. But, one thing, the business about the stones. From what the FBI instructor said, it was never made public. Of course, eventually a lot of law enforcement people knew about it and probably told their wives, girl friends, or who have you. But it evidently never came out in the media. And the position of the body. He said as far as he knew the media only referred to it as a ritualistic position. That could mean anything." His face had regained some of its normal swarthy color. He made another feeble smile. "One thing for sure, if it is him, you or someone in authority will be hearing from him. Probably as soon as one of your names hits the news."

Cloud perked up, sat up straighter. "You means he sends letters?"

"No. He calls. Telephone. At least he always has before. In New York he used to call and tell them what night he was going to kill. He never missed once."

"Jesus Christ!"

"Yeah. And it still took them more than two years to catch him. He finally got too reckless, started telling them what area he'd be working. They got lucky and nailed his ass in the act. Otherwise . . ." He let it fade away, and shrugged.

"This thing about him calling intrigues me. Why couldn't they trace his calls?"

Rafferty smiled wryly. "He was too damn smart. He was never on the phone long enough. Except once when he managed to get the home phone number of the detective in charge. I guess they had quite a chat that day. They later bugged the cop's home phone, but after that first time he'd only talk a few minutes. He probably talked to the guy fifty times before they caught him. The same thing happened in Chicago. 'Course, that time they knew his name, but they still never caught him. The killings just suddenly stopped. That's been over a year ago by now. As far as I know, he hasn't shown up anywhere else since."

Cloud shrugged. "There must be hundreds of young girls raped and murdered that we never hear about. If he kept moving around, hitting one or two in each large metropolitan area, he could keep busy for years without a lot of furor. Particularly if he quit using the stones, stopped playing with them afterwards."

"I don't think he'll do that," Rafferty said. "The uproar and notoriety is a part of it for him. At Quantico they thought he was killing to fulfill some sort of maniacal compulsion. He's trying to say something, and having people know about his work is important to him. Maybe it's something simple like 'Hey, look at how smart I am. The stupid cops are too damn dumb to catch me'.''

Cloud bounced a rubber-tipped pencil on his desk, then hunched forward toward his visitor, his dark eyes alight with interest.

"We both went to the same profiling class at Quantico. How do you read the murder scene? I know you were emotionally out of it the other night, but you must have done some thinking since then.''

Rafferty stared at him silently for a moment, his lips pursed in a whistle as soft as a baby's breath, his eyes quiet and steady within their dark, sunken sockets.

"I've thought about nothing else,'' he said. "I think I know what you're getting at. It's almost as though there were two killers. Ramona was blitzed. A savage attack that was over quickly. Afterwards, her killer treated her gently, even to the point of covering her, going to a lot of trouble to do so. Except for taking the ring, he probably didn't touch her again. Certainly her clothing wasn't disarranged in any way. That seems to indicate an older man, one with some degree of humanity, maybe someone who knew her, a relative or a friend. She was more attractive than the Elliot girl, yet he didn't rape her, molest her in any way. He simply killed her. And took her ring. I believe he may have taken the ring as a memento, a way to relive the incident later.'' He stopped.

"How does that equate with your theory about Arrowstone?''

Rafferty sighed heavily. "It doesn't. But it could be a first for him. They never mentioned any double slayings attributed to Arrowstone. He was obviously after the Elliot girl—the right age, auburn hair. I think Ramona came up on him afterwards, or during, and he had to kill her. Maybe it bothered him because it wasn't in his script. His scenerio was a young girl, auburn-haired. And here he had two. Maybe he killed Ramona before the Elliot girl, and he couldn't stand her dead—'' His voice faltered, and he looked away. "Her dead eyes watching him,'' he finished quietly. "So he covered her up.''

"And the Elliot girl,'' Cloud said, his dark brown eyes intent.

Rafferty massaged the bridge of his nose, trailed his fingers down to smooth his moustache, tug lightly on a slightly misshapen nose that had been poked into too many barroom brawls.

"The Elliot girl,'' he echoed. "A different scene entirely.

Obviously his emotional focus. He played with her. Dominated her. Probably had her paralyzed with fear because she evidently made no attempt to fight him; she scratched the concrete instead. He probably took his time, enjoying it, acting out his fantasy, whatever it is. Making her do things, doing things to her. He probably killed her slowly, and after she was dead, worked on her features to make them as pretty as possible. And then his signature—the stones and the obscene position.'' He wagged his head slowly. ''Crazy. Crazy. Maybe they were right, some of them. Maybe he's got a split personality. Maybe the neat compassionate one only comes out when he's needed.''

''That would explain a lot of things,'' Cloud said. ''But whether he's one man or half a dozen, we need to find out if he's *our* man.'' He pushed back from the desk. ''I'll get a query off to New York and Chicago.'' He hesitated, smiling crookedly. ''Then I think I may become a TV star.''

Rafferty's bushy eyebrows lifted, but before he could speak a rotund figure in the open doorway. Red-faced, a two-day growth of beard, earlobe-length hair in wild disarray, he looked exactly like the homeless derelict he was supposed to be.

''Hi yuh, Jake, Ben.'' He lifted a dirty hand to his forehead in a snappy salute.

''Doneli,'' Cloud said. ''Jesus, are you still working for us? I heard you'd died and gone to wino heaven.''

Doneli grinned and blew his nose into a ragged blue bandanna. ''I don't get in from the front lines much. You spit-and-polish rear echelon assholes make me nervous.''

Rafferty snorted. ''Don't let him kid you. He's found a home. I saw him on the street the other day with his hand on a bag lady's ass.''

''Turned out to be a narc in drag,'' Doneli said. ''Ben, I have a message from little Sammy Keeler. Says he needs to see you ASAP.''

Rafferty and Cloud exchanged glances. ''Me?'' Cloud said. ''Did he say what it was about?''

''Nope. Seemed nervous, jumpy, you know. Said you'd know where.'' He lifted a meaty hand. ''Hey, you guys, don't let your meat loaf.'' He bellowed a laugh and disappeared.

''I wonder why me?'' Cloud turned to Rafferty. ''He's your snitch now. You set up the bust the other night.''

Rafferty shrugged. ''Knowing Sammy, he probably laid back

somewhere and watched us set up the stakeout. He probably knows you were in on it. He always liked you, Ben.''

Cloud nodded. ''Only one way to find out.'' He rocked back in the chair and grinned. ''I'll check in with him right after I make my comeback on TV.''

11

Like many of the small cities in the Dallas and Fort Worth suburbs, Trinity Square had never expected to amount to much. A small farming town in the early fifties, two thousand inhabitants more or less, no industry worth the name, it just sort of grew like an unattended fungus. The original downtown Trinity Square was in a small valley bordered on its southern edge by the Trinity River, on its northern limits by a range of low, scalloped hills covered with sagebrush and post oak suitable only for the grazing of cattle.

Highway 183, once the major artery between Dallas and Fort Worth, bisected the downtown area. The rest of the town grew in haphazard clusters south toward the river or swarmed northward into the lower reaches of the hills. The homes were small, frame houses for the most part, with an occasional two-story clapboard or brick veneer usually inhabited by the town's businessmen, the movers and shakers, such as they were.

Signs of growth began in the late fifties. In fits and starts. Modest tracts of homes appeared almost overnight. Cheap construction and low prices, usually located in the less desirable southern section of the town where the land was cheapest. It was also level and could be razed easily by bulldozers, the homes stacked neatly along its arrow-straight streets with little need for costly contour planning.

But it wasn't until the sixties that the big developers began to take notice of little Trinity Square, its rolling, wooded landscape north of the highway, its proximity to the proposed Dallas/Fort Worth Airport, its ideal location close to the midpoint between the two cities. Land values boomed. Residential building resumed with a vengeance. Better houses this time. Invariably brick veneer, each house with its own modern elevation, the more savvy builders leaving the existing trees where they stood, finally seeming to understand that instant shade in Texas was well worth the extra effort.

A city began to form. City planners were hired. The city council expanded from three to six and hired a city manager. The police department initiated a steady expansion that wasn't to stop until the mini-depression of the early eighties.

People poured in, bought the new homes. Engineers, buyers, salesmen and executives from bustling firms such as Bell Helicopter, LTV, General Motors; from as far away as General Dynamics, twenty-five miles to the west.

Growth and prosperity. It was a heady tonic. A generous citizen, one of the ranchers who had grown rich from the sale of his land, deeded a thirty-acre tract on the southwestern edge of town to the city for an industrial park. A concerted effort began to attract small business. A successful effort as it turned out. However, Trinity Square, with its ideal location between two large, prosperous cities, appeared destined from the beginning to become a bedroom community, a service community for thousands of people seeking the good life away from the congestion, smog, and crime of the inner cities in the seventies.

It was part of the American dream, a fine house in suburbia, a decent place to raise kids, a place where young mothers could walk their babies down the street without fear of being accosted by muggers, rapists, or degenerates.

But, insofar as Benjamin Cloud and Rosie Simple were concerned, it was only a dream. Trinity Square, no longer little, no longer sleepy, had its full contingent of muggers, rapists, and other assorted degenerates. With very little coaxing, they would have stood up and testified to that. With almost no coaxing at all they would have stood up and told you that muggers, rapists, and other degenerates were predators, that predators must have victims, and that suburbia was rapidly becoming the most lucrative hunting ground of all. Like the soft underbelly of the porcupine, suburbia was one of America's most vulnerable spots.

But thoughts of muggers, rapists, and degenerates were only dim shadows of awareness in the minds of both men as they left

Trinity Square for Dallas, Rosie driving as usual, a two-year-old
Pontiac just off the mechanic's rack, a blue-black cloud of smoke
hanging on behind them like a persistent winter cough.

"Just once, by God," Rosie growled, "I'd like to get a car
that didn't look and smell like it had diarrhea."

"Our own fault," Cloud said. "We're getting a late start, and
the bad ones are always left for last."

Rosie snorted and whipped around a pickup loaded with bales
of hay. "There ain't no damn good ones."

"Uh-huh." Cloud lit a cigarette, cracked a window, and
looked out across the rooftops of Irving. Another town much
like Trinity Square, he thought, only a little bigger, more harried
people scurrying to nowhere to do nothing.

They topped a rise and dipped into the gentle curve fronting
the Texas Stadium, home of the Dallas Cowboys. Built during a
time when the Cowboys thought of themselves as America's
team, it had a gaudy, unstable, futuristic look about it, a look
that exemplified the disorganized team's current roller-coaster
style of playing.

"No bowl ring this year," Rosie said, uncannily reading
Cloud's thoughts. "Them shithooks will be lucky to make the
playoffs."

"Don't look good."

They climbed another small rise and entered the bridge across
the Elm fork of the Trinity River. Ten miles ahead of them,
Dallas rose out of the rolling plains, its horizon unimpressive
from this viewpoint, a city of angles, modest squares, and soaring quadrangles of concrete metal and glass, a city aspiring to
sophistication and elegance, the best that money could buy.

A low-slung blue Ford flashed in from two lanes to their left,
cut into the small safety space ahead of them, then ducked right
to make the freeway exit.

Rosie tapped the brakes and swore. "Oughta run that dipshit
down and whip his ass."

"Looked like a little old lady to me, Rosie," Cloud said.
"But I'll hold her for you if you want." He leaned right to peer
around the van in front of them. "Next exit. Regal Row. It's off
to the right somewhere in among all those small businesses."

"Yeah. I think I know about where it is. My wife used to
work out here. I picked her up a couple of times."

"Who's the guy from Dallas?"

"Sergeant named Lafitte, Jerry Lafitte. Said he'd meet us in front of the place.'' Rosie eased the cream-colored Pontiac out of the traffic flow into the curving exit. ''Didn't sound too happy about it.''

Cloud shrugged. ''Par for the course. As long as he's there. He can sit there and suck his thumb, for all I care. All I want is his presence, not his input.''

''Typical Dallas bullshit,'' Rosie said, turning off the service road onto a winding street bordered by small brick and concrete buildings. ''They don't hesitate a minute when they need our help for something.''

''Any idea how big Cinetex is?''

''Not very, according to the Elliot girl's mother. Forty or fifty employees, maybe, along in there.''

''This guy Coover give you any flack?''

''Naw, not really. He was kinda . . . cautious, I guess. Can't say I blame him with his rap sheet. He wouldn't come in for a talk, but he said he'd be glad to see us at his office.'' Rosie turned left at the first intersection, drove slowly past several businesses with ornate facades and neatly cropped lawns. ''It's right along here somewhere, I think.''

They drifted along the almost deserted street. Cloud spotted the building first, rust-colored block with a glass-brick entranceway, a small, unpretentious sign above a portico supported by two white, metal columns.

Rosie pulled into the curb behind a tan-colored Buick with sagging springs. A man sat slouched behind the wheel, a baseball cap pulled over his eyes.

''There's our man Lafitte,'' Rosie said. ''Looks like their cars are even worse than ours, if that's possible.''

They got out and walked up beside the Buick. The man appeared to be asleep. Cloud knuckled the window lightly. The man moved, one hand coming up to lift the cap, the other reaching for the keys dangling in the switch. He looked out at Cloud and nodded, unsmiling. He dropped the cap on the car seat and opened the door. He climbed out, looked across the car top at Rosie.

''Glad you guys could make it.''

''Sorry we're a little late,'' Cloud said easily. ''We appreciate your cooperation. I'm Ben Cloud, and this is Rosie Simple.''

''Jerry Lafitte.'' He shook Cloud's proffered hand. ''This gonna take long, you think?''

''Not long,'' Cloud said.

"As long as it takes," Rosie said, leaning his forearms on the car top and staring at the tall, thin cop. "You Dallas boys work by the hour, do you?"

Lafitte turned to look at Rosie, one narrow hand coming up to rub his chin, his long face revealing nothing. Dark, benign eyes met the big man's gaze calmly.

"Simple. You're the guy who called me."

"No. I called Captain Dunworth. He transferred me to you. He said we'd get full cooperation."

Lafitte spread his hands. "I'm here. I'm at your disposal." He smiled faintly, revealing a row of overlapping upper teeth. "I have to tell you though, I think Coover's got his lawyer in there. I saw a criminal lawyer named Dellcroft go in about ten minutes ago." He buttoned his jacket, a lightweight, navy blue blazer with shiny brass buttons. "I know you guys are working that double homicide you had. You think Coover's the perp?"

Cloud shrugged. "Just routine. Chances are he was the last one to talk to her before she was killed. She called her mother at six and told her she was working until eight on some hot project for Coover. She had steak and lobster not long before her death, and it's logical to assume he may have taken her out to dinner. Her mother said Coover had been pressuring her to go out with him."

Lafitte nodded. "You read his sheet? He's been charged twice with assault on a female—young female—in the last three years. There's a civil suit in the courts now charging him with sexual harassment in the workplace. Another young girl. Old boy can't seem to learn."

"That's why we're interested," Cloud said.

"Okay," Lafitte said, brushing a lank swatch of blond hair off his forehead. "Let's do it."

12

Jared Coover was tall and spare, a bony triangular face with flat planes and hollows, a humped beak of a nose, dark eyes that moved ceaselessly between slow, deliberate blinks. His hair was pure white, thick and wavy, obviously freshly styled. An ugly man—near fifty, Cloud guessed—his skin glowed with the healthy bronze patina of a much younger man. Manicured hands and impeccable tailoring fleshed out the image of successful businessman.

He was alone in the office, but Cloud had a feeling that help was close at hand.

Introductions over, Coover waved a hand at the plush leather furniture arrayed before his ornate wooden desk.

"Please be seated, gentlemen. Could I offer you something to drink?" His voice was deep, pleasantly harsh.

"No, thanks," Cloud said. "We don't want to keep you longer than absolutely necessary, Mr. Coover." He gave the white-haired man a disarming smile. "Just a few routine questions, if you don't mind."

"Of course, of course. What a terrible thing. We were all very fond of Laura—such a terrible thing to happen to a young girl like that. We were . . . . shocked."

"Yes," Cloud said. He took a small notebook and ball-point pen out of his pocket, balanced the pad on his knee. "We have reason to believe, Mr. Coover, that you may have been the last person to talk to Laura—except for the killer, of course. I understand that you and Laura worked late that evening. How late was it?''

"Somewhere between seven-thirty and eight. I don't remember exactly, but I would say offhand until about seven forty-five.''

"Why?''

"Why? Oh, you mean why were we working? Well, I had a lot of correspondence piling up, you see.''

"Then Ms. Elliot was your private secretary?''

"Yes . . . just barely. She had only been promoted two days before. The job had been vacant for almost a week while I made up my mind about a replacement. My previous secretary—''

"Any particular reason why you chose Ms. Elliot?''

"Yes, of course,'' he said firmly. "Laura was a good worker, punctual, conscientious, and she had a good work background.''

"Let's get back to the night she was killed, Mr. Coover. What happened after you quit work?''

"After? Well, nothing really. I asked her if she was hungry and she said yes and we stopped off at the Steak and Ale on Six Flags Road and had a bite to eat.''

"And after that?''

"After that? Why, nothing. I waited until she drove off the lot, and then I got my car and went home.''

"Where is home?''

Coover smiled faintly. "I suspect you already know that, Lieutenant Cloud.''

"I have a faulty memory. Could you tell me again?''

Coover rattled off his home address.

"That's in Dallas, isn't it?''

"Yes, Dallas, North Dallas.''

"What time did you arrive home, Mr. Coover?''

"Oh, I'm not sure exactly. I guess around nine-thirty or so.''

"Anyone there when you got home?''

Coover wet his lips. "Of course, my wife and my two kids.''

"They were all still up and about, I suppose?''

"Sure, of course. My kids are fourteen and seventeen. They— along with my wife—were in the family room watching TV.''

"And you sat down and watched TV with them.''

"Well, no, I went on to the back . . . our bedroom. I'm not much for TV. At least the kind of stuff the kids like to watch, sitcoms and the like.''

"You went to bed? At nine-thirty?''

"No—no, I read for a while then tuned in the news. After that I—" He broke off, flicking a glance at a closed door off to Cloud's left. "Look, I'm doing my best to cooperate here, but I don't like the direction these questions are taking. Why are you interested in what I did? I thought you wanted to talk about Laura—Ms. Elliot."

"I thought we were," Cloud said mildly. "Just background, Mr. Coover. Routine stuff for the report. I'm sure you understand."

"Well, okay. It's not like I have anything to hide, you understand, it just seems to be an invasion of privacy—"

Cloud saw Rosie move forward in his seat, and he broke in hurriedly. "You *did* talk to your family when you got home that night, didn't you, Mr. Coover?"

"Well, hell yes, I did. My house isn't that big. I had to go right through the family room to my bedroom—"

"And you didn't leave again . . . for any reason?"

"No. I told you what I did."

"Yeah, he did do that," Lafitte put in amiably. He crossed his legs and took a pack of cigarettes out of his pocket. He turned to smile at Rosie's scowling face.

"You guys are asking the wrong questions," Coover said. "You oughta be asking about Laura, what she told us a couple of weeks or so ago."

"All right," Cloud said, "what did she tell you?"

Coover picked up a small silver pen from his desk and worried it with his long, thin fingers. "She was upset . . . not hysterical or anything like that, but pretty upset about some guy who had been following her home—"

"From here?"

"No, well, she wasn't sure exactly where he started, but she'd notice him usually after she stopped in Trinity Square at this supermarket she traded at . . . Safeway, I think she said."

"How often?"

"I don't know that. Three or four times I think over a three-week period."

"She say what he looked like?" Rosie came forward on the edge of his seat, pad ready on his knee.

Coover wrinkled his brow. "Big and ugly, she said. Casual clothing. Drove an old car, an old beat-up car—"

"She get his plate numbers?" Cloud detected the skepticism in Rosie's voice and wondered if the other two men could.

"No, if she did, she didn't tell us about it."

"Us?"

"Yes, my office manager Mabel Langworth and . . . and I guess anybody who'd listen. She was worried about it."

"Did she contact the Trinity Square police?"

Coover shook his head. "I don't think so. That's what I suggested, but I don't think she ever did."

"Didn't it occur to you," Rosie said coldly, "that you should have come forward with this information when you heard she had been killed?"

"I—uh, yes, well, I suppose I should have, but it had sort of slipped my mind until you fellows came with your questions."

Cloud stood up. He put his notebook and pen away and stepped to the front of the desk, hand outstretched.

"Thanks for your time, Mr. Coover. We appreciate your cooperation."

"Hey, you bet," Coover said, pushing to his feet, catching Cloud's hand with obvious relief. "Glad to help anyway I can."

Cloud dropped the damp, wiry hand. "You think of anything else, Mr. Coover, we'd appreciate a call."

"I sure will." He came around the desk, then stopped short as Rosie and Lafitte turned toward the door. "Yeah, I sure will," he added lamely.

Cloud nodded and smiled, catching sight of Rosie's disapproving scowl as the big man made the turn at the door. He closed the office door and paused in the corridor to light a cigarette, allowing his two companions to pull ahead.

When he got outside, Lafitte was already climbing into his Buick, talking to Rosie who was standing beside the car. The Buick's engine roared, belched a cloud of smoke. Lafitte put on his baseball cap and leaned sideways to wave at Cloud as the car lurched away from the curb.

"What's his big hurry?" Cloud slumped into the passenger seat, listening bemusedly to the clattering whir of the Pontiac's starter motor.

"Has to meet his old lady for lunch. Said to tell you you did a good job in there."

Cloud studied the strong line of Rosie's jaw. "But you don't think so, do you?"

Rosie shrugged, jockeying the car away from the curb, tapping the gas pedal to keep the motor going. "You covered it, I reckon. It's just that I think you shoulda hit him with his record, shook him up a little. He was too damn smooth to suit me. He's a womanizer, Ben, and we treated him like he was an ordinary, decent human being.''

Cloud laughed and shook his head. ''His morals are his own, Rosie. It was too soon to come on like badass cops. After we check out his story, his wife and his kids, that woman in his office, Mabel Langworth, then's the time to come down on his ass if he's doing a number on us.''

''I still say, by God . . .'' Rosie's voice rumbled on, but Cloud was only half listening, his mind tumbling backward across the years. Another time, another place, a ten-year-old boy watching a tall, white-haired man very much like Jared Coover—almost *exactly* like Jared Coover, in fact—walk hunch-shouldered and staggering out of a courtroom in Dallas, on his way to a six-by-ten hole in Huntsville Prison.

Cloud had watched the old man's departure with burning eyes and a bursting heart, his head high, not crying—not yet—but fully understanding that he would probably never see the gangling figure again, knowing that without knowing why, also understanding that the three-year segment of his life, the only part that had ever seemed real, was over. Gone. Lost in the murky limbo of his tender years.

He had not understood all they had asked him—not until later when it no longer mattered—but he had sensed that they had not believed him when he told them that Leonard Brinx, foster parent, accused child molester, the only real father he had ever known, had not touched him *there*, had *never* touched him except with hands of love, touched him with his deep baritone voice, reassuring, instilling pride, demanding always his very best.

Later, when he fully realized what had happened, he felt no shame for Leonard Brinx, only a consummate pity and an abiding hatred for the system that had taken him away.

''Well?''

Cloud became aware that they were at the intersection near the freeway, that Rosie was watching him with an expression half-annoyed, half-amused.

''Sorry, Rosie. What did you say?''

''I said are we going to Coover's house now to talk to his old lady?''

Cloud glanced at his watch. ''Better not. We've got a command performance with Captain Summers in less than an hour. Better head for the barn.''

Rosie grunted and passed through the intersection, signaling a left turn.

''Wish we had a little more time. Be better to hit her cold before he has a chance to prep her.''

Cloud sighed and found a cigarette in his shirt pocket. ''Be even better if wishes were wings, Rosie, then all of us could fly.''

13

"Good evening, ladies and gentlemen," Amy Reed said for the third time, smiling easily into the beady eye of the camera. "We have with us tonight, Lt. Benjamin Cloud of the Trinity Square Police Department." She hesitated a beat, smiled at Cloud, then said, "Tell me, Lieutenant, have the police come to any definite conclusions regarding the murders of Laura Elliot and Ramona Butler?"

Cloud cleared his throat automatically, although he had promised her he wouldn't. Trying desperately to ignore the blind, relentless eye he could feel closing in on his face, he bobbed his head like a small boy who has, for once, memorized all the answers.

"Yes, Amy," he said, not moving anything but his mouth, "we have come to some very definite conclusions." *Jesus*, he sounded like an ass. "First of all, we're sure the slayings were the results of a robbery that got out of hand. A confrontation that led to murder. It happens frequently. A thief goes into a situation he is comfortable with, one he feels is relatively secure. He finds himself confronted with an irate citizen, or even a frightened citizen, and he panics. His first thought is flight. If, perhaps, he is stymied, as we believe he was in this case, he strikes out, often resulting in death." He turned glassy eyes toward the camera. "A citizen should never, never try to apprehend an intruder in those circumstances."

"But weren't the victims strangled?" Amy asked innocently,

65

deviating from the script. She looked a little glassy-eyed herself. "That doesn't seem to be the spontaneous reaction of a frightened burglar. One woman, perhaps, but surely not two."

Cloud managed a condescending smile. "Oh, it can happen," he said fatuously. "You have, in this case, in all probability, a young, inexperienced bumbler, a hoodlum with a dope habit, no doubt, looking for a few dollars for a fix. Addicts are notoriously unstable, erratic. They are, by definition, weak people, selfish and irresponsible. Being slaves to their cravings, they will sometimes do unspeakable things to acquire the means for relief." He paused, wet his lips preparatory to continuing, but she stepped in smoothly.

"Thank you very much, Lieutenant Cloud, for your very interesting insights into the criminal mind. And now, Norma, back to you."

"There was a little more," Cloud said tentatively, watching her unclip the mike from her blouse. "I think I was getting the hang of it there at the end, don't you?"

She gave him a fleeting glance, then lifted her head and called into the gloom beyond the cameras. "Think we got it this time, Charlie?" Her tone stated clearly that it was tough shit if they hadn't.

"As good as it'll ever be, I reckon," came the laconic reply. "You wanna run-through?"

"Not right now," Amy Reed said, her voice clipped and precise. She turned to Cloud. "This won't run before the ten o'clock newscast. We'll have to do some work on it." Her lips twitched. "You did fine," she added, a waspish edge to her voice. "But what you said was unadulterated bullshit. You didn't add anything at all to what we already know about the murders."

Cloud grinned. "I know. It wasn't accidental. I know I sounded like a pompous ass, but that's the way I wanted to sound. I didn't enjoy it."

"You couldn't prove it by me," she said crisply, slipping into the rust-colored blazer that matched her pleated skirt. "You were really hamming it up there at the end. Mugging is what we call it."

"Aw, come on, I hate it when people brag about me."

The corners of her mouth tilted upward, then dropped precipitously as she frowned. "I know you're using me, and I resent it. Maybe I wouldn't mind so much if you'd tell me why."

He laughed. "Now, who's conning who?"

Her eyes flashed, then disappeared into shadow as the bright lights went off. They walked out of the alcove with the two chairs, a low, free-form table, and a potted palm. She fumbled in her purse for a cigarette, ignored his proffered light, and lit up with a disposable butane lighter.

"Hey, you're the one who's been humping for an interview. Why are you pissed off at me?" He lit a cigarette of his own, wincing inwardly at his choice of verbs.

"I'm not humping for anything," she said acidly. "I didn't expect you to reveal any state secrets, but all that pap about bumbling burglars and erratic addicts is just so much drivel. We've heard all that stuff a million times before." She paused significantly. "And from a lot better speakers than you." She whirled and headed for the door.

"Hey, wait!" He caught up with her in two swift strides, put his hand on her arm. "Okay. Maybe I owe you an explanation. And I won't even bother asking you not to repeat anything. I know you're smart enough to know that. I'm trying what we call a reactive technique. The guy was clearly in control, knew what he was going to do, and did it. Ramona Butler must have startled him a little, but he handled it, then went on with his business with Laura Elliot. He walked away clean, just the way he had it planned. If we're right in what we think, it wasn't the first time. This guy must have a monumental ego. He's not going to like what I've said about him. Not at all. A lowly burglar or an addict getting credit for his work? Not likely. To him it was a mission, meticulously planned and executed. Flawlessly, to his way of thinking. I'm hoping his ego will compel him to refute what I've said. I'm hoping he'll get in touch with me."

She wet her lips with the tip of a pink tongue, her face pale. "What makes you think he will?"

"He's done it before," Cloud said quietly. "In other places, other times. I'm trusting you with this, Amy. I hope I'm not making a mistake. None of this can be used. If he's who we think he is, he'll do it again . . . and again, until we stop him. And it'll have to come out. It always does. When that happens, I'll do my best to give you a jump on the competition. Deal?"

She nodded wordlessly, green eyes wide, burning up at him with disconcerting intensity.

"Whenever I can," he said, "I'll let you know what's going on."

Her parted lips closed; she wet them again, giving him a smidgen of her marvelous smile.

"Shit, Cloud, you don't even know how to talk like a cop. That's 'what's going down'."

14

Spencer Price watched them gleefully, the tall, good-looking cop and the pretty girl. She giggled a little at the way the cop fidgeted, his hands tightly clasped in his lap like a little boy in church.

"The son of a bitch is scared shitless," he chortled aloud, laughing uproariously when the cop turned his face to the camera and delivered his solemn warning about confrontations with burglars in the home.

He pounded his thigh and giggled helplessly when the cop prattled on about hoodlums and addicts, warming to his subject, obviously relaxing, smiling, casting sidelong glances toward the camera.

He thought the cop was funny, better than Archie Bunker and Fred T. Sanford combined. He laughed until his sides ached.

The girl was pretty; she wasn't at all funny. Lovely hair. A beautiful smile. Outstanding teeth. Lips like . . . Elizabeth Taylor? No, maybe the lower one. Dyan Cannon? No, not quite that full. Lana Turner? Yeah, Lana Turner. Exactly like Lana used to look. He wondered how they would taste . . . soft and velvety and hot and wet . . .

He sat upright. She was speaking directly into the camera, smiling. God, she was beautiful. Regretfully, he watched her image fade.

He sat still for a moment, knees pressed together, feeling the exquisite rush of power, his fingers drumming on the chair arms.

The cop was stupid. A salamander on a string. A bumbler like the bumbling hoodlums and addicts he kept prattling about.

He dismissed the cop, went back to the girl. He wished he had seen her standing. She was slender and graceful, lissome and pliant, and would respond to him as they all did ultimately. He pictured her short, sturdy neck that flowed so smoothly into the rounded shoulders.

He closed his eyes and he could feel it, his thumbs tracing the firm yet soft musculature . . . the arteries pulsing against his thumbs like the fluttering heart of a frightened dove.

His hands clenched convulsively; his blood sang. His back bowed, then straightened as the pleasure-pain surged through him, gushed out of him.

A long while later, he staggered to his feet, dizzy and weak. He went into the bathroom, disconsolate and afraid.

Sleep was a long time coming. He lay wide-eyed on the bed, staring at the dirty, textured ceiling, the light from the bathroom a bright triangle across the foot of his bed.

He couldn't sleep without the lights. He had tried, often. Laid with his eyes squeezed tightly shut, willing himself to sleep, willing himself not to hear the sounds—the creeping things that peopled the dark, that rustled and chirped just beyond the edge of his hearing, scaly things with ropy tails and red-rimmed devilish eyes blazing with their own dark fire. It was not logical; he knew that. There were no hobgoblins, no wyverns, no monsters with dripping fangs and slimy claws. It was all in his head. Amanda had told him that a thousand times, no, maybe ten thousand times. And he had always believed her, until she turned off the light and the dark came.

Slithering things were what he dreaded most: anything that crawled. Kittens crawled; little kittens, fat-bellied little dogs, snakes, spiders . . .

He stirred restlessly, looked around the room. Despite the gloom he could see everything clearly. Satisfied, he returned his gaze to the ceiling.

Why couldn't he sleep? The pleasure-pain had come; that almost always did it. All he wanted was a quick nap. But instead of the usual serenity, he felt an empty keening inside that he abruptly realized was guilt. Guilt. After all the years, she could still make him feel guilty about the dry pleasure-pain.

She had warned him what it would do the first time she caught him, shamed him, then made him finish while she watched with bright, wise eyes. Then she had washed him lovingly and they had prayed together.

He tried to remember if it was later the same night that the storm had come and she had appeared in his room, shivering and frightened. She had crept into his bed like a little girl, and he had comforted her the way she showed him, her eyes dark and mysterious in the light from the hall, her lovely hair cascading around their faces like golden prayer shawl. They had made the pleasure-pain together, again and again, until he was so exhausted he didn't mind that she turned off the light.

Awash in memories, he drifted toward sleep, the image of the girl with the cop wafting gracefully into his mind, blending with the old, dimmer memories of dancing auburn hair, shimmering supple body, and dark eyes that laughed and teased . . . and cried.

He could picture her clearly, ripe lips taunting, smiling an invitation, looking up at him, cupped hands holding rich, full breasts, her knees drawing up, spreading.

No, he thought dimly. Too soon for her. She was special. There were others. Plenty of others . . .

Almost asleep, her image burning in his mind, he drew slowly into a fetal knot, locked his arms around his shinbones to keep himself from drawing up the pleasure-pain.

"Thanks for a very nice dinner," Amy Reed said primly, her hand groping for the door handle, "and I'm glad we got all the way through it without a fight." Her hand moved to a different area, and then she looked down. "Okay, I give up. Where is the dumb thing?"

Cloud laughed. "On the floor probably. It falls off. I'll have to let you out." He climbed out and walked around the front of the car. He opened the door.

"I'll walk you to the door," he said, smiling. "It's dangerous for a defenseless woman to be out after dark. Anyhow, I'm already out."

She hooted softly, then let it expand into a throaty laugh. "You're sneaky, Cloud. I would never have thought of that, but then I'm not a conniving male." She tilted her head to the light, dark eyes filled with irony. "I'm not defenseless, either."

Nevertheless, she held his arm lightly as they went up the

walk. She unlocked her door and turned, gave him a smile without teeth.

"This is my door, Cloud."

He nodded soberly. "Could I ask you a question?"

"Sure. That's what you do best."

"Do you kiss on the first date?"

"I didn't think this was a date, Cloud. I looked at it as more of a business . . . thing."

"It was a date for me."

She looked at him, the smile fading a little. "I do sometimes; sometimes I don't."

He stood quietly waiting, his face unsmiling, revealing nothing of the tumultuous upheaval inside him.

She looked back at him, the meager smile gone, her shoulders squaring minutely. His heart missed a beat as she turned away; she hung her purse on the doorknob, turned back, her expression enigmatic, eyes faintly gleaming.

"Well, hell, Cloud, *I'm* not going to kiss *you*! If there's any kissing done, then you'll have to do . . ." It ended in a smothered gasp as he swept her into his arms.

Her lips were exactly the way he knew they would be: firm and full, yet warm and soft, dissolving as his opening mouth demanded more, as the raging fire in his blood became a palpable thing, a magnetic flux flowing through the point of fusion, radiating outward, something indefinable prowling the air around them, charging the night with a bright, sparkling electricity.

She stood rigid in his arms for one eternal moment, then made a sound deep in her throat and came against him, timidly at first, then firmly, voraciously.

He bent and caught her behind the knees, gathered her against his chest; the kiss went on.

She swung down an arm and retrieved her purse, opened the door. He carried her inside and pushed the door closed with his foot, stood waiting for night vision.

She broke the kiss. "I don't *do* anything on the first date, either, Cloud," she said plaintively, her warm breath huffing against his neck, lips following.

"You won't have to," he promised huskily.

15

She lay on her side, left leg drawn up into a figure seven, the right extended to its fullest shapely length. Her arms were intertwined in front of her face, right hand beneath her cheek. Her hair spilled loosely across her face and shoulders, one russet tuft almost concealing her breasts.

He had been surprised by her breasts. Surprised and delighted. Larger than he had suspected; he could still feel the satin texture, remember the taste of the strawberry buds. Even after the long, tumultuous night, looking at her made him weak, stirred the craving . . .

She moaned and rolled over on her back, spread-eagled, and Cloud looked away guiltily, feeling like a peeping tom, feeling a flash of shame at his adolescent voyeurism.

He finished dressing quietly, wanting to wake her, tell her what the magical night had meant to him, wanting, in truth, to make love to her again. He didn't dare. She might be a surly morning person and destroy this mystical aura of contentment that surrounded him, buoyed him with sweet memories of soft darkness, easy laughter, and incandescent love. She might stare at him blankly and say, "Who the hell are you?"

He found pen and paper in a desk in a small alcove off the living room and left her a note. He fought mightily the impulse to indulge in glowing metaphors, a fanciful sonnet or two; he kept it short and, he hoped, funny:

Sleeping Beauty!

Awoke with the sun! A new man! Trust you feel the same.
I'm off to rescue fair maidens and joust with the bad guys.
I'll call you at six. If you just can't wait that long, track me
down. I'll understand. I'm easy.

                              The (new) Centurion.

Capt. Eli Summers probed the inside of his right nostril with
a slender, hairy finger, seemed suddenly to realize that he was
picking his nose in front of two grown men, and turned the
action into an innocent scratching gesture, evolving finally into
a vigorous massage with thumb and forefinger. His eyes wa-
tered. He dropped Cloud's report on his desk and leaned back
in his chair, clasping his hands behind his head and staring at
the lanky detective with blurred intensity.

"Julian Arrowstone. Sounds like one of them swish designers
to me. You telling me this asshole is here in Trinity Square?
Killing our girls? This squirrel from a nuthouse in New York?"

"No, I'm not telling you that," Cloud said, nettled at the little
man's tone. "I'm telling you it's a distinct possibility based on
the stones, the position of the body, and the fact that he spent
time working on the features of the victims. New York and Chicago both confirm that's Arrowstone's MO. I don't know it's
him, but we're in no position to discount it, either."

Summers chewed on his lip and glanced at Rosie Simple holding up the wall with one beefy shoulder. "How do you feel
about this, Rosie?"

Rosie managed a shrug despite his awkward position. "Can't
really say yet, Captain. I don't know any more than you do about
this guy Arrowstone." He sounded slightly aggrieved, and Cloud
gave he a quick, probing glance. He had sensed a diffidence in
Rosie long before the murders, an undercurrent of animosity
directed at Jake Rafferty that he had concluded was a form of
jealousy of Cloud and Rafferty's close relationship. Aware that
Rosie liked and respected him and wanted to be his friend, he
had on several occasions included the big man in activities he
and Rafferty had planned. It had not worked out well. Rafferty
had tried graciously to accept the situation with humor, but Cloud
was certain he considered Rosie's presence an intrusion into their
friendship and was not totally immune to a little manly jealousy

himself. Balancing the two on the fulcrum of his patience had proved too physically taxing and too emotionally frustrating, and he had stopped.

Summers bent his head over the report and grunted. "Not much of a description. Five-ten, one-seventy-five, regular features, light brown hair, no distinguishing marks—hell, that could be half the men in the country. Dye his hair black and grow a moustache, and he'd stick out about as much as a pair of cowboy boots at a rodeo. How about pictures? They got anything on the way?"

Cloud winced without being aware of it. "Only one. Mug shot taken when he was first arrested at eighteen—"

"Jesus Christ! Eighteen! And he's what now? Thirty-four, thirty-five?"

"He never stood trial. He went almost directly into a mental institution for the criminally insane. In there for fifteen or so years. I guess there wasn't much reason for pictures. Particularly since they never expected him to be released."

Rosie Simple deserted his post at the window, walked to the other chair, and sat down. He cleared his throat self-consciously.

"Maybe it ain't him. Maybe somebody's imitating him. There musta been a lot of writing about him back then. All these *True Detective* magazines and like that. They publish stories all the time about famous killers."

Cloud nodded, pursing his lips sagely. "That's a good thought, Rosie. But from what New York and Chicago told me, there was never anything released about the stones or the way he left them. That doesn't rule it out as a possibility, though. A lot of people had to know."

Summers leafed rapidly through the Elliot file and came up with another F.I.R. held gingerly between slender fingers. "How about this clown Coover? His alibi hold up?"

Rosie cleared his throat. "Pretty much, I guess. I took his wife, and Graves talked to his kids. Their stories tallied as far as the time is concerned. He came home around nine-thirty and went on to his bedroom. Just before the ten o'clock news came on, his wife took him a glass of milk and some chocolate chip cookies. His favorite snack, she said. She talked to him a few minutes, then went back downstairs to watch the Johnny Carson show with her kids. He don't like Johnny Carson. Anyway, his house in north Dallas is at least forty-five minutes from the murder scene—unless he went by helicopter, and even then I don't think he could have made it.''

"Did you take somebody from Dallas with you?" Summers asked.

Rosie looked annoyed. "Cop named Lafitte. He stayed with Ron and the kids. I don't think he trusted Ron alone with the Coover girl. She was a little beauty, and you know how that affects Ron.''

Summers eyebrows lifted. "No, I don't. How—?"

"How about the office manager?" Cloud interjected smoothly. "What's her name . . . Langworth?"

"Yeah, we talked to her, too. She told about the same story as Coover. Some joker followed the Elliot girl home a few times. Coulda been an ex-boyfriend or something. She never got a good look at his face. Description the same as we got from Coover, rough-dressed man in a beat-up old car. That oughta lead us right to him.''

Summers pursed his lips and fingered the papers in the file. "I didn't see a report in here about any of this.''

Rosie shrugged. "We ain't had time, Eli. Ron's working on it right this minute . . . or should be, anyhow.''

Summers nodded thoughtfully and made a half-turn in his swivel chair.

"Well, how's everything else going?" Summers wanted to know, his fingers creeping toward his nose again, stopping to fiddle with his lower lip, quivering, building suspense.

"We're about through the list on the Elliot girl." Cloud nodded toward Rosie and smiled. "Ron Graves and Rosie have been working like Trojans on this thing, fourteen, fifteen hours a day." He paused. "We could use some more help," he added without much hope.

"Hmmm," Summers said, rearing back in his chair, getting his hands out of temptation's way behind his head. "How about the Butler woman?"

Cloud sighed. "I guess we'll have to wring her out, too. We figure her for an innocent bystander, but . . ." He shrugged and let it drop.

Summers's eyes gleamed. "Caught your performance on TV. Good job. Think it'll work?"

Cloud shrugged again, feeling defensive. "Time will tell.''

"He's getting to be a real celebrity," Rosie said with heavy humor. "Don't know as I'd mind myself with that pretty little redhead doing the questioning."

"He'll probably be leaving for Hollywood any day now," Summers said, smiling, but with a little more cynicism than was necessary, Cloud thought. "Maybe with the redhead," Summers added.

He grinned quietly, picturing their reaction to where he had spent the night—and how. He lit a cigarette and shoved to his feet, feeling a warm glow as he pictured it himself.

He lifted a hand at Summers and faked a punch at Rosie's stomach. "Come on, Simple, we've got work to do."

"And miles to go before we sleep," Rosie said, coming up beside him in the hallway.

"What?" Cloud asked vaguely, his mind fuzzy with visions of limpid green eyes and supple thighs.

"And miles to go before we sleep. Didn't you see *Telefon* last night on the tube?"

"I saw it the first time."

"Charles Bronson and Lee Remick. Jesus, he must be a lot older than her. Unrealistic. Can you see them making it together?"

"Sure, why the hell not?" Cloud said, grinning.

16

Spencer Price watched the pizza parlor from his vantage point in the recessed doorway of the abandoned building that had once housed a bustling business. Reaganomics, he thought idly, stiffening as the trim redhead came into view through the large plate-glass front of the pizza store.

She stopped behind the cash register, her head canted, and he knew she was counting the day's take, balancing the money with the register tape. She had locked the front door five minutes before; the two boys who cooked the pizza and cleaned up were gone. She was alone, and in five more minutes or so, she would be walking down the sidewalk in front of him. She never varied her schedule by more than two or three minutes either way. He had watched her often; he knew.

He had noticed her the first time a few weeks before, a sweet-faced girl with hazel eyes and wine-dark red hair. His heart had leaped crazily in his chest, but that had been during the dead time, and he had forced himself to smile and take his pizza and leave, almost choking with the desperate need to touch her, make the hazel eyes widen, brim finally, and spill over onto his hands fitting themselves around the silky smooth neck, his thumbs probing oh, so delicately for the quicksilver pulse, pressing, hearing the first small gasp, seeing the exquisite anguish as she realized, and the tears began, the sobbing, and the tears burning on his flesh . . . and the tears . . .

He shuddered and wrenched himself back to reality. He looked across the street and saw the hunch-shouldered wino where he was supposed to be, looking halfway presentable in the old tattered blue blazer and the cheap straw cowboy hat. The derelict had washed and shaved, just as Spencer had instructed, and he carried the map clutched in his left hand.

Satisfied, he turned his gaze back to the pizza parlor. He saw the lights go down, saw the girl appear at the door again, unlocking it, stepping out, locking, rattling the knob to make sure, then whirling to stride down the street with her long-legged, lazy gait.

Haughty bitch, he thought and grinned, his lips cotton-white with dryness, his heart thumping almost painfully in his chest.

He pressed back into the shadows.

The girl neared the corner, turned without pause, and started across the street. Out of the corner of his eye, he saw the wino walk out into the brightness cast by the streetlight, the map unfolded in his left hand, his right tipping the straw hat as the girl reached the curb.

"Pardon me, miss, but could you tell me where Sycamore Street is?" He took off the hat and held it in his hand, a harmless old man lost and bewildered in the city.

Price saw the girl pause, hesitate while her eyes scanned and assessed the slight figure a few feet away. He saw her head bob, and she stopped. The wino put on his hat and opened the map, and they bent their heads over it. He could faintly hear the rumble of their conversation, but he was no longer paying any attention.

He stepped out of the doorway, walked quietly to the corner, and started across the street. He could see the wino's head canted to one side, watching for him, and as he neared the curb, the wino folded the map and slipped it into his pocket. The girl was talking animatedly, pointing.

He was within a dozen feet of the pair when the wino's voice broke in: "Fifty dollars? Dang, Missy, that's way too much! Now, I got twenty here . . ."

He stopped beside them, reached for the girl's wrist, and slipped the handcuff around the slender arm in one practiced motion. "You're under arrest, miss." He held the leather case with the shield in her face, then dropped it into his pocket.

She leaned away from him, mouth flying open, eyes springing wide. "Wha—my, God, what are you talking about?"

"Solicitation, ma'am." He turned to the wino. "Did this lady offer you sex in return for money, sir?"

The wino ducked his head, grinning. "Well, I don't wanna get the pretty little lady in trouble—"

"Did she or did she not?" The damn fool was padding his part.

The wino looked at the girl and grimaced apologetically. "I sure can't go lying to the law. Yes sir, she sure did, right enough."

"He's crazy! I did no such thing! He wanted to know—"

"I'm sorry, ma'am. We don't want to cause a scene out here on the street. My car's just around the corner."

"No! He's lying. I was helping the old bastard! He—hey, he's getting away!" She took a step after the wino limping off down the street. "Hey! You dirty little—"

He tugged on the cuff. "Come on, lady. Don't make it hard on yourself. I won't call a patrol car. I'll take you down myself. You can post bond and be on your way."

"But, I didn't do anything!" She bent forward in frustration, near tears. "I'm not a . . . I'm no prostitute!"

He smiled sadly. "I'm sure you're not, ma'am. But we'll have to let the judge decide that. Now, come along." He turned and started walking; the girl followed reluctantly, dragging, crying now, and he had to thrust his free hand into his jacket pocket to keep from grabbing her by the throat, had to think about creeping crawling things to keep the pleasure-pain from bursting forth.

17

He seated her on the passenger side of the car, handcuffed her hands in front of her, raised them, and hooked the chain in the heavy eyebolt secured high on the post of the old two-door car. Not a particularly uncomfortable position since her arms were supported by the hook, but it rendered her helpless, left her midsection and breast area vulnerable.

That was important. He was certain he wouldn't be able to wait; he never could before.

He wished she would quit sobbing. It was making him too excited. The pulsing agony was building in his loins, and he thought he would explode. He kept his eyes away from her, wished there was some way he could shut out the sounds.

It was too soon. Much too soon. They were still within the city limits, a good thirty miles from their destination, and already he could feel the mewling deep in his throat, the convulsive waves that heralded the pleasure-pain he had never been able to control.

Goddammit, he had to make her stop crying!

He twisted and reached into the back seat for the old Indian blanket. He dragged it into the front and spread it across her lap and the seat between them, bunching it a bit at his right thigh. If she noticed, she gave no sign.

The mewling rose higher in his throat, became a whimpering grunt. He clenched his right hand into a fist and drove it into her stomach. The crying stopped with an explosive gasp.

He held up his end of the blanket to protect himself from the vomit, watched her dispassionately as she writhed and gagged and retched. When he thought she was finished, he folded the blanket over the mess in her lap. He could see her eyes, dark, murky splashes of light in the gloom.

"If you cry again before I tell you, I'll hit you again," he said matter-of-factly. "It's for your own good. When you cry, I get . . . agitated."

She moved her head first one way and then the other, wiping her mouth on the puffy sleeves of her blouse.

"Who—who are you?" Her voice was thick with fear. He felt a faint tremor; next to tears, fear was best. He smiled without looking at her. They were well out into the country now, there was no further need for pretense.

He turned onto Stillwater Road, a long, straight stretch of highway following the Trinity River. Fifteen more miles, he thought, I'll show you who I am. He snickered, an obscene, whispering sound born of vivid imagery, rich anticipation.

"Please . . . my arms are going to sleep. I won't try to escape."

He laughed uproariously, but obligingly pulled to the side of the road. He put the car in park and scooted across the seat toward her. Using both hands, he ripped open her blouse, then cocked his head and grinned.

"A little trade? You get to lower your hands, I get to see your little pretties." He moved his hands over her breasts, stroking, prodding, tugging.

"Lovely, lovely," he crooned, but nothing stirred inside him. He put his hands in the thick, silky hair and held her head and thrust his tongue into her mouth. Still, nothing moved in his vitals. He felt her shrink, and he thrust harder, covering her mouth with his, sucking, chasing her twisting tongue. She moaned, and he told himself it was from pleasure; but he knew it was fear, and he felt a swift surging deep in his loins.

He broke away. He released her hands from the hook, worked the blouse down over her shoulders to her elbows.

"Leave it there," he said gruffly, then quickly scooted back behind the wheel.

They rode in silence. An occasional farmhouse back off the road, a glimpse of the dark, murky river through the trees, an infrequent car—the rest of the world was theirs. He slowed for a series of signs indicating highway repair and watched her surreptitiously search for the door handle under the guise of rubbing her right thigh with her hands.

He snickered again, this time allowing the sounds to rise to an audible level.

"It isn't there, sweetie." He clucked his tongue. "After promising you wouldn't try to escape, too. I see you can't be trusted. I'll have to punish you, you know. Little bunnies have to learn to obey." He leaned and gripped her left breast with his right hand. "I could rip it off, you know," he said softly.

"Oh, please . . . please, don't . . ."

He relaxed his grip, stroked. "That seems severe, doesn't it?" He straightened and grinned, slowly raised his hand and began sucking his thumb. His cheeks billowed. Without removing his eyes from the road, he took out the thumb and held it out to her; it dripped with saliva.

"Suck it," he said. "Take it into your mouth and suck it until I tell you to stop."

She made a whimpering, gagging sound and shrank, shoulders hunching, eyes dark, wounded holes in the pallid blur of her face.

"Do it," he said, "or I'll do the thing with your titty."

It felt nice, pleasant, he thought. Warm and wet and sensual, her tongue unavoidably caressing. It was a new thing; he had never done that before. It was definitely sensual, and she would think twice before trying to defy him again.

His arm grew tired; he withdrew his thumb.

"Wasn't that nice?" he said, almost kindly, smiling at her, snapping his head forward again as he saw the fear.

"Oh, God . . . who . . . who are you? Who . . . ?"

"Who I am doesn't matter. It's what I am that should make you piss your pretty little drawers."

"You're—you're not a cop. Oh, God, what do you . . . you want with me?"

He looked at her then, grinning. "What do you think I want with you? Let's see now, perhaps I'm taking you to meet Mother—no, wait, Mother dear's all dead. All wormy and dead. Perhaps just a little drive in the country—a picnic! Of course, we'll have a picnic! No, wait, it's dark outside. We couldn't see all the little creepy crawly things—tell me, dear, what do you think I want with you?"

She was quiet for a while. When her voice came, it was surprisingly calm, almost under control. "I think you will probably

rape me. I can see why you might want to do that. It must be
. . . exciting to have someone in your power. Listen. I can understand if you want to rape me. I'll do it any way you want,
anything you want. I'll cooperate if you want me to, or I'll fight
back if you want me to. I'll do anything to make you feel . . .
secure and happy. If—if you just please won't hurt me . . . hurt
me bad.'' Her voice quivered and broke on the last few words,
and he threw back his head and laughed.

"My God, a speech! A pretty little speech for the crazy rapist.
Where did you learn that one, little bunny? The rape prevention
center?"

"I'll do it! Just like I said. I'll do anything for you, to you.
Please . . . please . . .'' Her voice clotted and he saw a glistening shine in her eyes. He trembled, humped his shoulders, a
gibbering whine forcing itself past his clenched teeth.

"Don't cry, dammit!'' Just a few more miles. God, don't let
her spoil it now. He groaned deep inside, clenched his fingers
on the wheel until they ached, burned.

"I won't! I won't! Please just . . . if you'll just please not
. . . hurt me . . . afterward!''

"Don't—don't worry," he said, breathing strangely, in short
gasps. "Afterwards . . . afterwards, I promise I'll bring you
back.''

18

She felt him kick her in the side with his bare foot. Not hard. Just enough to snap her wide awake, pluck her out of the seductive folds of lethargy that imprisoned her. He had been at her for two hours . . . or three, she couldn't be sure, and more than anything now, she was exhausted.

He hadn't hurt her. Not once, and she was no longer paralyzed with fear. He would turn her loose. She was sure of it. It was disgusting, sickening, the things she had had to do, the things he had done. But they wouldn't kill her; and after all, she wasn't a virgin, was she? Everything they had done, someone at one time or other had tried to get her to do. But she never would. She had been raised a certain way, and that was that. But now she didn't have a choice, and now she knew about all those dirty things . . . and there had been once or twice there—

He kicked her again. Her eyes opened. He was straddling her, his feet pressed against her sides. The *thing* jutted, rigid and swollen.

"Oh, no," she groaned, "not again."

"Oh, yes," he said, grinning the wild grin that had scared her to death until she realized that must be the way he grinned all the time. He sank slowly until he was sitting on her hips. He traced a ring around her left nipple. "This will be the last time, I promise." He lifted his member and let it slap against her stomach. "We can't leave him like this, now can we?"

"Oh, all right," she said crossly.

He raised easily to his feet, watched her position herself the way he had taught her so painstakingly. When she was ready, he lowered himself, still watching raptly as she fitted them together. She felt a curious thrill of surprise at how easily he went in.

"Please try to come this time," she scolded, mouthing the words he had told her. "Mother doesn't have all day."

"I will," he said, his voice small and subdued. "I promise, Mommy."

"That's the way," she crooned, faltering, forgetting the next words, groping. "That's the—oh, now Mommy's headache will go away." She felt his tempo increase, his body tense, relax, tense, felt a silent spasm deep down inside her own body, shrank from his hot breath on her ear, his panting breath, his garbled words—something like "fly", "high", something like that.

"Cry," he gasped. "You have to cry!" His hands were clasped behind her neck, thumbs rubbing her jaws from her chin to her ears. Shaking; she could feel them shaking.

"I—I can't," she gasped, filled with a fleeting horror as her own orgasm burst suddenly inside her, and incredible flood of pleasure engulfing, holding her rigid, dissolving, radiating outward in consuming waves, raw ecstasy that pulsed and tumbled and soared until her body writhed, quivering, almost in pain.

"Cry!" he screamed, frothy spittle spraying her face, his body hunched and bucking. He hung over her face, mouth gaping, slobbering, his eyes wide and bugged. "Cry—goddamn you, I can't come unless you cry!"

It was then that she understood he was going to kill her, read it in the insane eyes, realized almost wearily that he had meant to all along.

"Cry!" His thumbs were on her neck now, racing up and down the smooth, firm flesh, pressing, clenching, moving again. "Cry, goddamn you!"

Her body still throbbed, unmindful of the humping beast trying to feed. She brought her hands up and gripped his sides, dug in. She smiled into his raging face.

"Fuck you!" she screamed. She clenched her hands and raked her nails through his flesh.

He howled in insane rage: closed his hands on her neck in savage fury.

She had only a moment to revel in her small victory before the darkness swooped, blinded her, covered her, covered the world.

19

"Goddammit to hell!" Trinity Square Chief of Police Patrick Donleavy pounded a hairy, freckled fist on the chipped and scratched surface of his mahogany desk, his choleric face the color of old, burnished copper, pale blue eyes alight with cold fire, raking the assembled men with scathing malevolence.

"What kind of police department do we have here? A goddamned crazy dumps a murdered girl practically on our doorstep, and nobody, repeat, nobody, sees a goddamned thing! Six people here, right here in the building at all times, another thirty coming in and out all night long, and it takes a couple of school kids taking a shortcut across our lawn to find her!" He glared around the room, fiery eyes settling on a tall, gangling man leaning against the wall near the door. He had thinning blond hair and a long, patient face deeply scored by nature and long years of working for people like Patrick Donleavy.

"Well, Larry?" the chief said coldly. "You have Night Watch. What about this shit?"

Capt. Larry Belden returned the pudgy chief's glare steadily, refusing to be intimidated before his peers.

He nodded. "That's about what happened," he said. "It's dark around the wall of the fountain at night, and he'd covered her with newspaper. If anybody had seen her, and probably some of us did, we'd have thought it was a wino. You know they sleep around there sometime behind—"

"Goddammit, they're not supposed to! What the hell is this,

87

a police station or a flophouse for winos? I want that shit stopped
as of now," he added in a more moderate tone, acknowledg-
ing a custom they were all aware of. The derelicts felt secure in
the close proximity to the police department, and as long as they
remained in the shadows cast by the waist-high stone wall and
caused no disturbance, the police officers passing back and forth
to the parking lot a few yards away left them alone. Locking
them in the small, usually crowded jail served no real purpose,
using man hours and space sorely needed for the confinement
of real criminals.

"I wonder where they were last night?" Lt. Glenn Sourbane,
Robbery, fiddled with the dimple in his plump chin, looking
studious and grave.

"We're checking that now," Capt. Eli Summers said. "So
far, nobody will admit to being there. There's four or five more
or less regulars, and we've talked to three. They're a timid bunch.
That's why they sleep there. Anyone could have rousted them,
cop or not. I think maybe that's what happened. But now with
this dead body turning up, they're scared shitless. They won't
talk, even if they know anything. After all, they have to live out
there where he is. I can't say I blame them."

"Lean on them!" Lt. Gil McReady, Traffic Control, snarled
the words, his black, bloodshot eyes on Benjamin Cloud sitting
quietly in one of the three padded chairs in the room. "A tap in
the nuts, and they'll jabber like a monkey. You damned dee-
tectives are too soft!" A burly, beetle-browed man Cloud's age,
he had a loud mouth, a drinking problem, and an intense hatred
for his mundane job, an unshakable conviction that Cloud had
somehow purloined the Homicide job right out from under his
heavily veined nose.

Cloud looked into the hot, blaring eyes and smiled.

"They'd break," Eli Summers said mildly. "Like a candy
cane." A caustic edge came into his voice. "Maybe you can
catch one of them jaywalking, Gil. Take him out in the boonies
and break his legs with a fence post—"

"All right!" Donleavy said testily. "End of ass-chewing. All
of you clear out of here, except you, Eli. But remember this.
This bastard is playing with us, making us look like a bunch of
boy scouts. I don't much like being made a fool of. I know you
don't, either. So pass it along to your men. Lean on their
snitches, contacts, friends, whatever. Whores, pimps, snow-
birds, and even the goddamned pushers—they finger this asshole

for us, and they get a free ride. So get the word out—I want this asshole!''

Cloud filed out behind Jake Rafferty. In the corridor, he poked the shorter man in the ribs, made a menacing face, and growled, ''You hear me! I want this asshole!''

Rafferty smiled wanly. ''He's a little piqued, all right.'' He looked tired, the plum-colored splashes under his eyes a little darker, the blue eyes lusterless. ''Anything turn up yet on this one?''

Cloud sobered, fished out a cigarette, and lit it. ''Brenda Sue Dickerson, worked at the Pizza Place out on Northcross. Her mother reported her missing when she didn't show up from work last night. She drove to the store, found it closed, and came right to the station. She came back down and identified her this morning. Hell of a thing. One of the hardest parts of this god-damned job is official identification. It sucks.''

''Like the others?'' Rafferty asked.

''Like Laura Sue. Just like Laura Sue. Stones, position, the whole lousy bit. This one was marked up a little more. He really did a job on her neck. Marks like big black plums, vertebrae shifted out of line, nail marks penetrating the skin. More savage than Laura Sue, I'd say. M.E. said she looked like the whole Cowboy defensive line had been taking turns with her, but funny thing, he didn't find any traces of semen. He'll autopsy her this afternoon, and we'll know for sure. He probed enough to find the stones, but he left them in there. I expect he'll find five, just like the other one.''

They stopped in front of Cloud's office. ''One other thing. Stovall said it looked like she may have marked him. Her nails had been cleaned, but not good enough. He said he has traces of human flesh and a little blood. He's working it up in the lab now. Won't matter a hell of a lot, maybe, unless she tracked his face. This kind of cool weather, everybody's wearing jackets, and unless she got his face or hands, it's not going to show.''

''It's something,'' Rafferty said.

''Yeah.'' Cloud mashed the cigarette against his heel, dropped it on the floor. He glanced at Rafferty's morose face and felt a rush of empathy. He clapped him on the shoulder.

''Well, how's the snowbird squad?''

Rafferty shrugged. ''We're making a run at them every chance we get.''

''How's your buddy Strobish?''

Rafferty crimped his mouth wryly. "Black."

Cloud laughed. "Not getting prejudiced in your old age?"

"I don't mind that he's black. I kind of enjoy it, as a matter of fact. He's a funny guy sometimes. It's just that he can't leave it alone. Being black, I mean. Black jokes, racist jokes. He's forever denigrating black people. I get embarrassed for him. It's like he's always apologizing for being black, as if making fun of them somehow makes him not-black."

"You easy with him?"

"Oh, hell yes. He's tough as rawhide, not afraid of anything, and he can be mean as hell when he needs to. I never worry about my back." He smiled crookedly. "It's not like the old days with you, but, what the hell, things change."

"That they do," Cloud said solemnly, as embarrassed at the compliment as Rafferty had been in giving it. He took out another cigarette and moved to his office door. "Well, better rattle the box a little. I'll see you, Jake."

Rafferty glanced past Cloud's shoulder. "Where's all your troops?"

"Out beating the bushes. It's where I ought to be, but I've got a stack of field interrogation reports ass-high I've got to wade through. I'd sooner fight a mad dog with a water pistol."

Rafferty nodded soberly. He lifted a hand and walked off down the corridor. Cloud stood in the doorway watching him, the slumped shoulders, lead-footed walk. He wondered how long it took to get over losing someone you loved enough to want to share your life with.

20

"Hi. This is Ben Cloud."

"Who?"

"Now, come on, Amy, don't give me a hard time. I'm sorry about last night. I got tied up on this damned Arrowstone thing . . . you know how it is."

"No, I don't know how it is. I know how you are well enough. You're not a man of your word, Ben Cloud. What is it? Are you getting horny again? You want to ravage me again?"

"Could be . . . Anyhow I think the word is ravish."

"Well, whatever the word, you caught me with my defenses down and took advantage of me when I plainly told you I didn't do things like that. On top of that, you stood there and looked at me when I was totally naked."

"Is that why you turned over on your back?" Shit, he was beginning to think she meant it, that she was really angry.

"That's when I woke up and saw you leering at me like I was a piece of raw mutton."

"I don't even like mutton. I wouldn't leer at a piece of mutton. A steak, maybe."

"You're not funny, Cloud."

"Amy?"

"What, dammit?"

"I only wanted to see you tonight."

"Okay! What time? Your place or mine?"

Cloud was still alone in the office. Ron Graves and Rosie Simple were working a new list of names that had evolved out of the Brenda Sue Dickerson murder. A detective named Lou Tolbert had been assigned from Robbery to help out.

Cloud had spent the better part of an hour poring over the new interrogation reports, looking for something, anything out of kilter. He felt it was a monumental waste of time, but it was procedure, and sometimes it was the drudgery that paid off.

Not this time, he thought. This killer was not one of the big three: relative, lover, or friend. These were stranger murders. Wanton, willful, and without reason, except for the inexplicable compulsions in a madman's brain.

But was he a madman? Could a madman plan so methodically, execute so brilliantly, so coolly? And with malice aforethought, as the prosecuting attorneys were so fond of saying. All killers were not classified as madmen. And killing one of fifty was, in principle, the same. A predator preys, and man was a predator. The most efficient of all the predators. Did the degree of madness increase proportionately with the number of people killed? No, it did not, Cloud thought. If a demented person killed, he did not necessarily become more demented. If a sane man killed, he did not necessarily become insane.

So what? So what did it mean?

It could mean, Cloud thought wryly, that Julian Arrowstone didn't have to be a nut. He could be as sane as anyone Cloud knew—himself, for instance. Maybe saner. It was a cinch that Julian Arrowstone wouldn't let a redheaded slip of a smart-mouthed reporter tie him in knots. Hell, no, he'd simply strangle her ass.

He shuffled through the stack of papers and found the mug shot of Arrowstone from New York. Clipped to it were several copies of a composite made up by the Chicago police during his rampage in that city some fifteen years later.

There was little resemblance between the two. As a boy, Arrowstone had had an ordinary face, plain, even features, the mouth perhaps a trifle too large for his face. Dark eyes under the thick, bushy brows of an older man, nondescript light hair combed straight back from his brow.

The composite had been assembled from the memories of assorted hospital personnel. The change was remarkable; no longer angular with indeterminate planes and angles, the face had become square, brutish, the mouth smaller, thinner, a knife slash under a curved nose. The eyes dominated the face, deep-sunken and sullen, the bushy brows now almost nonexistent. The pointed chin, now squared, jutted arrogantly, a fitting colophon to someone's preconceived notion of what a mad rapist-killer's face should look like.

There was no way the boy could have made the man, he decided, wondering if anyone had ever actually compared the two images before. He had little faith in composites, particularly those made up from details supplied by more than one person. He had yet to see one bearing a recognizable resemblance to its subject.

He lit a cigarette and leaned back in his chair. He closed his eyes and let his elbows dangle over the arms of the chair. This latest murder bothered him in a way he was hard put to define. Maybe it was the sheer audacity of the killer, the cold nerve it would have taken to carry the dead body across twenty feet of well-lighted space to its final resting place behind the fountain. A bold, cunning act, it had about it an air of invincibility, exhibited at the same time a sublime contempt for those who would hunt him down.

Cloud doubted that he had the guts to do what the killer had done. That was assuming he had had the guts to kill the girl in the first place.

Guts. Was that what it took? Was that the difference between a killer and a nonkiller? He doubted that.

21

He had once killed a man. Shot him three times in the chest. Guts had nothing to do with it. Fear had been the motivating factor. Fear for his life, and a cold, savage rage aimed at the man who was trying to destroy it. He could still close his eyes and see it: the bright flashes from the gun held in two mammoth hands, the snarling face and hating eyes, the man marching toward him, firing . . . marching . . . firing—

The phone rang; he jumped.

"Shit!" he said aloud, his heart pounding, feeling foolish. Grinning a little, he picked up the phone.

"Cloud."

A moment of silence.

"Lieutenant Cloud? Lt. Benjamin Cloud?" He recognized the voice immediately: the peculiar intonations, liquid, sibilant, distinctive. A voice out of his past—somewhere—but the name eluded him.

"Yes, this is Lieutenant Cloud. Who are you?"

Another moment of silence.

"Does the name of Julian Arrowstone mean anything to you, Lieutenant Cloud?" A hollow, almost ethereal echo, a faint, metallic resonance; Cloud's heart began to pound again.

"I've heard it, yes," he said, keeping his voice even. He stopped and waited.

A moment of silence again.

"Then I have no need to explain. You are undoubtedly aware

of my work. I suspected as much after seeing your rather transparent subterfuge during your interview with the lovely Ms. Reed. Particularly when it appeared twice again the following day. You needn't have bothered. I would have contacted you sooner or later, in any case. I enjoy keeping on friendly terms with my, ah, adversaries, as it were.''

"You are Julian Arrowstone?" He thought furiously during the seemingly inevitable moment of silence. The voice. *Goddammit, he knew the voice!* It flitted around the tip of his mind like a hummingbird around a rose. In and out, before he could grasp the amorphous image and transform it into coherence. Shit! Of all times to be alone in the office. He looked at the phones on the other desks. Too far.

A low laugh. "But, of course. Let's not kid each other, Lieutenant. You were expecting my call. Not quite so soon, perhaps. I'm sure you have by now assimilated all pertinent data from New York and Chicago. You are familiar with my propensity for . . . shall we say, garrulity. I enjoy tremendously discussing the finer points of my work with those individuals who are in a position to appreciate them. You are aware of this, and you were soliciting my call. Otherwise, there would have been no need for that absurd display on television the other night.''

"Not absurd," Cloud protested, stalling, standing up to peer into the empty squad bay outside the plate-glass front of his office. "Amateurish, maybe."

Cloud cursed silently. He sat back down, then leaped to his feet again as a slender female figure marched sturdily through the squad bay doorway. She hesitated, looked around the empty office, then angled across toward one of the offices at the other end. Cloud waved wildly.

Cricket Bloom paused, waved back, then continued on her way. Cloud pressed the receiver hard against his stomach and shouted, "Cricket!"

She stopped. Cloud motioned frantically. She turned and came toward his office.

He pressed the phone against his ear.

". . . should never hold the receiver against your body anywhere near the diaphragm, Lieutenant Cloud. I should think you would know that. I didn't quite understand what you shouted, but it sounded somewhat like 'Trace it'. What a pity. I had looked forward to having an interesting chat this first time. However, we have approximately four minutes, allowing a slight margin for safety's sake. Is there any one thing that you would like to ask me?"

"All right, Julian," Cloud said. "I'll cancel the trace if you really want to talk." He motioned to Cricket standing in the door and mouthed the words: "Trace it", pointing to his phone. She nodded, bright smile vanishing, brassy red hair spilling around her hands as she cupped Rosie Simple's phone to her mouth.

Julian Arrowstone chuckled. "I'd like to believe you, Ben—May I call you Ben?—but something tells me you wouldn't hesitate to tell me a teensy white lie—"

Peter Lorre! Peter-goddamn-Lorre, for pete sakes! He had been listening to a dead man's voice. A perfect imitation—inflections, nuances, tone—it was damned eerie.

"You're a goddamned fake!" Cloud snarled. "Look, buddy, if I ever get my hands on you—"

"I am not a fake!" Peter Lorre's voice hissed indignantly. "I killed your silly women, and I am Julian Arrowstone." A hint of petulance infiltrated the syrupy voice at midsentence.

"Prove it," Cloud challenged.

A moment of silence and then a deeper, harsher voice that Cloud recognized at once: "Five smooth stones, friend. If you've done your homework, you'll know about the stones." Humphrey Bogart, perfectly done.

Cloud's blood chilled. He sagged into the chair and stared at Cricket's strained face hanging over the other phone, birdlike black eyes fastened on his face. She grimaced, her slender body bobbing up and down in impatience.

"What makes you do it, Julian?" Cloud asked listlessly, his temples throbbing. He reached for a cigarette, discovered he already had one going.

"You wouldn't believe how many times I've been asked that question over the years. The simple truth is that I enjoy it. You won't believe that, of course, but it's the truth. I don't question it any more than you do the urge to eat, or have sex. I just do it because I can and I want to."

"It sucks, Julian. You suck." He glared at Cricket Bloom; she grimaced again and shook her head.

"But it doesn't make me a bad person," the voice said, a perfect Paul Lynde, a low, good-natured chuckle.

"Get out of my town, Arrowstone," Cloud said. "Go to Fort Worth or Dallas, goddammit! Go to Houston or Los Angeles.

They'd love you in Los Angeles. You'd feel right at home. We don't want you here; *I* don't want you here. We don't deserve you. Get the hell out!''

The delayed chuckle gave him a clue before he heard the voice: ''I don't give a damn what you want, pard. The dart landed on Trinity Square, and that's that.'' Gary Cooper. He laughed gaily. The line went dead.

22

Cloud looked at Cricket and shook his head.

She spoke into the receiver and hung up. "I'm sorry, love."

Cloud brushed absently at ashes littering his khaki-colored twill slacks, unaccountably shaken by a mixture of anger and dread, an atavistic tension stirring the air around him, closing in on him like a high-intensity fever. He was barely aware of Cricket moving to stand beside him. She wore designer jeans, knee-high boots, and a wool sweater at least five sizes too large.

"Was it that bleedin' psycho Arrowstone?" Her tone expressed revulsion, but her avid face made a liar out of her voice.

Cloud stirred, looked up at her. "Where did you hear about Arrowstone?"

Cricket flipped a short, thin arm. "It's all over the Dallas newspapers. Julie Harper heard two of the detectives talking about it yesterday. Why, is it supposed to be a bloody secret?" Huge, heavily mascaraed eyes and a pointed nose gave her the look of a small, startled owl.

"Not bloody now, it's not," Cloud said. He picked up the phone, then held it dangling in his hand while he tried to remember who he was going to call. He remembered and began dialing.

"What are you doing here so early?"

Cricket made a prissy face. "Miss Angelpuss Dougherty is having her monthlies again. A bleedin' sissy, if you ask me. The muckin' brass had better be getting us another girl or I'm jolly

98

well going to pack it in." At a certain angle, her overbite and slightly oversized teeth gave her the appearance of a perpetual smile.

Cloud nodded sympathetically and listened to the phone ring. Four rings and it clicked.

"Rafferty."

"Did I wake you? What the hell you doing sleeping on your day off?"

The sound of a yawn. "Another bullshit stakeout last night. Just dropped off to sleep here on the couch."

"Is Arrowstone a mimic?" Cricket wiggled her fingers, then blew him a kiss and left, high heels cracking a tattoo on the tiled floor.

"What?"

"Did you come across anything about Arrowstone being a mimic?"

"You mean voices, or what?"

"Mimic. Voices. What else is there?"

"Sorry, I'm still half asleep. No, I don't remember reading or hearing anything like that. Why?"

"I just got a call."

"From Arrowstone? Remember, I told you—"

"Actually it was from Peter Lorre, Humphrey Bogart, and Gary Cooper . . . and, oh, yeah, a cameo appearance by Paul Lynde."

"I'll be damned."

"It was eerie as hell. The son of a bitch is good, I'll give him that. Even Rich Little is off-center on some of the words, but I didn't hear a false note. And he talked quite awhile."

"Not long enough for a trace?"

"Sure. Plenty of time. Not a damn soul in the office, and I couldn't reach the other phones. Cricket Bloom finally came along and we gave it a shot, but the bastard heard me yell at Cricket and he cut it off in time."

"Jesus. He won't give you a second chance. You should have put a tap on your—"

"Yeah, I know. I screwed up." He paused to light a cigarette.

"Ben. Maybe it wasn't him. Maybe some kook."

"It's too soon. Arrowstone didn't become general knowledge until this morning. Somebody talked to the newspapers. Anyhow, I thought of that. I called him a fake. He came back with the stones."

Rafferty made a sound like steam escaping from a valve. "We can expect an invasion from the media this afternoon. With all the potbellied old gossips in that meeting this morning, they'll have a field day. We're in for a firestorm, buddy."

"We? You can consider yourself lucky you're Narcotics."

"I'd trade, Ben, gladly."

"I know it, Jake. You know, there was something funny about Arrowstone's voice. Aside from the mimicry, I mean. It had a flat, mechanical sound, an echo quality. You think he may have had a throat operation and they gave him one of those voice boxes to speak through?"

"Should be easily checked. Unless he had it done since he escaped."

"There seemed to be some sort of pause before he responded. A precise, metered pause." Cloud changed sides with the receiver, wiped his sweaty palm on his pants. "I don't know. Maybe I imagined it. I've never talked to a mass murderer before. It's an unsettling experience. He didn't talk crazy, Jake. Well, maybe a kind of craziness. He said he did it because it was there to do, or at least I think that's what he meant. I wasn't hearing too good, to be honest with you. I was in a kind of shock when I finally knew it was him. I know you warned me, but it was too sudden. I think even after going on TV and trying to piss him off, I never really expected him to call."

"I'd give a lot to talk to him myself."

"It would be futile, Jake. I don't think he could tell you why he kills. We know why he killed Ramona. She was there and a threat to him. But all the others. Sex?"

"Maybe sex, maybe something else. What the hell's the difference. Just get him for me, Ben."

"I'll do my best. Go on back to sleep, you lunkhead."

"Take it easy, Ben."

23

Julian Arrowstone first saw the Dallas newspaper in one of the open-air newsstands off Hollywood Boulevard. He spotted the headline from ten feet away and stopped dead still, creating a momentary dam in the flow of restless humanity along the sidewalk. His breath caught, constricted by a squeezing sensation inside his chest.

MASS KILLER ARROWSTONE IN TRINITY SQUARE

Only the headline was visible, the rest of it hidden behind the rack and a copy of the *Washington Post*. Arrowstone stood rooted, oblivious to disgruntled glares and muttered curses. Slowly the shock began to fade; saliva flowed again and consternation overwhelmed fear. He crossed to the newspaper rack, lifted the heavy Sunday paper, and moved down the walk to the cashier.

The *Dallas Morning News*. He knew about Dallas, Texas. He had passed through there with his parents once a long time ago. But where, or what, was Trinity Square?

The girl rolled the paper and dropped it into a plastic bag. Arrowstone gave her a five-dollar bill and waved away the change, his mind teeming with questions he hoped the newspaper would answer.

It wouldn't be the first time the deaths of young women across the country had been laid at his door. But usually he was blamed in a speculative sense, when some bumbling police department was stymied and desperately looking for an out, a scapegoat.

He crossed Hollywood Boulevard and walked toward his room, smiling thinly. Who better than he, Julian Arrowstone, a perfect patsy for any inept detective with a difficult murder case on his hands?

He felt a turgid rill of indignation at the injustice of it, holding himself stiffly erect as he walked, ignoring as much as possible the milling humanity around him, hustlers and whores, flamboyant pimps and ragtag derelicts with runny noses and rheumy eyes, soft-faced men with shifting, lusting eyes darkly shadowed by years of furtive perversions, ubiquitous druggies nodding peacefully on the upper edge of their high or knotted painfully on their way down.

He felt like a lion prowling a herd of witless, bleating sheep, an avenging predator stalking unwary prey. He walked faster, adrenaline pumping, breathing the putrid smog-laden air in rapid, shallow drafts.

Inside his room he spread the paper on the sagging bed. He lit a cigarette and read the stories beneath the headline, anticipation and growing tension tightening the muscles in his chest.

When he finished, he crushed the paper into a ragged ball and threw it to the floor. He cursed tonelessly, in a weary voice.

The bastards were doing it again.

Three women dead and he was being set up to take the blame, police releases claiming that certain physical aspects of the crimes matched beyond a reasonable doubt the MO of one Julian Arrowstone, a psychopathic killer recently escaped from a mental institution in New York.

Psychopathic killer my ass, he thought savagely, wondering what physical aspects of the killings they were talking about.

Could it be the stones? The silly damned stones he had started using on a whim, then continued to use simply because it amused him to do so and gave the cops and the shrinks something to puzzle over.

That would mean a copycat, someone who had found out about the stones and was deliberately using them to shift suspicion and blame. Some unimaginative brute who killed out of uncontrollable rage or lust, or some other equally vulgar reason. His lip curled in disdain.

His own trespasses came out of a deep need to possess, a depthless hunger for domination, control. He had no desire to mutilate, to degrade. He craved the inexpressible thrill of complete subjugation to his will, total submissiveness, out of which he molded beauty far surpassing the original, a transcendent beauty that bore his mark as surely as the inimitable strokes of the old masters betrayed their artistry. He did not destroy beauty; he created it. When would they understand? When would they recognize the unique artistry and perfect symmetry of his work and stop confusing it with the wanton destructiveness of madmen?

He went out of his room and down the hall to the telephone on the wall by the window. He dialed airport information and learned that Trinity Square, Texas was a ten-minute cab ride from the Dallas/Fort Worth Airport. He made a reservation on a six o'clock flight.

He stood by the window for a time, smoking and watching the wretched specimens walking and sauntering and staggering by outside.

Three teenaged girls huddled near the curb, short shorts and knee-high boots, halters and dangling earrings. They made obscene, suggestive gestures at passing male motorists, flaunted their tender wares with surprising frankness, laughing and jeering in high, shrill voices.

He sighed. Youth and beauty and innocence. All wasted, beyond redemption. God, there were so many of them.

He mashed the cigarette on the windowsill and went back into his room to pack.

As he worked, he felt a tiny thrill of impending epiphany, a rising tide of awareness. He felt cool and invincible, a feeling usually associated with the beginning of a hunt, the initial stages wherein he carefully searched for a subject of worth, culling and sifting, eventually making his selection based on some esoteric formula he could never clinically define.

Somewhere in Dallas there would be a perfect specimen, a subject worthy of his special talents. And he would find her, show this presumptuous upstart up for what he was, a poor imitation of the real thing.

And, and the thought set his blood racing, he would do something he enjoyed doing almost as much as creating his works of art: He would tweak the noses of the bumbling cops.

24

Amy Reed came out of the bathroom damply warm and glowing. Nude, her hair freshly fluffed and tumbling, she leaped lightly onto her side on the king-sized bed, stuffed a pillow in the small of her back, and leaned against the satin-lined headboard. She lit a cigarette and drew up her legs. She tilted her cheek against her knees and regarded him gravely for a moment, her face quiescent, a trace of humor in the glint in her eyes, the curve of her lips. She reached out and raked his shoulder with clawed fingers.

"I'm not at all sure I want to get all tangled up with you, Cloud."

Benjamin Cloud, sprawled limply, ungracefully, in postcoital lassitude, uttered a small, plaintive groan and turned on his side facing her. He took the cigarette out of her fingers and swiped a puff.

"You make it sound like a wad of leftover spaghetti."

"You know what I mean. Things are moving awfully fast for this timid little country girl. You overwhelmed me again."

"Ravaged?"

"A couple of times there I felt like a tiny bonito being hit on by a grinning barracuda."

"Did it bother you?"

She smiled broadly. "No. And *that's* what bothers me."

He held the cigarette to her lips, then slipped his hand down along the taut stretch of her thigh. "I'm a jellyfish, actually, in disguise."

"You're a cop, is what you are," she said, as if that might be an interesting bit of news. "I'm just now getting over a three-year hitch as house mother for a swaggering bunch of little boys with big guns and bigger egos."

"Your husband was a cop? I didn't know that."

"I don't brag about it. He simply never grew up. He got locked in at the stage where little boys wear cowboy hats, play with six-shooters, and practice fast-draw in front of the mirrors. The Roy Rogers, Lone Ranger syndrome."

"I was partial to Hopalong Cassidy, myself."

"I was never sure from one night to the next whether I was the perpetrator, the suspect, or the victim."

"What kind of cop?"

"Highway Patrol. We lived in California."

"Yeah, those highway cowboy types tend to be a bit arrogant. They hand it out with the big hats and the boots."

She smiled wryly. "He didn't wear a big hat."

"They do here in Texas."

She bobbed her head. "I guess he did, too, only nobody but him could see it." She ran a hand through her hair and made a giggling sound. "If he and I had done some of the things you and I did tonight, he would have arrested us both."

"Straitlaced?"

"Hidebound. Missionary style, a kiss or two before, a little rooting at the boobs, and then tight-lipped silence and blank eyes. It wasn't manly to groan or gasp, and absolutely no post-coital conversation. We *never* talked about it. I don't think he even knew it was supposed to be fun for me, too. As a matter of fact, we didn't do it a lot."

"Maybe there was a reason for that," Cloud said, rolling on his stomach and propping himself on his elbows. "I spent four years in a prowl car. It's a bad job even in a small town; in a big city it's a killer. Everyone you see is a potential enemy. I mean everyone. From the kids high on alcohol or drugs to some little old lady who just can't afford another ticket. At some time or other, somewhere, every segment of the population has tried to waste a cop. Far too many succeed. In some ways it's worse than Nam. At least there, if there was any doubt, you blew the bastard away and figured out later if he was friend or foe. A cop can't do that. If you've never done it, there's no way you can understand. It eats at you, grinds you down. The really surprising thing is that cops don't shoot more people. Sooner or later, it spills over into your private life. You're wary of everyone except your partner, afraid to let go, to drop your guard.''

"Even with your wife?"

"Even with your wife. Even your own kids, sometimes. Cops are overexposed. They see all the things that supposedly moral, God-fearing, backbone-of-the-country types do to each other and to themselves, and they finally believe, rightly or wrongly, that we're all capable of anything given sufficient provocation. Cynicism trails the badge and always catches up.''

"Are you like that, Cloud?"

"I don't know," he said honestly. "I'm as cynical as most, I guess. But I'm lucky: I'm an incurable optimist, and I got out of a squad car in time, maybe. Being a detective is different. Not much better, but different. Everything's usually after the fact. I haven't shot it out with a bad guy in almost a month now.''

She stared at him, blinked, then looked away. "Dammit, Cloud, you're supposed to cheer me up, make me laugh, not make me feel guilty and sad.''

He reached across and gripped her shoulder and pulled her down. He kissed her. "I'd rather make you swoon with pleasure.''

"We've done that. What're we going to do for an encore?"

"We could play Scrabble or discuss existentialism.''

"I can't even say it, how could I discuss it? Tell me what it means.''

"We're here and it's now and that's all that matters.''

"Oh, I thought that was fatalism.''

"Fatalism is when you buy a new car and it breaks down three days after the warranty runs out.''

"Oh, I thought that was capitalism.''

"Now you've got it.''

She laughed and wriggled down beside him. She hoisted a slim leg and climbed on his back, stretched out. She nipped the side of his neck and licked his ear.

"Hmmm. Isn't this nice? How does it feel?"

"Soft and warm and . . . heavy.''

"Now you know how a woman feels.''

"Nooo, I don't think it's quite the same thing, somehow.''

"Maybe we've discovered a new position.''

"For what?"

She grunted passionately in his ear, rotated her pelvic region on his buttocks. "Isn't this exciting?"

"Exciting maybe, but it'd be a lot more productive if you'd let me turn over."

"You men," she hissed scornfully, "you think you know it all. A woman's body is a delicate instrument, and there's more than one way to make it sing." Her breathing had subtly changed. The kisses on his neck and jaw were warmer, wetter; her center oscillated furiously.

He could feel the tips of her breasts, engorged, pressing against his back. He twisted his neck and tried to grin at her; she kissed half his mouth, tried to get at it all, but his neck would only swivel so far. He felt her shudder, heard a low, strangled moan. Then a gasp, and she was arched above him, supported by her toes and outspread arms.

"Oh, shit, Cloud! Turn over, turn over! Hurry!"

25

Ron Graves watched stolidly as the young, bespectacled M.E. crouched beside the two dead bodies. Very nearly the same size, they lay stretched on the ground beside the Dempster Dumpster where they had been found. A young, grinning black man and a large, potbellied man in overalls stood near the gaping door of a garbage truck, alternating their attention between Rosie Simple and the dead men. A small crowd had gathered across the street on the parking apron of the Seven-Eleven, and a uniformed policeman stood in the middle of the street impatiently gesturing at the slow-moving cars.

Graves had recognized one of the dead men immediately: Sammy Keeler, part-time grifter and pickpocket, full-time snitch. An addict always in need of money, Sammy had sold information to whoever was buying. Even Graves had done business with him on occasion. He was aware that Sammy had dealt with other detectives, and since snitching was possibly the highest risk occupation in the world, he had not been particularly surprised to see the nattily dressed little man with his throat cut.

The other one, obviously a derelict, puzzled him more. A drifter, clean-shaven, dressed in a worn, but expensive, blue blazer and khaki pants, he had been killed in an identical manner. Not that it was all that unusual to find a wino with his throat cut. That sort of thing happened with disturbing frequency. But to find two dead men, one a derelict, the other a small-time hoodlum, in the same location and, as far as Graves could tell, killed at the same time, gave rise to the inevitable conclusion that they were somehow connected. A drug deal gone sour? Retaliation? Maybe the stranger was also a snitch. Maybe he had had the misfortune to be hanging around when the killer caught up with Sammy Keeler. Maybe a lot of things, Graves thought, grunting as Rosie came up beside him and poked him in the ribs.

"Got it solved yet, Sherlock?"

Graves shook his head. "No, you got any ideas?"

"Sure. They were back in here doing a sixty-nine and some latent homo—probably a weightlifter—come along and iced them."

Graves grinned and poked him back. "You recognize the guy in the seersucker suit—Sammy Keeler?"

"Yeah. You ever see the other one?"

Graves rubbed his chin, his long-sleeved shirt stretching tight across huge biceps. "I think I have. That blazer looks kinda familiar. Down on Northcross. Guy was wearing a cowboy hat, though."

Rosie nodded. "So was this one. It's still in the Dumpster. We don't want to forget it. It fell of when they lifted him out. Anything else?"

"No. He was kinda hobbling along. Far as I know, that's the only time I ever saw him."

"Probably another damyankee come down for some of our sun." Rosie moved away before Graves, an ex-New Yorker, could respond.

He squatted beside the young, pinch-faced M.E. "Anything, Doc?"

The M.E. grunted and glanced up, then down at Sammy Keeler's bare back. The other one lay on his stomach also, his shirt bunched at his shoulder blades.

"Judging from postmortem lividity, this one has been dead at least a day, maybe more, longer than his friend here. See these purplish striations here . . . and there. They were both lying on their backs. The blood settles to the lowest point. In this one, the lividity is considerably more advanced."

"Any idea when?"

"Two days on this one, day to a day-and-a-half on the other one. Guesses. I can tell you more after we get into them."

Graves had come up to stand beside them. "That knocks hell out of your theory, Rosie."

The M.E. glanced up curiously. "What theory?"

"Never mind," Rosie growled. "He's being a smartass, as usual."

Graves laughed.

Rosie rose to his feet. "Looks like somebody's found himself a dumping ground for his spare bodies. I can't figure two people using the same spot. Too much coincidence."

Graves shrugged. "I don't know. It's handy to downtown. This is a mean area. With all this lumber and machinery, it's almost private."

Rosie swiveled slowly in a full circle, then looked at Graves. "Which you want? The businesses across the street or the residences up there behind us. Take your pick."

"Doesn't matter. I'll take the residences. But nobody down here ever sees or hears anything."

"That's for damn sure," Rosie said. "But we still need names for the reports. Let's hook 'em."

Spencer Price prowled Northcross from one end to the other. A leisurely stroll, taking his time, checking all the likely places.

A solid mile of sleaze, he thought contemptuously, striding down the center of the sidewalk, watching them break around him, giving way like a squawking flock of chickens before a marauding lion. He checked the two shoddy supermarkets carefully, strolling along the front windows, catching more than one flirtatious glance from the line of cashiers, mostly young women.

But no redheads. Some of them were pretty enough—but no redheads. He chafed under this self-imposed limitation, longed for the time when it would no longer be necessary.

Disappointed, he crossed the street and started down the other side. A scouting expedition. Reconnoitering. Find the subject, then find the routine. They seldom varied from their pattern. Especially at night. Familiar sights and sounds gave them comfort, made them feel safe, or, at least, safer. Their complacency was his best ally. That, and his own intelligence, of course.

But first, the subject. The world was full of redheads: auburn, russet, ocher, copper. He wondered suddenly how it would be with a wig. Maybe that was the answer. With a wig, the list would be endless; there were three or four girls in the supermarkets alone who would fill the bill for face and figure. No, he decided. No point in taking chances since everything was going so well, exactly as planned. Later on, after Arrowstone was caught, and inevitably he would be caught, he would be free to take anyone he pleased. But no, he thought, suddenly disconsolate. When Arrowstone was caught, he would have to quit.

A police car came slowly toward him along the street. Abruptly, he turned into a bookstore. He wandered along the aisle, watching the squad car pass slowly down the street. Stupid pigs! He had nothing to fear; he could walk right past their noses and they would not suspect.

He went around the end of the rack and started back up the other side. He stopped, startled, found himself staring down into a lovely freckled face.

"Excuse me," she said, pulling the book cart out of the aisle. She gave him a fleeting smile and went back to shelving books, turning her back, the heavy mass of wine-red hair filled with flashing pinpoints of gold hooking his eyes with a heavy, mesmerizing force.

His heart began to pound. He took a step forward, hands rising, fingers clawed. He stopped, locked in a moment of blind panic.

His blood seethed. His vision blurred.

He had to get out!

He whirled and almost ran back the way he had come. He thrust his hands deep inside his coat pockets.

Jesus, he had almost screwed up! Coming on her like that, he had been overwhelmed, all the careful defenses crumbling in one blinding flash of time. He forced himself out of the building, walked rapidly toward his car, his heart jumping crazily.

He laughed shakily. Another few seconds and he would have had his hands on her. God!

"Soon," he promised himself, "soon."

26

Capt. Eli Summers glanced up from his littered desk as Cloud, Simple, and Graves trooped into his office. Graves carried a straight-backed chair in one massive hand as effortlessly as Cloud carried his clipboard. He deposited it beside the other two, facing away from the desk, straddled it, and folded his corded arms across the back, his unlined, ridiculously youthful face serene.

"Good morning, gentlemen," Summers murmured, scrawling his initials across the bottom of a report and closing the folder with a flip of slender fingers. He placed the folder on a stack at his right and carefully capped the ball-point pen. He studied the three faces arrayed before him, then reached into a desk drawer and withdrew a clean, glass ashtray. He leaned forward and placed it on the corner nearest Cloud. "If you just have to," he said.

Cloud grinned and reached for his cigarettes. "Thanks, Eli, I'd forgotten all about them."

Summers snorted softly, one hand straying to his chin. "Infantile habit," he proclaimed. "On par with sucking your thumb. I oughta know, I did it myself for twenty-one years." The hand crept to his mouth, flicked the end of his nose like a cat playing with a mouse.

"Poison," Graves volunteered, lifting an arm, flexing, watching with visible pride the ropy muscles writhing like tortured snakes beneath the bronze skin. "Screws up the muscle tone, murder on the lungs."

They all looked at Rosie, who shrugged noncommittally. "It's his life."

Summers laughed and reared back in his swivel chair. "Okay. So much for Ben's problems. We've all got enough of our own. Did you see this morning's papers? Hell, you'd think we'd been invaded by Attila the Hun. Let's see, the *News* said: 'MAD STRANGLER IN TRINITY SQUARE???' They, at least, made a question out of it. *The Telegram* wasn't quite so reticent. 'PSYCHO KILLER STALKS TRINITY SQUARE'. You ever hear such a pile of shit?" His eyes snapped belligerently. "Seventy-five goddamned calls we've had already this morning, and it isn't nine o'clock yet. Donleavy's wound up tighter'n a banjo string. He's called for another of his asshole-reaming meetings at ten o'clock. Department heads only this time. You know what that means. The bastard's gonna get out his bullwhip. The mayor and the city council's been on his ass all morning, and he's gonna pass it along. Who to? Me, that's who. I'm sitting here like a trussed-up gobbler at a turkey shoot with no log to hide behind. Not even a goddamned blade of Johnson grass. Now, I may be just another dumb cop, but I've been over all your reports and I don't have one blessed thing I can take in there to prop up my head with—"

"The hell you don't," Cloud said, bristling. "We know who he is. We know approximately what he looks like—"

"Are you absolutely sure of that, Ben?" Eli Summers watched the flushed face of the lanky detective intently. "You're positive it's this guy Arrowstone?"

"I am," Cloud said firmly, a tremor racing along his back. "Dammit, Eli, I've talked to the man! I thought he was a fake, too. I braced him with it. But he knew about the five stones. How else could he have known about that? Nobody outside of Homicide and the Medical Examiner's office knows about the stones—except Rafferty, of course." He felt another shiver as he thought about Amy Reed. But it was absurd to think she would have mentioned it to anyone. It was the nucleus of her story-to-be.

"We have the composites flying all over the Metroplex," Rosie said heavily. "Sooner or later, somebody's gonna pick up on the bastard."

"There's the pubic hairs found on the Dickerson woman," Ron Graves said. "Stovall said they came from an adult caucasian male, somewhere between thirty and fifty—probably. And then there's the fibers. Stovall says he thinks they're wool, but he's gonna run them through the Dallas lab.'' His face brightened. ''Incidentally, the M.E. said that although she had all the appearances of being raped repeatedly, there were no pecker tracks—semen.'' He looked around, a questioning frown on his guileless face. ''You think that's significant, Ben?''

''Maybe he wore a rubber,'' Rosie said. ''Or beat off in his hand. He's a damn nut, no telling what a nut will do.''

''I don't think so, Rosie,'' Cloud said. ''In all the other cases he raped them to completion. So far as I understand, anyhow. It doesn't make sense unless something happened, an interruption, something went wrong. Maybe she got a handful of cock and balls and did some damage. That could account for him not finishing.''

''Maybe she bit him,'' Graves said. ''He had oral contact with the Elliot girl.''

Eli Summers propped his elbows on his desk and washed his face with both slender hands, one bony forefinger dipping fleetingly into his left nostril.

''What about his guy's motivations? Donleavy's a sucker for psychological bullshit. Maybe I can sidetrack him. He saw a rerun of 'The Boston Strangler' on television the other night, and he just finished reading about that psycho Bundy who killed all them girls in Utah and Seattle, and now he thinks he's some kind of expert on the psychopathic mind.'' He sighed heavily. ''Anyhow, it's worth a try.''

Graves and Rosie looked at Cloud.

''Oedipus complex,'' Cloud said, blithely expanding on the skimpy information in the New York files. ''They say he's killing his mother—stepmother, actually—over and over again. They're not sure exactly why. There was some mention of possible incest, something about the mother being a tramp of sorts, an alcoholic, given to fits of depression. Some incidents in Arrowstone's earlier life about sadistic treatment of animals, an attempted rape at a very early age, a beating at twelve by the father that put the boy in the hospital. That's the only time the father was mentioned, so maybe he left, I don't know.'' He stopped and pursed his lips, thinking. ''And, oh, yeah, one of the most significant things, I think, he only kills redheads. His stepmother was a redhead.''

''Ramona Butler wasn't a redhead,'' Summers snapped.

"Ramona Butler was an accident—well, not exactly an accident. An unfortunate encounter, a by-product."

A look of resignation passed across Summers's face. He fingered the three file folders in the center of his desk, then slid them across to Cloud. "All right," he said morosely, the voice of a man who has been to hell and back and remembers every halting step with painful clarity. "If you see them taking my name off the door, you'll know I finally cracked up and blew Donleavy away."

Cloud stood up and wagged a cautioning finger. "Remember the pension, Eli. It's out there somewhere, just over the horizon."

Graves picked up his chair with one muscle-bound finger. "Yeah, boss, it's always brightest before the storm."

Rosie gave Graves a ponderous, disgusted look. "Darkest before the dawn, dummy."

"Not in my saying," Graves said indignantly. "You got your sayings, I got mine. In my saying—"

"Let's go," Cloud said. "Give Eli a chance to get his act together."

They filed out silently, the small man watching them darkly, fingers drumming, dancing on the desk top.

The moment the door snicked shut, the fingers stopped, poised motionless, then darted for his nose like a frightened spider heading for its hole.

27

Jake Rafferty leaned in toward the pole, putting the dark, creo-soted wood between his face and the two men hunkered at the rear of the Buick in the shopping mall parking lot. He keyed the walkie-talkie.

"It's a happening, bro," he said. "Move in. Give me ninety seconds to get in position. Then hit them. Keep your head up."

"Gotcha, whitey. Be cool. Nelson, you dig?"

"Roger," came the terse reply. "Moving in."

Rafferty jerked the blades out of the post and began his de-scent. It was slower going down, he discovered. Shit. He should have allowed more time. He stretched his legs, slipping once as the shiny metal gouged a chip of wood instead of biting in. Four feet from the ground, he said the hell with it. He unlocked the safety belt, hugged the post, and jerked both feet free. Kicking against the wood, he threw himself out and down.

He landed in ankle-high weeds, felt the sharp, lancing pain even before his brain registered the object beneath his left foot. He fell headlong into the shallow drainage ditch that bordered the alley. He rolled, came to his feet cursing the pain, glancing at his watch and realizing he only had thirty seconds to make the end of the alley.

Ignoring the pain, he kicked out of the pole boots, started forward at a sprint, fell sprawling, the packed gravel in the un-paved alley ripping his palms. He cursed and rolled to his feet and dimly heard the sound of shouting voices, the sound of a gunshot—another.

Whining with agony, he forced himself down the alley at a hobbling walk, the excruciating pain blotting the sound of running feet, the soft *thump—thump* of rubber-soled shoes on the hard-packed surface unheard until the man was almost on him.

Running full out, the man glanced at Rafferty without interest, arms pumping, the blue-black gun a glinting arc in the sunlight.

Rafferty yelled, scratching frantically inside the voluminous coveralls for his gun clipped to the belt of his pants. The man ignored him, almost even, ten feet away across the alley—so close, Rafferty could hear his rasping breath and pounding feet.

Rafferty yelled again, "Police! Stop!" The gun was in his hand, but he was turning too fast, and his ankle gave way.

He was already falling when the running man seemed to twist in midair and fire.

Rafferty felt an almost gentle tug an inch or so above his hipbone. He ignored it. He rolled on his stomach and yelled again, "Stop, goddammit! Police!"

The man kept moving, head down, legs pumping. Rafferty steadied his right hand in his left and sighted along the barrel.

He squeezed off a round. He blinked and saw the man stumble. He squeezed off another.

He was in midstride, long leg reaching for distance, another yard toward freedom. He seemed to hang there suspended; when his foot touched the ground, the man followed, crumpling, tumbling end over end.

Rafferty saw something fly into the air, catch a glimmer of light, and bounce into the weeds a few yards away from the fallen man. He knew it was the gun, but he lay without moving until Strobish came puffing up the alley, his gun sighted on the motionless lump among the weeds.

"Jesus Christ, Jake . . . did the son of a bitch get you?" Strobish fell to his knees beside Rafferty, grunting with pain as the sharp rocks took their toll. He grabbed Rafferty's shoulders.

"Get them damn big black paws off me," Rafferty said. "I'm okay. Just twisted my ankle. Go check on that mother."

"Shit!" Strobish said, his voice filled with relief. He hit Rafferty lightly on the shoulder and climbed to his feet. "You're a lucky mother honky. That'd been me, that asshole'd probably blowed a hole in my ass." He walked off up the alley, grumbling.

Rafferty sat up. He pulled back the edge of the jumpsuit and tugged his wet shirt out of his pants. It was beginning to burn, a long, red, ugly groove just above his hip, slowly oozing blood. He wrestled his handkerchief from his pants pocket and folded it into a wide pad. He held the pad over the wound and tugged his pants into place to hold it.

It was painful as hell, but he decided he would live. He climbed to his feet.

Strobish ambled back down the alley, carrying the pusher's gun by the trigger guard. "Nailed him both times. Last one dead center, looks like. Good job, man."

"What happened out there?"

Strobish shrugged thick shoulders. "Everything looked just dandy at first. They froze on signal. Then I guess this asshole thought he could make the alley. He pulled this gun and punched one in my direction. I answered, blowed the hell out of that Buick's rear window. The other guy—Bellows—he went down on the pavement like he was taking a Sunday afternoon swim. Nelson's got him. I couldn't risk another shot and . . . well, you know the rest." He stared intently at Rafferty's face, then put out a hand as the white detective swayed. "Hey, you sure you all right, man? You sure that bastard didn't nip you?"

Rafferty nodded, his face blanched. "This goddamned ankle's killing me. Give me a hand to the car, will you?"

Spencer Price crossed Northcross slowly to the west side. Bars and massage parlors, porn bookstores, and an occasional flophouse. Pool halls and arcades filled with stuttering cacophony. None of it interested him, not even the brassy redhead who loitered in the recessed doorway of a Million Delight's massage parlor, standing hipshot and seductive in hot pants and a bandanna bra.

"Come on in here, honey. I'll make you feel real good. How about it? A nice, slow rubdown . . . all over, then anything else your sweet little heart desires. You like balloons? A golden shower? A chocolate swirl? Popping pearls? You name it, sugar, we do it . . ." The shrill-husky voice trailed off behind him, ended in a casual, muttered obscenity, rose again as another potential customer sauntered into view.

He ignored it all, his eyes searching for the narrow bookstore across the street. He stopped a few yards from the corner, leaned heavily against a lamppost. His heartbeat increased even before he spotted her behind the cash register, the thick mass of hair pulled back, constricted behind her shapely head, fanning out over her shoulders and halfway to her hips like a dark, rippling waterfall of blood.

His heart began to pound, his throat dry. He was grinning so hard, his cheeks felt stiff and his jaws ached.

The noise around him diminished, faded, became silent. He could see her clearly, smiling toward the street.

Smiling at him.

Nothing moved in his world. There was only the girl and himself.

His hand clenched spasmodically in his jacket pocket, closed around the hard, smooth handle of the knife.

This time.

This time he would do it his way.

28

Slightly taller than medium height—but less than six feet, Cloud guessed—he wore tan denim pants, a western-style sport shirt, and a corduroy jacket. He carried a pearl-gray flat-crowned hat in his left hand, and his rolling gait along with a muted concussive rap of heels at each step told Cloud he was wearing high-heeled cowboy boots. He carried a scuffed brown briefcase in his right hand.

The narrow, handsome face and light-colored hair worn straight back from the tanned forehead told Cloud nothing. He watched him walk across the few feet from his office door, Eli Summers's words still echoing in his ears: "I'm sending a man down to see you. He's a cop from Chicago. Cooperate!"

He had barely had time to hang up and light a cigarette before the man had appeared, a pleasant smile on a face that Cloud suspected wasn't given to levity. He had an uncomfortable feeling the dark eyes staring steadily out of their deep sockets were assessing him as carefully and ruthlessly as the beam of an electron microscope. He shoved back from the desk and stood up.

"I'm Ward Callum," the man said, taking Cloud's hand, grip firm but not ostentatious, the smile vanishing as if it had never been, leaving the sober countenance that Cloud had suspected.

"Ben Cloud," Cloud said. "You're the cop from Chicago."

Callum nodded. "Captain Summers said you were the man to see."

"Have a seat." Cloud sat down and plucked his cigarette from the ashtray. "About what, Mr. Callum?"

"About Julian Arrowstone," Callum said quietly.

"What about him?"

"He's here in your town," Callum said patiently. He crossed his legs and placed the hat on the floor beside him.

Cloud smiled wryly. "We're acutely aware of that." He crushed out the cigarette. "I can see a connection, of course. You're from Chicago. Julian Arrowstone was reputedly in Chicago a couple of years ago. But this is Texas, Mr. Callum."

"Not reputedly, Lieutenant. He was there. We let him slip through our fingers. That's why I'm here. I know more about Julian Arrowstone than any man living. I want to help you catch him."

Cloud pursed his lips in a soundless whistle, gazing at the calmly waiting man in front of his desk, trying to decide whether to be pissed off or not. He decided not. It would be childish to begin with, and only a fool questioned the motives of a helping hand when he was going down for the third time.

He nodded slowly, frowning. "Texas would have first claim. You understand that, of course." Christ, he sounded as pompous as Donleavy.

"I don't care who puts him away. All I want is to help make it possible."

"I could arrange to have you deputized, I suppose, but you still wouldn't have any authority, not really—"

Callum shook his head. "I didn't bring a gun. I wouldn't want—" He stopped, a shadow passing across his face, the dark eyes suddenly darker. "If I should happen to be in at the . . . capture, I wouldn't want a gun. I wouldn't trust myself."

"Mind telling me why?"

Callum took a deep breath, nodded. "One of the women—girls—he killed in Chicago was my sister . . . my little sister Celia Ann Callum. The last one he killed before he disappeared. She was not a random choice, Lieutenant Cloud. He sought her out, deliberately, cold-bloodedly. I was his contact, you see. I headed the task force. I talked to him maybe fifteen times. We had a certain . . . rapport. I thought I was close to . . . to something inside him . . . some insight into that remarkable mind. He does have a remarkable mind, no matter how distorted, how perverted. He is extremely intelligent—cunning. He made fools out of us for eight months. Celia Ann was his *coup de grace*, his way of telling me he had been toying with me, playing with us all, his way of showing off his superior intellect.''

Cloud felt a chill coursing in his blood. He lit a cigarette, sucked deeply. ''I remember reading her name,'' he said softly. ''A high school senior, a gymnast.''

Callum leaned forward in his chair. ''Six months ago I went out on indeterminate leave. I've read everything ever written about Arrowstone. I know a lot about him no one else knows. His habits, his likes and dislikes, his preferences in food. I can be a help to you, Lieutenant Cloud.''

Cloud stood up and crossed to the window. He made an unnecessary adjustment to the Levelor blind, wondering why he was hesitating. Summers had said to cooperate. That meant he knew what it was all about. It also meant that Summers was telling him in his not-so-subtle way that he needed a little extra help. Well, he could use a little help, a *lot* of help, if you came right down to it. He went back to his desk.

''You're hired, Mr. Callum. The hours are long, the pay is nonexistent, but it's for a worthy cause.''

Callum almost smiled. He stood up and shook Cloud's hand again. He picked up the briefcase and slapped it on the work table adjacent to Cloud's desk. ''Everything I know is in here. And just call me Ward.''

Cloud smiled and pulled his chair behind the table. ''Okay, Ward, show me what you've got.''

29

Rosie Simple stopped just inside the entrance to Barney's Den. He took a step to one side and waited for night vision, unwrapping a stick of peppermint chewing gum, folding it twice and popping it into his mouth. He unwrapped another.

Off to his left he could hear the clink of glasses, a subdued mumble of voices, an occasional laugh. He chewed methodically, the way he did everything, savoring the taste of the peppermint, sharp and sweet on his tongue. He closed his eyes to hasten the transformation, opened them again to find the bar materializing to his right, vague shapes spaced along its concave outline like lonely spirits patiently awaiting their next incarnation.

He walked along the bar illuminated primarily by beer and whiskey signs, bellied up two stools away from the nearest wraith. He ordered a draft beer and a double shot of Irish whiskey. He drummed his fingers in time to Marty Robbins's voice coming from somewhere behind him in the gloom, glanced along the bar, and saw Alan Strobish's blacker-than-night face two stools away.

He paid for his boilermaker, downed the whiskey, a long, cool draft of the beer, then got up and moved down the bar. He elbowed Strobish in the ribs and sat down beside him.

"Hey, you black mother. Why didn't you trip me when I came by?"

Strobish grunted and took a sip of beer. "I didn't notice. Hell, anyway, you know all you white mothers look alike."

Rosie took another shot of beer. He reached up and rubbed his hand briskly through Strobish's tightly curled hair. "Shit, I've missed that! No wonder my luck's been so damned bad lately."

Strobish bellowed a laugh, spraying beer. He elbowed Rosie on the shoulder, almost knocking the big man off the stool, his flashing teeth a white slash across the dark mass of his contorted face. "Shit!" he said, then bellowed again, pounding the bar.

"Goddamn, I miss you, you honky mother! My new pardner don't say sweet things like that."

"Maybe he's not a sensitive type like me. Maybe he's not into dark meat."

Strobish howled again, beating the bar with a fist as hard as a black rock. His head bobbed up and down over his beer, guffaws dwindling to gurgling chuckles.

After a while, Rosie said, "Come on, man. It wasn't that funny."

Strobish huffed a gusty breath. "Yeah, man, it was. Shit, I don't get to laugh much anymore since they broke us up."

"Rafferty's a little solemn."

"Aw, it ain't that so much. You know all that stuff me and you 'usta do. Man, it was funny. A lot of it was silly, but mostly it was funny."

"He don't have a sense of humor?"

"Naw, it ain't that, either. He busts his ass laughing. It's just that he tries too hard, laughs at the wrong times. It's just mostly sad."

"I heard you and him had to buzz a pusher today?"

"Not me, man. Rafferty dusted his ass. I only tried. Glad I missed, the way it turned out. Better ol' Rafferty than me. He can handle it a lot better'n I can."

"I heard he got hurt."

"Twisted ankle. Emergency room doc said it'd be okay in a day or two." He stared thoughtfully at a ring of circles he had made on the bar with his sweating glass. "Funny thing. That asshole shot at him point-blank. Rafferty went down like a sack of dirt. Man, my old heart dropped. I thought he'd got him for sure. I still think he nicked him. I saw some stains on that old jumpsuit he had on. He said it was old paint stains and told me to mind my own business. Nobody has to tell me that twice." He shook

his head. "Man, you the only white man I ever understood."
He flicked a sidelong glance at Rosie and grinned. "It took me
a long time to figure out why. You ain't prejudiced. You probably
the only man I every met who ain't, black or white. I even
figured out why. You wanna know?"

"Sure," Rosie said, looking faintly embarrassed, realizing
suddenly that the black detective was drunk.

"You're so damned big, you ain't afraid of us. And if you
ain't afraid of us, you don't have to be racist; you can meet
everybody on their own level without worrying about the color
of their skin. Good or bad, that's your only yardstick. That's
great, man. I never told you, but that's great."

"Aw, shucks," Rosie said, "that's sweet. Look, you wanna
go out back? By God, I'd like to shake your hand!"

Strobish howled again, dropping his head forward onto the
bar. He made gurgling, choking sounds, thick shoulders shaking.

Rosie pounded him lightly between the shoulder blades. "Hey,
man, come on, straighten up. First thing you know, somebody's
gonna notice you ain't white."

Strobish didn't respond. A shudder rippled through his thick
torso; he muttered something inarticulate, began to snore.

Rosie looked at the scowling bartender, walking slowly toward them, wiping a glass. "What's the matter with him?"

"He's tired."

"This ain't no motel."

"It's not the Stork Club, either," Rosie said. He lifted the
sleeping detective's coattail and tugged his wallet out of his
pocket. He took out a sheaf of bills and counted them. He tossed
the wallet across the counter.

"There's two hundred and eighty dollars in there. He'll wake
up in an hour or so and be looking for this. See that he gets it."

The bartender bridled. "What the hell you think this is? Who
the hell are you?"

Rosie slid off the stool. "You're new here, asshole, or you
wouldn't have to ask. But since you did, I'm the big son of a
bitch who'll beat your ass bloody if there's a dollar missing out
of that wallet."

Rosie turned on his heel and strode toward the door, not waiting for the bartender's reaction. No point in wasting words. The
bartender would find out soon enough who he was, that he didn't
make empty threats.

"Hey, you . . ." There was more, but a sudden burst of laughter drowned the bartender's voice. Rosie whirled and stalked back to the bar, stood looking at the short, squat man.

"Say what?"

The bartender's eyes shifted first; he wet his lips, snaked out a hand, and picked up the wallet.

"I said I'd see he gets it."

"Sir," Rosie said quietly.

"I'll see he gets it, sir."

"That's a good little barkeep." Rosie smiled benignly, nodded at the watching faces along the bar, and turned to leave again.

Nobody called him back.

30

Cloud went through the material in Callum's briefcase while the taciturn Chicago detective studied the files of the three murdered women. Despite Callum's claim that he knew more about Arrowstone than any man alive, Cloud found little that he did not already have from New York and Chicago. A few psychological profiles from noted psychiatrists and psychologists who differed vehemently as to the causative factors of Arrowstone's murderlust; one from the FBI's Behavioral Science Unit at Quantico, Virginia. That one he read thoroughly.

The FBI's profile avoided excessive use of psychological terminology and was concerned more with "how" than "why", concentrated on details of individual crimes, autopsy reports, crime-scene photos, and post-offense behavior of the killer.

Requested by the Chicago police after the first three slayings which occurred within a period of ten days, the profile had been completed and returned shortly before Arrowstone's first verbal contact with Ward Callum.

It had been uncannily accurate, suggesting an age between thirty and thirty-five, a cold-nerved, controlled individual with higher than average IQ, an organized personality with a strong overlay of sadism, a superego with a deep-seated perception of invincibility.

From what he knew of Julian Arrowstone, Cloud could not disagree with any of it.

Callum seemed particularly interested in the Ramona Butler

murder. He studied the crime-scene photos minutely, pored over the autopsy report, then finally looked up at Cloud with shining eyes.

"The first deviation," he said, unable to keep the excitement out of his voice. "Out of thirty-one murdered women that we know about, this is the first non-redhead, the first one not raped, not left like the whore of Babylon, no stones, not strangled."

"And it doesn't mean a damned thing," Cloud said quietly.

"I can't believe that." Callum fished a package of unfiltered Camels out of his pocket and lit one with trembling fingers. "I can't believe it," he repeated.

"An innocent bystander. She was attracted to the scene, probably by noise. Arrowstone was startled or scared, or both, and he blitzed her, caught her head in a hammerlock, and broke her neck. It's not hard to do, if you know how. Thousands of men have been taught to do it efficiently, quietly. I learned how in Vietnam. You probably did, too."

"Arrowstone wasn't in Vietnam, or any other war. He was never even in the service."

Cloud shrugged. "It doesn't matter. You can find out in any library and most bars."

"That's just not his style," Callum said, his tone weakening, the fire in his eyes flickering out.

"You think there could have been two of them?"

Callum shook his head wearily and rubbed the bridge of his nose. "No, that wouldn't be his style, either. Arrowstone would never team up with anyone. No one else could measure up. He has style."

"He also has a colossal ego and more damn nerve than a cottonmouth in a goldfish pond."

"You mean dropping the Dickerson girl at the police department fountain?"

"That, and the way he took her. We have an eyewitness—not too reliable, since he was half-loaded at the time—but an eyewitness who saw two men on the corner of Peabody and Northcross about a block from where she worked. He said one of the guys was above-average height, average looking, and the other one wore a blue blazer and a cowboy hat. We pulled a wino wearing a blue blazer and a cowboy hat out of a Dumpster a day or so later. Mr. Average-looking must have been Arrowstone. Our witness thinks he remembers a moustache and a beard, but he can't swear to it. Arrowstone ever grow a beard?"

"Not that I remember hearing about. You think Arrowstone used the wino in some way, then went back and killed him?"

"We think he killed him. We don't know if he used him or he just happened by and somehow got mixed in. But our witness positively identified the girl. He buys pizza there all the time." He rolled the few feet to his desk and rummaged in a middle drawer. "We made up a composite with a moustache and a beard." He rolled back and dropped the paper in front of Callum. "Doesn't look much like the one from New York."

Callum lit another unfiltered Camel and studied the black-and-white sketch. He shook his head and pushed the paper back toward Cloud. "I've got a mental image of him burned right in here." He tapped his forehead with a finger. "And that's not him." He tilted his head and exhaled smoke toward the ceiling. "No fingerprints at all," he said, more a statement than a question.

"No. We think he may have worn gloves. Actually, there was very little at the Elliot–Butler scene that would have taken prints. Everything was cloth, even the Elliot girl's purse. He obviously went into the house for the sheet, but we found nothing on the inside. He may have just been careful."

"That's out of character for Arrowstone. Although, we didn't find a usable print until the third murder in Chicago, either. That's how we traced him finally, through the FBI files in Washington." He stopped and uttered a sharp, humorless laugh. "A week later, I was talking to him on the phone. He told me who he was. Up until that time we hadn't released his identity to the media. We had only learned a day or so before that Julian Arrowstone was an escaped loony from a New York mental institution."

"Too bad they didn't have a recent picture."

He snorted and stubbed his cigarette viciously. "That place was a warehouse. Underfunded and understaffed. Not enough guards or doctors or attendants. Like a lot of institutions, they relied on drugs to keep their patients in line."

"It's the same all over—" Cloud broke off as a figure appeared in the open doorway. He leaned back and lifted a welcoming hand.

"Hi, Jake. What the hell you doing here this late . . . or at all? I heard you had a High Noon today."

Jake Rafferty limped through the doorway. "Am I interrupting anything?"

"Come on in. Ward Callum meet Sgt. Jake Rafferty. Jake's Narcotics."

The two men shook hands, standing eye to eye. Callum unearthed his fleeting smile again; Rafferty nodded perfunctorily, his deep-sunken blue eyes studying the other man intently.

"Ward Callum. From Chicago? You headed the task force during Julian Arrowstone's rampage a year and a half ago. Right?"

Callum nodded slowly, his high forehead wrinkled. "That's right. If we've met, Sergeant Rafferty, I don't recall—"

"We haven't," Rafferty said, smiling.

"Jake was at Quantico during that period," Cloud said. "The FBI class in psychological profiling. Arrowstone was a class subject. He probably knows about as much about him as you do, Ward."

"I doubt that," Rafferty said, his voice suddenly harsh and strident. "I've never talked to the son of a bitch." He sat down abruptly on the corner of Rosie Simple's desk, his face strained, colorless. He took out a pack of chewing gum and methodically unwrapped two pieces.

"Ramona Butler was Jake's fiance," Cloud said quietly.

Callum nodded in understanding. "I'm sorry," he said.

Rafferty bent down and rubbed his left ankle, scratching lightly at the bulky, tightly wound elastic bandage. He spoke without looking up, his voice slightly muffled.

"I came by to tell you, Ben, I don't think you were talking directly to Arrowstone the other day."

31

"It's called Echofone. Made by Synco in Japan. It's some kind of sound synthesizer made to interface with almost all types of small home computers on the market. Johnny Donetti's kid got one for Christmas. That's where I saw it. Only his has a cast of Walt Disney characters. Daffy Duck, Donald, Mickey Mouse, and like that. You talk into a telephonelike receiver, and your words come out in someone else's voice. A perfect replica, although it sounds a little metallic. That's what got me to thinking. You said Arrowstone's voice sounded mechanical, tinny. I called the computer store in Dallas that handles them. He said you could get discs with the voices of almost all the movie stars and celebrities over the last forty years. All the biggies, anyhow."

Rafferty reared back in his chair and glanced from Callum to Cloud, then back to Callum, his eyes bright.

Callum looked at Cloud, frowning. "You didn't mention talking to him."

"Hadn't got around to it. Nothing much to it. A little ego trip on his part, a little bragging." He lit a cigarette and quickly ran through the gist of Arrowstone's conversation, what he remembered.

Callum was still frowning. "He never bothered disguising his voice before."

Cloud shrugged. "He evidently likes to play games. It's a new game for him. A very effective one, if you want the truth. It raised my hackles a little, hearing all those dead voices, knowing who was at the other end. I don't think disguising his voice had anything to do with it. I believe it was the psychological effect he was after.'' He barked a short, humorless laugh. ''He got what he came after.''

Callum rested his elbows on the table and probed the corners of his eyes with his thumbs. ''That computer store in Dallas— you ought to get a man over—''

''He's also the local distributor for Synco,'' Rafferty broke in curtly. ''He has at least three dozen retail outlets in the Metroplex, including most of the big department stores.'' His voice had a scratchy quality, and Callum glanced at him, almost smiling.

''I'm not trying to horn in on your investigation. It was just a thought.''

Rafferty nodded perfunctorily and pushed back his chair. ''It's not my investigation,'' he said pointedly, looking at Cloud. ''I'm too emotionally involved to be able to think rationally.'' His voice dripped with carefully constructed sarcasm.

''You're doing just great,'' Cloud said, smiling. ''Everything we've got so far, you've dropped in my lap. You're doing better on the fringes than we're doing slap dab in the middle.'' He spread his hands. ''It was Eli's decision, Jake. It's departmental policy.''

Rafferty smiled reluctantly and stood up. ''Departmental policy's a lot of bullshit, but at least it says I get three days off.''

''You okay?'' Cloud asked quietly.

Rafferty bobbed his head, grinning crookedly, understanding that his lanky friend was not concerned with his ankle. ''I'm okay. At least nothing that a couple of Harvey Wallbanger's won't get me through.'' He limped toward the door. ''Stopping by Barney's Den later?''

''Maybe,'' said Cloud, knowing he wouldn't, thoughts of why he wouldn't bringing a warm, creeping flush of pleasure.

''See you, then.'' He turned in the doorway. ''Nice meeting you, Callum.'' His tone was relaxed, friendly, the lopsided grin downgraded to an enigmatic smile.

''Sure, you bet. Same here.'' Callum seemed flustered, Cloud thought wonderingly, the unflappable flapping, as if Rafferty's curt rebuke and subsequent affable manner had disoriented him in some small way. He'd better get used to that if he wants to work here, Cloud thought, smiling inwardly. Quick to interpret advice from yankees as a form of condescension, Texans were just as quick to excuse it after a moment of thought as just some more of that inexplicable and sorry social mystique that afflicted everyone born roughly above the Mason-Dixon line. Hell, they couldn't help it, could they, being born up there?

Callum recovered quickly; he lit another cigarette and began gathering his material and arranging it in a neat stack. He looked tired, a slight rounding of square, compact shoulders, the color darker beneath his eyes.

"I'm bushed," he said, as if reading Cloud's thoughts. "I took the red-eye flight out of Los Angeles. I can't sleep on airplanes. Too chicken, I guess."

"You have a place to stay?" Cloud asked, then wanted to bite his tongue. Taking the Chicago detective home would spoil some very ambitious plans with a certain redheaded TV reporter.

"Yes, thanks."

Cloud locked up his desk and accompanied Callum to the parking lot. "You said you came in from L.A. You have relatives out there?" It was clear and cool and dark, the promise of winter in the tingling bite of the breeze.

Callum glanced at him and almost smiled again. "No. They had a killing a few days ago that had some of Arrowstone's characteristics. At least it seemed so from the newspaper account." He stopped beside a dark blue Camaro. "It was a washout. I was at the airport when I saw the headline in the Dallas paper. I changed my ticket."

Cloud shivered in his light corduroy jacket. "I hope your trip here isn't a washout."

Callum opened the car door before looking at him. "It isn't," he said quietly. "He's here." His eyes swept the glowing horizon, the collective illumination of three million souls. "He's here. I can feel it. I guarantee it. Somewhere."

They nodded at each other and shook hands. As he stood watching the blue Camaro drive off the lot, Cloud shivered again, this time from the inside out.

32

"That was a very lovely dinner, Cloud," Amy Reed said, sliding across the seat and kissing him lightly on the cheek while he fitted the key into the ignition. She dabbed at the lipstick with a Kleenex as he drove off the restaurant parking lot. She took his box of Carlton's out of his jacket pocket and lit two, laughing when he looked at the smear of lipstick on his and grimaced.

"God, you're an oddball," she said, thumping his thigh with her fist, leaving her hand there to squeeze with splayed fingers. "You go down on me like a famished bear at a honeypot, and when I get the end of your cigarette a little damp and smeary, you grouch."

"That's different," Cloud said. "Somehow."

She patted his leg and removed her hand. "You're sweet, anyway. A sweet oddball, but transparent."

"Transparent?"

"Sure. You've discovered that I love eating out in nice restaurants. You know it makes me all soft and smarmy, so you take me out and ply me with exotic food—"

"Lobster tails aren't exactly exotic."

"They are on my salary. Anyway, the point of this is that you've taken me out three times in a week, and it isn't at all necessary. You're not a rich man, and I like making love with you at least as much as you do with me—"

"How do you know?"

"How do I know what? That I like making love—?"

"No, that I'm not a rich man?"

"Well, I think that's obvious. You're a police lieutenant, and this old car—"

"What's wrong with this old car?"

"Well, nothing is really wrong—well, the damn door handle won't work half the time."

"That's a minor malfunction. This is a hell of a good old car."

"I didn't mean to imply that it wasn't. Actually, I suppose it's better than my little new one. At least it doesn't bounce all over the road."

"Exactly," Cloud said. "And it's paid for. New isn't always better, you know."

"I didn't start out to knock your car, Cloud. We've gotten completely away from the point . . ." She hesitated, then laughed. "What was my point?"

"You were saying how much you liked making love with me, and about me being a poor man who doesn't have enough money to buy a new car and take you out to dinner."

"That's not true! I didn't say you were a poor man. I said you were a police lieutenant and I know how much you—" She broke off and sighed, looking straight ahead. "I didn't look it up, Ben. It so happens I did a story on the inequities between Trinity Square employee salaries and Dallas and Fort Worth."

"So? Next time you can pay for dinner."

He glanced at her in time to catch the radiant smile that lit up her face. "I can't afford it, either. Not the way I eat."

"So what's the answer? Do we quit making love or quit eating? Or both?"

"Perish the thought," she said.

"Okay. What?"

She leaned forward and stubbed out her cigarette, then glanced over her shoulder and giggled.

"What?"

"Nothing. I just had a silly idea. It's really too silly to—"

"Tell me," he commanded.

"Well, you have that new condo with all that shiny new kitchen equipment. Why don't you cook for us once in a while?"

"How do you like your TV dinners? Medium or rare?" He cut his eyes sideways, smiled at her.

"I'll bet you broil a mean steak." She giggled again, nervously, Cloud thought, and wondered where she was headed. He

thought he knew, but that could be old paranoia alive again and
working.

"I have a better idea. Why don't you use my shiny new kitchen
and cook for us?"

She paused to consider that. "Well . . . that would be fine,
except I never get away from the station before seven-thirty or
so. By the time I came home and changed, drove to your place,
and cooked, it would be nine-thirty. By the time we ate and
cleaned up the mess, it would probably be eleven o'clock." She
clicked her tongue. "I have to be up at eight-thirty to get to the
station before ten. That means I have to be in bed by one—to
sleep. Counting driving time back to my place, bath, cleaning
my face, and what-not, that doesn't leave us much time for the
important stuff, Cloud."

"It's a quandary," Cloud said.

"Yes, it is," she agreed solemnly, her expression on the verge
of a smile.

They rode in silence for a while.

"Well, what do you think?" she asked after a time, taking his
right hand from the wheel, pressing it tightly between her own.

"About what?"

"About . . . our quandary?"

"It's pretty nice the way it is. We eat out. It doesn't take long.
No fuss, no bother. We have plenty of time for the important
stuff."

"I agree with that, but . . ." She wiggled a little, laced her
fingers with his.

"But I'm not a rich man?"

"That's right. I feel guilty seeing you spend all that money
on food that would cost only a fraction as much if we cooked it
ourselves." She moved her hands to his upper arm.

Cloud sighed. "It's a quandary."

She shook his arm, squeezed the biceps, and chuckled.
"You're repeating yourself."

He handed her the pack of cigarettes and watched her light
two from the dash lighter. He stopped at a light. He lowered a
window to let out some of the smoke and watched the way her
skin tone changed with the dim reflection of the low-hanging
light.

"I have an idea," he said as they passed through the intersection.

"What?"

"You could move in with me."

She was silent for a moment. "I'd like that, Ben, I really would. But there's the problem of my house. I'd hate to leave it sitting empty. Vandals and thieves . . ."

"Yeah, you're right. Well, it was just an idea—"

"On the other hand, there's my friend Emily and her new husband. They've been looking for something besides an apartment. I'm sure they'd jump at the chance to rent it."

"There you go," he said.

Her hand tightened on his arm and she leaned forward to see his face. "You really sure you want me to move in with you, Ben? You've been living alone a long time. You want panty hose drying in the bathroom, bobby pins all over, bottles of lotion and hair spray?"

"I want you," he said. "If all that stuff goes along with you, then I guess I can tough it out. I've been married before, you know. I'm not exactly a virgin."

She chuckled and squeezed his arm again. "You really want me to, then?"

"Of course I do. I wouldn't have asked you otherwise."

She snuggled against him, bobbed up to kiss his cheek near the corner of his mouth.

"Great. It's all settled then."

"You bet."

He drove. She pressed his arm against her breast, hummed along with "You Light Up My Life" on the radio, tapping the rhythm on his thigh with slender fingers.

Well, he had found out where she was headed.

He watched her come out of the bathroom toweling her impeccable body, a little annoyed with waiting, but pleased at her propensity for cleanliness. Instead of leaping into bed as she usually did, she walked around the end and stood beside him, wiping under her arms, staring down at him with a bemused expression. She dropped the towel and straddled him in one fluid motion, hooting a chuckle as his stomach muscles tightened, long legs drawing instinctively upward in a protective motion.

"It's my turn to ravage you, Cloud." She leaned back against his knees, eyes sparking green fire, growling, long nails raking lightly across his chest."

"I still think the word is ravish."

"Whatever," she murmured, falling forward on his chest,

tossing her head, her shining mass of hair tumbling around their faces like a silken shroud. She kissed him lavishly, spreading her lips, working his apart, pressing her body downward, her small breasts swelling, firming up, taut, yet softly resilient, nipples stabbing his chest in gentle coercion.

She broke free, sat up straight. "Dammit, I can't do it!"

"What?" he said groggily, blinking, eyes swimming with confusion, lust.

"I conned you, dammit. And I'm not that self-serving. I'm not a conniver and I maneuvered you into asking me to live with you and I can't let it go at that. I feel like a . . . a cunning tart!" She started to slip away, but he gripped her thighs with iron hands.

"Stay, woman! Don't the connee get a chance to talk? You think I'm simple, or something? I've been conned by experts, people who make their living at it. You're not even hard candy, you're soft fudge. I even had to help you a little. I'm tickled to death that you want to come live with me, Amy. I would've gotten around to it sooner or later. As soon as I got over this bad case of chicken guts. I was afraid you'd reject me, or what would be worse, laugh."

"Jesus Christ."

She slipped backward, found him, engulfed him, then dropped forward onto his chest again, her breath jetting against his lips, warm, exotic, her eyes large and luminous, exuding a captivating magnetism that assaulted his senses like a rippling shock wave.

"I'm going to make you feel good, Cloud," she whispered. "Did you know that?"

He sighed gustily. "I suspected as much. I'm not a detective for nothing, you know."

33

Ben Cloud rapped sharply on the pitted door of the small, ram-shackle frame house for the third time in two days. Not really expecting an answer this time, either, he stepped back to the edge of the shaky wood porch and studied the scudding clouds that carried the threat of more unneeded rain. Not for a couple of hours, he decided, and walked back for one more try at the chartreuse door.

It opened. A man stared out at him. A big man, towering, square-jawed. He had blue eyes and black hair cropped close to his scalp, A Zapata moustache. Thirtyish.

"Yeah?" He wore black motorcycle boots and a leather vest, dirty corduroy pants, and a black tank top with three-inch letters that said: "Rattlers".

Cloud felt his blood quicken. "You Percy Kilgore?" he asked politely.

"Yeah, so what? Who wants to know?"

Cloud gave him a bashful grin. "Me, I guess. I'm the only one here."

Kilgore looked at him for a full thirty seconds. "Buzz off, asshole," He began to close the door.

"No," Cloud said, taking a half-step forward, putting his left palm against the door. "I'd like to talk to you . . . please."

He heard Kilgore grunt and braced himself for an assault. It didn't come. The door swung wide. Kilgore stared at him in amazement.

"Hey, mac. You crazy or something? Man, I told you to get the fuck off my porch!"

"I'd really like to talk to you," Cloud said earnestly. "Honest."

"Honest?" A feminine voice, thin and shrill with derision. A face appeared behind Kilgore, narrow and painted and pretty, a petite body in a tight cerulean sweater and electric-blue pants. "Watch out, Muggsy, he'll beat you to death with his sash."

"Muggsy?" Cloud said, mimicking the girl's tone. "I thought your name was Perceeeee." He rolled his eyes and let his left hand drop limply from the wrist.

Cloud expected a headlong charge; a kick was what he got. A shiny, pointed boot on the end of a yard-long leg that came within a monkey's whisker of wrecking his sex life for the foreseeable future.

But he moved in time and the boot missed and that was that.

He let the leg's momentum carry it to the zenith of its arc, clenched his hands together, and brought them slashing upward. He caught the leg near the ankle, thrust upward and out. Kilgore grunted again, clawed frantically at the doorjamb to keep from falling.

Cloud took one short step and kicked him flatfooted in the balls.

Turnabout's fair play, he thought, watching the big man do a slow-motion pirouette, hands clutching his groin, mouth open wide, sucking for air. Face twisted in supreme agony, he slammed flat on his back on the wooden porch. The porch shook and Kilgore screamed once, a high, keening bleat. He tried to curl himself into a tight little ball.

The woman sidled through the door, her mouth open, eyes wide. "Well, kiss a wild boar's ass," she said.

"He must have slipped," Cloud said.

"Uh-huh. Toad frogs don't have warts, either."

"What's your stake in this, lady?"

"I don't have one. I just met him yesterday. I think I'll go shopping . . . in Denver. He won't like having anyone around who saw this." She went back through the doorway. She returned a moment later with a blue nylon backpack and sheepskin coat. "He has halitosis," she said, as if that might be a vital bit of medical history.

"I don't suppose he mentioned a girl named Brenda Dickerson?"

She shrugged thin shoulders. "We didn't talk much. Muggsy likes his women quiet and accessible." She stepped down off the porch. She looked at Cloud, her face expressionless. "Watch the big mother, he's shifty."

"He's awake, too," Cloud warned.

She nodded. "It don't matter. I got my own ride out back. He can't catch me." She turned and walked around the corner of the house.

Cloud stood watching Kilgore. A few minutes later, he heard the snap of a kick starter, a roar, and she appeared again. She revved the motorcycle's engine, then let it wind down to idle.

"So long, pig," she said.

Cloud wasn't absolutely certain who she was talking to.

She gunned the motor across the hard-packed dirt yard and into the street. She revved it again and went screaming off into the coming storm.

Cloud took out his gun and squatted beside Kilgore. "This is a .357 Magnum, in case you're playing a little possum. It makes a loud noise. Scary. You've got one more minute of R and R, and then me and you are gonna talk about a girl named Brenda Dickerson. You were seen with her shortly before she was slaughtered. We're gonna talk about that and anything else that comes to mind. Oh, by the way, I'm a cop."

He rose and stood staring down at the ashen-faced big man, acutely aware that he was thrumming with a fine buzz of excitement, his blood singing.

Shit! It was times like these that he really loved being a cop.

34

Spencer Price was aware that the redheaded girl had awakened and was covertly watching him from the pocket of shadow formed by her hair and her arms suspended from the hook in the doorpost. He ignored her, keeping his eyes on the rain-slickened road, trying not to think about the night ahead, still feeling a faint residue of the thick, exquisite pleasure that had washed through him like flowing lava when he had beat her into unconsciousness because she wouldn't stop crying. He had to avoid looking at her or he might lose control again.

He didn't want to spoil it; not with wild, flailing blows that undeniably brought quick spasms of joy, but would leave him feeling empty and unfulfilled. It had been so long. The others had helped, this one would be for him alone.

He thought of the dead years and shuddered. Playing at living. Getting through the days, mouthing empty words, smiling empty smiles, occupying empty space. Saying the things *they* wanted to hear, doing the things *they* wanted him to do. Dying. Feeling nothing.

The girl whimpered, and he growled savagely without looking at her.

"Who—who are you? You're . . . him . . . the one in the . . . Arrowstone."

He looked at her and grinned, stuck his tongue through glistening teeth, and wiggled it at her. "How did you guess?"

"Please . . . please . . . what are . . . what—oh, God, what are you going to . . . to do to me?"

Speaking in a dry, thick monotone, he began to tell her. Minute detail, in living color, he told her what to expect, savoring intensely the choking moans, the thin whines of pure animal terror, the slender body uncontrollably spastic.

Finally, she began to scream and could not stop.

He drove, his hands shaking on the wheel, absorbing the sound, grinning.

She had long since stopped crying. That was good. He was past the need for tears, wrung out, peaceful, weightless, as his body began its lazy, spiraling reentry from the dizzying orbit of the last three hours. And yet, he had never felt so alive, so vital.

God, he had almost forgotten the pure and absolute joy of it. Power. Total power and letting go. That's what it was about. It was more than suffocating lust and frenzied release; you could get that with a hooker.

It had to do with taking and not having to give, with playing and not having to pay.

It had to do with the flame of life, and smothering it. It had to do with Death, the inexplicable seductive mystery of it, the inexpressible yearning to worship and administer it.

He had no clear idea why; he seldom wondered.

It felt good and he did it and it brought him back from 'the dead.

He glanced over at the girl.

He would do it again.

He stood up, his muscles swelling, bulging with the force of the power.

It was time.

A feeling of infinite sadness swept through him; he wondered if he could make her cry again.

Ben Cloud stalked Northcross Street. Up one side and down the other, haunting the area around the Pizza Palace, making everyone nervous, disrupting commerce, drastically reducing the daily take of both legitimate and illegitimate businesses. A peripheral crowd of disgruntled entrepreneurs swirled and eddied around him like a herd of skittish roebuck fascinated by a stalking lion.

Cloud was putting out the word. The same way he had always

done it when he wore a uniform. He wanted something. Someone. And until the street coughed him up, nobody was safe. It made people anxious, created a certain amount of paranoia. Pressure and stress; Cloud knew how to create both.

But it wasn't working. Two days now and a thousand words. Nothing. And all that square-shouldered walking like Clint Eastwood was making him tired.

If Julian Arrowstone was hiding in Trinity Square, it wasn't among the thieves, perverts, derelicts, and whores. They would have given him up by now, worked him to the surface, and spat him out like a peach pit in a batch of fermenting wine. Loosely knit, a community within a community, a stranger might well go unheralded on Northcross Street, but never unnoticed. And, too, Brenda Lee Dickerson had almost been one of their own. She had worked among them, walked among them unafraid. There was a certain amount of pride and allegiance in that alone.

Near dark of the second day, Ben Cloud went home, frustrated and weary after almost forty-eight nonstop hours of fruitless intimidation.

Northcross Street drew a deep breath of relief; Cloud fell into bed and dreamed a quiet dream about a place where people never had to walk, carry guns, or kill other people.

35

Amy Reed hummed happily. Wielding dustrag and furniture polish, burnishing the dark, heavy wood in Benjamin Cloud's somber living room, she found herself immersed in thoughts of domesticity the likes of which she had never dreamed of before. Cloud did that to her. Brought out a nesting instinct she hadn't known she possessed. Espousing the causes of womankind was one thing, shouting the slogans, beating the drums, but there was nothing like a pair of brawny arms to make a girl feel safe and secure. Girl? She stifled an impulse to giggle. Two weeks ago she would have resented such a sexist appellation. Maybe she would again. But right now she wanted to be, wanted to do, something outrageously girlish.

Satisfied finally with her handiwork, she found her cigarettes and lit one, staring around her for the umpteenth time in two days at her totally masculine surroundings and wondering how, in some small, subtle way, she could bring a dash of color, a touch of femininity to the functional, no-nonsense atmosphere of the apartment.

A few vivid paintings would help, she decided, a potted plant or two for the fireplace mantel, a multihued afghan, perhaps, for the low-slung leather couch, bright antimacassars, white lampshades, new lace curtains—

The telephone rang.

—maybe a bric-a-brac shelf with colorful ceramic figurines in that bare corner, she thought, mashing out her cigarette and crossing to the phone at the end of the couch.

"Hello."

Silence; a faint sizzling as if the wires were being consumed by tiny flames.

"Hello." She counted to five and was taking the receiver away from her ear when the voice responded.

"Lieutenant Cloud, please. Lt. Benjamin Cloud."

"I'm sorry. Lieutenant Cloud is not available at the moment. Could I take a message?" She had an uncanny feeling that she knew the voice: slightly high-pitched with a distinctive British quality.

"I think not. Would this be Mrs. Cloud, perhaps?"

"No," Amy said. *That damned voice! Who was it?* "May I take your name and number and have Lieutenant Cloud return your call?"

"Ah. A lady friend, then?"

"May I ask who's calling, please? Your voice is very familiar. This is Amy Reed. Have we met by any chance?"

A low, polite chuckle, and Amy Reed suddenly had goose bumps. "No, I don't believe I've had the honor, my dear, but I don't mind at all telling you who—"

"Just a moment, sir. I believe Lieutenant Cloud is available now." She put her hand over the receiver as Cloud came through the front door followed by a slender, compact man with dark salt-and-pepper hair and a limp. He was carrying a large white paper bag.

"Hi," Amy said, smiling at Cloud. "I know this is crazy, but I'd swear you have David Niven waiting for you on the phone."

Cloud and the dark-haired man exchanged glances. Cloud took the paper bag out of his hands. He seemed not to notice. He stared intently at the phone while Cloud spoke rapidly in his ear. The dark-haired man nodded, crossed to the door, then disappeared. Cloud seemed to hesitate, as if killing time.

Amy watched him, bewildered. "Hurry up, Ben, he's waiting."

Cloud nodded and winked. He took the phone out of her hand and gave her the paper bag. "Chinese," he said softly, and lifted the phone.

"Hello." Amy walked slowly to the front door, clutching the

warm bag against her stomach. She peeked out at the landing. The dark-haired man was gone. She closed the door.

". . . just my cleaning lady. She comes in a couple of times a week and cooks dinner for me. Man gets tired of McDonalds." Cloud looked at her and smiled.

"No, nothing like that. Strictly a business arrangement. She's married and has three kids." Cloud was still looking at her; he grimaced this time, rolled his eyes.

Amy sat down on the end of the couch, the faintly sweetish aroma of the Chinese food making her mouth water. Her curiosity was drooling even more, a tiny bubble of indignation building as she realized Cloud was talking about her. Cleaning lady, my ass!

"I've been waiting. I thought maybe you'd decided to move on to greener pastures, after all." Cloud laughed, a peculiarly shallow, artificial laugh, Amy thought. She studied his face, realized suddenly that he was pale, the planes of his cheeks flat and taut. She felt a prickle of uneasiness.

"How did you get this number?" Obviously agitated, Cloud fumbled for his cigarettes and lighter. Amy put down the bag and took the cigarettes out of his hand. She lit one and gave it to him. She lit one for herself.

"When?" Cloud asked, his voice flat, dull. His eyes avoided Amy's. The thread of apprehension became a sharp dribble of fear. Amy watched him, transfixed, the cigarette halfway to her mouth.

"No!" he said sharply. "She's right here . . . No, I'm not . . . How the hell could I be tracing—?" He took the receiver away from his ear, dropped it carefully into its cradle. He sucked on the cigarette, glanced at her, and tried to smile.

"It wasn't David Niven, after all," he said.

"It was him," Amy said quietly. "Arrowstone."

He nodded without speaking. He sat down on the thick rounded arm of the couch.

"What did he want?"

"Lunch on Friday," Cloud said, then winced at the feeble attempt at humor. "He enjoys playing games. He wants to be my friend." He placed his hands on her shoulders and kissed her. His lips felt cold.

Someone rapped lightly on the door; it opened, the dark-haired man came in. He looked at Cloud and shook his head. "Not enough time, Ben."

Cloud nodded. He stood up, an arm around Amy's shoulders. "Jake Rafferty, Amy Reed." He smiled down at Amy. "Jake's our first dinner guest. Only he insisted on buying the Chinese. You can't beat that with a stick."

36

Amy smiled and shook Rafferty's hand. A cool, firm grip and a quick, flashing smile relieved the somber cast of the dark face. He's almost handsome when he smiles, Amy thought. Cloud had told her about Jake's connection with Ramona Butler, and she imagined she could see the tracks of recent pain and grief in the darkly circled eyes, in the twin grooves alongside his nose that disappeared into his thick, rectangular moustache.

"You're not exactly a stranger," Rafferty said. "Like most males around here between the ages of fifteen and eighty, I've fantasized a bit about that lovely face."

"Why, thank you," Amy said, flustered. The thought that men might see her image on the tube and have sexual fantasies had simply never occurred to her. It added, suddenly, a new dimension to her job. One that she wasn't at all sure she was pleased with. She sensed an undercurrent of teasing in his solemn tones, and a quick look at Cloud confirmed it. He was smiling broadly. Men. As transparent as little boys. Cloud was showing her off, seeking his best friend's approval of his taste in women. And Jake Rafferty had given it, couched in terms of a thinly veiled sexual compliment.

She hid her thoughts behind a lavish smile and picked up the paper bag. "This aroma has me drooling like a hungry wolf," she said brightly. "Why don't we eat before it cools?" She moved toward the kitchen, aware that her rear end was oscillating a bit more than normal, acutely aware, also, that she had an attentive audience of two. "I'll set out the dishes," she added unnecessarily.

"Great," Cloud said. "Jake, you want a quick one before we eat?"

"I think not," Rafferty said, limping to a maroon rocker-recliner set at right angles to the fireplace. He lowered himself with a sigh. He looked at Cloud. "What did he want?"

Cloud sat down on the couch and crossed his legs. "He didn't want anything. He had a message for me." His dark eyes met and locked with Rafferty's. Rafferty waited silently, his eyebrows upraised.

"He said . . . two days," Cloud said and cleared his throat. "The day after tomorrow. Another one. Another 'delicate morsel', he called it." He ran a hand across his face and mashed out his cigarette savagely. He uncrossed his legs and leaned forward, elbows on his knees, hands clasped. "I don't know, Jake . . . He didn't talk very long, but somehow he seemed . . . different. More . . . gloating, less articulate . . . something." He shook his head and lit a cigarette. It tasted as hot and dry as the wind off a forest fire.

"I assume from what Amy said that he used the machine?"

Cloud nodded. "You think maybe . . . several of the psychiatrists used the term dissociative reaction in their profile of Arrowstone. That means split personality, dual personality. You think maybe they could be right? Maybe this one was the other half, or the other self, or whatever the hell it is? The voice was David Niven's, but I had the distinct impression I was talking to him for the first time."

"Was it something he said?"

"No. That's what bugs me. I don't know why I feel this way unless it was his phrasing, the way he strung his words together. That's why I wonder if it could have been another side of him."

Rafferty nodded slowly, his lips pursed, his brow knitted. "I know what you mean about the profiles. The dual personality possibility was discussed in class. Nobody seemed to have a definite position, except the doctors who made the diagnosis." He smiled faintly. "That's par for the course. The FBI profilers tended to ignore that aspect of it. They concentrated on how instead of why."

"The sweet and sour pork is on," Amy said from the kitchen doorway, her forced smile and wan face telling Cloud she had heard their conversation.

"Let me at it," Cloud said, forcing a smile of his own. He stood up and waited for their limping guest. "By the way, Jake, how's the ankle?"

Rafferty grimaced through a smile. "Okay. I'm limping more out of habit than anything. Besides, it gets me a lot of sympathy. Nobody expects much out of a wounded man."

"Speaking of wounds, Rosie tells me Strobish thinks you took a hit from that pusher in the alley the other day."

Rafferty pulled a chair out from the dinette table. "Strobish is an old woman. A gossipy old woman to boot. It was a scratch. I doused it with disinfectant and stuck a Band-Aid on it. It's already healed."

"A bullet wound?" Amy sat down across from him; Cloud sat at the head of the table.

"A bullet burn is more like it," Rafferty said. "I've had worse scratches picking blackberries."

"He's macho," Cloud said, with gentle mock-derision. "It's the John Wayne syndrome. They hand it out along with your gun. Grit your teeth and shrug it off. Carry on until you drop dead from lead poisoning."

Rafferty laughed. "Look who's talking."

"Have you ever been wounded, Cloud?" Amy asked.

"Nope. I'm what you call your consummate coward. I studied it in school. I abhor violence, avoid it like the plague." He took a double spoonful from the first carton and passed it to Rafferty.

Rafferty snorted and looked at Amy, his eyes gleaming. "This pacifist here once walked in on a seventeen-year-old junkie who had just shot his old man with a double-barreled twelve-gauge and was threatening to shoot his mother and two little sisters. Old Gentle Ben here went in there and talked that spaced-out idiot into giving him the gun, brought him out in his arms like a ten-month-old baby."

"I think that's marvelous," Amy said, wrinkling her nose at Cloud, her eyes shining.

"Nothing marvelous about it," Cloud said, stacking food around his plate in neat, concise piles. "That little punk couldn't wait to throw down that gun and leap into my arms. He cried on my shoulder all the way to the car." He looked up and grinned. "Made a good newspaper photo. Looked like my shoulder was soaked with blood."

"Another time," Rafferty said, grinning at Cloud, "this coward here and I were—"

The telephone rang.

Rafferty glanced quickly at Cloud. Amy started to rise, and Cloud put a hand on her arm. "I'll get it. Probably for me, anyhow." He shoved back from the table, his expression noncommittal. "Go ahead and eat, it's getting cold." He stood up and left the room.

37

He was back before they could divide the remainder of the food. He came up behind Amy and gripped her shoulders.

"I'm sorry, babe, I've got to go. Jake, go ahead and stay—"

"What is it, Ben?" Amy twisted in her seat, stared up into his face, pale and taut again. "What's happened?"

Cloud's hands tightened on her shoulders, then relaxed. "I guess I may as well tell you. It'll be on the ten o'clock news, anyhow." He took in a deep breath. "It's another one . . . down on the Trinity River . . . some boys fishing—" He broke off and leaned down to kiss her. "I'll be back as soon as I can." He gave Rafferty a grim look. "He lied. He said two days." He squeezed Amy's shoulders again. "Will you be okay?"

She nodded mechanically, seeing Jake Rafferty come to his feet. "I'll wrap your plate . . . maybe we can warm—"

"Jake, you don't have to come. Stay and eat."

Rafferty shook his head, his dark face clouded, eyes shadowed by bunched brows. "I'll go," he said harshly. He looked at Amy and inclined his head a fraction. "Nice to meet you at last, Amy." He mustered a wry smile. "Thanks for the dinner."

"You didn't get a bite, either of you. Come back with Ben, Jake. If the Chinese is ruined, I can scrape up something, an omelet or something."

Rafferty nodded.

Cloud patted her shoulder and the two men left the room. She heard the door open and close.

She looked at the heaping plates of food, untouched, uninviting. Exasperation and worry tinged the edges of her sea-green eyes.

"Damn," she said under her breath. She got up to search for the aluminum foil.

Ron Graves was leaning against the rough, scaly bark of a twisted pin oak. Ward Callum stood a few feet away, dwarfed by the towering figure of Rosie Simple. The three men talked quietly, blinking at the occasional flash of bulbs a few yards away, keeping their eyes, as if by tacit consent, away from the torn and battered body posed obscenely in the approximate center of the wide, hard-packed path that bordered the river.

Ron Graves spotted Cloud and Rafferty first, pushed away from the tree, his boyish face hard and tight in the shadows cast by the Coleman lanterns and battery-operated lights. He spoke softly, and Callum and Rosie turned as the two detectives approached.

"What've we got, Rosie?" Cloud said tersely, brushing past the big detective and stopping at the tape strung across the path.

The girl lay five yards away and, after one swift, searching glance, he turned back to his partner. Without thinking about it, he found and lit a cigarette.

"Young female," Rosie said, his voice flat and emotionless. "Late teens, the M.E. thinks. Hard to tell, she's been savaged so much. Battered; stomped. Numerous puncture wounds; looks like a thin-bladed knife, an ice pick, and maybe a screwdriver. Raped. Numerous small, circular burns that could be a cigar or maybe a cigarette. No ID yet. No purse, no clothing . . ." He paused, flipping the page in his notebook.

"Not Arrowstone," Cloud said, exhaling a ghostly ball of smoke that the stiff breeze instantly whipped into the trees. His empty stomach rumbled angrily.

"Maybe," Rosie said, his tone noncommittal. "The M.E. checked the vagina. There were stones, Ben. He didn't take them out or count them, but there were stones."

"Goddamn," Cloud said, his eyes drawn irresistibly back to the girl, a rising sense of chaos threatening him with nausea.

"It doesn't make sense," Callum said from near his shoulder. "He's never done anything like this before. In thirty-four times, he's never done anything bad like this. He—"

"He's done it now," Graves said harshly. "Her legs are lying down now, Ben, but they were propped up with two small, forked sticks. The M.E. turned her to check lividity, and left her sprawled out like that, but she was propped up like the other ones.'' His voice was high and thin, with none of its usual deep resonance. Light reflections turned the convex surfaces of his eyes to glittering fire. ''Stovall's got the goddamned sticks. I don't know what the hell for!'' His voice had risen even more, and Cloud touched his arm fleetingly. Graves blinked at him, then looked down and backed away from the group bunched at the tape.

Cloud turned back to Rosie. ''Any idea how long she's been dead?''

''He said thirty or more hours. Rigor mortis has come and gone.'' Rosie shrugged. ''He'll give us his usual guess after the autopsy.''

''She wasn't killed here,'' Rafferty said. ''Even with the drizzle yesterday afternoon and last night, there would be some evidence of blood on the ground, on the bushes.'' He coughed. ''Jesus, there must have been a lot of blood.''

Rosie looked at him and nodded. ''We figured she was dumped sometime during the night. It quit raining about four this morning, and she had rainwater in that cavity there where he smashed her collarbone.'' Rosie closed his notebook and dropped it into his jacket pocket. ''She's missing a breast,'' he said. ''It wasn't cut off. Me and the M.E. figured it was stomped off with a sharp-edged bootheel, stomped loose, maybe, and pulled the rest of the way.'' He lifted the tape a couple of inches. ''You want a closer look, Ben? I think they're finished.''

Cloud nodded mechanically; reluctantly, he forced himself to bend and pass beneath the fluttering tape. He flipped his cigarette butt toward the dark, slow-moving waters of the Trinity and stared down at the grotesquely mangled thing that had once been a lovely, round-bodied, redheaded girl.

38

Capt. Eli Summers morosely surveyed the group of police officers arranged in an ill-defined semicircle in front of his desk. His bright eyes flitted restlessly from one solemn face to another, and finally came to rest on Benjamin Cloud.

"All right," he said grimly. "You damn well know this is gutting Robbery and Narcotics. The dopers and thieves are gonna have a field day out there. I hope I don't live to regret this, Cloud."

"Which is worse," Cloud said, striving to keep the irritation out of his voice, "a few more decks of dope changing hands, or another young girl getting butchered?"

"Some clerk getting blown away in a robbery don't matter, I suppose." Lt. Gil McReady looked at Cloud with sly, hostile eyes, the stub of an unlit cigar jutting from one curled-down corner of his mouth. "Dead's dead. It don't matter much how."

Cloud gave him a quick scathing glance, then turned back to Summers. "He's taking them out of the Northcross—Peabody area. All of them except Elliot and Butler. And even the Elliot girl was seen having drinks in the Green Room a couple of days before she died. That's on Albertson Street, just around the corner from Northcross. So it's the same area. This latest one, Melinda Cooper, was a clerk in Parker's Bookstore on Northcross. He may not be hiding in that area, but he's taking his victims out of there. So far. And he's promised another one tonight. Historically, he's always kept his promises. So, there's no reason to think he'll go elsewhere.''

''There's no reason to think he might not, either,'' Summers said irritably, flicking the end of his nose with a restless thumb. ''Fifteen men. You'll be stumbling all over each other.''

''Fifteen men won't exactly be high-level saturation. I wish I had fifty more. We're talking about a mile-long stretch of North-cross Street, as well as small patches here and there on Taylor and Spring. And all of it jammed with restless people. Fifteen men will be spread as thin as a drop of oil in a pan of water.''

''Exactly what'll we be looking for, Ben?'' Fred Toomer, Robbery, cracked the knuckle of his left index finger and leaned forward to peer down the line of men at Cloud. He had a large, veined nose and thinning sandy hair.

''You'll be briefed, Fred, but primarily we'll be looking for young redheaded girls. We've got six spotted already, and each one will be assigned a man. And, of course, we'll be looking for Arrowstone himself. But that'll be a tough one. Half the men in this room fit the physical description we have on him, and I don't put much faith in the composites from Chicago and New York. He obviously takes them somewhere else, so he'll have to have transportation. We don't know what kind. There again, that won't help much because of all the males prowling around down there looking for a hooker.''

''Shut off the goddamned street,'' McReady growled. ''Send the assholes back where they belong.''

''And Arrowstone right along with them,'' Eli Summers said, with carefully metered sarcasm. ''This is Lieutenant Cloud's operation, Gil. Why don't you let him get on with it?'' He turned back to Cloud. ''What time do we start, Ben?'' he said crisply.

Cloud glanced at his watch. ''As soon as we can get every-body briefed and assigned. He didn't tell me whether he meant today or tonight. I'm taking no chances. He's always worked at night before, but that could change. It's already almost nine o'clock. Let's hope he likes to sleep in.''

Whatever he may have been doing at nine o'clock in the morning, at three o'clock in the afternoon Julian Arrowstone wasn't sleeping. He was working. Working and humming ''Stardust.''

A real golden oldie, he thought, winding the two-inch gauze around and around his left forearm. Way before his time. Even so, his life seemed inextricably interwoven with the soothing,

magical strains of the tune. It had been her favorite. His very
first recollections were of cool evenings, a porch swing, open
windows with lace curtains blowing, and the sound of her piano
playing "Stardust". The blood-stirring tinkling of the keys and
her beautiful voice. A contralto, he knew now. Then he had
known it only as a lovely, lovely sound.

It was a soothing memory; one of the few pleasant ones.

He reached his wrist with the gauze, continued on across the
back of his hand and into his palm. He left his thumb free,
covering his fingers to the second joint. Enough to grasp and
hold if need be and yet present a helpless, vulnerable look.

He wrapped and hummed, thinking of voices and singing.

There had been one other—was it the fifteenth or the six-
teenth?—who had had a voice as lovely as hers. A beautiful
curving neck. Her startled eyes had given him a moment of great
sadness mixed with the incredible joy. She had been amazingly
strong for one so small, the sleek muscles of her neck resisting
his caressing hands, swelling and writhing as she fought to
breathe. It had been a time of overwhelming bliss, of sweet,
pulsing ecstasy that had left him shuddering with weakness afterwards.

For what seemed like hours, he had lain atop her still body
contented and at peace. He remembered taking more than usual
care with her fragile features, working painstakingly to restore
them to beauty. It had been difficult. He had rested too long;
she had already begun to stiffen, the eyelids particularly, defi-
antly resisting his most determined efforts to work them into
place over the staring gray eyes. Finally, in despair, he had found
a tiny pair of scissors in her sewing box and cut them off. She
had looked quite lovely, after all.

Thinking about it, his humming grew louder, a slow, stealthy
warmth spreading, growing, filling him with a feverish glow.
Power sang in his veins; his muscles swelled in anticipation. He
finished wrapping his arm, taped the gauze neatly.

He glanced at the clock. Two more hours. He wondered if he
could take a nap. He doubted it. He wondered if he could wait;
he doubted that, too.

39

Rosie spotted Strobish coming out of Poor John's Place. Garishly dressed in black-and-white checked gabardine pants, yellow Adidas, a bulky green sweater, and a pink watch cap, the black detective hit the sidewalk street-bopping, the bouncing, wrist-slinging, slouching gait designed to emulate the lazy, graceful pacing of a predatory cat.

He swept by Rosie's darkened doorway without a glance, head high and grinning.

Rosie fell in behind him, followed for half a block, then closed in on the blocky detective. He jabbed a sausage-sized finger into the small of a back that felt as hard as a block of frozen beef.

"Over against the wall, black guy. Let's see what you got."

"Shit," Strobish said without breaking stride. "You didn't think you was hiding in that little cubbyhole? Surely not. About like an elephant trying to hide in a dishpan." He swung a short, thick arm into Rosie's stomach. "Anyhow, you know what I got. You used to play with it often enough."

"Is that what that was? No wonder it was too limber to pick my teeth with."

Strobish barked a strident laugh and shook his head. "Man, this is a big-assed waste of time. I ain't seen a damned soul looked suspicious. Have you?"

"Not more than two, three hundred," Rosie said. "But none of them was grabbing redheads off the street."

"Where the hell is Lieutenant Cloud? I ain't seen him all afternoon."

"Moving around like the rest of us, I guess. I haven't seen him, either."

"You reckon me and you're the only ones out here busting our asses? Rest of them peckerheads probably knee-deep in suds somewheres laughing their fool heads off."

"Not the only ones. I saw Rafferty about three down on the corner of Northcross and Exxter. Looked like he was checking out the Northcross Hotel."

"These goddamned flophouses, man. I ain't going in them. They got little teensy things that crawl and bite. I had to take a mean wino out of one of them once. Sucker didn't want to come. I had to get a hold of him. I caught me the damnedest case of crabs you ever saw."

"That the story you told your wife, huh?"

"Yeah, why not? It was the damned truth."

"She believed you, huh?"

"Hell yes, she believed me. Don't your wife believe you?"

They were at a corner. Rosie looked at the light, looked down the street, then finally looked at the black detective, his face somber.

"Not much. Not since I told her about alum."

"Who's Alum?"

"It's not a who, dummy. It's a what. An astringent. Ever since Rosie Jr. was born, she's been griping about him being so big he stretched her all out of shape down there. I told her to smear a handful of alum around . . . you know, shrink things a little."

Strobish grinned. "What's the matter, did it burn?"

"I don't know if it burned or not, but did you ever taste that damned stuff?"

Strobish stared up at him blankly, then chuckled and shook his head. "See you later," he said and veered off across the street.

Rosie looked after him for a moment, then shrugged and turned to enter a drugstore on the corner. He was reaching for the door when the first braying peal of laughter rose above the cacophony of the street. He turned to see Strobish clinging to a lamp pole on the far corner, pounding the serrated metal with one big hand, mouth gaping with helpless laughter.

Rosie grinned and went on into the drugstore, thinking how

much he missed working with that black son of a gun. Nobody else thought he was funny.

For a while, Arrowstone thought she wasn't going to get out of the car. He stood well back from the partly rolled down window, talking easily, explaining how his pediatrician wife had been called to the hospital to attend one of her small charges suspected of having a ruptured appendix, explaining shamefacedly how the fool Doberman had wrapped the lead around his leg going down the stairs for his daily walk, displaying ruefully his broken arm bandaged from his elbow to his fingers.

He had purposely arrived twenty minutes late, giving her time to fret a little, to think about her commission on the quarter-of-a-million-dollar home he had made an appointment to see. He smiled a lot, sincerely, waved his right hand holding the brief-case in a funny demonstration of how he had fallen when the fool dog had dashed between his legs, went right on talking as if it was the most natural thing in the world for a Dallas millionaire oilman to stand on the lawn of an empty house carrying on a one-sided conversation with a pretty, redheaded young woman who was obviously thawing, rapidly losing whatever reservations she may have had.

The bandaged arm did it, he thought, following her into the house. And the briefcase. The briefcase always added a nice touch, gave him a businesslike air, a no-nonsense indication that he was ready to turn a deal at a moment's notice. And that's what this type was all about. Business and money. He watched the heavy mass of her hair swing as she turned inside the door, and told himself he would teach her there was more to life than business and money. Much, much more.

She led him out of the marbled entry hall into a high-ceilinged room crosshatched with dark wooden timbers, dominated by a sparkling crystal chandelier.

"This is a lovely room," she said, turning to him, smiling. She was a little older than he would have preferred. Rust-colored hair, a lovely white-toothed smile. Green eyes. Perhaps twenty-two. Slender. The age wouldn't matter in the end. *She* had only been young in her own mind and in his eyes. He knew that. He really did.

He put down the briefcase and pointed toward the ceiling at the far end of the room. "Oh, my, that is quite lovely."

Eyebrows raised in expectation, she turned, small, round chin lifting, lips parted, prepared to smile.

He stepped in behind her, circled her neck with his bandaged arm, tightened, pulling her head back against his shoulder, arcing the lovely neck, his right hand sliding through the silky mane of hair to find the wildly fluttering artery. He pressed gently.

A small, gasping moan was all she managed; no more or less than he had expected.

She didn't fight. That was a plus. Sometimes they fought, and it almost always called for violence, and he hated that. Violence left tracks, ugly black-and-blue marks to mar the pristine beauty. Some marks were unavoidable, of course. But they always came at the end, and he never looked at them.

"Shhh, little darling," he whispered a second before she went limp in his arms. "I'll take care of you. I'll make you even more beautiful. You will be proud. You'll see."

He stretched her on the thick, spongy carpet, stood looking down at her, smiling tenderly.

40

By two A.M. only a small group remained in the Seven-Eleven parking lot. One by one the others had straggled in sometime after midnight and had been sent home.

Benjamin Cloud leaned wearily against the side of Rosie's new Chrysler, watching the big detective check the list of names one last time.

"Everybody accounted for?" Cloud leaned his elbows on top of the car, propping his chin in cupped hands, staring moodily at the Dempster Dumpster across the street where Sammy Keeler had been found.

"That's it," Rosie said. He tossed the clipboard through the open window of the car and scowled at Strobish sprawled across the hood eating unprocessed peanuts from a small paper bag. Empty hulls littered the gleaming blue surface, and the thin metal popped and snapped under the husky detective's shifting weight.

"You're a sloppy bastard, Strobish. You know that?"

"Sure." Strobish grinned amiably. "That's part of my charm."

"You dent my damned hood and I'm gonna get part of your lame ass." Rosie leaned over the hood and blew peanut hulls to the pavement.

"Turnabout's fair play. I been getting part of yours for years."

Cloud laughed. He lit a cigarette and tried halfheartedly to figure out the man hours expended in the sixteen-hour operation. Sixteen times fifteen was what? Let's see. Fifteen times fifteen was two hundred and twenty-five. Add another fifteen. Two hundred and—Jesus Christ—forty hours. Two hundred and forty hours. For nothing. Talking about parts of asses, Eli Summers was gonna get a part of his for sure. Well, they'd tried. Gave it their best shot. You couldn't fault a man for that. He snorted softly. Donleavy could; Summers could. Without batting an eye.

He flipped the cigarette butt high in the air, watched it burst in a shower of sparks near where Rafferty and Graves and Callum stood talking quietly. Rafferty, facing in his direction, pantomimed fear of the exploding butt and gave him the finger. He said something, slapped Graves on a bulging bicep, and limped toward Cloud.

He leaned against the Chrysler and took out a pack of chewing gum. He opened the end and offered a piece to Cloud. Cloud shook his head. Rafferty folded two pieces together and put them in his mouth. He chewed for a moment in silence.

"We can't win 'em all, Ben," he said finally. "Any given Saturday . . ." His voice trailed off.

"Yeah, I know, but this was the Super Bowl, Jake. We needed to win this one bad."

"Just hang in there." Rafferty punched Cloud lightly on the arm. "We'll make that bastard sorry his goddamned dart landed on Trinity Square."

"He'll never be as sorry as I am," Cloud said morosely.

They fell silent again, listening to Rosie and Strobish argue amiably. Cloud lit another cigarette. After a moment, Rafferty shifted restlessly and spat out the gum.

"Do you think he . . . did somebody?"

Cloud scowled and loosened the bow tie that had been part of his executive-on-the-prowl disguise for the evening. He shoved the tie into his coat pocket.

"I think so. I have this goddamned feeling in my guts. I can't wipe the notion that he's playing with us again. Some more of his mind games. I thought we had a handle on him, but after the Cooper girl, I don't think so anymore. I think the switch in MO was deliberate. A kink within a kink. He kills thirty-five women in a more-or-less delicate way, and then he goes apeshit and literally destroys one. Did she make him mad? Fail him in some way? Is he losing control?" He barked a short, humorless laugh. "Jesus, I'm talking about him as if he were your average, fucked-up normal killer."

"Maybe he is," Rafferty said, "otherwise. At other times.

Maybe it comes and goes. Hell, maybe he can't help it. Might be he—'' He stopped, an odd look on his face. He rammed his hands in his pants pockets and wagged his head. "Hell. Look at me. Trying to make excuses for the son of a bitch when I want more than anything on this earth to stick a .357 in his gut and make it go boom." He shivered, grinning crookedly at Cloud. "Jesus, just thinking about it gives me chills."

Cloud nodded without smiling. "I know. I've had myself convinced for years that I could never kill another human being, but when it comes right down to the short and curly, in Arrowstone's case, I'd gladly make an exception."

"Holy shit!" Strobish slid off the Chrysler's hood and Cloud belatedly realized the other four men had been listening to their conversation.

"You white mothers too damned bloodthirsty for me. I'm going home to Momma." He grinned broadly.

"A sick nightcrawler's too bloodthirsty for you," Rosie growled, flicking peanut hulls off his new car, leaning in to inspect a scuff mark that looked suspiciously like a scratch.

"A good idea," Cloud said. "Let's call it a day." Impulsively, he shook hands all around, then, a little embarrassed by his strange behavior, he turned toward his car.

41

Six feet tall, a deceptively quiet-faced man with twinkling blue eyes, a wispy halo of fine white hair, and a ponderous paunch he detested, Dr. Jerome Collen tapped the large cardboard box on the corner of his desk with a blunt-ended, nicotine-stained forefinger.

"I've read it," he said, "most of it. Enough."

"Well, what do you think?" Cloud asked, watching the doctor's spatulate fingers groping in his shirt pocket for a cigarette, reaching for one of his own.

Collen grunted and lit his cigarette. "About what? The Cowboy game Sunday? The weather? What?" His voice had a thin, frangible quality.

"About Arrowstone," Rosie said, unperturbed by the peppery old fart's irascibility. He had been here before.

On a minimal retainer by the city, Collen was, in theory, and at drastically reduced rates, supposed to stitch back together the raveled psyches of burned-out street cops, perform massive bypass surgery on cops devastated by taking a human life, and lastly, smooth the quirks and kinks of cops who should never have been cops in the first place. He wasn't happy with it, but he considered it his civic duty.

"You must have formed some opinion, Doc," Rosie went on doggedly.

Collen rolled forward against the desk as far as his stomach would allow. "Sure. Hell, yes, I have an opinion. You already

ot forty other opinions in there. You want, I'll give you number
rty-one.''

Cloud leaned forward and dusted his ashes into an overflowing
htray. He cleared his throat. ''Actually, we're not as much
terested in another psychological profile as we are in some
dvice. To be honest with you, we're at a dead end. The son of
bitch is outsmarting us at every turn. This last killing, Lea
letcalf, he told us about it beforehand. Not who, of course,
ut when. We went for all-out saturation in the slum area where
e'd been picking his victims, and he kills a young woman in a
uarter-of-a-million-dollar house in one of the poshest sections
f Trinity Square. It's almost as if he knows what we're going
o do before we do it. It's damned uncanny. He calls me on the
hone, talks to me with Bogart, Niven, Peter Lorre's voices,
en gets off before we can trace him. The Cooper girl a few
ays ago—he savaged her, vandalized her body, dumped her on
riverbank. Lea Metcalf two nights ago hardly had a mark on
er. She was raped and strangled, and left spread out like a
hore, but he didn't mark her except for some small smudges
n her neck. It was almost as if he were trying to be gentle.''

Cloud stopped, his mouth dry. ''I want to try something.
omething the FBI calls pro-active technique. I want to make
im nervous, maybe get him on the same psychological hook
e's had us on. I want to make him think we're closing on him,
at we have new evidence. Try to make him believe that we
now exactly what he looks like now, that we have a witness
ho saw him with the Metcalf woman and can positively identify
im. That's been our big problem. We know his name, but our
hysical description would fit damned near everyone except fat
en and giants. We have two composites that don't look at all
like, and neither looks like the only picture we have, which was
ade seventeen or eighteen years ago. So, we have to make him
elieve we're up-to-date, that we have his ass nailed with a new
escription. That will either make him move on out or try to
hange his appearance. He's got to be living somewhere. Some-
ody has to notice if he shaves off a beard or moustache, or
ddenly turns up with one. We'll go public with that little item,
lso. Anyone suddenly changing his appearance is suspect—call
in! It's the only way I can think of. Get everyone in the city
volved.''

Dr. Collen seemed to be nodding, but it could have been the
cking motion of his chair. He swiveled a quarter turn toward

a window and laboriously lifted his legs to one corner of th
desk.

"Might work," he said crisply. "Might run him on out o
here. Somebody else's problem then. Maybe Dallas, maybe For
Worth."

Cloud shook his head. "No. Too close. If he runs, I think he
probably won't stop in Texas. Maybe not until he hits the Wes
Coast."

"If he goes that way," Rosie said laconically.

"I don't want him to run," Cloud said. "Not really. I wan
the bastard. But I'm realistic enough to know I can't have it both
ways. If I shake him up enough, he'll run. He did it in Chicage
when Ward Callum was nipping at his heels. If we start this
we'll have to go with it all the way. I don't see how we can de
it with halfway measures."

Collen nodded. "He's an unstable character. You stress him
enough, maybe he'll even do your job for you."

"What do you mean?"

Collen shrugged. "Kill himself. It's happened before. A ma
like Arrowstone doesn't function well in an atmosphere of un
certainty and fear. He'd be erratic, might even become disor
ganized enough to do away with himself."

"He's the most organized bastard I've ever seen," Cloue
said. "He has a genius IQ and obviously plans everything in ad
vance. As far as I know, he hasn't missed once."

"Doesn't mean a thing," Collen snapped. "It's all superficial
Inside he's candy glass. The only thing he has sustaining him i
an outsized ego and a certain amount of cold, calculating cun
ning. As long as he's in control of the situation, he's Jesus In
carnate; he can do no wrong in his own eyes. But he is terribly
flawed, gentlemen. He is not swayed by any of the normal hu
man traits: compassion, remorse, guilt, love, conscience. Non
of these things mean anything to him. He is controlled only by
the abnormal dictates of his desires. Which have, in turn, beer
formed by a life devoid of human feeling. Since he is unable to
love, he cannot conceive of being loved. I would think he woul
be emotionally incapable of sustaining a mature, intimate rela
tionship for very long. Self-doubt and suspicion would inevitably
intervene. Selfless love would be an enigma. He would be in
clined to make snap judgments about members of the opposite
sex, from almost instantaneous attachments based on superficia
qualities such as physical attractiveness and sexual desirability

His type of 'love' would be intensely possessive and all-consuming, and would be doomed to failure.'' He stopped, screwed his face into a frown, his lips wrinkling in a faint, cynical smile. ''Well, you didn't want my opinion, but you got it, anyhow. Except for some small deviations, he's almost a classic textbook case.''

''A sociopath,'' Rosie said, glancing sideways at Cloud.

Collen shrugged again. ''Names, tags. Psychopath; sociopath. He is an abnormal personality. He lives only for the moment, the here and now. He does what he wants whenever he wants without consideration for others. All things are for his pleasure, or they have no meaning. But being human after all, he genuinely needs to feel. That's a human trait. But he finds that he cannot. Except, as in this case, vicariously through the death of others. At some point in his past he discovered he could have feelings, possibly enormously intense feelings, by taking the life of young, redheaded girls. He has single-mindedly pursued that imperative ever since, and will continue to do so until he is dead or incarcerated.''

''He can't be cured?''

Collen smiled faintly and lifted his feet off the desk. ''They had him fifteen years. What do you think? He spent the entire fifteen years seeking approval for his actions, trying to get just one doctor to agree that since he is by definition a psychopath, it is his nature and his inalienable right to do what he did. He cannot stand rejection, and isolation and loneliness are his worst enemies. He wants people to know and appreciate what he does, but cannot tell them, of course, since it would result in society's disapproval and his incarceration. If he does not, periodically at least, have someone to manipulate—in this case, rape and murder—he feels dead.''

''What would be the best way to manipulate him?'' Feeling as responsive as one of Pavlov's dogs, Cloud watched the doctor light up again and reached for a cigarette of his own.

Collen stared at him thoughtfully through a haze of smoke. ''You've already named one way: fear. Despite his apparent calm, he is very fearful inside. He has no way of judging himself, his performance. He needs constant reassurance that what he does is noteworthy, thought-provoking, exciting. His only method of adjudication is society's reaction. The more hoopla in the media, the greater his sense of self-worth. He is manipulating, not just one person, but society as a whole. I think he would find this extremely ego-sustaining. At this moment, he is probably on a continuing high. Fully one third of the TV news air time and half the front pages of the newspapers are devoted to him.''

"I have very little control over the media," Cloud said dryly. "I seriously doubt that we could get the TV stations and newspapers to drop Arrowstone from their menu."

Collen nodded abstractedly, bouncing a thumb against pursed lips. "Rejection. If you can make him feel fearful and rejected at the same time, I think it's quite possible he would panic." He paused. "It's not without danger. He may cut and run, or he may feel in need of reinforcement. In which case he will likely kill another girl immediately."

"He'll do that, anyway," Rosie said. "He's stepping up the pace."

"That's not absolutely certain," Collen said. "Sometimes they quit. For no apparent reason. They just quit."

Cloud stood up and stubbed out his cigarette. He extended his hand across the desk. "Thanks. We appreciate your time and wisdom."

Collen shook his hand. "Don't mention it. And I mean that literally. At least the part about fear and rejection and compounding stress. As in all things that canker the human psyche, nature demands retribution, a balance in all things, and I realize that penalties must be paid, but I don't have to like using what little knowledge I have to bring harm to another human being."

"You got it," Rosie said, shaking his hand. "And thanks again."

"Don't mention it," Collen said again, smiling. "I'll bill the city."

42

"Hey, Ben, Rosie said you wanted to see me." Red Stovall, tall, thin as a cedar fence post, stomped across the asphalt tile and folded his seemingly boneless body into Cloud's visitor's chair.

"Yeah, Red." Cloud searched through the neat stacks of paper work on his desk, selected a single sheet, and held it between the thumbs and forefingers of both hands. "I've been going over your preliminary report on Lea Metcalf. You found some more hair, huh?"

Stovall nodded. He hooked the bill of a yellow-and-white baseball cap with two fingers and lifted it from a profusion of sandy hair that gave him his name.

"Two, as a matter of fact, Ben. Both pubic hairs." He grinned suddenly, revealing long, almost lupine, slightly yellowed teeth. "Shook you up a little, huh?"

"Are you absolutely sure about this, Red?"

Stovall shrugged. "All I know is, they don't match the cock hairs found on the Cooper girl's body. Hair don't tell you a lot. Not me, anyhow. I'm not a forensic pathologist. But I've had some training. Enough to know the cross-sectional samples don't match. Even the color's a little different, but that don't always mean much. Some guys with dark brown hair grow red beards, and vice versa. And then there's the powder. This last clown uses baby talcum powder on his cock and balls. Both hairs were loaded with it."

"That doesn't necessarily mean anything," Cloud said. "Maybe he just started using it."

Stovall rolled thin shoulders in another shrug. "Right. Anything's possible. The Rangers might take the pennant this year, too."

"Where did you find the hairs?" Cloud asked, unaccountably annoyed.

"Mixed in with hers," Stovall said, his pale eyes gleaming, a sardonic edge to his tone. "It's in the report." He crossed long legs and critically appraised the luster of an obviously new pair of boots. "It could have been planted, all right," he said, anticipating Cloud's next remark with uncanny intuition. "But for the life of me, I don't know why he'd bother."

Cloud rocked back in his chair and laced his fingers behind his head. "He likes to play games. He knows we know who he is, so the only thing left is to try to mess up our minds. My mind, since I'm in charge of the investigation." He took a cigarette out of his shirt pocket and held it cupped in his fingers. "No trace of fibers?"

Stovall shook his head. "No. I figure there wouldn't be. He didn't take her somewhere else like he did Dickerson and Cooper." He uncrossed his legs and shifted in the straight-backed chair. "I did a little more work on the fibers. I ran them over to Dallas and huddled with Sonny Tessler. Turned out to be raw wool, kinda' crude, old, brittle, the same kind of stuff the Indians used to spin before they started buying their Indian blankets from the mills."

"Indian blanket?" Cloud echoed hollowly, a fleeting blip skimming across the surface of his mind; a fractured image, instantaneous, gone before he could cinch it down.

"What's the matter?" Stovall was eyeing him curiously.

Cloud shook his head, more to clear it than to answer the thin man's question. "I'm not sure." He discovered the unlit cigarette in his hand and lit it, using the few seconds to blank his mind, make it easy for the provocative mind shadow to reappear.

Cloud exhaled smoke and rolled forward to his desk. "How about the stones? Any similarities there?"

"If you mean did they all come out of the same creek, I can't tell you that. I don't think anyone can. Some color differences, but you'd find that in any sampling of any pile of pea gravel in the county. There's some evidence of precise selection in that the sizes range from about three-quarter-inch in diameter down to roughly one-quarter-inch in all cases. Too much, I think, to be coincidence. He's obviously picking them for size." He slapped the hat back on his head and grinned. "That ought to lead you right to him."

"I'll pin the hero medal on you personally," Cloud said.

After Stovall left, Cloud rolled his chair to the window, lifted his feet to the narrow ledge beneath, and stared sightlessly into the bright, clear October day.

Two men? Two madmen running wild in one small Texas city? The possibility staggered his mind, formed a tiny boil of nausea in his stomach, an expanding sickness that radiated outward like the creeping filaments of some evil spider's web. He discovered that he was shaking his head.

No! The odds of one Arrowstone picking little Trinity Square were astronomical; two—impossible! Stovall must be wrong.

Forensic science appeared at times almost magical in its arcane revelations from bits and pieces of seeming trivia, but as Stovall had readily admitted in previous cases, the study of hair was an inexact science, to say the least. Race, sex, approximate age, condition of hair, and whether the subject used artificial substances for control, were about all you could expect. Factoring minute differences in the shape of the circumference, and chromosome testing. That was about it.

Yeah. Stovall must have goofed.

When Amy Reed's face appeared on the screen, Spencer Price got up and turned down the sound. He sat back down on the edge of the chair and began to fondle himself, watching avidly the sensuous mouth forming soundlessly into suggestive circles, mouthing sweet obscenities that triggered his imagination, filled him with a wild, coursing delight; the pounding thrust of blood gathering force, bubbling and seething, fired his veins with coruscating pinwheels of flame.

He closed his eyes and pictured the gold-toned, willowy body, kneeling, slim, tapered legs and outthrust breasts. Eyes shimmering with liquid fear, supplicating. Tears. A frenzy of terror. Whimpers. Pleas. Promises of rapture untold. A licking tongue and a soft, engulfing mouth, hot, wet, striving to please, to do good, to not be hurt, to stay alive.

A whine began deep in his chest, built into a keening crescendo as her face loomed large, bigger than life on the screen: limpid eyes and curving lips, a glimpse of the dark, mysterious cavern behind sparkling teeth, enticing, finally, the pumping, jetting release. He shuddered, watched her image fade with blind, mindless eyes.

Later, he rose unsteadily from his sprawled position in the chair, his naked body sallow in the unearthly glow of the set. He went into the bathroom and bathed, his mind humming with emptiness.

43

They had pizza and beer in front of the TV set, watching the
Cowboy-Viking game with the sound reduced to a barely perceptible drone. As they ate, Cloud stole surreptitious glances at
her face. As always, it was perfect; a complex blending of in-
tricately fashioned parts. The same as always, but yet he thought
it had subtly changed in the past few minutes since he had
broached the subject of another interview. A remote look in her
eyes, head tilted as if listening to some far-off voice whispering
her name, or some fascinating memory she was trying desperately to recall.

The Cowboys were down seven to nothing. He swallowed a
bite of pizza and took a drink of beer.

"You haven't told me what you think."

"I have this funny feeling I'm being ravaged again."

"You mean I'm using you?"

"That's one silver dollar. Do you want to try for two?"

He took another bite and chewed for a while. Too many olives;
he hated damned olives. He took a drink of beer and washed it
down.

"Isn't that what people do? Use each other? Husbands and
wives, lovers, friends? Everybody using everybody else. I use
you every time I make love to you. You do me. Don't deny it.
It's the human condition. Animals use each other all the time.
What makes you think we're any different?"

"I can do without the pop psychology," she said, watching a

Cowboy running back disappear under a couple of tons of Minnesota beef. "Okay, let's forget the part about my career maybe going down the drain. Let's talk about the important stuff. What if he doesn't do what you expect? We're talking about an insane killer here. What if he decides not to run and picks up another girl and makes mincemeat out of her the way he did the Cooper girl?"

"Don't you think we've considered that? It's a calculated risk."

She laughed; a short, chortling, mirthless sound. "That's easy for you big macho cops to say. He's not after you. You might feel differently if you were a young redheaded girl."

"If you don't want to do it, Amy, say so. I just thought it would look less contrived to him if I went on your program since I've been there before. But I wouldn't want you to do anything you don't want to do."

She gave him a cynical smile, eyebrows pushing grooves into the smooth, unblemished brow. She broke off a bit of pizza crust and nibbled daintily, silently, still smiling.

A faint cheer drifted in from the TV set; the quarterback had just been sacked; the Viking fans were ecstatic.

"Exactly what did you have in mind?" she asked finally, delicate fingers dusting crust crumbs onto her half of the pizza. "If he's as smart as you seem to think, won't he be suspicious if you get on TV and start making speeches?"

"No speeches. That's the last thing I want to do. He's smart, and he'd pick up on anything phony. We'd have to orchestrate something."

"Like what?"

"Like a hostile interrogation by you."

She frowned, brows arcing delicately, slowly shaking her head. "Not convincing, Ben. Why would a policeman let himself in for something like that? That's assuming you can act well enough to bring it off. I've never met a cop yet who didn't back off when the questions got sticky, or personal."

"I couldn't back off because it'll be live."

She stared at him, aghast. "Live? Are you out of your—"

"Live," he said firmly. "On the ten o'clock news. I'd like to make it earlier, but you'll have to use the six o'clock newscast to set the stage."

"Set the stage? Cloud, what the hell are you talking about?"

He grinned. "You were right. The only way Arrowstone will

buy this is if I'm convincing. The only way I can be convincing is if I'm defending myself, if I'm obviously pissed off enough at what you say at six o'clock to make me get on TV and make my rebuttal. If your broadcast is scathing enough, if you flay the whole damned department in general and me in particular, isn't it logical that I would want to defend myself and the department? And how better to do that than to confront the mouthy broad that started it all? See?''

They stared at each other through a silence broken only by another tiny cheer as Dallas turned over the football.

''It won't work, Ben. People know we're living together.''

''Only a few. I seriously doubt that Arrowstone knows. Or cares.''

She sat up straight, her hands clasped on her thighs. ''It frightens me, Ben. I don't want to be even remotely responsible for some girl . . .'' She shivered and looked at him, her features soft and unformed, lips tremulous.

He scooted down the couch and put his arm around her. ''I'm scared too, Amy. Enough to tie my guts in knots if I'd let it. We're dealing with a psycho, and I can't be sure which way he'll go. He may retaliate by killing again. But it's my job to stop him, and I've got to do something. I can't just sit on my hands and hope we get lucky, pick him up for speeding, or something.'' His hand moved across her back in slow, rhythmic circles, and he felt the taut muscles begin to relax. ''He's smart. Like an animal is smart. But he's had a hell of a lot of luck, too. And as brilliant as he may be, he can be manipulated like all the rest of us. It's hard to believe sometimes, but he's human. He has weaknesses. He did what I wanted the other time. He got in touch with me. It was my own damn fault I didn't believe in my own strategy enough to be prepared with a phone tap and an automatic trace. My only excuse, if there is one, is that I've never been confronted with this kind of thing before, this kind of madness. All the rules go out the window. Physical evidence, the other routines of investigation don't matter a damn. We know who he is. What we don't know is how to catch him.''

Amy pulled his arm around her shoulders, slipped back against his chest. She groped for his right hand and pressed it against her stomach, worked the silk blouse out of the way, and sighed as his broad palm flattened on bare flesh.

''What are you trying to get him to do this time?'' she asked, her voice subtly different, her belly slowly expanding and contracting under the pressure of his fingers.

Cloud exhaled audibly, rested his chin on the crown of her head, the sweet smell of her hair diluted faintly by the spicy aroma of cooling pizza. The score flashed on the screen; the Cowboys had made a touchdown.

"Give himself up," Cloud said, only partly aware that she had maneuvered his hand beneath the elastic band of her pants. "Since that's a bit much to hope for, maybe to make him mad enough, or agitated enough to call me and forget about watching the time." He paused as his fingers encountered a mass of tightly curled silken hair.

"Or get reckless, make a mistake," he went on almost absently. "I intend to have four policewomen with backup teams on Northcross a half-hour after the broadcast, just in case he goes wild and decides to pick up one off the street in retaliation." He stopped again, gauging her breathing, the almost imperceptible quivering of velvet muscles as his fingers probed and plucked, grinning foolishly over her head as a Cowboy's bullet pass was intercepted. He slipped his left hand up under the blouse and molded a small, firm breast. She hissed softly and twisted until she was lying across his thighs. He had to change hands.

She smiled up at him and arched her body. "You've got good hands, Cloud. Did you know that?"

"Sure," he said, using one of those good hands to lift her, the other one to remove blouse, pants, and panties. "They're famous throughout the Southwest. I'm considering an offer by the Texas Society for the Preservation of Natural Assets and other Artifacts. They want to cast them in bronze. I'd do it, but I'm afraid it might interfere with picking my nose."

Her laugh was rich and full, but short-lived.

44

For the first time in a very long time, Amy Reed felt a thickening in her throat, the acid sting of fear in her stomach as she watched the upraised arm, acutely aware of the unblinking black eye staring at her balefully, moving in, focusing.

A red light snapped on; the finger descended, jabbed at her; she smiled.

"Good evening, ladies and gentlemen. I'm Amy Reed. For the first time since the inception of the 'Reed Report', I have no story for you. No guest. I'm all alone out here and believe me, it's frightening." She smiled again, briefly. "It's not from lack of trying that I do not have a guest for you this evening. I invited one. I asked him very politely to appear before us tonight and answer a few simple questions. But I am sorry to say, he declined." She smiled again, dryly. "Very forcefully. I am speaking, ladies and gentlemen, about Lt. Benjamin Cloud of the Trinity Square Police Department. Lieutenant Cloud is in charge of the Homicide Division. He is in charge of the ongoing investigation into the recent brutal slaying of five young women. Unfortunately, Lieutenant Cloud could not be with us. Pressing police business, I believe, is the way he phrased it. I am sure, of course, that Lieutenant Cloud is busy. I would hope that each and every police officer on the Trinity Square Police Department would be working around the clock to find and remove from our streets this monster who walks freely among us, selecting his victims at will, killing at his leisure before crawling back into the slime from whence he came." She paused, green eyes cool and intent.

"Julian Arrowstone. They say they know who he is. One man against fifty. And yet, he kills with impunity, disappears like a wraith." She picked up a single sheet of paper from the corner of her desk and held it in her hands.

"Since Lieutenant Cloud could not be with us, I will ask my questions, anyway. Perhaps he will appear at a later time to answer them." Her lips quirked and she slowly, deliberately lowered her eyes to the paper.

"Lieutenant Cloud, would you please tell our audience what has been done and what is being done to apprehend Julian Arrowstone?

"Is it true, Lieutenant Cloud, that you have had several conversations with this man?

"Is it true that, in one case, Julian Arrowstone told you when the next murder would occur? And yet, knowing this, you were powerless to prevent it?

"Is it true that you have only two other detectives assisting you full time in this investigation? If so, is that what you consider an all-out effort?

"And last, but not least, Lieutenant Cloud, do you know beyond a possible doubt that the man you are searching for is, in fact, Julian Arrowstone? And if so, how?"

She looked directly into the camera and smiled a meager smile without showing her teeth. "Good evening, ladies and gentlemen."

She watched her image fade from the screen, dug into her purse on the floor beside her for a cigarette as the station disclaimer rolled, then in turn, faded into a commercial. She looked at Drew Rollins, the director, and said, "That's what I like, loyalty, guts."

Drew Rollins shrugged. "Only way they'd go for it, sweetie. You want to attack the establishment, you're all alone out there."

"Dammit, the establishment wanted me to attack the establishment. It certainly wasn't my idea."

Rollins grinned, watching the time. "Good job, though, babe."

Amy picked up her purse and stalked off the set. She stepped through the doorway into her dressing room and felt herself engulfed in a pair of long, strong arms.

"Great job, honey," Cloud said exuberantly, tugging back a swatch of hair and kissing her cheek. "And that eyebrow. That was a touch of genius. Gave it just the right tone of cold disdain. What do you think, Jake?"

Jake Rafferty nodded and smiled. "Good job, Amy."

"What eyebrow?"

"Your left one," Cloud said, laughing. "Each time you asked one of your icy little questions, it shot up about a quarter-inch." He squeezed her and let his arms drop to her waist. "Cute."

"Do you think he'll buy it?" Amy asked, talking to Cloud, but looking at Rafferty. He was watching the rest of the newscast, his dark face in repose, a fist-sized hand of hair spilling across his forehead, giving him a dark, brooding look. A look filled with infinite sadness, Amy thought as she felt a queer fluttering in her stomach.

She wished he would smile more often. It lit up his face in a way that struck a responsive chord somewhere deep inside her, a radiance that she found strangely compelling. She wondered if seeing her in Cloud's arms brought painful memories, and she moved spontaneously to break out of the lanky detective's grasp. She held up her cigarette to Cloud. "Here, you finish this."

He took it and she moved away, slowly, naturally. She fluffed her hair with both hands, straightened her blouse, tugged it smooth across her breasts, feeling suddenly girlishly coquettish, feeling also the weight of Jake Rafferty's eyes as she glanced up and caught him watching her, smiling. She returned the smile, then whirled on Cloud.

"Okay. You got what you wanted. Now it's my turn. Cloud, you're going to buy our dinner. Mine and Jake's. And I warn you, I'm starving. I want a big steak and a bigger potato, and maybe even a side order of crab's legs or lobster tails—" She broke it off, realizing suddenly that she was talking too fast and too much, seeing the quizzical expression behind Cloud's indulgent smile, his fleeting glance at Rafferty's beaming face. She felt her own face getting warm, a quick, sliding quiver inside her chest. She smiled brightly and reached for her coat. Rafferty took it out of her hands and held it for her.

"Sounds like a winner to me," Cloud said easily. "Steak okay with you, Jake?"

"Thanks, but I'll have to take a raincheck. I promised Strobish I'd meet him down at the Den for a couple of brews. I had a cheeseburger earlier."

"Better catch him while he's hot, Jake," Amy said, wondering if her voice sounded as unnatural to them as it did to her. She slipped her arm through Cloud's and formed her lips into a cool, impersonal smile.

Rafferty lifted a hand. "Next time. I'll catch your act on the tube tonight, Ben. Do a good job, hear. You too, Amy." He limped off down the corridor, and they stood watching silently until he pushed through the exit door.

"Why does he make me feel so sad?" Amy murmured.

Cloud looked down at her, a glint of something in his eyes. "I didn't notice," he said wryly.

"He does," she said. "Next to an uncle of mine, he's the saddest looking man I've ever seen. My uncle drank like a fish. Does Jake drink?"

"Not much. Drinking's a problem for Jake." He turned and led her toward the exit.

"You mean he's an alcoholic?"

"No, nothing like that. He just doesn't know when to stop when he gets started. He's the kind of drunk who goes down to the corner for a beer and wakes up in a jail cell in Helena, Montana, with a two-inch beard and cowshit on his boots."

"Doesn't that bother you?"

"No. Why should it? He's the one who has to clean his boots." She laughed. "I thought he was your friend."

"He is. Probably as good as I'll ever have. But he's also a grown-up adult. I'd back him all the way, but I won't babysit him or any other man." He held the exit door for her.

She tucked her hands inside the coat's pockets, and they walked across the parking lot without touching.

"You mean male friendship doesn't include things like tenderness and sympathy?"

"Sympathy, yes, tenderness, no. Jake's going through a very hard time and I feel sorry for him. I'm around if he needs me. I'll watch a ball game with him, go fishing, or maybe have a few beers and argue politics. But I won't hold his hand. If I tried, he'd probably bust me in the mouth."

She made a sound halfway between a snort and a chuckle. "Macho baloney. You have tender feelings. I know, I've seen them."

He opened the car door and looked down at her, smiling faintly. "Sure. Women and kids, horses and dogs. It's allowed. But you're forgetting something. We've been conditioned for centuries by women."

"It may not be as easy being a man as I thought," she said. "Having all those fine lines to walk." She climbed in and sat down. "I'm just glad I'm a woman."

He had the motor going before he replied. He looked at her with an evil Groucho leer. "So am I."

45

"Good evening, ladies and gentlemen. I'm Amy Reed, and this is the 'Reed Report'. Earlier this evening I made a number of comments and asked several questions relative to the ongoing investigation being conducted by the Trinity Square Police Department into the recent murders of five young Trinity Square residents. I am very pleased to announce that Lt. Benjamin Cloud, the officer in charge of the investigation, has consented to appear before us tonight to answer my questions and to assure us that everything possible is being done to apprehend this cold-blooded murderer. Lieutenant Cloud?" Amy smiled sweetly and swiveled slightly to her right, and Cloud felt the unrelenting eye swing with her. Maintaining his stony, uncompromising look for a few more heartbeats, he allowed his features to relax and reform into the aggrieved expression of a man unjustly maligned. He hoped he didn't look petulant.

"Thank you, Amy," he said crisply. "I'd like to say here at the beginning that you and the citizens of Trinity Square have every right to question your police department. You are, after all, our employers. And I want to assure you that I will answer with all candor any and all questions compatible with the exigencies of the continuing investigation."

"Exactly what does that mean, Lieutenant? 'Compatible with the exigencies of the investigation'?"

Cloud frowned heavily, then smoothed it into a condescending smile. "Exactly what it says, Amy," he said genially. "There are certain aspects of the investigation that must necessarily re-main classified. "I'm sure you can understand that."

"Yes, of course. Since time is limited, Lieutenant Cloud, why don't you tell us as briefly as possible exactly where we stand in the pursuit of alleged murderer Julian Arrowstone."

Cloud gave her a confident nod and a fleeting smile. He turned to face the camera. "Until the murder of Lea Metcalf, I'll have to admit, we had very little beyond bits and pieces of physical evidence. Our killer is a very careful and methodical man. We strongly suspected he was an escaped mental patient named Julian Arrowstone. We did not, however, release that information to the public. It leaked, as such things have a way of doing. We are now absolutely certain. Julian Arrowstone made a mistake with Lea Metcalf. We have an eyewitness placing him at the scene of the murder with the young lady shortly before the time of her death. We have something we have sorely needed: an up-to-date description of Julian Arrowstone by a very reliable witness, a man trained to observe and record detail, a retired police officer. By tomorrow noon these new composites will be available to every citizen of Trinity Square in one form or other." He stopped, staring into the camera, squaring his jaw, his mouth a grim, purposeful line. "By this time tomorrow night, Julian Arrowstone will be in custody." His voice rang with confidence and determination—he hoped.

"That's very reassuring, Lieutenant Cloud," Amy said, a sardonic gleam in the green eyes that met his when he turned away from the camera. "You are certain then that the man you are looking for is, in fact, Julian Arrowstone."

"Absolutely," Cloud declared. "As I said, he made a very serious mistake. He left his fingerprints at the Metcalf murder site."

"Isn't it possible," Amy said innocently, "that he may attempt to alter his appearance?"

"Uh, yes," Cloud said, realizing he had forgotten a portion of his prepared text. He turned back to the camera. "Some of you out there know Julian Arrowstone. By another name, of course. He's living somewhere, eating somewhere, buying gasoline—in other words, he's coming into contact with some of you each day. If anyone you know, male, between the ages of thirty and forty, around one hundred and seventy-five pounds, suddenly changes his appearance in any way, we urge you to call the police department. Do not in any way attempt to question him or to take him into custody. That is very important. Call the police! Remember, this man is a cold, calculating killer. If he feels threatened, he will kill without compunction. He is a psychopathic personality, totally devoid of human compassion, human feelings. He is a human parasite who preys on the weak and the vulnerable. He has the cunning of a weasel, the stealth of a cottonmouth snake. And he is fully as merciless as both combined.''

"Yes," Amy said brightly. "Well, Lieutenant Cloud, it seems our time is up. I want to thank you for appearing this evening. I'm sure we'll all sleep a little sounder in our beds tonight.'' She smiled into the camera. "Especially us redheaded ones. Good night, ladies and gentlemen.''

"Goddammit, Cloud!" Chief of Police Patrick Donleavy slammed a meaty hand on the two-inch slab of curving mahogany wood that made up his desk top, his round face rubescent, eyes like two flakes of splintered ice. "You have any goddamned idea what you've done?''

"I think so," Cloud replied diffidently, wondering how the battered desk had survived all those years of constant pounding by the fat Irishman's fist. "I hope I scared him badly enough that he'll come at me or run like hell.''

"Whatever he does," Donleavy snapped. "It's for damned sure you've prejudiced the state's case against him, if and when he ever comes to trial.''

"What trial, Pat?" Capt. Eli Summers asked. "You know as well as I do that he'll never make it to a trial. An insanity hearing, maybe. With his background, there won't be anything but a quick slide into Terrell for the rest of his life.''

"And you," Donleavy said truculently, "you had no business authorizing something like this without clearing it with me and the DA.''

Summers cut his eyes sideways at Cloud. "You weren't available, Chief. And I wasn't aware that brother Cloud here was going, uh, quite so far.'' He smiled at Cloud. "It's my fault. I should have requested a copy of the script.'' He squirmed into a more upright position and polished the side of his nose with a forefinger. "I really don't see what Lieutenant Cloud did that was so far out of line. He made an appeal to the citizenry to help in the apprehension of a killer. I see nothing wrong with that. If he went a bit overboard in his . . . ah, description of the killer, I think that is understandable under the circumstances. He felt it necessary to stress the ruthless qualities of this man in his warning to the public not to interfere in a physical sense. I feel that is commendable and well within the scope of his job as a guardian of the public.''

"Bullshit," Donleavy said, almost without rancor. "You can really turn out the bullshit, Eli, you know that?" He glowered at Cloud. "Dammit, there must be something wrong with it. I never heard of a cop getting on TV and talking like that before. The DA's pissed, anyhow."

"When isn't the DA pissed," Eli said, grinning.

Donleavy almost smiled. "Now about what you said. Is there any damned truth in it at all?"

"Very little," Cloud admitted. "I'm banking on Arrowstone believing it. I don't know. Did I sound convincing?"

Donleavy nodded grimly. "You sounded convincing. Especially that part about having his ass in jail by tonight at ten o'clock. My damned phone hasn't stopped ringing, nor the mayor's, nor the council's." He pointed a stubby finger toward his phone; all four lines were blinking. "Cricket Bloom said she's been jammed since last night about ten-thirty. Every son of a bitch in this town must be shaving off a beard or moustache. They're calling in on guys changing their damned pants, for chrissakes!" He cupped his fat cheeks in his hands, gently massaging his temples. "Okay. For the record, I've chewed both your asses to ribbons, threatened you with suspension, a firing squad, and castration." He looked up and smiled faintly. "I'm setting both of you up as scapegoats for when and if this thing blows up and bleeds all over us. So don't think you're home free yet."

"Understood, Chief," Summers said, snapping to his feet. "I regret that I have only one pair of balls to give—et cetera, et cetera."

Donleavy put his head back in his hands. "Bullshit. Always bullshit from you, Eli. You want to make me happy? Get out there and catch this cocksucker."

"Right. I'll detail men to surround the bus station and the men's rest room in the park. If he's truly a cocksucker, he's bound to be one place or the other." He nodded briskly and headed for the door. Cloud trailed along behind him.

Donleavy sat with his head in his hands and watched them go, a perplexed expression on his face.

"You'd better watch it, Eli," Cloud said, lengthening his stride to overtake the strutting smaller man. "One of these days—"

"Naw. Donleavy's a big fat Irishman. I'm a feisty little Jew. He condescends, and I needle. That's the way he thinks it's supposed to be." He made a short, barking sound. "Besides, he thinks I'm cute." He was almost snarling. "The asshole told me so."

46

The ringing telephone yanked Julian Arrowstone out of a deep, troubled sleep and, for the short increment of time between rings, held him suspended, thinking he was back at the institution, pastel walls and endless corridors, the maddening cacophony of the day rooms, the soul-shattering silence of what they had jeeringly called deep therapy.

By the end of the second ring he was wide awake, cognitive, sitting upright in the bed, his vitals burning with icy fear, tiny blisters of cold perspiration springing full-blown along the edge of his hairline.

His phone shouldn't be ringing!

Who?

Not them. They wouldn't call, they would come. Who? A wrong number? Yes. That was it. It must be a—

The third ring, he stared at the ugly, black instrument outlined in the wedge of light from the bathroom, watched it with the compelling fascination of a mesmerized bird awaiting the strike of a snake.

The fourth ring; shuddering, he eased off the bed and stood hunkered, the icy ball in his stomach radiating outward into numbness that held him rooted, almost beyond movement, almost beyond breath, his mind blurred with grayness, his heart galloping with fear.

Who, goddammit? Who? He should have run! Who?

The fifth ring, he jumped, whimpered, hugged himself in an

ecstasy of fear, cursing dully, monotonously his damned stupid arrogance, his infantile bravado.

He should have gone after Lea Metcalf. Right then.

The sixth ring, he made a high keening noise, watched in horror as his hand snaked out and jerked the foul black thing from its cradle.

He listened, pressing the receiver against his ear with both hands. Nothing. A hissing noise; a faint rustling sound. Breathing?

"I know you're there," the voice said softly. "I know you're there, Julian."

Paralysis held him; he swayed unable to breathe, unable to think, unblinking.

"No need to be afraid, Julian. I know you are. I know about fear. Fear isn't your enemy. Fear keeps you alive. Take a deep breath. Back up and sit down on the bed. The phone will reach." The voice spoke softly but with a husky, harsh resonance that plucked at his memory.

Obeying blindly, he did as he was told. He took another breath, inordinately pleased to discover the voice was right: the phone cord did reach to the bed. How did he know that?

"I mean you no harm. I only want to talk. This is a remarkable opportunity, Julian. We mustn't allow it to pass unused." The voice was normal, increasingly familiar, titillating, diverting him from his fear.

He took a deep breath, expelled it, and took stock, surprised to find some semblance of order emerging out of the chaos in his mind.

"Who are you? I—I think you . . . you must have the wrong number."

The voice laughed. "We're way past the point for indignation, Julian. You're Julian Arrowstone and, even though it won't mean anything to you, I don't mind at all telling you my name."

"What?" He was sounding better, he thought, blood circulating again, the vast region around his heart pulsing with a glow of warmth. The crisp, rich voice resounded in his mind with bell-like clarity and finally jogged his memory cells. He gasped. "You're Clark Gable!" He realized instantly what was happening and barked a short, involuntary laugh. "But, of course, you can't be. You're playing some sort of . . . trick."

"You don't mind, do you, Julian?" There was now a mocking

edge to Clark Gable's voice. "What's fair for the hunter . . ." The voice trailed off into that husky, harsh chuckle.

"I know, of course. You're using an Echofone. But why, if you don't mind telling me your name?"

"I wanted you to see how it sounds to Cloud. A very clever idea, if I do say so myself."

"Then who are you?"

"My real name is Spencer Price. Does that mean anything to you?"

"No."

"I didn't think it would."

"You—you're the . . . the copycat."

Spencer Price laughed. "Yes, I'm the copycat. You're not angry, are you, Julian? You know what they say: 'Imitation is the sincerest form of flattery.' And I do admire you. I want you to know that."

"I'm not all that sure I'm flattered," Arrowstone said, a thread of petulance creeping into his voice. He was warm, the numbness was gone; he was clicking along on full charge. He was speaking to an inferior, an imitator, obviously a man with no imagination, no style.

"You mean the Cooper thing?"

"That was . . . gross. Animalistic. Not that I mind that sort of thing occasionally, but I certainly wouldn't put my signature on it, either." He paused, trying to visualize the face behind the voice. "You must have been in a . . . a frenzy."

Price chuckled. "An animalistic frenzy, Julian. I like to wallow, to let out the beast . . . Don't try to tell me you don't know what I mean." Clark Gable's voice had grown thick, furry.

"Of course I know. But there are ways and there are ways. There are such things as delicacy, finesse. One doesn't have to be a butcher to enjoy chateaubriand."

"Don't get antsy with me, asshole." Price's voice was suddenly hard, ugly. "I'm not the one the cops are swarming all over the place after. I'm trying to be your goddamned friend. If you don't want it that way, say so."

"Hey! Hey, come on! I was only trying to point out . . . hey, everyone to his own kick. You do your thing your way, I do mine. Right?"

"All right, and don't you forget it. Look, I've never talked to anyone like . . . well, like myself before. Like you. I've read all the damned books, but they're all so much horseshit. They never get past causes, motivations. Actions and reactions. Everything has to have a cause, be symbolic of something else. There's not a damned thing in my childhood to cause me to be the way I am. I was the way I am before I ever knew there was such a thing as childhood. When I was two and a half, I sat on my pet rabbit and choked it to death. When I was four, I killed seven kittens with my foot, stomped them to death. And I remember it, man! It was great. I killed dogs and cats and chickens and canaries, anything I came across all through my childhood. And I almost never got caught. I learned quick, man, that other people weren't like me. I got off the first time killing a pet calf that belonged to a friend of mine. I was twelve. I tied its legs and shoved a broken mop handle up its ass. I came in my pants. I raped my first girl a few months later. I'd have killed the bitch, but her brothers came along and I had to run.''

Arrowstone thought he would burst. "That's me! That's me exactly! I love to . . . to choke things . . . to feel them quiver, to watch their eyes. The girls . . . that's what blows me away . . . their eyes . . . the terror in their eyes, their sweet, sweet eyes.''

"Tears,'' Price went on as if he hadn't been interrupted. "I need tears. That first little bitch cried and I had this . . . this overwhelming urge to smash her, to rip her, see her blood. And . . . and when I thought of that, I went off like a bomb. I blew myself apart. If I hadn't been so weak afterwards, I'd have found a rock and got her before the goddamned brothers came.''

"I gentle them,'' Arrowstone said softly. "I soothe their fears. It's entirely possible, you know, if you have sufficient time, to make them want you, to love you even. I've had them lay there with their legs open and beg me. I really have. And that's what turns me on. I calm them like a skittish colt. And pretty soon they begin to see . . . begin to see that I have the power, their power, and they begin to bargain, to barter. They understand that I am their God . . . their God of life or death. That I can make them live or not live, as I choose. *As I choose.* I let them hope until the very end.'' He made a sucking liquid sound. "And at the end, the very end, when I'm deep inside them, I look into their lovely eyes and smile . . . and they know. Somehow, they always know. I see the terror . . . welling like tears . . . Ah, it's indescribable! I absorb their life through my hands and it's . . . it's . . . sometimes they seem to push their

lovely necks into my hands . . . they seem to choke themselves
to death.''

''Why do you do it?'' Price's voice was so suddenly listless
that Arrowstone wondered.

''For the same reason you do,'' Arrowstone countered.

''Because you like it, right?''

''Of course. I can't imagine any other reason.''

''What's the significance of the stones?''

Arrowstone chuckled. ''For the shrinks.''

Price laughed. ''I thought so. They get so excited about things
like that. I've read a dozen theories all the way from the symbolic stoning of whores like they did in biblical days to you having
a severe castration complex due to mother-dominance when you
were a child.''

''I never knew my mother. But my stepmother was a doll.''

''That's another similarity in our lives.'' Price paused. ''I had
sex with my stepmother beginning when I was about eleven.''

''How odd. So did I. With my father as well, as a matter of
fact. Neither of them knew about the other, of course.''

''My father was an asshole. I always thought he hated me,
and eventually he did. I finally had to kill him when I was eighteen.'' Price was silent for a moment. ''I killed both of them. I
hated to do her. She loved me, I think. But she was there, and
I couldn't leave her to tell them.''

''Of course not. I'm sorry, you do seem to have had a disas-
trous childhood.''

''Not at all,'' Price said, an icy edge to his voice. ''I had a
very wonderful childhood. I didn't kill them until I was eighteen. I was a man.'' His breath hissed over the line. ''I've read
your history, Julian. Our lives are remarkably paralleled. We
could almost be twins.'' The harsh, menacing quality was back
in Clark Gable's voice.

''Of course,'' Arrowstone said quickly. ''I didn't mean to imply . . . I meant, it must have been a very traumatic experience
to have to . . . to do them.''

''No,'' Price said dispassionately. ''I detested him. I enjoyed
killing him. Actually, I enjoyed her, too. I didn't waste her . . .
in some ways, she was better than the young ones.''

''Did you see the 'Reed Report' the other night?'' Price asked
abruptly.

''Yes,'' Arrowstone said uneasily. ''I was wondering—''

''Don't pay any attention. It was all a lot of bullshit. They

don't have doodly-squat on the Metcalf woman. It's all horseshit
to spook you into running or getting careless.''

''Are you sure?''

''Of course I'm sure,'' Price snarled. ''You're my friend. I'd
tell you if they had anything.''

''That's quite a relief,'' Arrowstone said awkwardly, trying to
remember how long it had been since someone had called him
friend—or if anyone ever had. ''I was seriously considering leaving—''

''Don't. At least, not for a while. I've enjoyed talking to you.
I've never had anyone I could talk to before—not about this.
You're the only one I've ever met who understands.''

''I know,'' Arrowstone said gently. ''I met a few in the institution . . . but they were hopelessly deranged. One couldn't carry
on an intelligent conversation with them. I did meet one who
was . . . was like us. But he killed himself right after I met him.
I never really got to know him.''

''We're special, Julian, you and I. You know that, don't you?''

''Yes, I know that. I've known it all my life. I haven't always
been exactly sure why, but I've known it.''

''Do you know now why we're special, Julian?''

''Yes. I know now. It's actually very simple. We're more aware
than they are. We understand the value of power. The power of
life and death. We do the things we want to do, the things that
make us alive. That makes us *feel*. We are all living dead, but
at least you and I have discovered how to come alive, to feel the
exquisite feelings. We do the things they would like to do but
are afraid of. We live by our own rules. That's why we're different, why we're special. Do you agree?''

''It's so close, we'll call it a ringer.''

''Did you come here because I was using your MO?''

''Yes. I couldn't believe it when I saw the Dallas papers. I'm
used to that, of course. My name is in the news quite often. I
get named for murders all over, but only as a possibility. This
was different. They were saying I *was* the mad killer, that they
had definite proof. It made me furious, but it intrigued me as
well. I simply had to come and see for myself.''

Spencer Price laughed. ''I thought it was something like that.
I almost pissed my pants when I saw you and realized who you
were.''

''Do I know you? Your phrasing sounds a wee bit familiar.
But I can't . . . I certainly don't know anyone named Spencer

Price.'' He paused. ''Who are you?'' Another pause. ''Are you a cop?''

Price chuckled again. ''I'll tell you next time. I have to get a little sack time. I go to work early.'' He paused. ''I'm surprised you haven't convinced Cloud that you have an imitator. Just don't tell him too much. It's easy to get carried away.''

''Oh, no,'' Arrowstone said indignantly. ''I'd never tell them anything. In fifteen years I never told them a single thing other than what I wanted them to know. Incidentally, I thought the Echofone was a nice touch, mystical voices talking from the dead.'' He laughed. ''Especially now that I've heard it myself. It's quite chilling.''

''Maybe you can do me a favor with it sometime,'' Price said. ''Be cool, Julian. I'll keep in touch.''

The phone went dead.

Arrowstone gently cradled the receiver and lay back on the bed, trying to sort out his feelings, his mind seething like a wad of worker bees bustling around the queen.

47

Ben Cloud drank the last of his oily, evil-tasting coffee and hunched over the Lea Metcalf file, began reading the laboratory report paper-clipped to the front of the manila folder.

Typewritten, neat, it reiterated substantially what Stovall had told him about the loose hairs found on the murdered woman's body. Impatient, still unwilling to believe there had not been some kind of mistake, he skipped down the page, and suddenly found his eyes riveted to a single phrase:

Analysis of semen found in subject's vagina indicates attacker has type A-positive blood.

Feeling a faint numbness building behind his eyes, Cloud reached for the Elliot case file, leafed hurriedly to the lab report.

Type O blood. Vagina, mouth, and anus.

He opened another file, the Cooper girl.

Type O blood.

Slowly, the numbness segueing into a steady, nagging pain, he checked the other folders.

All type O blood.

All except Lea Metcalf's killer.

He reeled back in his chair. Another mistake? Two mistakes on the same case, first with the hair and now with the semen? He didn't think so. Red Stovall, despite his seeming indifference, was a top-notch technician, by far the best they'd ever had. They could always run the samples to Dallas or Fort Worth and have then checked again, but he had no real hope that the results would be different.

So what did it mean?

Cloud lit a cigarette and stared bleakly at the open folders on his desk, the throbbing pain behind his eyes spreading to encompass his entire forehead, seeking to escape through his temples.

He didn't want to think about it. No more than he had when Stovall had told him about the hair.

He sighed, rocked forward in the chair, and stubbed out the cigarette. He didn't *have* to think about it. Not much, at least. The answer was there before him, as chilling as an unexpected summer frost.

There *was* more than one of them.

A silent partner perhaps, finally making his presence known, a tagalong Arrowstone student soloing under the watchful eye of the old master. Maybe that accounted for the lack of brutality, mutilation—a beginner's squeamishness.

There was a precedent. By his own account, Henry Lee Lucas had had a younger partner during a part of his murderous rampage across the country, a follower, an eager oracle in the fine art of indiscriminate murder.

On the other hand, if Ward Callum and the historical data from Chicago and New York could be believed, Arrowstone was the one who always showed a certain amount of restraint, a disinclination to savage his victims. Until the murder of Lea Metcalf, they had assumed that he was changing, growing more violent in his depredations.

Cloud's eyebrows arched. Perhaps that wasn't true. Perhaps he had killed the Elliot girl and his partner and snapped the neck of Ramona Butler. Perhaps his pupil had assisted in the Cooper and Dickerson murders and then he had gone solo again with Metcalf.

Crazy, Cloud thought. But it could well be true. Crazy is as crazy does, and psychopathic personalities were not exactly famous for rational lines of thought.

Another thought struck him, brought him out of his chair to the gray metal filing cabinet where he had stored Ward Callum's data.

Back at his desk, he leafed rapidly through the mass of paper work until he found a copy of one of Arrowstone's medical reports while he was in the New York hospital.

His eyes raced down the page. He discovered he was holding his breath, his fingers trembling. He found what he was looking for and let his breath loose in a gusty sigh.

Arrowstone's blood type was listed as A-positive.

48

Cloud stalked the dimly lighted street. Hands knotted into powerful fists, swinging easily at his sides, the feel of the pavement beneath his bare feet cool and gritty. All senses on full alert, his piercing eyes swept the darkened doorways, invaded the dense shadows between buildings, penetrated walls.

He was here—somewhere. Cloud was certain of that. He paced, devoured distance with yard-long strides. A powerful predator after a cunning prey.

Startled, he whirled at a movement in a darkened doorway, whistled softly at the full-bodied, redheaded woman who moved slowly into the light. She smiled a garish, red-rimmed smile, stroked her hands down along sagging breasts, across a mounded belly, into the forbidden patch. Cloud came closer.

"You are safe," he said, "he only diddles the young ones."

The woman pouted prettily and stuck out her tongue. Behind her something moved, and another one appeared. A twin to the first. Voluptuous. Everything in excess.

Cloud shook his head. "You are both too old and fat and ugly. He likes them young and fresh. I'm sorry, better luck next season." He watched them fade into darkness, curiously poignant. He shook his head wearily. "They all want to get into the act."

"You're right, of course," Arrowstone said, and Cloud looked at him with no surprise and no eagerness, only a faint sense of inevitability. "But they looked rather nice. Perhaps just this once I might make an exception. After all, I've never had two before.

Sometimes one likes to wallow.'' Arrowstone smiled winningly, a stunning smile with dark stone teeth, sparkling pinpoints of light spinning off the convex surfaces of slitted eyes, meticulously groomed hair surrounding a narrow face.

"You lie, sir," Cloud replied firmly. "You forget Elliot and Butler. One and one makes two. Lying is against the law. I have come here to kill you.'' He lifted the gun, holding it in both hands the way they had taught him, spreading his feet a bit for proper stability, gritting his teeth and squinting his eyes against the brilliant zigzags of lightning just over the shoulder of the ringing telephone—

He jerked awake, lathered in sweat, a knot of bed clothing gripped between tightly clenched hands, his mouth open, sucking air through dry, clotted membranes.

The phone rang again.

Amy made a snarling sound, jerked her pillow over her head.

Cloud reached across her and picked up the receiver, swallowing noisily, feeling a swirling flow of sour panic clinging with the residue of the dream. He worked his mouth to summon saliva.

"Hello.'' It was a hoarse, hollow croak.

"Benjy? Sorry about the time, love, but it seems the stalwarts have themselves in a bit of a dither.'' Cricket Bloom's nasal voice slashed through the mist in his brain like a red-hot wire. "A bit of a hostage situation—''

"Dammit, Cricket, why call me? We've got Summers and Belden for just—''

"I'm sorry, love, but he's asking for you.''

"Who's asking for me?'' A tiny fist pounded methodically at his right temple.

"The gent with the redheaded lady,'' Cricket said, unable to contain a current of excitement. "Some bloke they think is Arrowstone,'' she went on, as if she hadn't heard the name a hundred times.

Cloud scooted and hopped across Amy's widespread legs, one hand groping through the pile of clothing on the floor beside the king-sized bed. "Where?'' He glanced at the clock: 6:25.

"Jetson's Market. That twenty-four hour Mom-and-Pop store on—''

"I know where it is. What's the situation—no, never mind.'' He hung up and flipped on the bedside light, clawing jeans and shirt out of the tangled mess. He dressed swiftly, stomping bare feet into his boots when his socks eluded him.

Amy lifted a tousled head, looked at him with squinted eyes. "What's going on? Where you going?" She shifted to look at the clock, groaned, and covered her eyes.

"To the store," Cloud said tersely, buttoning the shirt with one hand, stuffing it into his pants with the other, his face tightening as he recalled her unreasoning fit of temper at bedtime the night before.

"My God, at this time of night? What on earth for?"

"We're out of olives," Cloud said, wondering at his perversity. "I can't sleep knowing we're out of olives."

"Aw shit!" She flipped over on her stomach and buried her face in the pillow.

He leaned down, lifted her hair, and kissed her neck. "Go back to sleep. I'll be back in time for breakfast—probably."

She didn't move.

Chuckling, he trotted down the hallway to get his coat. He was opening the front door when she yelled, "Dammit, Cloud, you'd better tell—"

The closing door cut off her voice. He grinned and sucked in a lung full of crisp, cold air. By God, she'd think twice before she picked a fight again when all he had on his mind was tender loving.

49

Rosie was there when he arrived, stalking the perimeter of a semicircle of squad cars with blazing lights aimed at a small, shabby grocery store sandwiched between a beauty salon and a boutique. Hair in wild disarray, a slice of blue pajama top with white piping showing through the V of his lightweight sheepskin coat, Rosie wore his usual phlegmatic expression as he opened Cloud's car door and stepped back.

Cloud climbed out and lit a cigarette, studying the big man's face. "You think it's him?" He glanced over the cars at the grocery store, ancient and decrepit, its plate-glass windows cluttered with placards and posters proclaiming sales. Nothing moved inside.

Rosie shrugged. "We don't know for sure, Ben. Jim Barton and Sid Gilmore spotted him on East Roosevelt Drive. He was in that red Ford over there. They saw him punch his woman companion two or three times and push her toward the floor. They made a one-eighty and ran the license plate. It's on the hot sheet. Stolen late yesterday afternoon. Barton was sure the girl's hair was red, so they called for a backup and went after him, figuring they had Arrowstone for sure." He looked tired, his skin sallow in the early-morning gray.

"What's he doing in the store?"

"He went in there with the girl. McAllister and Powell set up a block down at the corner. Barton and Gilmore were riding his tail, so I guess he decided he was boxed." He turned and pointed toward a maroon Ford LTD canted sharply across the sidewalk with its right front fender almost touching the plate glass of the market. "He came out of the car shooting at Barton and Gilmore. Barton took a round—didn't look bad, but he was bleeding a lot. The girl broke free and ran into the store, so Gilmore let loose a couple. He thinks he winged him going in the door."

"Anybody tried to talk to him?" A shrill whistle swung his eyes to a tall, bulky office carrying a rifle. He made a series of complicated-looking arm signals directed at two men sitting nonchalantly on the edge of a roof across the street from the store. The two men didn't move. The tall cop cupped his hands around his mouth and bellowed, "All right, you guys. Off your asses and on your feet! We got a serious hostage situation here."

The two men looked at each other and slowly climbed to their feet.

"Some goddamned swat team," Rosie said.

"Anybody talk to him?" Cloud repeated his question.

Rosie grunted sourly. "I did just a couple of minutes before you got here. He didn't answer. Sergeant Pronti tried awhile ago, but all he'd say was he wanted you."

"How about the store clerks? They still in there?"

Rosie smiled faintly. "No. They went out the back door the minute they heard the commotion and shots out front. They've been robbed a few times; they're a little gun shy."

"Then there's only Arrowstone and the girl?"

"That's what Jetson said. There's only one other exit, the back door. We've got some men back there. So he's damned sure still in there. Arrowstone's got the rear door barred."

"If it is Arrowstone," Cloud said.

"Yeah, if it's him."

Cloud dropped his cigarette butt and methodically ground it beneath his shoe. He glanced along the row of men and machines to a noisy group of people milling beyond a squad car and several uniformed officers forming a barricade of sorts across the street. A dark-clothed figure detached itself from the group, paused momentarily beside one of the officers, and then walked toward them. Cloud recognized Ward Callum.

"He must have some kind of damned radar," Rosie said, nodding toward the approaching Chicago cop. Beyond Callum a raucous cheer erupted from the crowd as an obviously drunken youth tiptoed behind one of the cops and headed across the street toward the store. Two cops lumbered out from the group around the squad cars and intercepted him.

"Asshole," Rosie said absently, and went back to watching Callum.

"He's staying at the Holiday Inn down on Rosecrans," Cloud said. "He's on the second floor, and he could probably see this from his room." He shifted restlessly, moved around in a small half circle. "Okay, I've got it to do, I may as well get it done." He lit another cigarette and inhaled deeply. "Get a man over near the door with a horn. Tell him I'm coming in." He bobbed his head in greeting as Callum walked up and stood silently listening.

"You don't have to, you know," Rosie said harshly. "We can go in and get the mother."

"This is not the time for John Wayneing it, Rosie," he said, regretting it instantly as the big detective's face tightened and turned away. "He's got a hostage in there. We don't need another dead girl."

"Is it him?" Ward Callum asked softly.

"We think so. The squad car locked in on him because he was beating a girl in his car. Looked like he was trying to subdue her."

"He doesn't beat them," Callum said, turning toward the store. He appeared perplexed, a look approaching sadness on his angular face. "He uses fear. Terror."

"He beat this one," Rosie snarled, turning, stalking toward a short, beefy cop holding a bullhorn. They conferred briefly and the short cop started across the street. Rosie came back, a truculent look on his face.

"You bring your gun?"

Cloud smiled and winced. "Too much of a hurry, Rosie. Didn't have time to look for the damned thing." He realized belatedly that his remark about John Wayne had stung the big cop more than he had thought.

Without a word Rosie reached inside the sheepskin coat. "No problem. You can use one of mine." He flipped open the cylinder on a large black revolver, twirled it, then snapped it back in place. He held it out, butt first. "Shoots a hair to the right," he said. "Hold low on his breastbone, and you'll get it about right."

Cloud hefted the big gun in his hands and shook his head. He unzipped his jacket and shoved it into the waistband of his pants. He started to zip up.

"Don't bother," Rosie said. He turned to a tall, lanky policeman standing nearby. 'Who's wearing a Daisy Mae, Turnbow?''

The tall cop shook his head. "Macy'll have one. He always wears it."

"I don't want it, Rosie," Cloud said.

Rosie ignored him. "Tell him to shuck out of it, will you?"

Turnbow looked at Cloud, then back at Rosie, a silly smile on his dark-skinned face.

"You damned hard of hearing or something? Get the vest!" Rosie glowered, and the cop departed hastily.

"I don't want it, Rosie," Cloud repeated patiently, trying again to fit the zipper together.

"You're gonna wear it," Rosie said. "That is, if you go in. If you don't go in, then that's fine. We'll all go in and get the bastard, and I'll wear it. But if you go by yourself, you're gonna wear the damned thing if I have to hold you down and put it on you all by myself."

Cloud stared up at him, astonished. There was an odd look on the broad, square face he had never seen before, half smile, half sneer, eyes hard and shiny and unflinching.

"Goddamn it, man, I outrank you," he snapped, realizing with a small pang of dismay that the hulking lout meant exactly what he said. He visualized himself being undressed and redressed in the bulletproof vest by long, spatulate fingers and shuddered inwardly.

Callum's gaze swung back and forth between them, his face expressionless, his eyes sparkling; an unlit cigarette dangled from one corner of his mouth.

"Rank don't mean shit," Rosie said. "Not between friends." His eyes were even brighter, and Cloud decided the odd expression was a kind of fiendish glee. "Departmental regs," he went on, giving Cloud a way out without losing too much face. "Donleavy'd have your ass sure." He turned as the tall cop came trotting up with the vest. Rosie took it and stood looking at Cloud, bushy eyebrows cocked.

Cloud snatched it out of his hand and held it between his knees while he took off his coat. He looked at Callum. "What would you do with an old-maid asshole like him?"

Callum smiled. "Be thankful," he said.

Unable to wear the gun in his waistband because of the vest, he dropped it into his jacket pocket. He zipped up and looked at Rosie, feeling bulky and unwieldy and a little foolish.

"All right, Mother, you think I'm ready now?"

Satisfied with his small victory, Rosie smiled amiably. "Keep a low profile," he advised. "By the way, they're somewhere behind that second island of shelves. We can see everywhere else."

Cloud gave him a grim look and squeezed between two of the squad cars. "You can turn off the headlights," he snapped at the watching policemen. "It's broad daylight."

50

Cloud stopped in the center of the street and nodded at the man with the bullhorn leaning against the brick front of the beauty salon. The beefy cop sidled closer to the door.

"Hey! In the store! Lieutenant Cloud is here, he's coming in!" He lowered the bullhorn and listened, then repeated his message. He listened, then looked at Cloud and shrugged. "He ain't answering, Lieutenant." He put down the bullhorn and took out his gun.

Cloud nodded and ducked his head to light a cigarette, a rapidly growing sense of anxiety fluttering in his chest. All at once he felt immensely grateful to Rosie for making him wear the vest. Surrounded by fellow policemen, he suddenly felt all alone, incredibly vulnerable. He was inordinately pleased to find that his hands were steady.

He exhaled smoke and crossed the rest of the way to the door. He paused, scanning the interior through the plate-glass entrance. Nothing moved.

He opened the door a crack.

"I'm Lieutenant Cloud. You wanted to talk to me. I'm here, so let's talk." He took a last puff and dropped the cigarette to the sidewalk, listening. Nothing.

"You wanted me. Now I'm here. I'm coming through the door. Talk to me if you want to get out of here. I can't help you if you won't talk."

He took a deep breath and stepped through the door, his body cringing, the skin pulling taut across his cheekbones, something crawling upward into his throat, drying his mouth. He fought down a maddening desire to take out the gun. Instead, he stretched his arms high above his head.

"Look. I don't have a gun." He cleared his throat noisily. "Look, if you're Julian Arrowstone, you must know we're not going to let you out of here. I'm being honest with you. The only thing left to decide is whether you come out under your own power or we come and get you." He fell silent, feeling giddy, almost disoriented, a wash of anger creeping in to adulterate the fear.

"Send out the girl, Julian. Then come out yourself. It's your only option. I'm supposed to con you, lie to you, promise you anything, bargain. But you're too damned smart for that bullshit, and I'm too impatient. I'm a homicide cop, and I want your ass for murder. You know it, and I know it. Everything else is bullshit. So if you called me here to try me, have at it. Otherwise, I'm coming after your ass. Now!" He took out the gun and crouched, eyes working like a metronome back and forth along the tier of shelving. "Ten seconds, Arrowstone. Make up your goddamned mind!"

Out of the corner of his eye he glimpsed movement out in the street. He risked a quick glance. Rosie Simple, backed by a phalanx of cops, was coming across the street. Cloud raised a hand. Rosie stopped just outside the door.

"You hurt the girl now, Arrowstone, and I'll kill you." He took a silent step forward, a sickening knot of uncertainty uncoiling in his mind. It was all wrong. He had handled it wrong, and he was going to get himself killed . . . or the girl.

"Please don't hurt me." It was a feminine voice, oddly subdued, and Cloud stopped, transfixed, the boil of anger bursting inside him like acid rain.

"Don't hurt her, Arrowstone!" he yelled. "I told you—"

"Not him!" the voice screamed. "You! He—he's dead!"

"What?"

"He's dead. That goddamned cop shot him. He's not nobody named Arrowstone. His name is Mike, Mike Boyle."

Cloud slumped, the tenseness draining out of him. He knew Mike Boyle. Had known him, at least. A sleekly handsome man with a fiery temper, he had made his living off the bodies of women since dropping out of school at fifteen. Tight-fisted, a strict disciplinarian, he had gone a little overboard in chastising one of his whores, and Cloud and Rafferty had arrested him for murder a few years back. Plea-bargained down to manslaughter, the last Cloud had heard of him, he had been serving time in Huntsville.

"Who are you?" Cloud walked to the end of the island and stopped.

"I'm his . . . woman. My name is Velma Ford."

"Throw out the gun, Velma."

Something skittered along the tile floor; a small, black revolver slid into view.

"Come out slowly, hands behind your head." Cloud stepped back and to one side, halfway behind the island of shelves.

The woman walked slowly into view, hands locked behind a heavy mass of dark brown hair. She was young, no more than twenty-one, a lean face with pockmarked skin and dark, brooding eyes. Her face was wet, and a bright splash of blood stained the front of her blouse.

The front door burst open, and the small store was abruptly swarming with cops. Rosie came up behind Cloud. "Whatta we got?"

"Cuff her," Cloud said tersely. "He's a pimp named Mike Boyle. He's supposed to be dead back there, but take it easy. She's his woman, not a hostage."

Rosie nodded and turned her over to another cop. "I'll take a look," he said casually, passing in front of Cloud and stepping into the aisle before Cloud could object. A few feet into the opening he looked over his shoulder and grinned. "Yep, he looks dead, all right." Cloud started after him.

"Was it him, Lieutenant Cloud?"

Cloud turned. Ward Callum walked toward him, his expression curiously blank, suspended, as if awaiting some awesome and eternal judgment.

Cloud shook his head. "No. It was a man I helped send to the pen a few years ago. I don't know what he wanted with me." He watched Callum light a cigarette and took out one of his own. "Unless he wanted to even the score."

Callum inclined his head. "I didn't think it would be him when they said he was beating the girl. That's not his style. He deals in terror, paralyzing terror. They don't fight back." There was something approaching awe, almost reverence, in the tight-lipped man's face, and Cloud wondered if Callum's obsessive pursuit of his sister's murderer had resulted in some sort of mystical bonding between the hunter and the hunted.

Cloud looked past him and saw the girl being led out of the store. "Excuse me a minute." He caught up with them on the sidewalk. "Powell, mind if I have a minute with Miss Ford?"

"Sure thing, Lieutenant." The officer moved a few feet away and leaned against the plate-glass window.

Cloud smiled at the girl and held out his cigarettes. "You smoke, Velma?"

"Yes, thank you." There was something extremely sensual about the dark, brooding eyes, Cloud thought. Mother nature hadn't been totally neglectful.

Cloud lit the cigarette and put it between her thin lips. "I don't have herpes," he said.

She nodded without smiling.

"Why did Mike run, Velma?"

She sucked on the cigarette, tilting her head to keep the smoke out of her eyes. Using her tongue, she rolled it to one corner of her mouth. She looked back at the store, then turned to Cloud with a shrug.

"You'll find out anyhow, I guess. Mike and two other guys hit that supermarket in Dallas night before last. He thought the cops were chasing him for that. And too, the car was stolen."

"Why was he hitting you?"

She shrugged thin shoulders again. "I was mouthing off too much, I guess."

"Why did he want me?"

"I don't know. He just said he had something to trade. Something he got from Sammy."

"Sammy Keeler?"

She nodded. "He never said what it was. But he seemed to think it was enough to maybe get us out of this."

"You're sure it was Sammy Keeler?"

"Yeah, I'm sure. I knew Sammy. Little man. Snappy dresser for a junkie. Him and Mike were pretty tight, you know."

Cloud took the cigarette stub out of her mouth. "You like to tell me who the two guys were with Mike?"

She smiled faintly and shook her head. "I don't think so."

Cloud offered her another cigarette. She nodded, and he put it in her mouth. He reached for his lighter, but she shook her head. "I'll keep it for later." She glanced at the crowd still milling in the street, then brought her gaze back to Cloud. "Why are you arresting me?"

"Suspicion of robbery, accessory after the fact."

She spat out the unlit cigarette. "I'll deny I said it."

Cloud nodded. 'So would I, in your case. But you did say it." He shrugged and took a half-step away. "It's out of my hands."

"Wait." She cast an uneasy glance at the patrolman leaning against the window. She moved closer to Cloud. "What if I told you something else, something about those two women who were killed out on Crescent Lane? Could you cut me loose then?"

"Depends on what it is," Cloud said, feeling a fluttering sensation in his stomach, a coolness on the nape of his neck. "I can't make blind promises."

"Sammy told Mike" She hesitated and wet her lips, her voice barely above a whisper. "Sammy told Mike it was a cop . . . a cop did it."

"He didn't tell Mike who, of course."

"No, he didn't."

"And Sammy Keeler is conveniently dead." He shook his head. "I'll have to pass on that one, Velma. There are people who say Oswald didn't kill Kennedy, too. We have to go with what we've got, and what we haven't got is any evidence pointing to a cop." He motioned to the waiting policeman.

"You sorry bastard," she said.

"Okay, Velma. Good luck." He stood watching them get into one of the squad cars. He wondered if the information about a killer cop was what Mike Boyle had had on his mind, or if the woman had made it up on the spur of the moment.

He walked across the street to his car, shucking his coat and the bulletproof vest. He tossed the vest to one of the uniformed officers and climbed into his car. He sat for a moment experiencing the curious mental and physical interaction that invariably followed moments of extreme tension, the slowing down of the senses. He felt light-headed, giddy, somehow cleansed.

51

Amy Reed was still asleep when Cloud let himself into the condo apartment. Sprawled inelegantly across the middle of the bed, ice-green shortie crumpled about her waist, small mouth pursed in soundless astonishment at some startling facet of her dream, she was his ultimate conception of the sensuous woman. Part gamin, part sophisticated lady, she continually kept him off-balance with mercurial mood shifts, spontaneous displays of keen perceptions, and high humor infrequently interlaced with cool sulkiness and egregious disdain.

Her moodiness, he knew, stemmed at least in part from the tenuous nature of their relationship, the fact that she harbored an undercurrent of resentment because she had been the one to initiate their union. No amount of reassurance from him seemed to touch that; it was a *fait accompli* in her mind and could not be changed. Why it bothered her so much he couldn't fully understand, nor could she explain it to him in rational terms on those occasions when she worked it into the conversation. It seemed to plague her like a running sore, and he sometimes found himself wondering guiltily if her constant harping on something he considered insignificant might not be just another subtle tactic in a grand campaign to push him into a deeper commitment. But he was wary, too uncertain of himself and of her to risk her eventual rejection.

He heated water and made a cup of instant coffee. He went into the living room and parked himself in front of the picture

window overlooking a square block of dusty, spiritless woodland
that had been depicted in the artist's conception as a lush, semi-
tropical wonderland of pools and tennis courts and jogging trails.
The last condo had been sold two years before, and the pin oak
woods was still a pin oak woods. A closer look at his sales
contract had revealed that no mention had been made of pools
and tennis courts and jogging trails. Surprise, surprise. The
builder's rationale was that the artist's conception was what the
park *could* look like if the condo owners decided to make it so.
And anyhow, everyone knew what dreamy, whimsical folk artists
were.

He was on his second cup of coffee and fourth cigarette when
he heard the soft swish of feet in the deep pile carpet; he felt
warm arms slip across his shoulders and lock beneath his chin.

"If you're a lady burglar after my family jewels," he said
solemnly, "I'm sorry, I've already got a redheaded woman in
yonder I'm crazy about."

She laughed, puffing warm breath into his ear. "Beast. You're
not getting around me with such obvious B.S. as that."

"Around you? In you, maybe."

Her arms tightened. "You think we're even now? You've had
your little revenge for my temper tantrum last night." She vaulted
lightly over the arm of the chair and into his lap.

"Temper tantrum? What temper tantrum? I thought you were
just being your usual ornery self."

She kissed him, then pulled back and squinted her eyes
thoughtfully. "No, I guess not. I was really a little shit. I think
you have some more coming."

"Good, I'll collect it right after breakfast. Uh, some more
what?"

"Some more revenge." Her eyes sparkled. "Maybe you ought
to spank me."

"I'd probably like that, all right, but I don't think so. Forgiving is too nice."

"That's one of your problems. You're too forgiving. You're
too nice to run around loose. You let people take advantage of
you. People like me, for instance."

"Not all that much. I'm just a normal easygoing slob. You
haven't seen my bad side."

"Do you have a bad side?"

"Of course. Everyone has a bad side. Some more than one."

"What's yours?" She squirmed; ostensibly to find a better

seat, but he thought he knew better, the small, round bottom sending a blatantly eloquent message to his vitals.

"I have a temper, too. It's not as volatile as yours. It comes slower, but it stays awhile. My ex-wife thought I was too possessive, but then she thought I wasn't upwardly mobile enough, either." He paused, reflecting, then cupped a breast through the filmy material of the nightgown. "And I desire little women that tempt me too much."

"Oh?" Her eyebrows climbed, twin arches over snapping green eyes. "You think I'm easy, huh?"

"I didn't say that. But eager yes. There's a world of difference."

"You're right," she said, and began kissing him, light, fluttery kisses as soft as the brush of a butterfly's wings. "Let me show you how eager I really am."

"Sure," he said, pondering a bit, remembering his persistent efforts the night before to placate her, pampering and babying, all to no avail. Remembering also, her lacerating, waspish voice telling him he was a wimp, a nerd, and that it would be a cold day in July before he got in her pants again.

"Sure," he said again, and stood up, dumping her on the floor. He grinned down at her shocked face. "See me next July."

52

"Ladies and gentlemen, we have with us today, Dr. William S. Worsdorfer. Dr. Worsdorfer, founder and director of the Psychiatric Research Institute, is perhaps most noted for his work in the area of sexual psychopathology. Dr. Worsdorfer has also on numerous occasions been called upon by the state to assist in the determination of the mental attitudes of defendants before the courts, and has, as a consequence of his adjudications, been sometimes referred to as 'the hanging doctor'."

Amy Reed turned slightly in her chair and smiled winningly at the tall, ugly man seated to her right. Heavily moustached, bearded to the upper tips of his ears, the impeccably dressed man's dome-shaped head gleamed like polished stone, thick, unruly brows guarding bright black eyes bunched in annoyance. The good doctor was clearly not happy with his host's introduction.

Cloud hooted aloud into the empty living room and took a sip of beer.

"Dr. Worsdorfer, on behalf of our TV audience and myself, please allow me to extend my thanks to you for volunteering to appear on this, the third segment in our series dealing with the murders of five young women here in Trinity Square. I am sure your expertise and vast knowledge will provide us all with at least a modicum of insight into the perverted mind of a person capable of such atrocities."

"Good girl, Amy," Cloud said aloud, finishing the rest of his beer and stretching lazily on the couch. Amy Reed had been furious with her producer's acceptance of the well-known doctor's offer to appear, and Cloud expected fireworks.

Dr. Worsdorfer lifted a long, bony finger and wagged it playfully at Amy Reed. "I must correct," he said with heavy humor. "Not necessarily perverted, my dear. A sick mind, certainly, but one very much like yours and mine with, perhaps, one small but, of course, significant difference." He smiled benignly and took a pipe from his coat pocket. He stuck it into one corner of his almost lipless mouth, unlit.

"And what would that difference be, Doctor?" Amy's voice was soft and warm and silky.

He pursed his lips and blew invisible smoke. He jabbed the pipestem at her for emphasis. "Deprivation," he barked. "A mind deprived is a mind in want, in need. We are born with inherent needs. They are basic needs, of course. The need to obtain sustenance, to be comforted, to be loved. Both physical and psychological needs. They are, in essence, the same thing in the end. If the organism is not maintained in a reasonably comfortable condition, i.e. is allowed to go hungry, to be left cold and wet and unattended in its crib, it will, after a certain lapse of time, feel bereft and abandoned, suffer almost continuous pain. Since its primary motivational force at the moment is to sustain itself, to remain alive, it will be forced sooner or later to ameliorate the pain by shutting down these antithetical feelings, to divorce itself from these unfulfilled needs."

Amy Reed leaned slightly forward. "Are you saying then, Doctor, that the subject of this discussion might be killing young women because he was not properly cared for as a child?"

Dr. Worsdorfer smiled indulgently. "A severe oversimplification, my dear, but yes, in essence, I am saying just that."

Amy smiled thinly. "Environmental, Doctor?" Her eyebrows lifted.

"Twenty-five years ago we were told that reason and not discipline was the humanitarian way to rear our young, to allow them to grow up with uncluttered minds, untrammeled souls, free of prior generations' hidebound ethics and morals. We have seen the results of that: the dropout generations of the sixties and the seventies, the escalating crime rate among the young, the early pregnancies and abortion rates. Perhaps I am oversimplifying again, but isn't it just possible he is doing what he is doing simply because he likes to do it? And not because Momma or Daddy didn't act properly appreciative of his dedicated efforts in the third grade?''

Dr. Worsdorfer frowned and sucked on his pipe, the other side of his mouth billowing as if ejecting smoke, a row of thick inverted V's spiraling upward into his endless brow.

"Yes, my dear," he said crisply. "You are oversimplifying again. One does not commit this sort of depredation against another human being simply because one enjoys it. It is the result of what we might term an irresistible compulsion brought on by perhaps an underlying demonic rage that has been seething in the subconscious and can no longer be contained. He stands as helpless before his eruptions as a leaf in a windstorm."

"Uh-huh," Amy said. "He's been erupting a long time. There is evidence of extreme cruelty and destruction of small animals at an age when most of us are still playing with dolls and toy trucks."

Dr. Worsdorfer waved his hand airily, the condescending smile back in place and working. "The needs of the organism begin at birth. This is simply a manifestation of early deprivation combined, no doubt, with aggression against the budding senses. In the interest of self-perpetuation the infant, or child, submerges into the subconscious these wants and desires that have not been fulfilled; buries them to lie and ferment, exerting finally draconian pressures that can no longer be denied. Since the causative factors are in the past and can no longer be addressed, the organism must seek substitute or symbolic expression in an effort to relieve the tension."

Amy nodded wisely, her eyes glinting. "Oh, I see. Then it's quite possible that Melinda Cooper was raped, beaten, mutilated and killed because a small boy somewhere was once spanked for beating up on some little girl."

Dr. Worsdorfer sucked furiously on his pipe, wagging both his head and a forefinger. "You are certainly given to—"

"—oversimplification," Amy said, turning and smiling into the camera. "That's it for the 'Reed Report' for today, ladies and gentlemen. I would like to thank Dr. William Worsdorfer for his powerful contribution to our growing awareness of the killer who lives among us. And remember, ladies, if you should be confronted by Julian Arrowstone, take heart, treat him with loving kindness. After all, he may well be an overgrown, misunderstood little boy."

53

A few minutes after Amy's mocking sign-off smile had faded on the screen, Jake Rafferty showed up at Cloud's door bearing gifts of beer and pretzels and beer nuts, and the two men settled in to watch, in the time-honored tradition of American males everywhere, the deliberate and premeditated mayhem of twenty-two gladiators caged between opposing, howling, blood-thirsty mobs who would have done justice to any arena in ancient Rome.

Rafferty settled in, munched on some pretzels, and looked over at Cloud. "I've been meaning to tell you, you've been looking pretty gaunt. Is it the murders or too much nooky too often?"

Cloud gave him a sour look. "You don't look so damned hot yourself. You could probably get prune juice out of those wrinkled bags under your eyes, and I'm damned sure not going to sit here and discuss my sex life with you."

"Why not? You always have before." Rafferty grinned. "You're right, though. I'm beat. I can take just so much of this happy crime-fighting shit and I've got to bust out. As soon as this thing is over, why don't me and you take off up to my cabin? Run around half naked, cuss and spit on the floor, talk dirty, and maybe even knock some of them stripers in the head."

"Sounds great, but I think it's a little cold to be prancing around naked. Besides, you don't look all that great with your clothes off." He canted his head and grinned. "Matter of fact, you don't look all that great with your clothes on."

Rafferty cocked one arm in a classic bodybuilder's pose, tentatively felt his biceps with two fingers, and then sighed. "Luckily that don't seem to matter much to the ladies." He spoke lightly but with an underlying edge of sorrow that made Cloud wince inwardly at the direction the good-natured exchange had taken. Despite the smaller man's iron control, Cloud sensed a deep inner turmoil, and innate sorrow that would be a long time waning, that even now sent out waves of almost palpable pain.

After a partnership that had lasted more than five years, he felt he knew the other man better than any other living person, and he had been mildly surprised to see that steely reserve disintegrate before the sultry beauty of tempestuous Ramona Butler. Personally, he had found her likable enough, but her beauty seemed to have a fragile quality, the never-ending vivacity a shade too ferocious, almost voracious. Her eyes had been her best feature: dark, lazy eyes that suggested age-old secrets, suntanned gods, and nubile maidens, languorous nights of illicit delight. She had known their value and had used them well.

"Jesus Christ," Rafferty said disgustedly. "I got better hands than that. That shoulda' been six points, man. He had that damned ball right in his hands. Shit, Tampa Bay is oh for five and they're gonna beat Dallas's ass."

"They're due," Cloud said absently. He picked up the two empty beer cans and went into the kitchen for refills.

He was on edge: an indefinable something that stalked his consciousness the way a black cat prowls the night, unseen, unheard, unfelt, a fleeting, ghostly image like a wisp of deadly fog above a murky swamp. A shimmering blip appeared on the lip of his mind, expanded into a comic character's balloon—

"The dart landed on Trinity Square and that's that."

Arrowstone's words. He tried to recall on which occasion they had been spoken, but his recollection was suddenly vague and threadbare, as if a horde of voracious ants had been feeding on the fabric of his memory. The harder he tried, the more disoriented he became. And why was it important? Why did the words themselves heighten his sense of uncertainty? Broaden the scope and dimension of the anxiety they engendered? Taken in or out of context, they meant nothing more than the convoluted logic of a madman. But was Arrowstone a madman? The answer to that was a qualified no. Not in the accepted sense. Cool, cunning, a remorseless killer. Yes. But not a madman. Then why would he use a map and a dart to select the locations of his merciless slaughter? The answer to that had to be—

"Hey, those beers too cold or something?" Rafferty slouched in the doorway grinning at him, and Cloud realized he was holding a can of beer tightly clenched in each hand. He relaxed and tossed a can at Rafferty.

"Cooling my hot little hands," he said. He pulled the tab on his beer and drank a long, cool sip.

Rafferty crossed to the refrigerator and put his can back inside. He patted his stomach. "I've had too much already. Gas up to here." He stretched and yawned. "Looks like the Cowboys are going in the dumper. Tampa-damn-Bay, of all people. Even Tom Landry looks worried." He strolled back to the doorway. "Reckon I'll cut out and get a little sack time. Tell Amy I said hi. Or have you run her off already?"

"She took part in a special this afternoon. That thing on Arrowstone. She oughta be in before long. Stick around and we'll burn some steaks and crisp up a few fries."

"Sounds good, but I'll take a raincheck. Speaking of that son of a bitch Arrowstone, is there anything new?"

Cloud shook his head.

"You haven't heard from him since your TV show?"

"Not a murmur. I'm beginning to wonder if he saw it."

"Catching any flack?"

Cloud lit a cigarette and exhaled slowly. "Eli's fielding most of it. We have a command performance scheduled tomorrow with Donleavy."

"So what? He can't eat you."

"He can make it damned uncomfortable to sit down."

Rafferty laughed and shook his head. He went back into the living room and crossed to the door. He glanced at the TV set and threw up his hands. "A damned massacre. I can't stand all this blood. I'll see you later, buddy."

"Take care," Cloud said. "Oh, by the way, do you remember the name of the guy who used to share an apartment with Sammy Keeler?"

Rafferty frowned thoughtfully. "Yeah, Mendosa. Julio Mendosa. Why?"

Cloud told him about Mike Boyle and what the woman had told him.

"You think it may have something to do with the aborted coke buy we sat on that night?"

Cloud shrugged. "I don't have any idea. More likely it had to do with Keeler's death. Boyle was no dummy. I can't see him trying to trade me information about a coke buy that didn't take place against the attempted murder of a cop. My guess is he knew something about Sammy's killer, or at least why he was killed. It doesn't make any sense, otherwise."

Rafferty nodded and took out a pack of chewing gum. He folded two pieces of Doublemint into his mouth and compacted the wrappings into small squares. "You want me to ask around, see if I can locate Mendosa?"

"If it's handy. Don't spend a lot of time on it. I know you're as busy as we are. I can put Rosie or Graves on it. After all, it's our cotton bale." He punched Rafferty lightly in the stomach and grinned. "Don't get me wrong. Any little thing will help."

Rafferty returned the grin, brightening his face. "I'll have a chat with a couple of my little junkie buddies. No sweat." He opened the door and stepped out onto the small concrete porch. "One of these evenings soon, I'll take you and your pretty girl friend out for a little pepperbelly food. How's that sound?" He flipped the gum wrappers out into the yard.

"Like a winner. Say when."

Cloud watched his friend until he was out of sight around the corner of the recreation hall, his walk jaunty and sure again, all traces of the limp gone. The flesh takes care of itself, he thought, it's the emotions we have to fight tooth and nail to conquer. Time was Rafferty's friend; the memories would gradually blur, become submerged beneath infinitesimal increments of soothing, healing time.

But time was Cloud's worst enemy; the chances of solving a murder dropped drastically after twenty-four hours, were further reduced with the passage of each day. The statistics were distressing enough, but what really depressed him was the almost certain knowledge that the passage of time would bring more murders. He sighed and walked out into the yard and picked up Rafferty's gum wrappers, shaking his head.

54

Amy stood in the open door of the bathroom watching him towel after his shower. Arms folded beneath her breasts, one slim ankle crossed over the other, she leaned against the doorjamb, head tilted, appraising him critically.

"You're not bad for an old fart of thirty-five, Cloud," she said, with just the right amount of raillery in her voice to dull its cutting edge.

"Thirty-four, but who keeps track?" He turned to look at himself in the mirror and sucked in his stomach. "You're right. I'm what my many admirers call a lean, mean machine."

"Friends can lead you astray. They pamper your ego, tell you what you want to hear. That's destructive, Cloud. It makes you complacent. A true friend would tell you that you're sagging a trifle there around the belly button, that you need to exercise more."

"You are a friend, indeed, my love."

She drifted across the space between them. Clear, sparkling eyes locked with his, she reached down and cupped his penis in her hand.

"I'm a friend in need, Cloud." She smiled crookedly, holding him without movement. "Do you think you have punished me enough? It was only a small temper tantrum."

He looked down at her without speaking, without smiling, feeling the absurd rush of blood drumming eagerly through his veins toward his center in response to her light, warm touch, resenting it in some dark, perverse corner of his brain, this spontaneous, irrepressible response to an almost casual caress. Power, he thought hazily, incalculable power in one small, warm palm. And they know it; they've always known it.

He stared deeply into depthless green eyes and felt his whole body begin to tumesce.

He took her in his arms. "I'm not punishing you," he said huskily. "I've been starving myself. Starvation purifies the body and cleanses the mind, they say. No telling what it'll do for my libido."

She melted against him, nibbled on his chin. "I like your libido just the way it is." Her hand tightened. "Exactly the way it is. Don't screw around with your libido, Cloud."

He picked her up, and she worked her mouth under his jaw to his neck. She bit down hard enough to make him yelp, then laved it gently with a warm tongue as he carried her to the bed.

Later, locked quivering and helpless deep within the consuming, quicksilver sheath, staring into the beseeching eyes, his mouth hot and dry and imploring, he thought fleetingly of power again and decided it all evened out in the end.

She lay nestled against his side, her body pliant and warm, her head tucked into his shoulder. They shared a cigarette, alternating puffs, slowly coming down from their sexual high. She raised her head suddenly and looked around the bedroom.

"You don't have any in here, either, Cloud."

"Any what?" He stretched an arm and stubbed out the cigarette.

"Pictures. You don't have any in the living room or the other bedroom. Not even on your fireplace mantel. Everybody has pictures on their mantel."

"Sure I do. I have three or four pictures in the living room. That watercolor of the deer at the lake, the pointer and the pheasant hunters, not to mention the Monet prints—"

"Not that kind of picture. I mean people. Don't you have any of your ex-wife? Your mother and father and brothers or sisters?" She sat up and crossed her legs Indian-fashion, knees pressing against his ribs.

Cloud brought an arm up behind his head, keeping his gaze trained on the ceiling. He felt a familiar tightening in his stomach, a vague stir of resentment.

"My wife took all the pictures. All we had were a few taken right after our wedding."

"How about family pictures? I have pictures all over my house. My parents, relatives, me."

"I don't have a family," Cloud said, keeping his voice carefully neutral. "My mother left me when I was six months old. With my grandmother. She died a few months later. I was adopted."

"I'm sorry, Cloud. I—"

"No need to be. It could have been worse. I could have been raised in an orphanage somewhere."

"I'm really sorry, Cloud. I didn't know—"

"Of course you didn't." He smiled wryly. "I'm not sensitive about it, if that's what you're worried about, and I got over feeling sorry for myself a long time ago. I was too young to know what was going on, anyway. The second time was a little harder to handle, though."

"The second time?" Her eyes widened, suspiciously moist.

He sighed. "When I was four my adopted parents decided to get a divorce. I guess it was pretty messy. Messy enough that neither of them was awarded custody. I never learned all the details—I guess I didn't want to know—but at any rate I became a ward of the court. I spent the next twelve years in foster homes. Some of them were okay, some not so good. I guess I didn't make things any easier for myself. I was bullheaded, and for a lot of the earlier years I had a gut full of rage I couldn't seem to get a handle on. I had a few fights and took some punishment and moved around a bit. By the time I reached eighteen, the army looked pretty good. The rest is history, as they say."

"You poor thing!"

He caught her arm and pulled her forward across his chest. "I don't want your pity."

She scooted around until she was lying straight on top of his body, hands coming up to cup his face.

"What do you want from me?"

"It'd take at least an hour to think of all the things I expect out of my women."

"Well, while we're waiting, why don't you give me a little hint?" She squirmed slowly, pressing tightly at breast, groin, and thigh.

He sighed again. "It'd make a deep impression if I showed you."

"Yeah, I'll bet."

55

Rafferty tapped the horn on the faded Plymouth and angled in toward the curb where Ron Graves waited impatiently, bouncing on his toes and pacing back and forth between a fireplug and a light pole. He leaned over and peered through the Plymouth's window, then yanked open the door and leaped inside.

"Hey, man, I was expecting a squad car. Thanks a lot."

"I was the closest," Rafferty said, easing back into the flow of traffic. "No sense wasting a working cop's time for taxi service when I'm just cruising around. What happened to your car?"

"Damned carburetor again. It's that blue Pontiac with the dented deck lid. Don't ever let them foist it off on you." He reached out and slapped the dash with a muscular hand. "This oil guzzler's not much better. I had it last week. I wonder when this cheap-assed city's gonna spring for some decent wheels."

"About the same time dogs quit licking their dicks," Rafferty said, turning into Lincoln Center, Trinity Square's second-largest shopping center. He drove a full city block between neatly pocketed cars and parked in front of an Eckerd's drugstore.

"I need to run in here a minute. You need anything?"

"Yeah," Graves said. "You think they got any wheat germ?"

Rafferty snorted and got out; Graves climbed out the other side.

Inside Rafferty bought a package of razor blades, a carton of Snickers candy bars, and a carton of Doublemint chewing gum.

On the way to the register he remembered he was low on beer. He retraced his steps and picked up a six-pack of Coors.

Graves was waiting empty-handed at the cashier's desk.

"No wheat germ?" Rafferty asked, stacking his purchases on the counter.

Graves shook his head dumbly, staring at the cashier, a slightly shell-shocked expression on his blunt features.

Rafferty followed his gaze. She was something to see, he agreed silently, a slender, sturdy body, well-rounded and firm-buttocked, a pretty-heart-shaped face surrounded by a glossy shifting mass of auburn hair. Arrowstone's type, he thought immediately, and glanced back at Ron Graves.

Graves was grinning; a silly grin, Rafferty thought, puerile and lascivious, but not unexpected and in its own way a compliment of sorts to the lovely young thing now watching him with an odd look on her face. He suddenly realized she had spoken.

"I'm sorry, how much is it? I was woolgathering, I guess."

She repeated the amount and laughed. "I haven't heard anyone say that in years. Woolgathering. My granddad used to say it all the time."

Rafferty gave her a ten-dollar bill. "Can't be all that many years. You can't be over . . . what? Nineteen?"

She nodded brightly. "Right on." She counted out his change, pressing the money into his hand, brushing his fingers with soft-warm skin. She lifted clear hazel eyes, her face slightly flushed. "Everybody was nineteen once," she said. "It isn't a permanent affliction."

Graves guffawed in Rafferty's ear, his response disproportionate to the humor in the girl's statement. "Some affliction! Old Rafferty'd give a lot to be nineteen again, wouldn't you, buddy?" He slapped Rafferty on the back, blithely ignoring the fact they were almost exactly the same age. He casually opened his jacket to give the girl a better view of his wide chest and bulging pectorals inadequately covered with a black T-shirt.

The girl brought her smile back to Rafferty. "Age is only important in wine and racehorses," she said, deepening the smile, bringing dimples to cheeks glowing with the healthy vitality of youth, flawless skin with the merest tracery of freckles across a short, straight nose.

Rafferty stared at her for a moment, as if making up his mind about something. He leaned forward and read the nametag pinned about her left breast.

"Lolita," she said, the smile going for broke, almost dazzling in its brilliance.

"Lolita," Rafferty echoed solemnly. "A lovely name. Lolita, I don't want to frighten you any more than you probably already are . . . but, the fact is, you are exactly the type our Trinity Square killer is looking for."

Her smile died a sudden, painful death. She stared at him, speechless, eyes spreading wide, mouth parting as if she might scream.

"We're police officers," Rafferty said hurriedly, slipping the leather case out of his jacket pocket and showing her the badge. "We're warning everyone like . . . well, everyone with red hair in your age bracket. Well, we should be, and I am you."

Surprisingly, she smiled again. "Thank you. I know about it, of course and, believe me, I'm careful. I get off at four-thirty and I have plenty of time to get home before dark." She stopped and dimpled up again. "I don't have to worry at home. My boyfriend is . . ." She hesitated and looked at Graves. "He's a weightlifter like you."

Rafferty could almost see Graves preening behind his shoulder. He picked up his bag of purchases and nodded, his dark face brightening as he smiled for the first time.

"Just keep on being careful, okay?"

"I will," she said. "And thank you very much. Have a very nice day."

Cloud and Simple spent part of the next few days working on the Sammy Keeler murder, primarily searching for Julio Mendosa. The Arrowstone killings were sitting on high center and, while neither man would have admitted it, they were doing busywork waiting for another one. Cloud expected little from Julio Mendosa, even if they found him. A small-time con man, part-time pusher and pimp, he had been in and out of jail since he was sixteen and was streetwise enough to know that an informer's life was a perilous one and that the only safe time to talk to cops was when they were selling tickets to the policemen's benefit raffle.

By Thursday afternoon, they decided the sidewalk telegraph had preceded them and that Julio had departed for parts un-known. They located his erstwhile place of residence, an evil-smelling, cramped apartment in an old, decrepit apartment building a half-block off Northcross Street.

The junkie prostitute he had been living with, and off of, thought he had been gone for a couple of days, but wasn't sure and good riddance; he wasn't anything but a no-good shiftless bum, anyway. He never balled her anymore and beat her up a lot because she wasn't bringing home more money. She hoped the sorry "sumbitch" never came back.

She told them she was only thirty and probably looked thirty-two or three and that she had to turn three tricks a day just to keep straight and that was great, man, 'cause when that bastard was here she'd had to turn six or seven before he'd dole out even a measly little old dime bag, and, hell, a dime bag with her habit was like a sip of Ripple to a fuckin' alcoholic, and if they were so inclined, man, she'd give them a two-for-the-price-of-one job, no hassle and no fuss and any little old way they wanted it, man.

Rosie told her they'd think about it and catch her later. She was nodding happily when they left, and Rosie bet Cloud a dollar they could go back five minutes later and she wouldn't remember them.

Cloud wouldn't take the bet.

By Friday, Cloud was nervous, irritable and jumpy, a vague, inexplicable sense of helplessness gnawing relentlessly at his insides. He couldn't shake the feeling that he was missing something, some essential ingredient, something indefinable prowling the periphery of his mind, elusive and taunting, nudging and probing for access. Despondent to the point of acute depression, he swung from the morose belief that Arrowstone had fled, to the firm, despairing conviction that he hadn't, that he was playing a cat-and-mouse game, allowing the pressure to build. Each time the phone rang, he expected Clark Gable or Humphrey Bogart, another promise, another death.

56

"Do you realize," Arrowstone said, "that you're the only person in this whole wide world I can talk to? I mean, really talk to, tell things, you know, the things that matter." He lay back across the bed and crossed his legs at the ankles.

"Sure," said Spencer Price. "You think it's any different with me? Nobody else understands. Oh, I suppose there are others like us. I'm sure of it. But how does one go about reaching them? Without being locked up in a jail or institution, I mean. Even then, ninety-nine percent are just crazies, compulsive psychotics who do terrible things and have no idea why."

"Weird," Arrowstone agreed. "They deserve to be locked up."

"I, uh, was wondering. You've been pretty quiet lately. Not letting all the hoopla get to you, are you?"

"Oh, no, indeedy. I find it terribly exciting. If you'll look at my record, you'll find that I often go quite some time between times. It varies. Sometimes I'll do one a week for several weeks, then none at all for simply months. The fact is, I've been looking around, and I haven't found anything that's up to my usual standards."

"I know of one," Spencer said, chuckling. "But I think I'll keep her for myself, if you don't mind."

"Stingy, stingy. What if I should find her and get to her first?"

"You'll have to hurry," Spencer said, his voice suddenly

thicker, a liquid resonance that made Arrowstone shiver. "I think I'll do her . . . maybe tonight."

"Really?" Arrowstone's breath caught, images spinning through his head, sweet mind pictures that brought a fever flush to his skin, a surging torrent of blood to his loins. He reached down and held himself tightly. "Really? Tonight? How—what are you going to do to her?"

"You really want me to tell you? I thought you didn't like the violent stuff."

Arrowstone laughed huskily, his hand around the receiver suddenly hot and damp. "I didn't say I didn't like it. I said I didn't do it—not very often. And I didn't sign my name when I did." He unzipped his pants and began squirming out of them. "Tell me," he said urgently, his tone low, rough, furry.

Spencer chuckled. "All right, if you insist." His voice tightened, but neither man noticed nor appreciated the incongruity of his words spoken in the nasal tones of Jack Benny. "First I'm going to strip her down . . ."

And it was still Jack Benny's querulous voice on the phone the next morning, a nerve-shattering call that yanked Arrowstone out of bed at dawn. He wrenched the receiver out of the cradle before it could ring a second time and pressed it against his ear, instantly awake.

"Hello, Julian."

"Spencer . . . hello." He sucked in his breath, his blood suddenly racing. "Did you do it?"

Spencer Price laughed. "Of course I did it." He paused, chuckling. "And, boy, am I tired." The chuckle exploded into laughter.

Arrowstone joined him, his voice shaky with excitement. "How—how was it? Tell me all about it."

"Later, Julian. I'll call you later and give you every little detail. But first, I want you to do something for me. Remember, I told you I might need your help."

"What?" Arrowstone asked cautiously, a nervous tremor rippling across the top of his scalp, his lips suddenly coated with dryness. "I don't want to do anything that might be . . ." His voice trailed off.

"Dangerous?" Jack Benny's voice managed to be both derisive and menacing at the same time. "Just being alive is dangerous, Julian. Not helping your friends is even more so."

"I don't want to do anything . . . violent or gross."

"Of course," Price said, his voice dripping with sarcasm. "I wouldn't want to offend your tender sensibilities. Now listen to me, you jerkoff. I'm asking you to do me a small, simple favor. Are you going to do it or not?" The sarcasm had dissolved into menace.

"I'll try . . . I'll do my best."

"It's simple, Julian, just like I said. I've got the Echofone all set, and all you have to do is call Cloud and read some lines. You think you can handle that?"

"Of course. I'm not stupid. I just didn't want—"

"Look, friend, you do this for me and later, next week, we'll get together and really have a good long talk. I want to know all about you, and I'll tell you all about myself. Does that sound okay?"

"Oh, yes. I'd like that very much."

"Okay. Here's the address: 1410 Beechnut Lane, Apartment C. You can go in the back way and nobody will see you. The door will be unlocked. I'll leave instructions and what you are to say to Cloud. Don't let him lead you astray. Be natural, don't force it. Just tell him exactly what I'll have written down, and then get off the line. Okay?"

"What's it all about?"

"Never mind. I'll explain it all to you later."

"Who does the apartment belong to?"

"What difference—okay, it's mine, all right? It's just a small place I keep for . . . for other things."

"I think I should know—"

"Dammit, Julian, I said later! Now, are you going to do it or not?"

"I didn't mean—of course I'll help you, any way I can."

"Good, I thought you would." The line went dead.

57

Saturday morning, Ward Callum wandered into the Homicide squad room while Cloud and Rosie were going over the week's reports on hapless males who had in one way or another decided to change their appearance. From shaving off beards and moustaches to buying a new suit, the reports kept coming in. A good many were obviously inspired by overzealousness or vindictiveness and could be discarded; the others had to be checked.

"Any way I can help?" Callum wanted to know.

"Don't think so," Cloud said. "We're about to wrap it up. I want to get out of here before something else comes up."

Callum nodded and turned to Rosie. "I want to thank you again for that dinner the other night, man. It was great. First home-cooked meal I've had in a long time. That pretty wife of yours knows how to set a table."

Rosie grinned and rifled the last stack of reports. "She gets plenty of practice. I ain't much on eating out. Too much hassle."

"Too much money, you mean," Cloud said. He looked at Callum. "Rosie's a close man with a buck. He's got the second dollar he ever earned. The first one went to buy a piggy bank."

"I ain't stingy," Rosie protested. "I'm just what you'd call a rigid conservative."

"He sets a heavy table," Callum said.

Rosie turned to look at Cloud, his eyes gleaming. "I'll have to admit, my old lady is a good cook, but you ain't had nothing till you've tasted old Ben's charcoaled steaks with baked potato

and mangled salad with them little endives and croutons and that
special sauce of his. How about it, Ben? Old Ward here's gonna
ruin his stomach eating all that Tex-Mex stuff and greasy fatbur-
gers.''

Ward looked embarrassed. "Oh, no, I couldn't impose—"

"As a matter of fact," Cloud said, stifling an urge to kick
Rosie's big ass, "I've been meaning to ask you over for dinner
some night. How about . . . oh, say next Tuesday? Give my
maid a chance to get in some supplies."

"Maid, my ass," Rosie growled. "You better not let Amy
hear you say that."

"I accept with pleasure," Collum said, smiling. "If you're
sure your . . . uh, maid won't mind."

"She'll be tickled. She's a good cook, but she says I don't
appreciate it. Give her a chance to show off a little."

"She don't need to show off a whole hell of a lot," Rosie
said. I'd let her sit around on my mantel just as a conversation
piece."

Callum laughed, obviously pleased with the invitation. "She
sounds like a lovely woman. What's her favorite flower, Ben?"

Cloud looked at him blankly. "By God, would you believe I
don't know?"

"I'd believe it," Rosie said, chortling. "You mean a big
spender like you don't bring her flowers? I buy my wife a bouquet every anniversary."

"Roses are always good," Callum said. "I'll bring some roses
and a nice bottle of wine. Red or white?"

"Probably be having steak, but don't worry about wine. I
think we have—" He broke off as the phone began ringing. He
looked at Rosie and grimaced. "We hung around too long.
Probably Eli wanting an update."

"Don't answer it," Rosie said. "We'll sneak out the back
way."

"Homicide," Cloud said cautiously, lowering his voice to a
deep gruff bass.

"Ben? You sound funny."

"Hi," he said in his normal voice, lifting an arm to return
Callum's wave as he went out the door. "I was all prepared to
say I was the janitor if it had been someone I didn't want to talk
to."

Amy laughed. "Having a bad morning? You're not planning

n working all day, are you?'' There was a note of petulance in
er voice.

"Why? What did you have in mind?''

"Well, you said you wouldn't be very long, and you did prom-
se to help me hang the new kitchen curtains.''

Cloud sighed. "Yeah, I did, didn't I?''

Amy laughed. "Yes, you did. Right before I let you do all
ose strange things last night.''

"This is blackmail. That's a serious crime in Texas. I could
aul your sweet little ass up before a judge for that. On second
ought, I might just kiss it and let it go at that.'' He grinned
s Rosie turned and gave him a slant-eyed look, his lip curling
mock-disgust.

"We'll see,'' she murmured. "But first, the curtains.''

"Okay, give me another hour. If nothing jumps out of the
oodwork, I'll see you then.''

"Okay, honey,'' she said softly, then after a small hesitation,
I love you.'' She hung up.

Cloud lowered the receiver gently, shaken by a sudden swirl
f unbidden emotion.

There it was, the three words they had been carefully avoid-
g, spoken clearly and simply as if she had been saying them
him for years. He reached for a cigarette. He wasn't at all
ure he was ready for that.

He bent his head over the papers on his desk, aware that Rosie
ad turned in her chair and was watching him again. He pre-
ended absorption in the report on top of the stack, and Rosie
urned back. He was still staring sightlessly at the same report
irty minutes later when the phone rang again.

He picked it up automatically, then grimaced as Rosie looked
t him and grinned.

"Lieutenant Cloud.''

"Well, doggone, if it ain't my favorite policeman,'' Jim Na-
ors said shrilly.

Cloud motioned to Rosie, signaled for a trace, then switched
n the speaker. "Well, I'd about given up on you. I thought
aybe you were out on the coast by now.'' He heard a tiny click
s the recording equipment came on and glanced at Rosie's broad
ack hunched over the other phone.

"Well, golleeee, I couldn't run off and leave my best friend,
ow could I? Just think how dull it'd be around here without
ne. Don't you sometimes wonder what you used to do with your

time? Come on, 'fess up. Isn't your blood racing a bit right now?''

Cloud forced a chuckle. ''Yeah, you really brighten my day.''

''Do I detect a note of sarcasm there amongst the desperation Lieutenant Cloud?'' A different voice, and for a moment Cloud couldn't place it.

''Not desperation, friend. Your days are numbered.''

''Oh, yes, I seem to recall your promise to the populace last week. A very stirring speech, sir. I enjoyed it tremendously. As a matter of fact, I have gone to great lengths to compose my rebuttal.'' Sonorous rolling tones, a slightly harsh resonance—Richard Burton—suave, menacing, reverberating throughout the room.

''What do you mean? Are you going on TV, Arrowstone?''

A harsh, grating laugh, and then silence.

Cloud felt a creeping chill, a spasm of fear rippling in his stomach, sweeping upward into his chest, scorching his throat. He could see Rosie's graven face staring at him over the phone.

''Fe, Fi, Fo, Fum, I smell the blood of a redheaded one!'' The harsh laugh again, and then: ''My rebuttal, my dear Lieutenant Cloud, lies in state at the junction of Dalworth Drive and Paris Lane. If she appears a bit, ah, shopworn, the dear, sweet thing had a hard night. Please excuse her—ah, shall we say slovenly appearance.''

''I'll kill you, you son of a bitch!'' Cloud was vaguely aware that he was on his feet, right hand clenched into a fist, pounding the desk lightly with a curious, rhythmic cadence. Rosie was shaking his head wildly, holding up one finger.

''Time's up for this time, boys and girls,'' Mister Rogers said, and the line went dead.

58

The weekend went steadily downhill for Benjamin Cloud. Feeling unaccountably aloof, an almost frightening sense of detachment, he supervised the removal of the mutilated dead girl and the subsequent search of the weed-and brush-infested lot where she had been deposited. He joined in the inch-by-inch survey of the surrounding area, feeling an eviscerating hopelessness, his mind stalked by long, dark shadows of guilt.

Arrowstone had called the girl's death his rebuttal, and while his reasoning mind told him that his scathing indictment of the killer had meant little, his emotions were not prepared to accept such logical exonerations; the fact was, he felt responsible for her murder, and he wasn't sure he could handle that.

Based on the few factors at his immediate disposal, rigor mortis and lividity, the M.E. estimated time of death at somewhere between seven and ten Friday evening.

Dismally Cloud tried to remember what he had been doing during that time, recalled with a small pang of dismay that he and Amy had ended the evening making love. The thought served only to increase his feeling of guilt.

Saturday afternoon he stoically endured a ten-minute harangue from Patrick Donleavy in front of Trinity Square's entire contingent of detectives. Red-faced and hoarse-voiced, the squat chief of police smashed meaty hands on his mahogany desk and demanded answers, demanded to know how one man, a goddamned nut at that, could paralyze the police force of an entire city, stalk undetected among its citizens, pick his victims with great care and exactitude, and cut them out of the herd without so much as a ripple or a cry of protest. He addressed his remarks to the room at large, but everyone understood that he was speaking directly to the small Homicide Division.

He hurled nameless threats and issued ultimatums, and when it was over the detectives filed silently out into the corridor, Cloud, Rosie, and Graves forming a tight-lipped, taut-faced triad forcing its way through the small group of uneasy men. Rafferty caught up with them before they had gone five paces, fell in step beside Cloud.

"That asshole," he said absently, unwrapping a package of spearmint gum.

"Yeah," Rosie growled, "grade-A first-class."

"Fat-assed, potbellied asshole," Graves amended, his muscles stretching, popping into bold relief through the thin fabric of the dark T-shirt. "You ever see such a sloppy looking bastard?"

Cloud was silent until they turned into the small Homicide Office. He dropped wearily into his chair and lit a cigarette. He looked through the smoke at the three men arrayed in front of him.

"That grade-A, first-class, potbellied, fat-assed asshole is right," he said. "We're not doing our job. If we were, we'd have the scummy son of a bitch behind bars—or dead."

Rosie looked offended. "I've been puttin' in twelve, fourteen hours a day, Ben. Same for you and Ron. What the hell else can we do? They couldn't catch him in Chicago with Ward Callum and a task force of fifty men looking for him. They only caught him in New York because he got careless and they got lucky. Jesus Christ! We're only three men here, with a little help now and then when they can spare it. Sure, we're a small town compared to them places, but eighty-thousand people is still a lot. And they're coming and going all the time. For all we know, he may live in Dallas or Fort Worth or anyplace in between. Maybe he only comes to Trinity Square to get his victims. Shit, he could live as far away as Waco or San Antonio—or Oklahoma City, for that matter. And we got three goddamned men full-time. We didn't deserve that ass-burning from Donleavy, and you damn well know it!" The big man's face was pale pink, the jaw firmly squared. He looked ready to fight a gorilla if somebody would hold his coat.

"Amen," Ron Graves said.

Cloud looked up and smiled faintly. "You two not happy in your chosen profession?"

Rafferty straddled a straight-backed visitor's chair and folded his arms across the top. "Everybody knows you guys are doing everything that can be done. Including Donleavy. He's catching hell, and he's the kind of guy who had to pass it on. Don't sweat it."

"Donleavy doesn't bother me," Cloud said. "Not really. He's right. But that doesn't stop the murders."

"Jake," Graves said. He got up from his desk and came around in front of Rafferty. "This last one. Do you know who she is?" He held a sheet of paper in his hand, his boyish face pale.

Rafferty shook his head. "I didn't know you had her identified."

Graves nodded. "We have. Her last name is Barnes." He paused and wet his lips. "Do you remember the other day in the drugstore? The redheaded girl?"

Rafferty stared up at him, his eyes narrowing, then springing wide. "Lolita? Jesus Christ, you don't mean Lolita?" His dark eyes filled with horror, face slowly blanching.

Graves nodded again, grimly. "Yes."

"Jesus Christ," Rafferty said hollowly.

"You guys know her?" Rosie asked. He glowered at Graves. "You didn't say you knew her," he said accusingly.

"I didn't . . . I mean, it didn't ring a bell until I just noticed that she worked at Eckerd's drugstore. Lolita. It has to be. There couldn't be two Lolitas working at Eckerd's, not with that color hair, anyhow." He turned to Rosie then looked at Cloud. "Remember, I told you guys about it?"

"I warned her," Rafferty said harshly. "Goddammit, I warned her."

"Yeah, you did," Graves said, looking down at the paper in his hands. "She said she was careful, that she had a boyfriend—" He broke off and looked at Rosie. "You talked to her boyfriend. Any chance that he—?"

"Who knows?" Rosie snarled. "He talked clean, looked clean, had an alibi a foot thick. He broke down when he saw her, all tore up like . . . like . . ." His voice failed him, gained strength. "But who knows, maybe the son of a bitch did it himself."

"Were the stones there?" Rafferty asked quietly.

Cloud sighed. "They were there. The boyfriend didn't kill her. It was Arrowstone."

"I don't believe it!" The voice came from the doorway, harsh and emphatic. Ward Callum stood a few feet inside the room, watching them calmly. He advanced to the front of Rosie's desk, leaned against it, and lit an unfiltered cigarette. He looked at each man in turn, his face pale, a faint hint of belligerence in the set of his mouth.

"It's not his style," he said, blowing smoke, his voice now soft and inflectionless. "He's a methodical, ritualistic killer. If his ritual isn't done right, it means nothing to him."

"How come you know so damned much?" Graves said waspishly, his bronzed face suddenly the color of ashes. "Who the hell are you, anyhow? You come in here out of nowhere telling us how to run our damned business. If I remember, you didn't do so hot catching him up there in Chicago—"

"Take it easy, Ron," Rosie said, dropping a hand on the stocky man's shoulder. "He's only trying to help, man."

Graves breathed deeply, massive pectorals cleanly etched through the tight shirt, the burst of anger bleeding into the mass of tensed muscle. He moved away from Rosie's hand, dropped the homicide report on his desk, and stalked out of the room.

"Sorry," Callum said, speaking into the awkward silence following the muscular detective's departure. "I should keep my opinions to myself."

Cloud shook his head. "He's just jumpy. We all are. The difference with Ron is he has to get rid of his tension every so often. He doesn't handle frustration well."

"Who does?" Rosie rumbled. "He didn't mean any of that shit, Ward. He's uptight and he dumped on you because you were handy."

"Of course, I understand. Nevertheless, he's quite right. I should keep my opinions to myself unless asked."

"No, you shouldn't," Cloud said. "You're here to help us catch him. You know him better than any man alive. So, why do you think he didn't kill the Barnes girl?"

Callum grimaced apologetically. "I keep saying this as if I could prove it, but he just doesn't savage his victims the way the Barnes girl was savaged. From the beginning his killings have had a certain . . . delicacy, a sort of flair that this one didn't have. I felt the same way after the Cooper killing, if you'll remember.''

"How do you account for the stones?" Cloud asked.

Callum winced again. "I know. That's a puzzler."

Rafferty pushed up from the chair, his face bleak. "I have to disagree with you, Ward," he said. "Arrowstone's a psycho. As such, he's unstable, erratic. This ritual you keep talking about. We don't know what it is. Maybe the Cooper girl and Lolita Barnes didn't go along with him, fought back, tried to escape, hell, anything could have happened to set him off. Once he started, there'd be no real reason to hold back. With his fantasy destroyed, he'd be in a dangerous, explosive mood. From what I've learned about it, bloodlust feeds on itself, escalates into a kind of mindless frenzy." He shook his head and dropped his wad of chewing gum into Rosie's wastebasket. "Ritual or no ritual, I don't see how it could be anyone but Arrowstone."

"I'll buy that," Rosie snarled. "The mother found out he liked something different when he killed Cooper, and he decided he'd do it again with Barnes."

Cloud pushed back from his desk and rose abruptly to his feet. "I don't know. The facts in this case just don't add up. Maybe Jake and Rosie are right somehow, Ward. It doesn't make much sense, otherwise." He walked around the desk and stood smiling down at the Chicago cop. "By the way, Amy has a staff meeting Tuesday evening. Okay if we make the dinner Monday instead?"

"Sure. You bet. Still seven o'clock?"

"Around there. Few minutes either way won't make much difference. We won't be eating until seven-thirty or thereabouts. I'll probably be home by seven. Donleavy's having his monthly ass-chewing session with all us brass at six. I haven't got much left, so it shouldn't take more than half an hour. If you make it before I do, go on in and have a beer with Amy. Maybe you can give her some pointers on how to make a good salad."

"Be careful, man," Rafferty advised solemnly. "Old Ben here's a jealous bastard. Last man tried to cut in on him ended up losing his cojones."

Callum looked startled.

Cloud shook his head and laughed. "Just a little Texas humor there, Ward."

"What's cojones?" Callum asked, then reddened as the three men laughed.

"Two-thirds of your three-piece set," Rosie said.

"I'll be there, seven sharp," Callum promised, as if Rosie hadn't spoken.

Cloud lit a cigarette and moved toward the door, walking flat-footed, arms dangling limply, realizing suddenly that he was unutterably weary. "I'll see you guys," he said.

"Get some rest," Rosie advised.

"Take it easy, man," Rafferty said. "I'll see you when I get back."

Cloud stopped. "Get back? Where you going?"

"Taking a week's vacation. Probably hang around my lake place. Sit on my duff and drink beer and contemplate the dubious destiny of mankind."

Cloud laughed and lifted a hand. "Bring me a mess of crappie."

He found his car and drove toward home through a day that had gone sour: muggy and dark and dripping. He turned on his windshield wipers at the first red light and watched them track sluggishly across the glass. He turned on his radio and tried to find something besides rock or country-western. He turned it off again. He drove through the intersection and the rest of the way home wondering if thirty-four was too old to start another career.

59

Sunday afternoon Cloud watched the stalwart jocks of Philadelphia take a double drubbing, alternating between the fifth game of the World Series featuring the Orioles and the Phillies and the Cowboy–Eagles game at Texas Stadium in Irving, Texas.

Amy, bored and restless, resentful of his absorption in this dual-headed monster of Sunday-afternoon sports, prowled the condo apartment sulkily, tried unsuccessfully to seduce him, then tight-jawed and stormy-eyed, dressed in fetching red-and-white running togs, hurled herself around and around the perimeter of the square block of pin oak woods.

Sighing, Cloud changed seats, positioned himself near the large front window where he could catch occasional glimpses of her slender figure flying through the trees and still maintain a watchful eye on both games by use of the remote control.

From his vantage point, Spencer Price watched Amy go tripping lightly across the street, the brightly colored, voluminous sweat shirt and pants masking the perfection of the lithe, slender body. Her hair, caught behind her head in a flaming ponytail, seemed to sparkle with a million tiny lights in the brilliant October sunlight.

His breath snagged in his throat; his heart began to pound. Moving away from him, her features were hidden, but he could imagine their crisp, clean loveliness, the luscious, pouting mouth, the darkly shadowed eyes that had pierced his soul, warm and bright and promising.

He watched her flash between the trees, pictured her face sweetly flushed and fearfully acquiescent, and felt a ballooning joy in his guts, a winnowing thrill of anticipation that made him shiver, brought a hot, thick gush of blood to his center, a wild, coursing energy that threatened to consume him like a moth fluttering above an open flame. He gasped with the force of it, gripped himself fiercely with both hands, then gasped again and surrendered to the exquisite sensations as his body took control, emptying his mind even as it emptied his loins.

He sagged limply, his shoulders slumping as though overcome by an intolerable gravitational force. He scanned the woods looking for a flash of red, his eyes blank and lackluster.

He found her again, followed her progress almost indifferently.

Soon. Soon she would be his in the only way that mattered. Then she would understand.

He licked dry lips and wondered if he could wait.

Yes. Only a little while more. He could wait. He had no choice.

Amy came back winded and sweaty, walked stiff-legged through the living room without once looking Cloud's way. He heard her get into the shower and, when it became eminently clear that the Orioles had taken the pennant, that the Cowboys were neatly plucking the Eagles' tail feathers, he shut off the TV and went into the bathroom.

He caught her coming out of the shower, pink and damp and glowing from a brisk rubdown with an oversized towel. She ignored him, snapping off the shower cap, fluffing her hair with quick, sure strokes of her fingers, shaking her head with a totally feminine gesture that somehow excited him.

He came up behind her, cupped her breasts, and kissed her neck.

"The damn ball game's over, I suppose," she said coldly, standing stiffly motionless, yet not resisting.

"No, not completely, but there isn't much doubt about the outcome."

"And now His Majesty deigns to notice me when there's nothing better to do."

He turned her, pressed her against the wall beside the shower

door. "His Majesty noticed you all along; it was damned hard
not to, you were making so much noise. And there's never anything better to do, it's just that we can't do it all the time—no,
I'll amend that: maybe you can, but I can't. In any given span
of time, I have only so many times at bat. I won't waste them
simply because one or both of us are bored. It's too much like
cheating, somehow."

She lifted her head to look up at him, an ironic tilt to her
meticulously arched eyebrows. She freed her hands and touched
his cheeks. "I like your face, Cloud. It's open; it doesn't hide
anything. You're like a little boy in that respect. You don't look
tough enough to be a cop, and yet they tell me you're a good
one. How come it hasn't touched you like all the others? How
come you can be the hard, tough cop they say you are, and still
be like a little boy with me?"

His hands tightened on her waist; he pressed her against the
wall. "We're all little boys when it comes to this." He chuckled,
tried to give his words humor they didn't have.

"Is this all I am to you?"

He looked into her depthless green eyes, studied her solemn
face. Finally, he said, "No, this isn't all you are to me."

It was her turn to try for humor, "Well, would His Majesty
care to elaborate?"

He stalled for time by kissing her, moving his hands up to
rest lightly on her shoulders, his thumbs caressing her neck,
feeling the strong, steady surge of her life force passing beneath
his hands. He broke the kiss and picked her up in his arms.

"Not yet," he whispered, their faces only inches apart. He
kissed her again, lightly.

"But soon," he promised, and carried her into the bedroom.

Later, still restless, he called Rafferty on the off chance the
detective hadn't left on his vacation.

He was still at his apartment. Cloud invited him over to eat,
and later in the evening they grilled hamburgers out on his mi-
nuscule patio.

But the evening couldn't seem to get off the ground. Amy was
subdued, glowing but indolent, signs that Cloud had come to
recognize as her normal reaction to heavy-duty lovemaking. He
smiled a little, inwardly, wondering what Rafferty thought.

But Rafferty was keeping his own counsel, reserved, friendly,
responding to Cloud's efforts at conversation, but contributing

little on his own. As a result, Cloud found himself talking too much, ranging far and wide for subjects that might prick the interest of his two lackadaisical companions. With a notable lack of success.

He wasn't at all disappointed when Rafferty made an early departure, explaining that he wanted to get an early start for the lake.

He was disappointed, but not surprised, when Amy went to bed soon after, explaining coyly that she needed a lot of sleep to regenerate the energy lost earlier in the day.

Cloud sighed, opened a bottle of Coors, and settled in front of the TV to wait for the ten o'clock news.

Fifteen minutes later, when the camera zoomed in on the saucy-faced newscaster, he was sound asleep.

60

Capt. Eli Summers watched cynically as the detectives and clerks filed desultorily into the open squad room outside his office window. Hollow-eyed and dispirited at the prospects of another long week ahead, they gripped plastic cups filled with hot-steaming bile from the coffee machines in the corridor, grouped in small listless knots grousing, no doubt, about their solitary day off, delaying the inevitable moment of truth with obscene gibes and filthy jokes.

His lips curled. He had been at his desk for over an hour, had already completed the equivalent of a full day's paper work for any one of the bumbling, inept slobs he commanded.

But that was as it should be, he thought. That was why he was in here and they were out there.

Beefy, slovenly louts, most of them, with cop written all over their lined faces and hanging bellies. No wonder they couldn't get anything done. Who could respect a man like that? Self-esteem was important. He understood that. If you didn't respect yourself, how could you expect respect from others?

He rolled forward and picked up the file folder on Lolita Barnes. He opened it and shuffled slowly through a stack of field interrogation reports until he came to the crime-scene photos. Lips pursed in a soundless whistle, he studied each one carefully, his mind recording with infinite clarity the most minute details of the savage brutality that had been visited on the hapless girl.

A shiver rippled deep within him, snaked upward through his diaphragm, into his throat, brought hot, thick dryness to his mouth. He swallowed audibly, stacked the pictures, and began dealing them again, face up, stringing them across his desk like the opening run in some macabre game of solitaire.

Ron Graves had come in early, also. He spent twenty minutes in the dispatch room listening to sleepy, waspish Cricket Bloom complain while he laboriously composed a message. He watched while her flying fingers sent his words across the country, then walked down the long corridor toward the Homicide Office wondering if he might not be making an ass out of himself. It wouldn't be the first time, he thought ruefully.

When he reached his desk, it was still ten minutes before eight, and he settled into his swivel chair and propped booted feet on one corner of his littered desk.

Best that he keep it to himself, he decided. Cloud would give him one of his friendly, sympathetic grins, and Rosie would probably snicker behind a ham-sized hand, then laugh unmercifully when he ended up with shit on his boots. And he would, of course. He was ninety-nine percent sure of that. It was a wild-assed idea in the first place, spawned of dislike and a fluttery feeling in his guts when he looked into the quiet eyes. A subtle shifting, stirring, inside him that he had finally interpreted as a kind of atavistic fear. He consciously feared no man or no thing, and it was that as much as anything that had made up his mind. He would conquer this fear—if that was what it was—as he had all the others: by meeting it head-on, quelling it with sheer, brute strength and iron will.

At eight-thirty he gave up on Rosie and Cloud and walked out into the moldy day. A true Blue Monday, it was gray and dripping, oppressive; people scurried, shoulders hunched, their eyes downcast as if the fault were theirs alone.

He strode confidently among them, upright and bouncing on his toes; shoulders squared, muscles swollen, as haughty and serene as a young messiah taking credit for the world.

61

Louis Wexell leaned a bulky shoulder against the doorjamb at the rear entrance to Wexell's Fine Meats and shook his head dolefully, his heavy, square face despondent.

"I haven't thought of anything else since I talked to you," he said to Rosie Simple, taking off the three-cornered paper hat and tucking it behind the bib of his white, bloodstained coveralls. He shoved a heavily corded hand through the neck opening of a thick-woven wool sweater and produced a package of Kents and a disposable butane lighter. He had small, round blue eyes and a dense thatch of blue-black hair cropped close to his skull. He lit the cigarette and turned his head to expel the smoke. "I'd have called you if I had," he went on quietly.

Rosie nodded. "I know, but sometimes after a guy has some time to think, he recalls little things, things that might not have seemed important even now that you've had time to think. Sometimes it's the little things that mean the most, Mr. Wexell."

"The last week or so," Cloud said, "did she mention anything out of the ordinary about where she worked? Some guy maybe, some stranger who seemed overly friendly, suddenly started coming in every day, someone who paid her more attention than normal, who seemed to be watching her?"

Wexell shook his head somberly. "Everybody—every guy watched Lolly. She was . . . something special." He shook his head again. "No, she never mentioned . . . Well, there was this one thing she thought was funny . . . well, kinda' of, I guess, but nice. These two cops. They were, you know, kinda' flirting with her. One of them warned about . . . about this nut . . . this goddamned nut who killed her." He took a deep breath and turned away for a moment. "She . . . she thought one of them, one of the cops, looked at her in a funny way. She laughed about it, but I think it bothered her in a way."

Rosie snorted. "That would be Graves. He looks at all women like they were some kinda' pretty little toy he'd like to tinker with."

Wexell smiled faintly. "I think she used the word leer," he said.

"Was there anything else? Someone hanging around the area of your apartment? Some stranger she saw more than once—anywhere?"

"Not that she mentioned. And I think she would have. She was pretty frightened by all this . . . all this stuff that was happening." He puffed furiously on the cigarette, the small eyes shimmering with moisture.

"Old boyfriends," Cloud persisted. "Anyone upset by her dating you? Any animosity, threats that you know about?"

"No. I gave you the name of the only boyfriend I knew about. That guy that went to school with her." He glanced at Rosie. "You remember?"

Rosie nodded. "He's living in L.A."

Wexell flipped the cigarette out into the alley. "I'm sorry. I wish to hell I could help you, give you something. I wish to hell I could have five minutes with the son of a bitch who killed her." His hands clenched into huge, knobby balls. "Not even that much—two minutes, one!" The color had drained out of his deeply tanned face, leaving a faintly yellowish tinge. Pain rolled off his thick, rigid body in palpable waves, his face contorting as if he might cry. He whirled abruptly and went inside the building.

The two detectives lingered under the overhang while Cloud finished his cigarette, disturbed and frustrated by still another fruitless interview, another dead end in the hopeless maze that Julian Arrowstone left in his wake.

Cloud flipped his cigarette butt after Wexell's and turned up his coat collar against the annoying drizzle. They walked to their car in silence.

"This is not the way to catch him," Cloud said morosely as Rosie pulled into the slow-moving traffic.

"You're goddamned right," Rosie said, suddenly snarling, his voice thick with savage rage. "And you know something else? We won't catch him. The son of a bitch will go on killing until he's had his goddamned fill. And there's not one damned thing we can do to stop him!" He faced straight ahead, his broad mouth a thin, compressed line, hands fisted on the wheel, knuckles gleaming like smooth white stones.

Cloud said nothing. He lit another cigarette, and they rode in silence through the rain-darkened streets. Cloud cracked a window to let out the smoke. He watched people scurrying, his thoughts troubled, guilt stalking his mind like wolves around a campfire.

He threw the butt out the window and settled back, spoke without looking at his compassion, spoke without conviction.

"You're wrong, Rosie. Jesus, I hope you're wrong."

By one o'clock in the afternoon the drizzle had become a downpour, and Cloud stuck close to his office, ostensibly to sift once again through their dishearteningly scanty hoard of physical evidence, yet knowing deep down inside that he was hoping Arrowstone would call again. Firmly convinced that the telephone was their only concrete link with the elusive killer, Cloud was determined he would find some way, find something to say that would keep him on the line those last few precious seconds needed to complete the trace. Twice they had been close, but he had slipped away. Knowing the general area would slice a few additional seconds from the time, and a few more words wrung somehow from the wary lips of Arrowstone might well make the difference.

But it was a two-headed coin. Another call would mean he had selected another victim, might mean that there had been another victim, already.

He pushed that thought from his mind, got up, and paced restlessly between his desk and the room's single window. He had spent an uneasy night, sleeping fitfully, snapping awake to stare into darkness peopled with jeering wyverns and hobgoblins, not always certain whether he was asleep or awake, never quite sure what was dream illusion and what was reality.

By morning he had felt anything but rested, his head heavy with a pall of malaise that was not alleviated by a shower and a shave and a breakfast of bacon and eggs that still lay unwanted in his stomach. The dismal day had done nothing to help the

vague sense of dread, and indefinable feeling of imminent di
saster. Rosie's impassioned warning had solidified the gray i
his mind into a sort of dense, humid smoke that flitted in and
around the peaks and crevices of his brain like dark storm cloud
tumbling along the mountaintops.

And now, stalking his office, chain-smoking, hating himsel
his murderous quarry, a system that had spawned such a creatur
then allowed him to run amok, he felt a growing savagery dee
inside his guts that frightened him, shook him with its growlin
demands for justice, for vengeance in the way of primeval max
with hands and teeth and clubs and stones.

He stopped before the window, his body taut as the string d
a bow, his mind a whirling maelstrom of concentrated rage.

Your run is over, animal! Wherever you are, I'll find yo
Wherever you go, I'll hound you until you are dead, dead, dea

The words rang so vividly in his head, he wasn't sure h
hadn't shouted them aloud. He blinked his eyes slowly and gr
maced, and the passion ran out of him; he propped an unstead
hand against the window frame, feeling foolish and melodra
matic.

But the resolution remained; Julian Arrowstone had finall
touched him, stroked an obscure chord, ignited a dormant nee
for righteous retribution handed down to him unseen and un
noticed by some forgotten ancestor.

Julian Arrowstone was his; he would fight the world for hin

62

Amy Reed put the finishing touches to her table setting for three around one end of the long, narrow table in Cloud's small dining room.

Fine linen napkins edged with lace, elegant and fragile, one of the few things left from her marriage that meant anything to her. A gift from her mother shortly before her death, they were doubly precious simply because her mother had not been a woman inclined to giving expensive, frivolous gifts. She had not been a woman who gave much of anything, Amy thought a little bitterly, not even love. There had been times during the last six months of her mother's life, while she lay dying in a nursing home, that Amy had looked at the decaying body and comatose face and wondered if this cold, reserved woman could truly be her mother. A mistake, perhaps at the hospital, careless nurses switching babies in their cribs, a malicious trick spawned from some demented mind.

As far back as she could remember, she had fantasized about a warm and loving mother-daughter relationship, dreamed of the day when she would do something *exactly* the right way, say some magic word that would forever shatter the inexplicable barrier between them, bring an instantaneous rush of warm, nurturing love, give rise to something more than sustenance and clinical care.

Many nights she had lain awake, dry-eyed and bitter, hating her mother, and the father who wasn't there, plotting her escape at the earliest possible moment. But the umbilical cord had been long and tenacious, binding her with its invisible strands, breaking finally when she was a sophomore at Texas Christian University. Clyde Upton Reed, a cold, country yankee, had swept her literally off her feet, carted her off to Las Vegas on a dazzling, whirlwind weekend, and married her. She had lived to regret the marriage, but never the breaking away . . .

Since Cloud had told her their guest would be bringing flowers, she removed Cloud's bouquet of mixed artificials and substituted a slim ceramic vase. She wondered who had brought him the dusty centerpiece. One of his lady friends, no doubt. She couldn't visualize him buying it for himself. Not practical, unromantic Benjamin Cloud. His idea of a romantic evening was dining out, a little necking on the sofa while they watched the latest trashy cable movie sizzling with sex and violence, a quick hot shower—preferably together—then right into the old sack.

But that wasn't all bad, she thought, smiling, feeling a faint, lazy warmth creeping upward out of her stomach. Cloud was a very good lover, gentle and considerate, as much concerned with her pleasure as with his own. A far cry from her younger ex-husband, a bedroom cowboy who had thought that being in there was all it took, who assumed that she received all the pleasure she required during his ramming, snorting assault on her unresisting body, who believed that a woman who liked it too much was either a tramp or a nympho and therefore wouldn't have married a hard-working, God-fearing cop such as himself.

She went into the kitchen and checked the rib roast. She unwrapped the foil and sliced a tiny sliver from the crusty brown edge.

Perfect. Juicy and delicious. Saliva flowed, and she rewrapped the tender meat hastily to avoid temptation. She suddenly realized that she was ravenous. Her day off, she had slept late, made do with a cup of coffee and a piece of toast, and spent the rest of the day grocery shopping and cleaning the apartment. Her first sit down, real, honest-to-goodness meal-with-a-guest since moving in with Cloud, and she wanted everything to be perfect.

She looked at the clock over the sink and decided she had time for a long, leisurely bath . . . well, maybe not a bath, but anyhow a hot, rejuvenating shower.

She hummed happily while she undressed and adjusted the spray. She washed herself meticulously, acutely aware of her slender, rounded frame, as always fervently thankful for some fortuitous blending of ancestors that had brought her such a trouble-free body, healthy and vital, velvety unblemished skin and fine-boned, well-formed features she realized matter-of-factly that most men found eminently desirable. Over the years, that had had its disadvantages, but there had been times, like now with Benjamin Cloud, when she gloried in her desirability, exulted in her sensuality with its innate power over the handsome detective's sexuality.

She wanted more, of course; she wanted the power that came with his love. But, like herself, he had been badly burned in the cauldron of marriage, and he was wary of commitment.

Tingling and squeaky clean, she turned off the shower and rubbed briskly with the furry side of a large crimson towel. She bent down and carefully wiped between her toes, dried her ankles, her calves, behind her knees, straightening slowly as she worked her way upward.

She freed her hair and fluffed it with her fingers, tossed the towel across one shoulder. She was reaching to hang the shower cap on one of the faucets when she caught the flicker of movement through the frosted shower door.

She gasped, turned, stood frozen.

Except for her eyes; they blinked rapidly, would not stop, would not turn away from the unmistakable figure of a man materializing through the semi-opaque glass, pressing against the pebbled surface, flat, distorted, except for the swollen cylinder of flesh forced downward by the forward thrust of hairy loins.

A naked man.

"Cloud? Cloud, damn you—" Her voice cracked, high and shrill, caught her in her throat; she heard dimly a low, rasping chuckle and ice water spilled into her veins, robbed her of strength; she pressed backward against the tile, put out her hands in an unconscious gesture of supplication.

"Cloud? Oh, God, Cloud . . ." Her voice withered to a moan, a plaintive whimper.

She watched, horrified, as the man's hips began to rotate, the distended tube of flesh rolling and bumping as his groin withdrew and reappeared, stabbed and gyrated in an obscene parody of the sex act.

She watched it, trying to remember, and she could not.

"Oh, God, please!" she pleaded, shuddering uncontrollably, wanting to believe that this was Cloud, some monstrous game he was playing, that any second he would open the shower door, see her helpless fear, and curse himself for a stupid, thoughtless fool.

"Please stop!" she moaned, the sound ragged with anguish, tearing through a clotted throat, a mouth dry as a handful of dust.

A harsh, grating laugh was her answer; a sound not quite human, a growling animal sound that became a hoarse, guttural incantation as the hips increased their frenzied attack, rolling and stabbing, impacting the frosted glass with incredible speed and force.

Weak with shock, Amy slid slowly to a sitting position in one corner of the shower stall; she pulled up her legs and buried her head in shielding arms, waiting numbly for the dark and terrifying thing that had always lurked at the edge of her life, the bad thing she had always known would someday find her.

The sounds diminished to short, huffing grunts and snuffles, liquid sucking sounds.

Silence.

And then the click of the shower door.

A low, husky laugh. "Hello, little bunny," a voice said softly.

Amy Reed didn't look up. She didn't have to. She knew who he was.

63

Dressed, his body gently thrumming with the pleasant resonance of satiation, his strength partially restored by a great chunk of the cooking meat he had found in the oven, Spencer Price stood in the doorway of the bathroom and surveyed his handiwork.

She had been one of the good ones. Maybe the best since Amanda. Not the prettiest, nor the youngest, but there had been something special, and he had wondered about that while he ate. Maybe it was because he had stolen her from Cloud, the same way he had stolen Amanda away from the queer bastard.

There had been a kind of soaring ecstasy, a wild, coursing energy fueling the passion that had not been present with the others. He remembered the hopeless fear in her eyes, the tears, and his body quickened.

He giggled aloud—and saw her stir, one broken, bloody hand scrabbling through a pool of crusting blood like the talon of a gigantic bird.

Not dead? he marveled. He shook his head in wonder. He had felt her ribs cave beneath his knees, saw the spark of life fade from the brilliant eyes, the lovely mouth open in a soundless rictus of pain as his fingers crushed her throat like a frangible tube of sugar glass.

Alive? Not possible. A reflex action, surely.

Nevertheless, he picked his way daintily across the bathroom floor, avoiding the blood, the smears and the pools, the shriveled bits of flesh.

He knelt beside her head, stared intently, and listened, looked up and made a face of amazement as he heard a low, whistling suck of indrawn breath.

"I'll be damned," he said, smiling down at her tenderly. "You're a tough little bunny."

Still squatting, his eyes lost the cold, blank look, glittering again he reached down and closed his hand on her neck. Carefully, using thumb and forefinger, he began to squeeze, listening, nodding with satisfaction as the faint sound subsided.

A tremor raced through his body as she twitched, a slight tightening of the neck muscles as her body made one last effort to survive. He snickered and squeezed harder.

It was ten minutes before seven when Cloud locked up his desk and walked out into the corridor. He paused to light a cigarette, the residue of recent anger hanging dull and heavy in his gut.

He had come late to Donleavy's meeting, and the beefy red-faced martinet had at first pointedly ignored him, then turned on him suddenly like an angry, snarling bear, vicious and cold, berating him with icy, calculated fury.

He had listened, tight-lipped, his guts coiling into a nauseous rope of anger, his throat trembling with the need to retort, to lacerate the pudgy man with the acid edge of his own contempt, to enumerate the fat slob's failings as his own were being so methodically detailed in front of his peers. But he had held his tongue, a miracle of control, rose during a lull and told the irate chief politely to go fuck himself, and walked out of his office amidst a deadly silence. He wasn't at all sure he was still a cop in Trinity Square.

He sighed, exhaled a ball of smoke, and picked up his pace. He swung past the dispatch room, then leaped to one side as Ron Graves came thundering out, his bushy head lowered over a flimsy teletype tear sheet gripped in both muscular hands. He drew up abruptly, his broad face alive with excitement, eyes flashing with effervescent fire.

"Shit, I was afraid I'd missed you!" He thrust the sheet of paper at Cloud, stood oddly grinning, his head bobbing with a curious, rhythmic cadence.

"What the hell is it?" Cloud asked, annoyed. Sometimes, not often, but sometimes, the irrepressible exuberance of this muscle-bound adolescent was hard to take.

"Read it," Graves said succinctly, his grin spreading, convoluting, almost simian.

Cloud read it, scanned the precisely articulated message, translating the numerous abbreviations, the solecisms of the law as he went along. He stopped once to look into Graves's shining eyes, returned to read again. He finished, raised his gaze to Graves's beaming, boyish countenance.

"Why did you—how did you know to ask?"

"I don't know," Graves admitted. "Just a hunch. Just a goddamned gut hunch!" He licked his lips and grinned again. He couldn't seem to stop grinning, stop bobbing. "Maybe because he don't look like a cop—that damned beard—"

Cloud put a hand on the hard, rubbery shoulder. "He's at my house. He's with my . . . Amy!"

Graves blanched, the inane grin finally gone. "Jesus Christ!"

"Call Rosie," Cloud yelled, already moving. "He lives closeby. Get a squad car out there!"

He hit the entrance at a run, almost lost his balance as the heavy glass doors fought back. Then he was free and running again, searching the lot for his car, cursing frantically when he couldn't remember, cursing Donleavy for keeping him, cursing the twilight, himself, and finally, when he fumbled the key into the ignition, cursing Arrowstone, begging God. Shouting curses and whispering prayers, threatening Arrowstone . . . promising . . . promising.

64

Rosie's car was there, flanked by two squad cars, their lights rotating, smoke pouring from their tail pipes. Even as he ran up the steps, he saw a third car turn the corner, siren winding down, another set of whirling lights. A dull, sick ache flowed through him like a fever.

He stopped at the half-open door, not looking, not sure he could force himself to go inside, telling himself that everything was all right, knowing it wasn't; there were too many cops and too many whirling lights. He looked away from the door, staring at, but not seeing, the inevitable knot of people across the courtyard, huddled, bowing before the cold wind like a throng of vultures patiently waiting their turn.

The flashing lights pricked his eyes, sent spikes of pain thudding inside his head.

"Turn off those goddamned lights!" he yelled.

The two cops alighting from the third squad car looked at him, then looked at each other across the top of the car.

"Goddammit, I said turn off those lights!"

One of the cops shrugged, reached inside, and the third car's lights went off; the other two whirled busily. The two cops stood looking at him.

Cloud threw up his hands and went inside filled with nameless dread, looking down at the floor, refusing to see anything except the small area immediately below his eyes.

What he couldn't see couldn't hurt him, couldn't be her, torn and bloody and . . . and there was nothing awry that he could see except a wrapped bouquet of red roses lying beside his rocker-recliner and two small squares of something that gleamed dully, marring the spotless bowl of his large, ceramic ashtray.

The fact that the living room was undisturbed penetrated; hope rushed through him like a small, hot wind. Surely if she had been—

"Ben."

Rosie's voice. Off to his left. He could see the giant blur in his peripheral vision. In front of the bathroom door. He tried to think back, to analyze Rosie's voice. Had it been gentle? Yes. Had it been reassuring? Oh, God!

"Ben."

She was dead. It was there in Rosie's voice. Compassion, pain, horror. Yes. And that meant the goddamned son of a bitch had killed her, had—it was only when he felt Rosie's arms around his shoulders that he realized he had been walking toward the bathroom door and that he had been talking aloud.

"You can't go in," Rosie said, and now there was determination in the gruff voice.

"Get out of my way," Cloud said, twisting angrily in the mammoth arms.

"You're not going in, Ben," Rosie said patiently, his voice thick and unnatural, his arms tightening, holding the smaller man as easily as a child.

"You son of a bitch, let me go," Cloud said wearily, feeling a splash of wetness on the back of his hand that had not come from his eyes. He looked up at the big man wonderingly, appalled at the contorted, tearstained face.

"Jesus Christ," he said hollowly. "Is it that bad, Rosie?"

Rosie nodded, unable to speak, the wide mouth a saber slash across his white face.

"I have to see," Cloud said doggedly, wrenching at the iron bands, bucking, heaving, almost toppling the two of them to the floor.

Rosie shook him then, gripped his upper arms with his giant hands, and shook him like a limp rag doll.

"Goddammit! Listen to me! You want to see her . . . like that? You want to see her, or do you want the bastard, the son of a bitch who did it to her? Tell me, goddammit!"

Cloud froze, transfixed by the bellowing voice, the fiery eyes dawning knowledge.

Rosie grinned down at him, a hard, merciless grin, his wet face shining. He nodded.

"Wha-what are you—where? Goddammit, where, Rosie?"

"On the roof of the rec building. The mother's treed! White and Anson and two other guys are holding him pinned down. They caught him coming out of here. He ran."

Cloud threw back his head and breathed deeply, opening his mouth wide and sucking air like a man drowning. A spasm of rage bloomed in his stomach, rippled upward, expanded, became a dark, saw-toothed edge of hate, perfectly honed, bringing a kind of calmness and a cold and deadly purpose.

He broke through Rosie's unresisting arms and headed for the door.

"You got your gun?" Rosie called softly.

Cloud stopped, whirled. "It's in my desk."

Rosie already had one in his hand; he tossed it to him, butt first. "Same one I loaned you last time. You remember?"

"I remember," Cloud said. He looked toward the bathroom. "You called in?" He felt pain welling through the cold fury and firmly forced it down. Everything in its own time.

"Tech squad's on the way. Let's go."

Cloud gave him a hard, level look. "Stay out of my way, Rosie."

Rosie shrugged and gave him back a tight grin. "I'm your partner, man, not your conscience. I'll be that shadow you'll see if you turn around fast enough."

They walked out the door together.

65

"He went up here, Lieutenant." Patrolman Chuck Anson
pointed to the vertical metal ladder extending up the side of the
two-story brick building. "If he was armed, sir, he didn't use
it." He stirred uneasily, his right hand holding his gun along the
seam of his pants pointed toward the ground. "I could have
picked him off, but we didn't know what . . . we didn't know
then that he had—"

"You did fine, Chuck," Rosie said. "Any other way off that
roof?"

"There's a trapdoor opens up in the loft," Anson said. "But
it's bolted on the down side. Anyhow, Wazenski and Pearl are
inside. Only way he's got down is to jump, and we got guys on
all sides of the building."

Cloud nodded and stepped to the ladder. He began to climb.
After a few feet, he stopped and looked down at Rosie whose
right foot was on the bottom rung. He was cramming his hands
into a pair of leather gloves.

"Better wait'll I get up. This thing might not hold both of
us."

He turned around and resumed climbing. He felt the ladder
tremble and looked down. Rosie was right behind him.

The big man shrugged. "So we'll fall," he said.

"You stubborn jackass," Cloud muttered, and began climbing
again.

By the time he reached the top, a spot in the center of his

head was tingling, and despite his icy calm, a trickle of cold sweat shivered its way down his backbone.

But no lupine face appeared over the parapet, no gun blazed in the night. He went up and over without hesitation, dropped lightly to the flat, gravel-covered roof. He took a pace forward, and Rosie stepped down behind him.

Cloud counted five places a man might hide: three large ventilation ducts five feet high as big around as a man's waist, a small, square platform half as high as the ducts that was undoubtedly the trapdoor housing, and a large, metal shed that housed the air-conditioning system. The balance of the roof was bare, glowing dimly in the illumination from a streetlight placed near one corner of the building.

Five hiding places; but Cloud did not intend to search him out. He took two swift paces toward the air-conditioning shed.

"Come out, Callum," he said, slightly surprised that his voice was calm and even.

"I can't do that," Ward Callum said. "Not unless you bring up some more cops. You two will shoot me down . . . and I didn't do anything."

"You've got it right," Cloud said. "But you got a choice. If we have to come and get you, you go over the edge headfirst."

"Either way, throw out your gun," Rosie said.

"I don't have a gun. I never carry a gun, you know that."

"Then how did you kill Ward Callum?"

"With his own gun. He was a stupid, stupid man with a drinking problem. After he resigned, the first thing he did was go out and get drunk. I followed him, waited for him. I hit him with a tire tool, then shot him and drove him and his car to the Ohio River—"

"Come out, Arrowstone. Don't make me come after you. You do, and I'll blow your scummy cock off. I'll laugh while I watch you bleed to death."

"Will you take me in? So I can get some help? Maybe the shrinks can help me this time. I only did the Metcalf woman, you know."

Cloud laughed, a sound he didn't recognize; out of the corner of his eye, he saw Rosie turn and look at him. He took a step forward, his foot grating loudly in the gravel.

"Wait! Wait! I'm coming out! But first, will you believe me when I say I didn't do your lovely girl friend? I told you, that's not my style. You invited me to dinner, after all. I wouldn't be dumb enough to do her, would I—?''

"Do? *Do?*" Without warning, the overwhelming rage seized Cloud again, ballooned inside, swept upward, clogging his throat, filling his mouth with howling, liquid curses.

"No! No, wait, I'm coming!''

And suddenly he was there, at the corner of the metal shack, his right hand still out of sight. "Look, Ben, I've still got—"

"Watch out!" Rosie roared. "He's got a —''

Cloud shot him.

Arrowstone staggered backward, right hand still grasping something that caught the feeble light and glinted. "Wait! Look—''

"Watch it," Rosie yelled again.

And Cloud shot him again.

Arrowstone went down, spread-eagled on his back.

Behind Cloud a gun fired twice; he whirled, stared dumbly at Rosie grinning at him, holding a snub-nosed gun pointed at the sky.

"Two for you, two for him," Rosie said matter-of-factly. "I think that's fair." He walked to the prone body and pressed the gun into one outflung hand. "Less fuss this way, Ben." He yanked off a glove and touched a finger to Arrowstone's neck, then pressed his hand against the bloody chest.

"Sumbitch's still alive," he growled. He looked up and grinned again. "But it's mighty thready," he said happily. He reached across the body and picked up the object Arrowstone had dropped.

"I'll be damned," he said. "The gritty bastard stole a bottle of your red wine.''

66

Benjamin Cloud couldn't sleep. Long after the condos around him were silent and dark, he prowled the small apartment, padding barefoot through the deep pile carpet, going over and over the events that had culminated in the death of Amy Reed and Julian Arrowstone four days before—and what had happened since.

Something was wrong. Something other than the terrible death of Amy Reed; something other than the righteous death of Julian Arrowstone a.k.a. Ward Callum. He felt no regret over the killing of Arrowstone. There was no doubt that he had killed Lea Metcalf. He had left fingerprints on the wide, plastic belt worn by the redheaded saleswoman, and a neighbor had identified him as the man he had seen talking to her on the lawn of the empty house shortly before the murder.

It was something else, an endogenous malaise that nagged and irritated like a splinter beneath a fingernail.

Small things, bits and pieces; big things.

And facts.

Like the fact that Ward Callum had been sitting in a booth in Barney's Den with Strobish, Graves, and Stovall during the hours when Lolita Barnes had been killed.

Like the fact that the M.E. had found no traces of Amy Reed's blood on either Callum's clothing or body. An impossibility, according to the M.E., considering the amount of blood splattered and splashed and streaked around the walls and floor of the bathroom. Smeared handprints and footprints indicated that

e had been nude during the murder, and not even the most
horough scrubbing would have removed all traces from the min-
te crannies and crevices of the killer's body. Besides, there
adn't been time for that.

Conclusion: There should have been traces of Amy Reed's
lood on Arrowstone's body. There were not. Why?

Because he didn't kill her, Cloud thought grimly. The same
vay he hadn't killed Lolita Barnes. Maybe the same way he
adn't killed the Dickerson girl, the Cooper girl, the ones who
ad been savaged.

From the first, as Ward Callum, Arrowstone had insisted it
vas not his style, and now in retrospect, it was easy to see the
ndignation in his protests, a trace of pride that he killed with
ignity, accorded his victims what his twisted mind perceived to
e respect, loving care. And right up to the end, he had denied
avagery in his acts.

Cloud stopped before the picture window that faced his slowly
ying patch of lawn. He stared distractedly at the bright glow of
Dallas on the horizon and tried to deny truth, irrefutable truth
hat brought despair, and fear that stalked his mind like a run-
way missile roaming the edges of the world.

There was another one out there.

Another one like Arrowstone, perhaps infinitely worse. A sav-
ge, without mercy, without pity, without remorse. As cunning
s evil itself, as merciless as nature's worst predator.

Guilt erupted inside him like a shout. The fault was his. He had
teadfastly denied what the blood and hair samples had shown. Two
illers. And he had dismissed it out of incredulity and fear.

Who?

He felt a chill sweep up across his back, trickle along his neck
nd into his scalp, the hair bristling like that of an angry dog.
He shivered and hugged himself with long, sinewy arms, his
tomach churning with nausea, the taste of hot bile washing up
nto his throat.

He thought he knew. God help him to be wrong, but he thought
e knew.

He glanced at the clock over the fireplace mantel. Midnight,
traight up. He wondered if Rosie was still up.

He picked up the phone and began dialing. Tough shit if he
wasn't; their work wasn't done. There was another crazy out
here, a psycho even more deadly and cunning than Arrowstone
ver hoped to be.

"Hello." The big man's voice was thick and furry with sleep

"Rosie, this is Ben. Sorry to roust you out, but—"

"I've been looking for you. Where you been all evening?" The deep voice had turned sharp, an octave higher.

"Fort Worth. They picked up Julio Mendosa on a drug bus this afternoon. I finally got a crack at him." He paused. "Samm Keeler told him that Arrowstone didn't kill Butler and Elliot that he knew who did. He told Mendosa he figured it was worth a pot full of dope." He stopped again, his mouth dry. "He told Mendosa it was a cop, Rosie."

He heard a muttered exclamation that sounded like a curse "A cop? Who?"

"He didn't tell him that."

"Do you believe him?"

"Believe who? Mendosa or Keeler? I tend to believe Mendosa Remember, I went to him, he didn't come to me, and it wasn't any kind of trade or anything. I think Keeler told him that, all right Whether it's true or not is another matter. Keeler also told him that it had something to do with a phony drug stakeout at the Seven Eleven parking lot on Northcross. He didn't say what."

"The one you assisted Rafferty and Strobish on?"

"That's the only one I know about."

"But, dammit, I don't see the connection—" He broke off Cloud lit a cigarette while he listened to the big man's heavy breathing. After a moment his voice came again, flat and quiet. "Could there be a connection, Ben? With Butler and Elliot?"

Cloud sighed, the sinking, defeated feeling back again. "We maintained radio silence. We keyed in every hour on the hour We couldn't see each other."

Rosie whistled softly through his teeth. "Jesus H. Christ."

"By itself that doesn't mean much, but two hours ago Stovall called me. He had just returned from the Dallas lab. They brought out two partial prints on the gum wrappers they found in my ashtray. Good enough to run the comparison check I wanted done. He called again thirty minutes ago."

"And?"

"And they matched."

"Matched who?" He made a soft, sibilant sound. "Strobish?"

"No, not Strobish," Cloud said tiredly.

"Then, who dammit? Quit playing—"

"Rafferty," Cloud said. "Jake Rafferty."

A moment of heavy silence, then Rosie exploded. "Dammit, Ben, come on! Jake was out at your place Sunday. Maybe he left the chewing gum wrappers then. If that's all you've got, a smart lawyer—"

"It's not all, Rosie. You remember me telling you what Arrowstone said the first time he called? About the dart landing on Trinity Square? It was the copycat, of course, and not Arrowstone, but that's what he said. Did you tell Rafferty, by any chance?"

"No, no I didn't. I didn't mention it to anyone."

Cloud sighed. "The night we staked out Northcross Street, Rafferty used those very same words to me, and I hadn't told him about it, either. He knew about it because he said it. The point of that whole Echofone thing was to keep me from recognizing his voice. He told me Arrowstone would call, then proceeded to make it happen. It all fits too well, Rosie. For whatever reason, he decided he had to kill Ramona and he set up that whole drug-bust scene to give himself an alibi. The Elliot girl came home unexpectedly, and he had to kill her, too. Then he set it up to look like Arrowstone—"

"How did Sammy Keeler fit in?"

"I don't know. Maybe he didn't kill Sammy Keeler."

"But he was there with you and Strobish at the Seven-Eleven—"

"We keyed in at ten o'clock and at eleven. That would have given him an hour. He didn't need nearly that much. Ramona lived no more than a mile away, a two- or three-minute drive, at most."

"And that's it?"

"No, not quite. Jake has a key to my place, and Amy's killer came in through the front door. There's evidence that Amy was in the shower at the time. The front door locks automatically. The killer would have had to have a key."

"Jesus H. Christ," Rosie said again, his heavy voice as empty as an echo.

"We need to toss his place, Rosie. Can you meet me there in twenty minutes? He's still out at his cabin on the lake."

"Sure," the big detective said mechanically. "But we don't have a search warrant."

"With shoulders like yours, who needs one?"

67

Cloud swung the wheel sharply, then cursed aloud as the old car bottomed in the gaping, muddy chuckhole. He gunned the motor irritably and almost spun into the bole of a large red oak as the rear wheels lost traction, spewing torrents of loose mud and water in twin fantails behind him.

"Shit! Wonder why that peckerhead don't fix up this damned road?" He got the car straightened out and grinned a little at the pointless question he had asked Rafferty a hundred times. He had always gotten the same answer.

"I fix up this damned road and there'll be more cops up here than you can shake a stick at. Messing up my cabin, pissing off my dock, getting jism all over my clean sheets with them groupies all you other cops can't seem to stay away from."

The spiel went on and on, but the essence was always the same kernel of truth: Rafferty enjoyed his privacy, solitude. And now, Cloud grimly realized, there had been a very good reason for that.

The cabin was a twenty-by-twenty foot rectangle with a rough cedar shake roof and masonite siding. Each side had its own window, long, narrow sliders to catch the summer breezes. The front had two, and a door, and faced toward the lake. Except for a small, square plywood partition in one corner which housed a portable toilet, the inside was one single room. Paneled in light birch with a white acoustical ceiling, it had a light and airy ambiance even on the gloomiest days. Weathertight and snug, it was comfortably, if not ostentatiously, furnished with odd bits and pieces donated by friends and fellow police officers. The only new piece of furniture was a white, ten-cubic-foot refrigerator from Sears. Cloud had helped him build the cabin, had spent many peaceful evenings there on his own.

Cloud parked beside Rafferty's Plymouth at the end of the cabin. He lit a cigarette and got out to find his friend advancing toward the edge of the porch, smiling broadly, his bushy, unkempt hair and bare feet mute evidence that he had not long been awake.

"Hey, man, glad you could make it."

Cloud nodded and returned the smile. "Me, too. There was some doubt in my mind about halfway up your road. It's getting worse."

Rafferty laughed and did a little dancing jig. "Come on, let's go inside. It's colder'n a witch's tit."

"Beautiful day, though," Cloud said, stepping up onto the porch, taking Rafferty's proffered hand as if he really needed help with the eighteen-inch elevation. Rafferty's hand felt warm and dry, as if he had just finished toasting it before a roaring fire. Cloud was positive his own must feel cold and clammy, but if it did, his smiling host gave no indication.

From somewhere out on the lake a boat motor whined like an angry hornet, the high, shrill sound disappearing as they went inside and closed the door.

"Get on over there and warm your backside," Rafferty said, tiptoeing across the linoleum floor. He dropped on the edge of a mussed-up bunk and began slipping on a pair of socks. "Jack up that fire a little. I just got it going a little while ago."

"I'm fine," Cloud said, peeling out of his jacket. He hung it on a peg on the wall and stepped to the fireplace. He poked at the burning logs a couple of times, then hung up the poker. "It's not really all that cold. You've just been sleeping. Anyhow, all you yankees have thin blood."

Rafferty laughed and pulled on his boots. He stamped his feet and slumped toward the end of the long room that served as a kitchen. "Sit down, Ben. I'll whip us up some coffee. You eaten?"

"Yeah. Enough." Cloud dropped into the dinette booth that he had helped build and propped his chin on folded hands. He looked through the long, narrow window toward the line of brush twenty-five yards away. No sign yet of Rosie.

Rafferty set two empty coffee mugs on the table and slid into the booth across from him. "Coffee'll be ready in a shake."

Cloud nodded and brought his gaze back to the other man's face. "I guess you've heard," he said tonelessly.

Rafferty inclined his head slowly, his features bunched in an apologetic grimace. He reached across the table and gripped Cloud's wrist. He squeezed once, then let his hand fall away, looking faintly embarrassed.

"I'm sorry, man. I only heard last night. My TV hasn't been working, and I heard it on the car radio last night when I drove to Medford for some supplies. They said she was . . . they said the burial was yesterday. I was planning on coming home today." His hands came up and combed through his shaggy hair, then came together and opened wide in a gesture that somehow conveyed sympathy. "Now you know how I felt when Ramona died," he said softly.

Cloud cleared his throat, wrenched his eyes away from Rafferty's dark, piercing gaze. He looked out the window; Rosie stood just inside the line of brush, looking directly at him. He raised his right hand and scratched his cheek. Rosie stalked across the yard toward the front door, the big gun swinging loosely in his right hand.

Cloud found and lit a cigarette. He cleared his throat again, a harsh, rasping noise to cover the soft sounds of Rosie's footsteps on the concrete porch.

"I'm quitting, Jake. I've discovered I'm just not cut out to be a cop."

"Come on, man. You're a damned good cop. And I'm the one who ought to know."

"No. I'm too trusting. Or maybe it's just laziness, or stupidity. I talked to Callum a dozen times and never thought to question him, his presence, his motives."

"You can't blame yourself for that. Seems to me he was sent to you by Eli."

Cloud smiled faintly. "And Donleavy sent him to Eli. Donleavy got a call from some 'captain' in Chicago. He never thought to confirm that, either. It was from Arrowstone, of course. I'll have to give him credit, the son of a bitch had smarts . . . and guts. Dumbass Donleavy told the 'captain' all about the Dickerson girl over the phone. I guess that's how Arrowstone knew that first time he called—" He broke off.

Rafferty's eyes sharpened, his brows knitting. "Why wouldn't he have known? He killed her."

Cloud shrugged and made a self-deprecating face. "Yeah, that's right. I wasn't thinking." He ran a hand over his angular features. "I'm not thinking clear lately."

"Well, you said he had a monstrous ego. What could be more ego-fulfilling than the fox sitting down with the hounds to help plan the hunt."

"He was an animal, but it wasn't a fox."

"What would you do, Ben? You've been a cop for . . . what? Ten, eleven years, counting the military?"

Cloud shrugged. "Go back to school for a while. I've got a degree in electronic engineering—I'll bet you didn't know that, did you? It's a little outdated, but a couple of years of concentrated—"

"Come on, man," Rafferty jeered gently. "You're no damned engineer. You're a cop. You're letting this thing spook you. I know. I felt the same way when Ramona was killed. I felt helpless, frustrated—" He broke off when Cloud suddenly raised a hand, a fisted hand that hung trembling in the air, then slowly relaxed and fell back to the table.

"It's not quite the same thing, Jake," he said. "I don't know how you felt when you killed Ramona, but I have a good idea how it was with Amy."

Rafferty stared at him, eyes spreading, mouth parted, poised to smile if there was humor to be found in his friend's incredible words.

"What?" he said finally.

Cloud wagged his head, looked down at the Formica table in front of him. "Five years and you'd think you'd know a man. I thought I knew you, Jake. I really thought I knew what made you tick. We were partners, man. In the best sense of the word." He stopped and smiled wryly. "We were more than that. We were friends."

"No," Rafferty said harshly. "We weren't friends. Not all of the time, we weren't. Only when you felt in the mood, when it suited you. I wanted that more than anything, but there were times when I didn't know you, times when I didn't know if you even liked me. About half the time I didn't know who the hell you were, man."

Cloud winced and smiled faintly. "One thing I'm not. I'm not a killer."

Rafferty slammed the table with fisted hands. "What is this shit? What did you mean about Ramona and Amy? Is this some kind of damned sick joke—"

"No joke, Jake. Or maybe it is. A joke on me. I'm so damned dumb I work beside a cold-blooded murderer for five years and don't suspect a damn thing. A sadistic son of a bitch who gets off killing little girls, little redheaded girls."

Rafferty stiffened slowly, his face blanching. "What? My God, Ben—"

Cloud silenced him with a lifted hand; he shook his head wearily. "Forget it, Jake. It's finished. Arrowstone's dead. He was one head of our little snake, and you're the other. Two Arrowstones. I thought it wasn't possible. But it was. It *is*. You started it all with Ramona and the Elliot girl. Why, I don't know. Maybe because Ramona was screwing around on you, maybe because you had held it in as long as you could and the Elliot girl set you off. But you killed them. You used me to set up your alibi. Your old buddy, Cloud, old gullible Cloud. You left me sitting out there on a bogus coke buy while you drove to Ramona Butler's house and killed them both. You even used the oldest scam in the world, a broken watch, to fake the time of death. At ten o'clock you were over there in that apartment parking lot, keying in with the signal, and at ten-fifteen you were killing your girl friend and her roommate."

"Shit!" Rafferty yelled. "Shit, shit! That's all this is." He slammed the table again, pushed to his feet, his face tight and writhing, eyes stark, burning holes. "You snorting, man, or taking it straight in the vein? I've never heard such crap in my life."

Cloud reached down and worked the short-barreled gun out of its sheath attached to his boot top. "Sit down, Jake," he said quietly. "You're not going anywhere. Rosie's just outside that door."

Rafferty's eyes flicked to the door, came back. "Bullshit. He wouldn't walk in from the highway, and I haven't heard a car."

"Boat," Cloud said succinctly. "Sit down, Jake." He replaced the gun and lit a cigarette. He spoke without looking toward the door. "Rosie."

68

The front door opened and Rosie stepped through, the big gun held negligently in his right hand. He pushed the door shut with his foot and faced the two men silently, his eyes like splintered chips of stone.

Rafferty sank slowly into his seat. "Jesus Christ, you really mean it!"

"Yes, I'm sorry to say I do. I take no pleasure in this, Jake. It makes me sick, if you want the truth. I valued your friendship. I let it blind me. Rosie wanted to check you out on the Butler and Elliot killing, but I gave you an alibi and he backed off. And then you so conveniently handed me the Arrowstone theory and I was off and running. Jesus. I made everything so damned easy for you."

"If this wasn't so goddamned crazy, I'd laugh. You can't believe all this shit—"

"Don't laugh, Jake. I'll shoot you if you laugh. You killed Amy and —"

"Goddammit, Arrowstone killed Amy! I heard it on the radio. You shot him for it, for chrissakes!"

Cloud's face was a cold, hard mask. "I shot him, but he didn't kill her. You got there first. You killed her and set him up for it. The only thing I don't know is how you knew Callum was Arrowstone. But maybe you didn't. If he hadn't panicked and run and if Graves hadn't had a gut feeling about him and sent off a query to Chicago, he could probably have bulled his way through it. At least long enough to run. That must have tickled the hell out of you, the way it worked out. Better than you could possibly have hoped for.''

Rafferty's head shook back and forth doggedly. "You're wrong, Ben. Jesus Christ, we were partners—''

Cloud leaned across the table and slapped him, a hard, ringing blow. "Don't lie, goddammit! You killed her, you killed all of them except the Metcalf woman. We found the bag of stones in your apartment, Jake. We found two gum wrappers in Amy's clean ashtray with your fingerprints all over them. And the clincher, Jake . . . we found Ramona's engagement ring in your bureau drawer. We found the Echofone. You're even more careless than I am gullible. Plain carelessness or arrogance? Were you so sure of me, of yourself? You started it all, and Arrowstone came here because of that. Someone was stealing his trademark, making him look bad. He had to show us the real thing, the delicate Arrowstone touch, so he killed Lea Metcalf. He told me he didn't kill Ramona and the Elliot girl, but of course I didn't believe him.'' He stared at the ashen face of his friend, a hard, curious glint in his eyes. "What would you have done, Jake? Would you have quit the killing now that your cover is dead? *Could* you quit?''

Rafferty stared at him, his face alive with anguish. "This must be a joke,'' he said shakily. "Dammit, Ben, it's gone far enough. You're talking crazy and I've had—'' He broke off and turned to Rosie. "Rosie . . .''

"And then there's Julio Mendosa. We found him finally. You made a mistake bringing Sammy Keeler into it, Jake. He was smarter than you thought. He followed you from the Seven-Eleven that night, saw you kill them. You—''

"Ben! Jesus Christ, Ben! You can't believe that!''

"You're taking a long time, Ben,'' Rosie said.

Cloud nodded and slid out of the booth. He straightened his lanky frame and stared down at Rafferty.

"I know. It's harder than I thought. I believed he would admit it to me.''

"Let's get it done,'' Rosie said harshly.

Cloud crossed the room toward him, walking stiffly, an old man suddenly, with fragile bones. His eyes met Rosie's briefly, flicked away. He turned back to face the slowly rising man in the booth.

"We need his gun," Rosie said. "Do you know where he keeps it?"

Cloud nodded listlessly. He turned to a battered bureau against the inner wall. He opened the top drawer and removed Rafferty's .38 Smith & Wesson and well-worn belt holster.

Rosie held out a big hand and Cloud silently gave him the rig. "Give me your cuffs," Cloud said.

Rosie smiled and turned toward Rafferty. "We won't need them. We killed Arrowstone, and this one is ten times worse. Besides, think of all the money we'll save the taxpayers." His voice was genial, the smile broad and friendly, only his cold eyes supported the harsh logic of his words.

"Come on, Rosie," Cloud said irritably. "Quit bullshitting around. Give me the cuffs." He felt suddenly tired, depressed, tension and an almost sleepless night catching up with him. "Let's get this over—"

The blast of Rosie's Magnum drowned his words, reverberated inside the room like the backlash of cannon fire. And once again.

He gaped at the big man's grinning face in the concussive silence of sound-deadened eardrums, whirled to see Rafferty sagging limply, an incredulous look on his handsome face, one hand pressed to his chest, the other pushing against the table where the force of the bullets had thrown him.

His mouth worked soundlessly, the dark eyes flashing white as they rolled back in his head. He seemed to hang suspended for one bloated fragment of time, then pitched forward on his face.

"Goddammit, Rosie!" Cloud's words seemed dim and far-away in his own ears as he raced across the room. He turned Rafferty's body and searched frantically for a pulse in the strong brown neck, knowing it was useless even before his fingers encountered warm, silent flesh. He was vaguely aware that Rosie had come up beside him.

"Forget it," Rosie said. "I hit him dead center both times."

Cloud rocked back on his haunches and stared up at the face towering above him. "What the hell's wrong with you? You just committed cold-blooded murder! Goddammit, he wasn't armed, he wasn't resisting, he was just—"

"Just a killer," Rosie broke in genially. "Fair's fair. You got one and I got one." He stepped back, grinning. He dropped his gun into its holster and slipped Rafferty's out of its sheath. He flipped open the cylinder and glanced at the bright cartridge heads. He nodded and snapped the cylinder back into place. "Keeps a neat gun." He looked at Cloud again, eyes glittering above the grin that suddenly seemed all wrong. "That's good. I'd hate to shoot a man with a dirty gun."

Cloud rocked up on his toes, rose slowly to his feet. "What're you talking about, Rosie?"

Rosie shrugged, the grin looking strained. "I have to shoot you, Ben."

"Shit!" Cloud threw up his hands. "Will you cut out the bullshit? Goddammit, man, this is serious. Even if Jake hadn't been my friend, I couldn't let you get away with this. We're cops, not executioners."

Rosie shook his head, his broad features suddenly grave. "No, Ben, you're wrong. We're all killers in one way or another. You killed Arrowstone—you *wanted* to kill Arrowstone. Why don't matter. And you enjoyed it, man, even if you don't believe it now. I saw it in your face."

"You're crazy," Cloud said harshly. "I thought he had a gun."

Rosie smiled thinly. "But you shot him twice before you knew if he did or not." He lifted a wide, open hand. "Hey, man, don't alibi it. You killed him because you wanted to. And that's okay. In the end, we all kill because we want to." He took a deep breath and raised the gun to waist level. "Except once in a while, when we don't have any other choice."

He brought back the smile, and pulled the trigger.

69

The sound appeared curiously attenuated, the sledgehammer blow to his chest demanding all his attention, concentration.

Time seemed to stretch, to skip; Cloud was next aware of being on his side on the smooth, vinyl floor next to the dinette booth, his face only inches from the soles of Rafferty's boots, his body tightly curved in a fetal clutch. In the swollen moment before realization caught up with him, he stared blankly at Rafferty's boots and wondered why he had never noticed before that they were made from sharkskin.

"Sorry, man," he heard Rosie Simple say, and memory swarmed in like an angry horde of hungry mosquitoes, pricking his mind with a million bits of recollection. He changed his line of vision and saw Rosie squatting a few feet away, the gun dangling from one thick, hirsute hand.

"You moved," Rosie said accusingly. "Throwed me off a mite. Otherwise, it'd be all over. Don't matter. You'll be dead in a few minutes. Sorry you got to suffer some, but two bullets in each of you'd be a little bit much." He pursed his lips and whistled soundlessly, shaking his head. "Shame. Our mad killer there gets off one unlucky shot before I got him down. Hits you instead of me. Luck of the draw."

Cloud licked his lips and coughed. He tasted something slick and salty inside his mouth. He swallowed convulsively and spat out the words in a liquid rush. "Why . . . Rosie?"

Rosie stared at him, his expression reflective. "Lots of reasons,

275

I guess. Biggest one is that with you and Rafferty dead, the whole case dies with you. Nobody's looking for nobody anymore. Another one is you, Ben. You're a smart man. You've just been a little dazed lately. Sooner or later you'd wake up and start wondering how Rafferty could be so dumb as to leave gum wrappers at the scene of a murder he committed, how he could be so dumb as to leave the rocks and the engagement ring lying around where they could be found. Ditto the Echofone. And, too, sooner or later you'd remember that old Indian blanket I used to carry in my old car, and that I had a key to your condo. Once you started wondering, Rosie Simple's goose would be cooked. Incidentally, my name is Spencer Price." He gave Cloud an affable smile, eyebrows cocked.

"You . . . killed them . . . all?" He as having trouble breathing and, deep inside, he could feel the blood flowing silently, steadily, into all the dark crevices of his body, his life juices slipping away.

The big man nodded, the smile fading, a strange look crossing his face. "All except Metcalf. She was Arrowstone's."

"My God . . . why?" He felt something shift inside and almost screamed with the pain and the fear that washed over him in numbing waves.

The leonine head wagged again. "I don't know why, Ben. I mean, I do and I don't. I *like* doing it. You won't understand that. I don't understand it myself. It's just something I've been doing all my life—killing things, killing people . . . and liking it. I feel dead the rest of the time, like I'm just going through the motions. I tried, man. When I came here six years ago, I told myself it was all over. I was gonna be like other people, live like other people. I found me a decent girl, got married, started having some kids. Six years. Jesus, you can't believe what that was like. It didn't mean shit to me. I had to fight it all the time, every damned day, man, every time I saw a girl, especially a redheaded girl—" He stopped and leaned forward, peering closely at Cloud's face. "Hey, man, are you still alive?"

Cloud opened his eyes in time to see the big hand come in to touch his neck.

"Not long now, partner," Rosie said and pushed to his feet. "Time I put in the call and they get out here . . ." His voice drifted away as if he were talking to himself. And yet, he lingered, stood looking down into Cloud's burning eyes.

"Butler and Elliot. That worked exactly the way I wanted it to. You were puzzled as hell about it, about them being killed outside and all. They weren't, you know. I killed both of them inside the house and carried them out later. I scraped the girl's fingers on the concrete, carried her clothing outside, and stacked it nearby. Why? Well, you ought to know why—to make it look like a nut working, to make it fit right in with the Arrowstone thing. Lucky for me, Rafferty remembered about Arrowstone. Saved me the trouble later on. That's one of the reasons I went ahead with it even after I found out that Butler was Rafferty's girl friend. I never liked Jake much, you know that. But I had to make sure he wouldn't come drifting in right in the middle of . . . of things. That's where Sammy came in . . . and the little bastard tried to blackmail me later." He paused, eyes cold and shining. "He was a ratty little son of a bitch, but he was a good snitch. Dependable, I thought." He took a deep breath. "I planned it, Ben, right down to the last detail. Only thing was, the girl almost screwed me up by working overtime. I wanted to spend a lot more time with her . . . you know, inside the house, but when it got so late, I had to hurry it up. I didn't know how long Jake would hang around the Seven-Eleven waiting on the drug buy. I'd been following the Elliot girl for about a month. I knew where she worked, where she bought her groceries . . . everything about her. And she was a redhead. I needed a redhead to fit Arrowstone's MO. I almost canceled out when I saw the Butler woman with Jake a couple of days before and realized she was the one Strobish had been telling me about, that she was Jake's fiancée. But I couldn't do it. It would have meant starting all over with someone else, and I just couldn't wait. You won't understand that. It's hard for me to understand myself, but it's the truth." He squatted and laid a big hand on Cloud's neck, moved it around, fingers warm against Cloud's pallid skin. "You're about there, old buddy," he said quietly and rose to his towering height, stood looking down at the lanky detective's pain-wracked face. "Sorry, man."

He whirled abruptly and walked to the small table at the end of the couch. He picked up the phone, dialed the operator, and asked for the sheriff's office.

Cloud watched him with eyes that went in and out of focus like a flickering light, the tall figure wavy and disjointed, dark and menacing against the spray of light from the window.

He inched his thighs toward his chin, curling his lean body tightly. Ignoring the pain that radiated outward from his chest, he slipped bloody hands between his knees and tugged at his pants leg, feeling the bulk of the snub-nosed gun through the thin denim material, despairing as his weak, blood-slick fingers lost their grip. Through the hollow roaring in his head, he could dimly hear Rosie's voice:

". . . the first lane past the intersection of Cowl's Road and the highway. No need to hurry, they're both dead . . ."

He felt the pants cuff tighten over the bulk of the gun, felt his trembling fingertips once again lose their hold. Through slitted eyes he watched Rosie turn and glance at him, still talking into the phone, the words indistinguishable amidst the myriad sounds inside his skull.

He lay immobile, as still as stone.

He saw the big man turn back to the window. He took a shallow, pain-filled breath, gripped a fold of denim, and pulled, squandering his last small reserve of strength.

He felt the pants cuff slide, tighten, hang for one excruciating moment on the bulge of the gun's cylinder, then slide again, fall free, the checkered grip cold and hard and comforting beneath his hand.

He slipped it free, held it in both shaking hands.

Rosie was still on the phone, winding down the conversation.

He had to do it now— now, while they were still linked with the outside world by phone.

He balanced the gun on the side of his knee, peered down the barrel with blurred eyes, the small movements of his arms creating new waves of agony that brought creeping paralysis.

He held the sight on the center of the broad back, watched it dance away as his spastic hands refused to obey his commands; a smothered moan escaped tightly clenched teeth.

Rosie began to turn, the phone still at his ear.

Cloud's target diminished, the wide back narrowing to a thick side, a crooked elbow, a beefy arm, a startled face peering down at him over a bunched shoulder.

Cloud yelled and yanked the trigger.

Faintly, through the ear-splitting din of concussion, he heard a hoarse, cursing bellow, opened his eyes to see the contorted face of Rosie Simple staggering toward him, huge body bent double, one hand appearing out of his silhouette with his Magnum, the other still clutching the phone.

Cloud fired again, then closed his eyes and pulled the trigger again and again, until the thunder seemed a living part of him, invading his mind like a physical force, a crashing swell of sound and darkness that pulsed with the dwindling rhythm of his heartbeat, bringing finally a kind of contentment—and oblivion.

70

"You were lucky, boss," Ron Graves said, grinning down at him from his perch on the wide window ledge. "An inch higher and a fraction to the left and Trinity Square'd be looking for a new Lieutenant of Homicide."

Cloud nodded minutely. "That's what they tell me. Just good, clean living, I guess."

"Most assuredly." Eli Summers squirmed in the hard-bottomed hospital guest chair, stretching his slender body to its fullest height in order to see Cloud's face. "We were all worried here for a while. They told us they lost you twice. Once on the way to the hospital, and then again on the operating table."

"Thanks, Eli," Cloud said dryly. "They hadn't told me that."

Ron Graves laughed. "Well, all's well that ends well."

"What about Rosie?" He had been waiting forever it seemed to ask the question that was there waiting each time he swam up out of the comforting darkness. Each time he saw a familiar cop face he had tried to form the words, only to feel himself sinking back into that warm, carefree world of silence and peace.

"Rosie," Eli said, "was a man named Spencer Price." He hesitated. "But I guess you know that. You did some babbling before you died that first time, and the deputy wrote it down. Enough to get us started on the right track."

Cloud wet his lips. "He's dead then?"

"And buried," Graves said. "You clipped him three times, Ben."

279

He stared silently at Graves's sober face, trying to think of another question. Finally, he asked, "How long . . . ago?"

"Eleven days," Eli answered. "We've got it pretty well figured out, Ben, but I don't think we should worry you with it this time—"

"Tell me, dammit!"

"Sorry, gentlemen. Time's up." The cheery voice rang with a familiar authority, and Cloud relaxed back into the pillow, feeling himself fading, hearing only faintly and without interest Grave's heavy-handed attempt at humor with the young nurse. He felt cool fingers on his brow and the soft murmur of a female voice, extrinsic indicators that meant little as he drifted once again into that safe, fuzzy other world.

"Okay," Eli said, "I'll have to talk fast. I only have about five minutes. You can just listen. You're not supposed to talk much, anyhow."

"All right."

"Rosie Simple and Spencer Price soldiered together in Vietnam. Military Police. They served almost two years in the same unit in Saigon and were discharged within a week of each other. They evidently got together again right away because they visited Simple's half-sister in Kentucky less than a week after Price's discharge. That was about twelve years ago. Simple's sister hasn't heard from him since. My guess is, sometime after that, Spencer killed Simple and took his name and identification. Physically, they were a lot alike, both big men, same color hair, approximately the same height, same build. They even looked a little alike, according to Simple's sister." He stopped and fingered the tip of his nose, studying Cloud's pale face. "I don't want to tire you out, Ben. I can come back again tomorrow."

"Go on, dammit, you just started."

Summers smiled faintly and nodded. "The first question that came to my mind was why he would want to do that—kill Simple, I mean, and take his place. The obvious answer was that he wanted a new background. Spencer Price had a bad record as a juvenile in California, mostly for assault on young females. The records were sealed, but there was a good chance he didn't know that, and even so, there were a lot of people in law enforcement who knew him, who believed that he had been responsible for the deaths of several young girls in and around Los Angeles. On the other hand, Simple had a clean record, even had two years as a deputy sheriff before he went into the army. At any rate, Rosie Simple showed up in Louisville, Kentucky six months later, and on the strength of his previous experience as a deputy and the military police, he was hired by the Louisville police.'' He stopped and shook his head, the austere smile returning. ''Their background check was about as cursory as ours. They talked to the sheriff he had worked for, and ran him through their state system, and reviewed his military records. Everything checked out fine. They didn't bother with the FBI.''

''I thought we ran everybody through the FBI? Wouldn't they turn up the discrepancy in prints?''

Summers nodded and sighed. ''We do, ordinarily. Donleavy hired Rosie on the strength of his letter of recommendation from the Louisville Chief of Police. Seems the chief and Donleavy were old buddies from Chicago. He did call him, I think. At least he said he did. His face is permanently stained red, by the way. First it was Arrowstone, and now Rosie.''

Cloud's head rolled fitfully on the pillow. ''I don't think this was the first time for Rosie, Eli. He talked like he had done it before.''

Summers nodded again, his sharp features puckering with distaste. ''Yes, we believe he has. During the five years or so he spent at Louisville, they had a number of unsolved murders. Young girls.'' He paused. ''Although there were no records of stones—''

''There wouldn't be. He only did that because of Arrowstone. He copied Arrowstone's MO to keep the heat off himself.''

''How did you get onto him, by the way?'' Summers relaxed into the chair and crossed his legs. He rested his elbows on the chair arms and steepled his hands, thin index fingers pressing against the sides of his nose.

Cloud's head rolled again. ''I didn't. He and I went up there to arrest Rafferty. Rosie set him up. He planted a couple of Rafferty's gum wrappers when he killed Amy. He planted a bag of stones and Butler's diamond ring. He even planted the Echo-fone he used to call me. We met at Rafferty's apartment to toss it. When I got there, Rosie was already inside. It's an old lock, and he slipped it with a credit card. I didn't give it a second thought at the time, but he probably took that stuff with him. But maybe not, maybe he planted it earlier. He knew Rafferty was up at the lake.''

"But why did he shoot you? Did something happen at the cabin?"

"Not the way you think. Rosie was just tying up loose ends. His frame wasn't all that tight, and he knew I was having trouble convincing myself that Rafferty was a killer. I was still in a kind of shock from Amy's death—and Arrowstone's—and he knew I was an easy target for a little deception. I was walking around in a daze, and I think he was worried about what might happen when I finally woke up. Then there was the matter of the Indian blanket and Julio Mendosa's—"

"Indian blanket?" Summers pursed his lips, narrow brow wrinkled. "There were some fibers—"

"That's the one. Rosie carried it around in the back seat of his old second car. Evidently that's the car he used when he went out prowling at night."

"Julio Mendosa. I seem to recall seeing his name in your notes."

"He was a friend of Sammy Keeler's. A fellow junkie. Keeler told Mendosa a cop had killed Butler and Elliot, that he was going to use it to get some drugs. Rosie told me he had Keeler tell Rafferty there was going to be a big drug bust in the parking lot of the Seven-Eleven that night. That was to make sure Rafferty didn't happen along while he was having his fun with the Elliot girl. Jake went over there almost every night. Everybody knew that. Rosie planned it, figured it out down to the last detail. The only thing he didn't figure on was Keeler following him. He didn't know that Sammy would suspect the motives of his own mother, didn't know him well enough to know that he was sharp as a tack."

"No, no, Mr. Cloud, you're not supposed to be talking!"

The nurse swept into the room, starched whites whispering around the matronly body, her broad, freckled face puckered in a frown. She clapped a hand to Cloud's brow and spoke to Eli Summers without looking at him.

"Time's up, sir. We have to rest now."

"Then go lay down somewhere," Cloud growled. "That's all I've been doing, for chrissakes."

"Behave yourself, Ben," Summers said, popping to his feet like an uncoiling spring. "The lady is right. I've overstayed my allotted time by three minutes."

"Big damned deal," Cloud snarled, watching Summers disappear through the door with a smile and a cheery wave of his hand. He turned to glower at the bustling nurse.

"I'll tell you one damned thing. I'm not going to sleep until I get a cigarette."

"Uh-huh," the plump woman said absently, lifting the sheet to inspect his dressing. "We'll see what doctor has to say."

"I don't give a damn what doctor has to say. Doctor doesn't smoke."

She smiled and patted his knee and swished toward the door. "We'll see."

Cloud started to call her back, then thought better of it. He didn't want to be alone with his thoughts, with the inevitable replays that haunted his time awake; but the nurse wasn't the answer, and in the days ahead there would be great chunks of time to muddle through, a million images he would be unable to keep out of his mind, so he may as well get used to it.

It was something he would have to learn to cope with alone, a part of living, part of being a cop.

He thought of Amy Reed and felt a spasm of internal pain, a dark blanket of misery descending. After a time, he forced his thoughts away from her, back to more immediate concerns: getting well, living with what he had helped do to Rafferty, and making up his mind about his future.

He wasn't sure he could go on being a cop. It was something he would have to think about.